Praise for Elise Hooper and *Angels of the Pacific*

"Absolutely riveting. A stay-up-all-night read about two very different women who discover just how strong—and daring—they can be during the brutal Japanese occupation of the Philippines in World War II. This story of endurance and sisterhood will have you turning pages late into the night."
—Lauren Willig, *New York Times* bestselling author

"Told in vivid detail and with tremendous heart, *Angels of the Pacific* is a deeply moving World War II novel. Hooper masterfully brings this little-known story of the heroic US Army nurses in the Philippines to life, weaving together fascinating history, an intricate plot, and characters you will be rooting for the whole way. A must-read!"
—Sara Ackerman, *USA Today* bestselling author of *Radar Girls*

"Hooper's eye for detail and skillful storytelling shine once more in her latest historical novel about the military nurses who risked their lives in the Filipino resistance during World War II. A powerful testament to female friendship and bravery, *Angels of the Pacific* is a gripping, satisfying read."
—Heather Webb, *USA Today* bestselling author of *The Next Ship Home*

"Elise Hooper's latest book is a meticulously researched, captivating story about military nurses serving in the Philippines during the Japanese occupation of World War II. In *Angels of the Pacific*, Hooper pushes past the boundaries of the traditional war novel to reveal little-known details of the challenges endured by an extraordinarily brave and resilient group of women. Infused with Hooper's trademark heart and bountiful narrative abilities, this is a tale that shocks and inspires."

—Lynda Cohen Loigman, nationally bestselling author of *The Two-Family House* and *The Wartime Sisters*

"Elise Hooper's *Angels of the Pacific* is a captivating and heart-wrenching portrayal of the US Army and Navy nurses in World War II. . . . This stellar novel is an ode to the power of female friendships and to the strength, bravery, and resilience women can have in the very darkest of times. Hooper has brought the true story of the Angels of Bataan to light in a way that both celebrates their unique place in World War II history and honors their many sacrifices. I loved it!"

—Jane Healey, bestselling author of *The Beantown Girls* and *The Secret Stealers*

"Hooper's latest is a powerhouse combination of heart-stopping battle scenes and heart-wrenching relationships. At the same time as she brilliantly illuminates the stage of the Pacific theater, she looks deep into the souls of the women who bravely gave their blood, sweat, and tears to a cause larger than themselves. An essential, eye-opening addition to World War II literature."

—Kerri Maher, author of *The Paris Bookseller*

"Absorbing and fascinating, *Angels of the Pacific* is historical fiction at its finest. With characters to root for, a story that keeps the pages turning, and a multilayered look into the history of the Japanese occupation of the Philippines during World War II, *Angels of the Pacific* is a story of sisterhood, resilience, and hope. Hooper's attention to historical detail and commitment to research is evident in every page."

—Susie Orman Schnall, author of *We Came Here to Shine*

ANGELS
OF THE
PACIFIC

Also by Elise Hooper

Fast Girls
Learning to See
The Other Alcott

ANGELS
OF THE
PACIFIC

A NOVEL OF WORLD WAR II

ELISE HOOPER

WILLIAM MORROW

An Imprint of HarperCollinsPublishers

P.S.™ is a trademark of HarperCollins Publishers.

ANGELS OF THE PACIFIC. Copyright © 2022 by Elise Hooper. All rights reserved. Printed in the United States of America. No part of this book may be used or reproduced in any manner whatsoever without written permission except in the case of brief quotations embodied in critical articles and reviews. For information, address HarperCollins Publishers, 195 Broadway, New York, NY 10007.

HarperCollins books may be purchased for educational, business, or sales promotional use. For information, please email the Special Markets Department at SPsales@harpercollins.com.

FIRST EDITION

Designed by Diahann Sturge

Map by Nick Springer, Springer Cartographics, LLC

Library of Congress Cataloging-in-Publication Data has been applied for.

ISBN 978-0-06-306890-2
ISBN 978-0-06-321272-5 (hardcover library edition)

22 23 24 25 26 LSC 10 9 8 7 6 5 4 3 2 1

In loving memory of my grandfather Donald William Baker

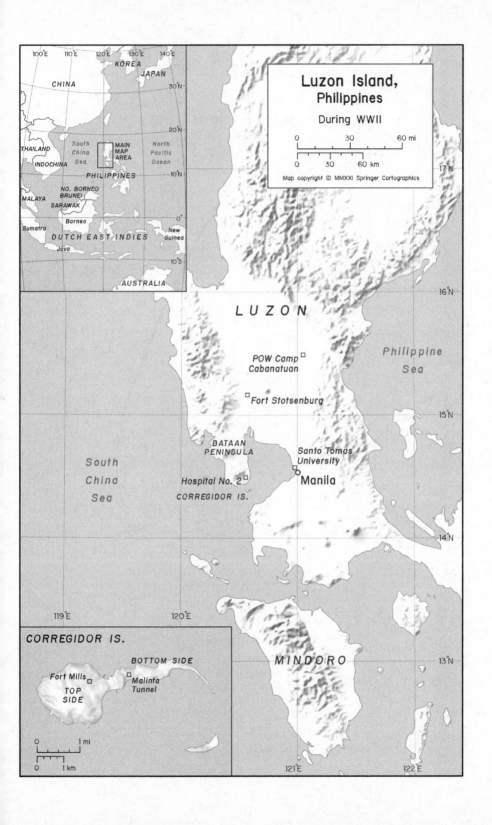

Luzon Island,
Philippines

During WWII

0   30   60 mi

0   30   60 km

Map copyright © MMXXI Springer Cartographics

100°E   110°E   120°E   130°E   140°E

KOREA

JAPAN

CHINA

30°N

20°N

South
China
Sea

North
Pacific
Ocean

MAIN
MAP
AREA

THAILAND

INDOCHINA

PHILIPPINES

10°N

NO. BORNEO
BRUNEI

MALAYA

SARAWAK

Borneo

0°

Sumatra

DUTCH EAST INDIES

New
Guinea

Java

10°S

AUSTRALIA

17°N

LUZON

16°N

Philippine
Sea

POW Camp □
Cabanatuan

Fort Stotsenburg
□

15°N

BATAAN
PENINSULA

Santo Tomas
University

South
China
Sea

Hospital No. 2 □
□

Manila

CORREGIDOR IS.

14°N

119°E

120°E

MINDORO

13°N

CORREGIDOR IS.

BOTTOM SIDE

Fort Mills
□

Malinta
□ Tunnel

TOP
SIDE

0   1 mi

0   1 km

121°E

122°E

1.

TESS

December 1941
The Philippines

We headed to Manila for an overnight escape from the countryside having no idea that our lives were on the verge of changing forever. Four of us piled aboard a commissary truck and motored southbound along the highway toward the coast, our shoulders jostling against each other while the rolling golden plains of Luzon retreated. The smell of ripe copra swirled around us, along with heavy diesel fumes, and though it would take several hours to drive to Manila, anticipation was running high for that evening's annual Christmas gala at the Army-Navy Officers' Club, the OC as we called it. Rumors of a coming war with Japan had consumed everyone for months, but they felt so far-fetched, so gloomy that all we wanted was to drown out the worrisome chatter with a few gin-soaked hours of jitterbugging and jiving.

Virginia and I sat on one side of the truck's bed with Sally and Darren opposite us. An olive-colored canvas tarp protected us from the direct intensity of the sun, but still, the air was hot. Though my cotton sundress clung to my back, it was a relief not to be stuck in our stiff high-necked army nurse's uniforms.

"Jeez, Virginia, what do you have in there? The cavalry?" Darren shook his head at the size of her suitcase.

"If you must know, Doc, I couldn't land on what dress to wear tonight. I wanted options," Virginia said in her heavy Texas accent. Gravelly, smoky, and deep, it belied the wholesome expectations implied by her blond hair and blue eyes and reliably created a swarm of admirers wherever she went. "A smart woman likes to have options. In fact, we're just waiting for Sal to come to her senses and give you the heave-ho so she can take advantage of playing the field around here."

"Now that's a load of hogwash. I'm afraid you're stuck with me," Sally said, tracing her index finger along Darren's ear as if preparing to nibble on it.

"Ugh, if you two lovebirds keep mooning over each other, we're going to throw you right out the back," Virginia growled. "Maybe less weight in this thing could actually make it travel a little faster. I don't know about all of you, but I'm champing at the bit to get back to the bustle of the city."

Though Manila had its advantages, we had also found plenty of entertainment at our new posting at Fort Stotsenburg. Riding horses in the jungle, golfing, tennis—our new rural assignment offered plenty of diversions. I'd arrived in the Philippines almost nine months earlier, only nineteen years old, but well-versed in the hardships of the '30s. My childhood consisted of Washington State's gunmetal-gray skies, of chilled toes and chapped fingers, and of the ever-present smell of wet wool.

From the moment we'd disembarked our transport freighter, the USS *Saratoga*, and landed on Manila's Pier Seven and the small city spread out before us—elegant coconut palms; seventeenth-century Spanish-style buildings; stucco walls dotted with vining purple bougainvillea; and fragrant breezes laced with frangipani—it was like we were walking into some sort of wonderful dream. Of course, we had no idea what was coming. None of us did.

"What time are we supposed to be at Nell's?" I asked.

Virginia shrugged. "Whenever we get there."

"But didn't we say four? We're going to be late."

"Tess, it'll be fine. Loosen up." Virginia yawned.

"You make me sound like such a stick in the mud," I said.

"It's just that you need to live a little. If you don't do it now, you'll regret it later," she said.

I made a squeak of annoyance and frowned.

"You're *not* a stick in the mud," Sal insisted, "but it's just that . . ." She tapped her finger on her chin, thinking. I waited, knowing her verdict was going to sting a little. This wouldn't be the first time I'd allowed these two to transform me.

WHEN WE'D FIRST met during our Pacific crossing and I'd introduced myself as Esther Abbott, Virginia had openly inspected me from head to toe. "Honey, you're too young to be an Esther. It makes you sound like a fifty-year-old orphanage headmistress who darns stockings for fun. Let's call you Tess instead," she said.

It was as if she'd proposed piercing my ears or swearing off meat—I'd blinked in shock at the proposed name change—but rather than be offended, I couldn't help but feel intrigued by the possibilities. *Why not?*

And that was just the beginning. I was *Pygmalion's* Eliza Doolittle to their Henry Higgins and Colonel Pickering. During our second morning at sea, as I'd washed my face, I'd turned to find Sally and Virginia appraising the long thick braid running down my spine.

"How would you feel about a new hairdo?" Sal asked.

I pulled my braid into my hand and wrapped it around my

wrist. My wavy chestnut-colored hair was my one vanity. "I don't think so."

"Did you see *Rebecca* or *The Women?*" she asked.

"I did. Loved them both. Why?"

"What if I make you look like Joan Fontaine?"

Virginia snorted. "Joan Fontaine? Are you kidding me? Let's shoot for someone a little juicier than that. With Tess's waves, she could be more of a Rita Hayworth than boring ol' Joan Fontaine."

"Hayworth it is," Sal said. "Although I really liked *Rebecca*. I know she was supposed to look kind of boring, but I thought she was pretty."

"Well, I also really liked *Frankenstein*, but that doesn't mean I'd suggest we turn her into Boris Karloff," Virginia said.

"Pay no attention to her, Tess. I'll make you look divine. Sit right here." Sally tapped at the floor in front of her. I hovered for a moment, uncertain of the familiarity and intimacy she was suggesting. I had no real experience with friends. Orphaned at ten years old, my childhood under the care of my older sister, Sue, had been lonely. Though Sue cared for me deeply, she was reserved and consumed with the industry of living on our apple orchard. Until leaving for the Philippines, I'd kept myself quiet and withdrawn, closed like a fist, but the thrill of leaving home split my defenses.

"Sit!" Sally insisted.

So I sat, my shoulders tensed around my ears, but she didn't notice my discomfort. "Don't worry, back in Michigan, I cut my brothers' and sisters' hair all the time. I'm the oldest of ten, so I have my work cut out for me—and they keep me busy with *everything*, not just hair. They're always begging me to make them meals or to referee a game. Our house is a zoo, an absolute zoo. Not a single moment of peace and quiet. It's why I've always liked going to the movies so much—I escape everyone for a couple of hours."

"Nine brothers and sisters? My word," I said. "I have a sister, but she's much older. I was basically an only child."

"I can't imagine being an only child, not even for one minute." Sally's fingers grazed my shoulders and the *snip snip* of scissors whispered near my ear. "Did you ever get lonely? My brothers and sisters drive me nuts but I think I'll miss them. They promised to write tons of letters. I left stationery and stamps and assigned each one a day to write to me."

"You're so organized," I marveled, trying not to wonder about what she was doing to my hair.

"Ha, if I wasn't, nothing would get done! In fact, I have no idea how Mother's holding down the fort with me gone. They must all miss me terribly. I don't even want to think about it. I don't mean to boast, but I'm a very essential part of my family."

I laughed before realizing Sal was completely serious.

And then I wondered: *Who would miss me?* Of course, Sue and her husband, Dan, loved me, but was I an essential part of daily life on the farm? I doubted it.

Sal must have seen my anxiety. "How about I get my sisters and brothers to write to you, too? Lord knows, a few of the younger ones need to work on their cursive. You may not be able to decipher much of their letters, but it would be nice to get more mail, don't you think?"

"It would. You're generous to offer."

And before I knew it, half of my hair lay on the floor surrounding me, but my new friends were right—my fresh hairdo felt perfect. It made me lighter. Freer. Did I resemble Rita Hayworth? Not really, but I didn't care. This was the new, more stylish me. *Tess.*

BOUNCING ALONG IN the back of the commissary truck, I fingered the waves of my shoulder-length hair and steeled myself for whatever improvement Sally was about to suggest next.

"Maybe you should change things up a little," Sal said. "What did you bring to wear tonight?"

"My pale yellow silk."

"But haven't you worn that a million times?"

"I guess so."

"Well, how about something that . . ." She pursed her lips, searching for the right words.

"Shows more cleavage," Darren said.

"Darren!" Sally elbowed him.

"Are you joking? I don't have anything that fits the bill for that," I said, half laughing, half indignant. I couldn't believe Darren—our mild-mannered family doctor from Portsmouth, New Hampshire—had just made such a risqué suggestion.

"Don't worry, Doc," Virginia said. "I've been trying to tell her the same thing for months now. Who doesn't appreciate a good view, right?" And with that, she leaned forward to rest her elbow on her knee in a way that gave everyone a view straight down into her ample décolletage.

Sally laughed, but Darren's face turned such a dark shade of red, I feared for his blood pressure.

"If Virginia brought a few different evening gowns, maybe you could try one of hers," Sally suggested.

Virginia arched a perfectly penciled eyebrow. "I think I've got some extra dimensions that will make that *tricky*."

Sal rolled her eyes. "I'm sure one of the other girls will have *something*. Maybe a strapless dress would be just the thing!"

"I don't know," I said slowly.

"I promise, nothing vulgar. You'll look classy," Sally said.

"But also, maybe a little trampy," Virginia drawled, resting her arm along the back of the bench and grinning. It was clear she was having a ball of a time at my expense.

"That's not helpful," Sally said.

"Trust me, when I'm done with her, she'll be a knockout."

"Fine, maybe a smidge"—Sal held her index finger and thumb an inch apart—"*daring*. Just for tonight."

I studied the delighted expressions on my friends. Despite how the late-afternoon heat was making us wilt, I felt a flicker of excitement, but tried to cover it up by smacking Virginia's knee. "Quit looking so smug."

She gave my leg a return smack. "Relax. Tonight is going to be the most fun y'all have ever had—I can feel it in my bones."

WE ARRIVED AT the house in Manila where the nurses lived, a tall ivory-colored stucco building with bright fuchsia bougain-villea crawling up its facade. Nell Farmington, Virginia's room-mate aboard the USS *Saratoga*, had invited us to stay with her.

When we explained my dress predicament, Nell looked at me and shrugged. The tall blonde had been a champion swim-mer back in Pasadena and was built like a prizewinning thor-oughbred, all long lines and muscle, a fine balance of power and grace. "You'll need stilts for anything I've got, so let's check with the other gals."

It didn't take long.

The new gown barely needed any alterations, but clung to me in places where I usually looked for breathing space. Also, it was strapless so I felt entirely exposed, which was cause for alarm, but also—I'll admit it—a bit thrilling. Soft pale pink satin crisscrossed in an artful drape across the bodice and cinched into a narrow waist before cascading to the ground in a four-piece full skirt. When I stepped into the boardinghouse's hallway and spun, sending up a pale pink cloud of satin into the air, a chorus of whistles from the other nurses greeted me.

Virginia applauded. "My, my, give the rest of us a chance, will you?"

"Don't worry, you gals are hard to overlook," I said.

She threw back her chin, laughed, and wrapped her arms around all of us in a dramatic embrace. "It's times like this when I realize how boring my life was before I met y'all. Now let's see what mischief we can scare up!"

With her call to action ringing in our ears, we pranced out of the boardinghouse and headed into the muggy evening, swanning behind Virginia and Nell, their two blond heads gleaming like lanterns leading the way.

We arrived at the holiday party, sparkling in our colorful gowns, stylish updos, and costume jewelry. Icy drinks were thrust into our hands, but it didn't take long before a group of officers invited us to another club. We lowered our glasses, now sucked dry of gin and tonic, and off we went, tottering outside into the crush of Manila's nightlife.

We rounded the corner onto a busy thoroughfare and sounds of yelling and a scream reached us. Ahead, a cluster of people gathered around a caretela. Despite the commotion, the shaggy calesa pony attached to the cart eyed the crowd balefully, swatting its tail back and forth as if it hadn't a care in the world.

We all paused, but it was Darren who swung us into action. "*Stand back! I'm a doctor,*" he shouted, plunging into the crowd. I followed, amazed at how he transformed from goofy friend to serious professional in the blink of an eye.

Within seconds, I stood above a small boy, perhaps three years old, lying next to the caretela. His right leg appeared crushed and a woman crouched beside him, screaming in terrified agony. My heart dropped at the sight of his delicate limbs splayed so unceremoniously on the cobblestones. His leg looked terrible. An astonishing amount of blood had pooled around him, reflecting the garish-colored lights from the surrounding shop and restaurant signs.

Across from me, Sally fell to her knees and yelled, "Hand me something to cover him!"

A scarf and blanket were proffered. She reached for the scarf and began to bind the mangled leg. Virginia wrapped a blanket across the child's shoulders and began talking to him in a low, soothing tone, but the boy seemed to register nothing.

"He's going into shock," Darren announced, crouching by the boy's side. He moved from checking the child's pulse in his hand to inspecting the leg. "Sal, wrap up his femoral. He's losing too much blood."

"Is there time to get him to the hospital?" Virginia asked.

"No," Darren barked. The mother's screaming sliced through the air around us. A man, perhaps the boy's father, started yelling at the driver of the caretela. Around us, the crowd muttered prayers. It was so noisy and hot that I could scarcely think. Darren ran his hands over the sweat pouring from his face. "We're losing him," he whispered, staring at the maimed limb.

Under my fingers, the boy's carotid pulse grew fainter. I lowered my face to his, saw the velvet softness of his baby skin up close. I wanted to simply whisper *Wake up! Wake up!* but we were well beyond that. Below my hands, he appeared lifeless and his eyes took on a glassy, unseeing stare. He was slipping away. But that's when I noticed the faintest flaring of his nostrils. My fingers on his neck detected a weak stirring of muscle. I stared at the boy's chest, squinting in concentration. Everything around us faded away. It was just me and the boy.

And then I saw what I'd been looking for: his chest strained to rise. It was slight, but it was something!

At that moment, a jolt ran straight through me as if someone had hit me with a live electrical wire. When we had arrived on the scene, we had immediately focused on the bloody leg, but we'd missed something.

I tilted his head back, opened his jaw, and leaned close. The smell of something sweet and sugary emanated from the boy.

"Tess, what are you doing?" Sal asked.

But I didn't answer. I stuck a finger between the child's blue lips. Sure enough, deep in the back of his mouth something was blocking his airway, something hard and slippery. I hesitated, knowing this was a critical moment. The last thing I wanted to do was push whatever was blocking his throat down deeper. I turned his head to the side so the object would fall out of his mouth rather than down his trachea. Channeling the most delicate of motions, I flicked at the object. And it moved! It popped away against my fingers and I scooped it out.

Lying on my palm was a glistening piece of butterscotch candy, but there was no time to dwell on it.

I leaned over the child, watching for a sign of life. Time seemed to stop. I held my breath. A twitch of his fingers, a trembling of his eyelashes. Anything.

And then, a cough. The boy convulsed with a gagging sound and then wailed. Never before had I been so happy to hear a child cry.

I stared in amazement. And then finally, I exhaled, shuddering. Goodness, we had come so close to losing him.

Beside me, his mother's screams turned into pants of excitement and the crowd cheered. "Thank you," she repeated over and over as she dropped her forehead to her child's chest.

Darren clapped my shoulder. "Smart thinking. Wow, I'm embarrassed I missed that."

"Holy hell, how'd you do that?" one of the officers asked in a voice filled with wonderment.

"Tess kept a cool head. The kid must have had the candy in his mouth when he got hit," Darren explained, easing the child onto a blanket and then nodding at Sally to stand and lift it as a stretcher. A Model T had stopped and the driver offered his back seat to the group.

"We'll take the baby to Sternberg Hospital and find you later," Sally called, before someone slammed the door. They sped off.

My legs quaked with adrenaline as I watched the car's tail-lamps disappear into the crush of street traffic. Every fiber of my body vibrated with energy. If someone had asked me to scale the side of the building beside us, I could have done it easily. I felt capable of anything! I was invincible!

"Bet you could use a drink."

I turned to see an officer with sandy-colored hair standing next to me.

"And they say mind reading isn't real," I said, glancing down to check on the state of my gown. At the sight of my cleavage, I felt my face flush, but then I realized: What was I so afraid of? I was invincible, remember?

"Please, allow me," he said, taking my hand. The next few minutes were a blur of smiling faces and listening to people retell the story of the accident. Still unable to believe what had just happened, I simply focused on putting one foot in front of the other. Suddenly I found myself in a hotel's gilded lobby. My new officer friend steered me toward the bar.

"That was the best thing to happen in ages!" Virginia crowed. "Someone get our gal a drink!"

An icy coupe was pushed into my hand and I lifted it to my

lips, ignoring the bubbles sloshing over the rim, the result of my unsteady hands. Cold champagne filled my mouth. Fizzing atop my tongue, I savored its refreshing tang.

"Cheers." With a satisfying clink, the officer nudged his drink into mine. Even in the buzz of my excitement, I glimpsed a smattering of freckles dotting the tanned skin under his white dinner jacket's cuff. My gaze continued up his arms to his broad shoulders and then to his face. He was tall with a square jaw and glowing light blue eyes—a looker, no doubt about it.

"How'd you know to check his mouth?" he asked.

"It just popped into my head. I realized we'd forgotten our first step of assessing the patient. Think they'll be able to save his leg?"

"You're the expert, not me."

"Oh, I hope they can fix him."

"The kid's alive and that's what's important."

"I suppose." I lifted my glass again only to realize it was empty. "Huh, guess I made quick work of this."

He chuckled, lifting a sweating green bottle to refill it. "So how'd it feel? You saved that kid's life. Now I'm rethinking this whole soldiering business, that's for sure."

"Until this evening, it's been pretty routine stuff. I've been on hand for the delivery of a few babies, which is thrilling, but this . . ." I trailed off, lost for words. In the past, I'd always been an assistant responding to directions. But back there with the boy? I'd figured it out on my own. For the first time in my life, I felt useful. I could really *help* people—*save* them even, and it was a big feeling for an orphaned girl like me who had spent much of life feeling like a burden. A *very* big feeling.

"So you're a nurse at Sternberg?"

"No," I said. "I'm at Stotsenburg. Heading back tomorrow."

"Tomorrow? Tonight's all we've got?"

"Well, how much time do you need?"

Those dreamy blue eyes locked on me. Tiny flecks of gold appeared to dance around his irises. "To do what?"

"To impress me."

He grinned and shook his head. "Somehow with you, I have a feeling all bets are off."

I was surprising him, and it was heady stuff. The dress, the accident, and now this man—all of it was causing a sense of daring to color everything. Sure, it was a foreign feeling, but I liked it. I wasn't even twenty yet, but I'd known more than my fair share of grief. This was my chance to start anew.

Here, in this far-flung corner of paradise on the other side of the world, I could leave everything behind, forget all the dreariness of home—the sadness, the hard times—and be whoever I wanted. And deep in my heart, I'd always wanted to be independent and adventurous. It's what prompted me to go to nursing school in search of a vocation and it was why I hadn't skipped a beat when asked if I wanted a transfer to the Philippines. I was capable of all kinds of things and now could be the time to experiment. I took a deep breath. "I'm Tess. Listen, you've got twelve hours to make an impression so let's see what happens, shall we?"

He laughed and I wanted to bottle the sound of it.

"I'm George." He held out his hand for me to shake. "Now, enough talk. And just so you know, this is a big leap for me. Normally I'm the kind of guy who likes to dot his *i*'s and cross each *t*, but tonight I'm tossing caution to the wind. So, come on, I've got to use every second with you wisely."

I laughed and he led me to the dance floor where Virginia was holding court with a group of officers, but she peeled herself away and approached us, appraising George up and down. I introduced her, but then he placed his hand on my waist and steered me away into a waltz. I couldn't believe it; not once did he glance back over his shoulder to look at Virginia. *Not once.* This was a first.

We spent the rest of the evening together in a riot of blaring trumpets and saxophones and clanking glasses filled with gin and scotch. We sang and told jokes and nonsensical stories. After a while I realized my shoes should have been pinching and my cheeks should have been tired from smiling, but instead champagne seemed to bubble through my veins. I could have stayed awake for days. As we wended our way from the hotel to a club and then to another club, I could feel George watching me as if he couldn't quite believe his luck. It amazed me, really, because I could tell he was older than me, maybe by ten years or so, and he had been to school and seen more of the world, and yet I was the one who was captivating him.

Eventually we found ourselves on the waterfront staring out at Manila Bay. Behind us the sun was rising over the city. The dawn air was brackish and thick with humidity, making the satin of my dress stick to the small of my back, but these discomforts were a small price to pay for the moment. I'd always been careful to not find myself alone with a man, to not risk any shadow on my reputation, but there was a frisson hanging over us, a sense of impending change on the way, so I decided to ignore caution for once and sighed, waving my hands at how the water and sky were aglow with the same breathtaking shades of dark blue, streaked with dashes of pink and gold. "Sometimes I wonder if the hard times at home were necessary so I'd be ready for *this.*"

"Me too," he said quietly.

"Where are you from?"

"Coast of Maine. Grew up on a lobster boat. I'm on my own

now. My parents died a few years ago so I left my small town and went to college and then law school."

Grief lowered his voice and I knew its weight all too well. The OC was filled with young people like us, men and women who were no strangers to rising on cold mornings, building things with our hands, and going to bed at night with not-entirely-full stomachs—we were the types who joined the army and then opted to be sent far away for a once-in-a-lifetime type of escapade.

"Let's just hope things never change," he said.

I glanced at his profile in time to see a slight frown darken his face. Though the evening's steady flow of drinks had left me unstrung, I could tell he was sober, an amazing feat of discipline given the reckless air hanging over everyone. "Are you thinking about the war?"

He shrugged. "Aren't we all?"

"Will we get drawn in?"

"There's a lot of saber-rattling coming from the Japanese."

"But wouldn't they be crazy to take us on?"

"Waging war isn't necessarily the result of rational thinking."

Silence descended upon us for a moment, but then he cleared his throat. "What do you say I borrow a ride and drive you back to Stotsenburg later?"

"Really? You can get one?"

"Sure, why not?"

"What do you do?"

"I'm in military intelligence." He winked. "All those years on a boat taught me how to be resourceful."

"Intelligence, huh? So you must know lots of special things."

"I only know I've never met anyone like you," he said.

It was the kind of thing officers said when they thought they had a chance at getting something more, and since arriving in the Philippines, I'd been surrounded by men and they were all in the market for something more. But as I gazed into his kind eyes and saw the way they widened with amazement as he looked at me, I shivered and reached out to stroke the enticing small cleft on his chin, the one irregularity on his otherwise classic features.

"Are you cold?" he asked in a low tone, but without waiting for an answer he pulled off his white dinner jacket and wrapped it around my bare shoulders while gently pulling me to him. He smiled almost shyly, and his earnestness inspired me to lean in and kiss him. Our noses bumped together awkwardly and we laughed a little, rearranging ourselves so we could continue to kiss. I twisted my hands together behind the nape of his neck and a patch of his closely shaven hair bristled against the tender skin on the inside of my wrists. Sparks flared inside me.

Our kiss deepened and his jacket slipped from my shoulders and fell to the ground, but neither of us cared. Instead he tightened his grip on the small of my back and pressed his lips into mine more intensely.

This—*this*—was beyond anything I'd ever imagined for romance.

When we pulled apart, I felt dizzy with the sense of tumbling into a different world, a magical one. Who knew what could happen next?

LATER THAT AFTERNOON, I found myself passing through the white gateposts to Fort Stotsenburg in the passenger seat of an army jeep with George at the wheel. When we reached the Officers' Commissary, George pulled into the shade of an acacia tree and Virginia, Sally, and Darren hopped out.

"Thanks, George. You're a sport." Darren gave a quick salute.

"Hope to see you soon," George said.

"Oh, I have a feeling we'll be seeing you again." Sally gave an exaggerated wink.

Darren raised his hands in apology. "Sorry, she doesn't get out enough."

Sally punched Darren on the shoulder and the two dashed away, laughing, while Virginia sashayed off with a little extra sway in her stride, but when I turned to George, he wasn't looking at her. His gaze was on me.

"You must be exhausted," I said.

"Not at all. I'm not the one who's been performing miracles. You raised the dead last night, remember?"

I smiled. That morning, when George had arrived in a jeep outside the front door of Nell's boardinghouse, he had surprised us with a picnic basket packed with sandwiches and fruit. Since we'd eaten it along the way, I wasn't hungry, but I also wasn't ready to let him go. "Want to come to the mess and get something to eat?"

"Do I ever, but I need to get back."

"So this is goodbye?"

He grinned, pushing the rim of his army cap away from his forehead. "Guess I made an impression, huh?"

I shrugged, feigning nonchalance. "Sorry, but what's your name again?"

He chuckled, shifted the gear, and killed the engine. "Tess, you haven't seen the last of me, not by a long shot."

"Is that a promise?"

He lifted my hand from where it rested in my lap and laced his fingers through mine. Up close, I watched him study the flyaway hairs escaping the silk scarf around my head, then he refocused on my chin, and then my cheek, and then he looked me straight in the eye. Normally such close scrutiny would have caused me to panic, but a surprising feeling took hold. I liked being the focus of his attention. Even hot and sweaty and covered in dust, I felt charming, smart, and interesting.

"It's a promise," he said.

And then he kissed me and even though we'd just met, I knew I'd found someone special. Right then and there, I decided the best kind of romance makes you not only fall head over heels for someone else, but helps you remember the best parts of yourself. Saving that young boy the night before had changed me. It made me feel powerful and clever and confirmed that nursing was my calling. That moment had connected me to a better version of myself, and George had been there to witness it. When he looked at me, I could see respect in his eyes. Like I was a force to be reckoned with. The feeling sizzled through my bloodstream like a shot of adrenaline.

And I was right. I was teetering on the precipice of a whole new adventure. The world was about to change for me—for everyone—but not in the way I anticipated. Not one bit.

2.

TESS

When my alarm first rang on Monday morning, I slapped it off, buried my head in my pillow, and fell back asleep.

I awoke again to the distant sound of planes taking off from the fort's nearby airfield and glanced at the clock. It was early for so much flight activity, but I thought little of it because I was running late. I tugged on my white nurse's uniform and headed straight for my shift at the Station Hospital, skipping my usual stop at the commissary to grab a sugar donut.

An unusual quiet hung over the parade ground as I hustled along its edges, but I barely noticed because I was replaying my final conversation with George from the day before in my mind. Goose bumps rose on my arms, just thinking about our kiss. *When would I see him again?*

At the nurses' station in the hospital, the assignment board was blank—strange. Normally Head Nurse Josie Nesbit would have written out a list of scheduled procedures in chalk already. Our nursing shifts in the Philippines lasted only four hours. The heat was too intense for anything longer. The expectation was that we'd treat US military personnel and their families for the occasional tropical fever, parasite, rudimentary surgery, and birth. Although we were military, we had never attended any sort of basic army training so our jobs were fairly straight-forward, and certainly not dangerous. Our limited work hours gave us plenty of time to enjoy the tropics by playing tennis, taking Spanish lessons, swimming, and admiring the aquamarine waters of the OC's pool, which we could visit because of our status as lieutenants. Our officers' distinction conferred no real rank, earned us half the salary of our male counterparts, and there was little chance of promotion. It was mostly intended to maintain our respectability by preventing us from getting too friendly with the enlisted men and it ensured our safety in the unlikely event we had any direct confrontation with an enemy.

Frowning at the blank assignment board, I hurried toward the supply room at the back of the hospital to sterilize surgical instruments. It was just a matter of time, I assumed, before Josie Nesbit would appear and order me to assist on a tonsillectomy or some other routine procedure so there was no time to waste on any more fiddle-faddling about. It was time to get organized. Humming, I spread out a row of shiny curettes, admiring the bright yellow orchids visible from the nearby ground-level window. It was moments like this when I couldn't believe how far I was from home.

When I was ten years old, my parents died in an automobile accident. My older sister, Sue, and her husband, Dan, settled with me onto the family plot, a small orchard on the outskirts of Tacoma. On my eighteenth birthday, eager for independence and a practical skill set, I enrolled in nursing school and eventually landed a position with the local Civilian Conservation Corps at nearby Fort Lewis. With a few extra dollars in my pocket, I'd begun frequenting the local cinema to see movies when I wasn't working. Films like *The Rains Came* and *The Hunchback of Notre Dame* and *Stanley and Livingstone* introduced me to a world wider than my small town, and an itch to leave and explore soon started nagging at me. When the offer to join the Army Corps of Nursing and transfer to the Philippines was dangled in front of me, I'd grabbed it with both hands and hung on for dear life with only thoughts of adventure and trying to make myself useful.

I was reaching for the first curette when Darren appeared in the doorway.

"What are you doing?" He mopped at his forehead with a handkerchief.

"The assignment board was blank so I thought I'd—"

"Jesus, haven't you heard?"

"Heard what?"

"The Japanese just bombed Hawaii."

I stared at him. "They bombed us?"

"There aren't many details yet. It's Sunday there, you know, but everyone's expecting an announcement we're at war now."

"War," I repeated, barely breathing.

"Do you have your gas mask? I was told to keep mine close."

I thought back to the previous month when the bulky contraptions had been handed out. "Maybe it's under my bed."

"When you get back to your room later, better make sure you've got it."

"Do you think George made it back to Manila safely?"

"Of course, he did. I'll bet he's with General MacArthur right now planning how we're going to strike back. Chin up, Tess. You'll see him again. It was obvious he fell pretty hard for you. I'll bet he'll be back this weekend, knocking on your door, flowers in hand."

I smiled at Darren and was struck by a similarity between him and my brother-in-law. Dan was quieter than Darren, but he always had a kind word for me, always tried to assure me that everything would be fine. I suddenly felt a wave of homesickness, the first one I'd experienced since arriving in the Philippines. The idea of facing danger while being so far from home left me shaken. I longed for the steadying presence of my sister.

"We're on high alert now and discharging able-bodied men. Go around and check charts. Anyone who can be put back into duty should get back to work." I must have looked alarmed because Darren said, "Don't worry, this whole thing will blow over in a couple of days. A week, tops."

"Really?"

"Sure, the Japanese don't stand a chance. The only reason they scored a hit on us was by playing dirty with a sneak attack. Hang tight. We'll knock 'em flat in no time."

I nodded, reassured. Darren was right. It felt impossible to imagine anything bad happening in our sleepy paradise.

AT MIDDAY, I went to the commissary for a sandwich and entered the building alongside a group of pilots from Clark Field. They swaggered in to get their food, rowdy with the news of the morning.

One airman, Dewey Bradshaw, nodded at the table where I ended up sitting with the other nurses eating lunch. "Gals, you've got nothing to worry about. We've been circling Luzon all morning and there's no sign of trouble. The Japanese must have decided they're in over their heads and gone back to Tokyo." He joined the other men, still in their flight suits, at an adjacent table and they grinned at us broadly, sprawling their long legs out in front of them, loose and unconcerned.

"Tell that to the crowd in Hawaii cleaning up the wreckage," Sally said glumly.

Dewey frowned. "It's a damned shame what happened there, but we'll get our revenge. The fellas back at the airfield are fitting our planes with bombs right now. We've gotten orders to head to the Japanese base on Formosa where we'll show them no one gets away with messing with us."

A nurse named Phyllis said, "Good, you boys better clean 'em up real quick."

The rest of us nodded. Though we were rattled by the news about Hawaii, the idea of a speedy counterblow suited us just fine. Our fear was quickly turning to anger.

One of the other pilots—I didn't know his name—leaned toward us to pipe in, "Y'all should come to the airfield and send us up in style. Bet our mission will go a lot smoother with a bunch of America's finest gals cheering us on."

"Yes," the other pilots called out. "That's the ticket!"

We looked at one another and Virginia pushed away her plate. "I don't have much of an appetite anyway. Sure, I'm in."

One by one we stood to join the airmen. Amid the cheering, I reached for my glass of lemonade and drank it down in one long gulp. Later, I'd look back at that moment and wish I'd slowed down and relished its icy temperature and tart sweetness while I'd had the chance. The memory of that lemonade stuck with me for years, a symbol of all that we had taken for granted, all that we would lose.

OUTSIDE, WE FILLED the jeeps. Several of us sat on the airmen's laps as we drove the few minutes to Clark Field, cheering and singing. When we arrived, several rows of B-17s were lined up neatly wingtip-to-wingtip as if on exhibit, gleaming in the bright sun, emblems of power and possibility. The high central plains of Luzon spread around us for miles and the air waved in the midday heat. Underneath the white cotton of my nursing dress, every pore on my body began to sweat, but who cared? I could change and take a cool shower later, but we only had one chance to send these boys off for action. I vowed to remember this feeling of adventure and excitement so I could describe it later in a letter home to Sue and Dan.

Before we hopped out of the jeep, Dewey turned to one of the nurses, a redhead named Mabel, his eyes glittering with mischief. "Hey, I've got a bet with Pax that the rumors about you being a wingwalker aren't true. How about we settle this right now so I can collect from this chump before our mission starts?"

Mabel gave a coquettish grin. "What makes you think they're not true?"

"Well, I can't imagine a pretty thing like you doing something that dangerous." He leaned forward toward the front seat to knock Joe Paxton's shoulder. "Like I said, Pax, pay up. I knew that rumor was a crock."

Virginia snorted. "You're a real sucker, Dewey. Mabel may look harmless, but the girl's got ice running through those veins of hers. If you didn't have to go settle the score with the Japanese right now, she could put on a real show for y'all that would knock your socks off. Mabel, remind me: What was your favorite trick back in your barnstorming days?"

"I had a lot of good ones," Mabel said. "But I guess my favorite was juggling bowling pins while I stood on the wing of the biplane two hundred feet in the air."

Dewey scratched his head. "So, wait, you really used to do that stuff?"

"I was also pretty good at walking back and forth along the plane's wings on my hands," Mabel added.

Under his breath, Dewey swore and dug around in his breast pocket to pull out a small wad of cash. He peeled off a few bills and stuffed them toward Joe Paxton.

Pax immediately handed Mabel one. "Thanks, buddy," she said, sliding it down the neckline of her uniform.

"What the hell?" Dewey said as everyone in the jeep burst into laughter. "You guys were hustling me?"

"Yep." Pax laughed. "Mabel and I grew up near each other in Kansas and I used to catch her shows. She was really something! When we both turned up here, I recognized her."

"And now you two are in cahoots?" Dewey asked.

"Sure are. No one believes that Mabel really did that stuff, but she did. I saw it with my own eyes," Pax said. "Our little racket's good money so far, huh, Mabel?"

She nodded. "You're keeping me in clover, Pax. Thanks, hon."

We were still laughing as the boys helped us unload from the jeep when a low droning sound rose over our voices. We looked to the sky, shielding our eyes from the glare.

In the distance, a swarm of planes in V-formation was heading in our direction. We all paused to watch them.

"Jesus, those are Zeroes!" one of the other airmen shouted. "Take cover!"

Of course in those days, I didn't know a Zero from a zebra. How would I? So I stood there, confused.

Pax grabbed my wrist. "The Japanese are coming! Get out of here!" he yelled, pointing toward the edge of the tarmac before turning and joining the airmen as they ran for their planes.

Sally, Virginia, Mabel, and Phyllis remained frozen in a cluster. "Come on!" I screamed to them, dashing for the low-lying brush at the edge of the field. I'd never sprinted so quickly in my life. My heart pounded, chest strained, lungs burned. We swerved off the pavement and dove under the few small straggly bushes poking out from the hot, dry ground, grunting as our knees and palms made impact.

The last thing I saw before crossing my arms over my head and pushing my face into the brush was the silver glint of the approaching planes and a flickering of something sparkly gliding to the earth below. It took me a second before I realized what those beautiful things were: bombs.

And then the world erupted into chaos.

Everything seemed to lift. The earth shuddered. A wall of wind crashed over me as I lay huddled on the ground. The air heated and thinned. It felt as though I was being turned inside out. Air was sucked from my mouth, nose, and ears. Even my eyeballs seemed to tug from their sockets. I could taste gasoline in the air and gasped, struggling to breathe. The weight of a tremendous force pulled at me and my hands scrabbled at empty space below. A bone-splitting crack rang out. And then, with a huge *THUD*, the pressure seemed to reverse and I was being flattened into the ground as if being crushed. After several beats of this, the pressure slid away, and I curled into a ball, praying for a miracle.

Explosions blasted. A thick slurry of dust and debris rose into the air, choking us.

I didn't want to die, not here, not anywhere. I willed myself to become as small as possible. My fingernails dug into my scalp as the rat-a-tat of nearby strafing rang out.

How long did this last? Ten minutes? Twenty? Thirty? It was a blur, hard to tell.

When the sound of plane engines faded, I nudged my face from the ground, blowing away blades of grass stuck on my lips. Every muscle in my body ached. *What the hell had just happened?*

Gone was the blue sky. Plumes of oily smoke rose, and flames appeared everywhere. Blackened smoking ruins burned along the tarmac where the planes had been. The surrounding hangars and ground installations had either been destroyed or appeared as mere shells of what they had been moments earlier. I drew myself to my knees, wobbly with uncertainty. Everything looked different.

The crackling sound of fire and a shrill ringing in my ears made me clap my palms to the side of my head as if I could push the sounds away.

Beside me, movement. Sally, covered in dirt and grime, struggled to all fours.

"Are you hurt?" she cried in a shaky voice.

Beside her, Virginia unpeeled from the ground. And then Phyllis and Mabel appeared, wearing dazed, fearful expressions.

"We've got to see if anyone needs help," I said. On quaking legs, we staggered to our feet, propping ourselves against each other for support, checking for injuries. Remarkably, we appeared unscathed.

Sally grabbed my shoulder. "What about Darren? Do you think he's hurt?"

"He's at the hospital. I'll bet he's fine."

Sally nodded, and the five of us, dizzy and disoriented, zigzagged closer to where we could see shapes of people moving against the smoke. Twisted slags of metal, too hot to touch, littered the ground. Hunks of acacia and nara trees that had once lined the airfield burned everywhere. And then came the grisly discoveries. Scraps of charred uniform. A helmet with a hank of hair hanging off the edge. A boot with the foot still inside, the ankle severed neatly as if with a butcher's blade. I froze, stunned.

Suddenly two trucks roared onto the airfield and orderlies

jumped out. "Sally, Tess!" one of the men—his name drifted just outside the edge of my memory—shouted, waving his arms frantically. "We were told we might find you here. Are you injured?"

We shook our heads.

He squinted, unconvinced. "Stay here and be ready to help as we load some fellas," he yelled. "Let's make this fast. The enemy will be back." The orderlies tied rags over their noses and mouths before disappearing into the smoke.

Dark smoke obscured the sky, but we peered overhead, stepping closer to one another in a pathetic attempt at protection.

Before there was time to think, two orderlies returned with a man on a stretcher. Smoke and grime darkened the injured airman's face, and a large gash, nine inches or so, had been torn in the lateral aspect of his left upper thigh. The muscle gleamed red and slick with blood. The orderlies lifted him onto the back of the truck and then gestured at us to climb up too. One of them tossed us a musette bag and Sally didn't wait for directions, but opened it and began pulling out bandages. Only as she leaned toward the airman did she gasp. "Dewey?"

We all froze, eyes wide. For once, Dewey didn't have a snappy comeback. He simply stared upward, his eyes glassy with shock. Without saying anything more, Sally started wrapping a tourniquet around his upper thigh and I held it in place, securing its tightness, as she tied it. His wound was ugly and cause for concern, but it wasn't life-threatening. Still, the gravity of seeing one of our own taken down by the enemy shook us.

Within minutes, more wounded airmen surrounded us. Virginia, Phyllis, and I moved to the second truck and crawled around the back, comforting the soldiers as best we could with the limited supplies of the moment. The choking smoke blended with the metallic tang of blood, along with something else, a bitter, sweet smell that turned our stomachs. Fear.

THE TRUCKS RACED along the main thoroughfare from the airfield to the Station Hospital as if the Japanese Zeroes were hot on our heels—and for all we knew, they were. At the hospital a group of doctors and nurses met us. The injured were rushed inside.

Head Nurse Josie Nesbit, pristine in her white nurse's dress, stopped us, her expression grim. For a moment, she reminded me of my sister and my knees weakened. I so badly wished for Sue at that moment, but Josie gave no time to indulge in homesickness. "Girls, are you injured?"

"No," we mumbled.

"Is Darren here?" Sally asked.

"He's inside, working." Josie's gaze roved over us, but stopped on Mabel and the stream of blood threading down her neck, soaking the white collar of her dress. Josie stepped toward her, deftly running her fingers along Mabel's hairline, investigating. She gestured at a nurse who hadn't been at the airfield to lead Mabel inside.

Josie turned back to the remaining four of us. "At the first sign of nausea or dizziness, sit down and let one of us know. Otherwise, let's carry on. Go to the nurses' station and grab syringes, vials of morphine, tetanus antitoxin, a pen, and a stack of index cards. We're triaging new arrivals. Check each patient, but there's no time for charts. Mark their conditions on those index cards and place them on their foreheads. One tells us they need a doctor's attention; two indicates you can treat the injuries yourself; and three means to keep the patient as comfortable as possible."

Triage? I hadn't heard that word since my training in Tacoma. Without looking at each other, we rushed inside to arm ourselves with medicine. That third category of keeping them comfortable—we knew what that really meant. We were no longer treating simple scorpion bites and other minor tropical ailments. War had arrived.

Once we had our vials, syringes, and note cards, we hurried into the first ward. Bodies, filthy and mangled, twisted on the beds.

Most of the men appeared to be biting back screams and when I approached the nearest one, he waved me toward the next cot, panting, "Check him out first. He looks worse off than me."

I gazed at the motionless man on the next cot. A ghastly stomach wound had already claimed him and I exhaled sadly before turning back to the first man, blocking his dead friend with my body. "How about I start with you instead?" I forced myself to sound lighthearted. "Those dimples on you are something else."

IT WASN'T LONG before air-raid sirens blared, prompting us to find cover wherever we could. I slid under a nearby cot. As I covered my ears from the whine and crash of nearby explosions, a trickle of blood began to pool on the floor inches from my nose. I swallowed hard. It was soaking through the mattress above me. War, I was realizing, demands *a lot* of blood. I pulled a towel from my apron's waistband and wiped away the puddle before sliding out from the cot to resume work.

Soon the hospital's wards filled beyond capacity, and the orderlies started lining up injured men outside on the grass. The wounded continued to be delivered on stretchers, in wheelbarrows and carts, and often in the arms of other soldiers. We sheared off filthy uniforms, cleaned lacerations and abrasions, dug shrapnel out of bloody gashes, and gave morphine injections. Meanwhile, our white nursing dresses were ruined. Dirt, blood, vomit—and worse—soaked and crusted us from head to toe. The business of repairing the human body was a messy affair. It was sticky, smelly, slippery, and surprisingly noisy. Forget the men's yells, curses, cries, and moans—the body itself makes a racket, wheezing, slurping, sucking, and squelching.

Until the last forty-eight hours of our nursing careers, patient chart data and doctor orders had informed our treatment decisions. Now, there was no time for any of that. Pulse, skin color, breathing tempo, and touch guided us—we had to reach into wounds for foreign objects, feel for broken bones, and assess blood loss. We needed to observe what was happening and respond quickly. Bodies have an overwhelming urge to survive, and despite our fatigue and shock, we needed to do everything in our power to help.

DUSK FELL AND the lines of patients became cloaked in darkness, and because of orders to maintain a blackout, we did our rounds in the moonlight.

At one point, I leaned over a man whose mangled arm dangled from his shoulder. The sight of his sandy-colored hair made me gasp. "George?"

The injured serviceman replied in a faint voice, "I'll be whoever you want, if you'll give me some water." I brushed his hair from his blood-encrusted forehead, noting the coolness of his skin, both relieved it wasn't George and deflated, knowing how grim this man's chances appeared. He gave me a look that was half grin, half grimace. "I've always thought I'm a ringer for Henry Fonda."

"Come on, you're far more of a dreamboat than him. Now buck up while I give you this shot." While he gritted his teeth together, I injected a syringe of morphine into his unharmed shoulder. "Now hang in there, handsome. The surgeon will be right over."

When I straightened, Virginia was next to me. "They're saying every plane on the airfield was destroyed." She wiped at her brow. "I swear, I'm practically dead on my feet."

"Well, you look a lot better than most of these guys, that's for sure." I shuddered, looking toward the sky.

Beyond the columns of greasy smoke still thickening the air, stars flickered. Where was George? What had happened to him? Around me, the other nurses circled, looking like ghosts as they floated among the lines of injured. Josie had told us more nurses and doctors would soon be arriving from Sternberg in Manila to help with our overwhelming crush of patients, but we understood it was a matter of days—maybe hours—before the capital would be facing the enemy too. There was no reprieve in sight. How would we keep up?

What surprised me more than anything was how quickly everything had changed. In an instant, our lives could be irrevocably altered—and even ended. And the future? There was no predicting it, no taking anything for granted anymore. No one knew what lay ahead.

3.

FLOR

Flor Dalisay awoke with a start. In a distant part of the house, the telephone was ringing, an unusual occurrence for so early in the morning, but she thought little of it because she was too busy wondering when had she fallen asleep.

The last thing she remembered was lying on her back at four o'clock in the morning, staring at the ceiling, praying the rosary. Now, with beams of sunlight slicing through her room, she rolled onto her side and squinted at her steamer trunk.

The last few months had been a whirlwind of emotions about today's departure—sometimes Flor was thrilled, other times anxious—but now that the day of her voyage was actually here, she felt nothing but dread. Why had she agreed to leave home? Yes, her parents and older sister had studied overseas, but Flor wasn't like them. She wasn't on the hunt for adventure and she had little interest in exploring new places and meeting new people. She preferred to stay home and attend classes at the university. She liked her daily routine to remain predictable and took comfort in keeping her family close.

Flor had agreed to study for a year in the United States because her father had spent four years there and the idea of following in his footsteps initially felt comforting. People always commented on how she took after him. Dr. Romeo Dalisay was widely respected for his calm, scholarly demeanor, the way he always appeared to think before he spoke, and his tendency to have his nose buried in a book. People often said that in another life, he might have been a judge, and Flor thought this to be a wonderful compliment. She took great pride in the parallels people drew between her and her father, although try as she might, she could never overcome her aversion to blood. Honestly, the idea of a career in medicine made her feel lightheaded and queasy, so she stuck with her love of numbers and planned to study mathematics at the University of California in Berkeley. So she wasn't *exactly* like Papa, but close enough.

Romeo Dalisay's primary occupation was running his private medical practice in a small office near their house, though he also served as an adviser to the Ministry of Health and was close personal friends with President Manuel Quezon, the man governing the Philippines during this decade of transition between the country's status as a US territory and full independence. Papa's love for medicine, his belief in the power of democracy and education, and his hope in full independence for the Philippines—all of it had taken root in California, so when the opportunity came for Flor to spend 1942 abroad, she embraced the formula that had served her father so well and agreed to leave.

But then the world became more complicated.

The war in Europe, though distant, was on everyone's minds. Emboldened by its successful invasions of neighboring European countries, Germany had turned its attention eastward and begun advancing on the Soviet Union the previous spring. Closer to home, the Japanese were making incursions in China and Indochina and rumors that they might launch wider aggressions circulated, though everyone seemed in agreement that the chances for their success appeared improbable.

Nevertheless, to be on the safe side, many Americans residing in the Philippines sent their families back to the States throughout the fall. As the January date of Flor's departure for California neared, her parents grew increasingly convinced that traveling to the United States was still a good idea, but Flor wasn't so sure. Although two Dalisay aunts lived outside of San Francisco, Flor didn't understand how being almost seven thousand miles *away* from her mother, father, and older sister could be considered good if war broke out. The original plan had been for her to sail for San Francisco after Christmas with her tita Angela, but as talks in Washington, DC, between Japanese and American diplomats stalled, Papa decided Flor and his sister should leave sooner so they were booked for passage to the United States on Monday, December 8.

Flor had spent her final weekend at home shopping and strolling through Luneta Park, eating Magnolia ice cream with a few friends and Ate Iris, her older sister, and putting on a good show of enthusiasm, though through it all, the sense she was on the verge of making a terrible mistake grew stronger and stronger inside her.

On her final night at home, a celebratory dinner was planned. Over the plates of adobo and sinangag and glowing votive candles on the dining room table, Romeo had raised a glass to Flor. "To our Flordeliza, may you spread your wings and learn to thrive in the United States," he said.

Pilar, Flor's mother, raised hers too. "Enjoy yourself, my love. Make new friends. It will be good for you to get away from your ate's social circle and make your own. Explore." She gave a dramatic sigh. "Oh, what I would give to be twenty years old again."

"Thank you, Mama." Flor had smiled, carefully pronouncing her mother's title with its usual French accent to hide how she bristled at the criticism nestled in her toast. Mama always seemed to feel that Flor was too serious, too consumed with her studies, too dependent on her ate.

Iris jumped to her feet and ran around the table. "Oh, Flor, I'm going to miss you so much," she said, embracing her tightly. "You'll always be the center of my circle. Is there an official name for that? Is it radius? Circumference? What do you call the center of a circle?"

Flor laughed. "I'm going to miss each of you, but I'm ready." And she was ready. At least, everything on Flor's packing list was checked off and safely stowed within her steamer trunk. Still, a sense of unease nagged at her. Was she really ready to leave everyone she loved behind? Seated in the dining room, surrounded by her family, Flor already felt homesick. How was that even possible?

After dinner, as Iris prepared to leave for her overnight shift at Sternberg Hospital, where she worked as a nurse, she had squeezed Flor's shoulders. "I'll be home in time tomorrow to send you off in style."

"Ate, you don't have to," Flor said. "You're always so tired after a night shift."

"Are you kidding? Nothing could keep me away from a final glimpse of you. *Nothing.*"

Flor bobbed her head up and down, not trusting herself to speak. When Iris had traveled all the way to New York City for university, had she felt anxious? Flor tried to think back, but all she could remember was her sister's confidence. Iris had been packed weeks prior to her departure, and the night before she left, one of her friends had thrown a big farewell party. For the morning her ship was to sail, Iris begged Luchie, their housekeeper, to make an American-style breakfast. By contrast, Flor had already requested Luchie to have her Filipino favorites on hand: a sweet and creamy cup of thick tsokolate and bibingka with shaved coconut and brown sugar on top. She knew American-style hot chocolate would not be the same as Luchie's, and once she was in California, rice cakes would be impossible to find.

"Are you sure you want to go? You don't have to leave," Papa had said, appearing at Flor's side to smooth down her Peter Pan collar.

"Don't upset her, Romeo! She'll be fine. Of course, she's going," Mama called from where she still sat at the table.

But when Flor finally retired to her room that night, she wanted to unpack everything. Her hands hovered over the latches of her trunk. What if she decided *not* to go? Would it *really* be so bad to change her mind?

She glanced at a photo beside her bed. In it, she sat on a sailboat beside Iris and two friends, all of them beaming for the camera. It had been taken four years ago, on Flor's sixteenth birthday. A friend of Papa's had taken the girls for a sail. Out on the water, a breeze tugged at the ribbons on their hats, their skirts snapped in the wind and made them laugh, and dolphins swam alongside them. That afternoon had been one of the best of Flor's life. Everything she needed had been hers: her ate at her side, a beautiful day, and the familiar skyline of home in the distance.

If she decided *not* to go to California, wouldn't her friends think she was crazy? Many of her classmates would kill for the opportunity to study abroad. And two years earlier, Iris had studied nursing at Columbia University, which was even farther away than California—would Iris think her a coward? How Flor longed to be brave! She had always admired Iris's courage. When they had attended the same school, classmates brightened when they realized Flor was Iris's younger sister, but in the weeks that followed, Flor could see everyone always lost interest in her when they realized she didn't possess her ate's same witty sense of humor, her penchant for storytelling, and her easy ability to make friends. None of that came naturally to Flor.

She preferred to study, to lose herself in a book, or even better, *numbers*. Flor was always at her most confident when she was problem-solving a long list of equations. Numbers moved easily through her mind the same way a skilled swimmer could carve through the water. The problem was that few people recognized number sense as a valuable skill for a twenty-year-old woman. If Flor were a man, she had little doubt her gift would be lauded. She would be offered training in engineering, physics, or architecture. Instead, it was less clear how she would be able to use her talents. So, she realized, maybe a onetime trip away from Manila to possibly expand her options wouldn't be the worst thing.

She moved away from her trunk without unpacking. Instead, Flor climbed into bed, her rosary beads clutched tightly in one hand, and she lay in the dark for hours trying to convince herself that California would be wonderful. At some point she must have finally fallen asleep.

NOW, FLOR ROSE. The ringing of the telephone faded.

"Today I leave for California," she announced to the figurine of the Blessed Mother Mary sitting on her bedside table.

She dressed in the jaunty navy blue poplin traveling suit Mama insisted would make her look chic, but when she left her room, the house felt quiet. Where was the usual clatter of breakfast dishes, the swish of newspaper pages being turned, and the low hum of her parents' conversation? Flor walked through the sala and passed the dining room. Place settings for breakfast lay on the table, but where was everyone?

It was then that she heard voices floating through the windows, so she went down the stairs and out the front door. There, underneath the butter-yellow trumpet blooms of the kampanilya spilling over the stone wall, stood her parents talking with their neighbors. Iris was next to Mama, her white nurse's cap askew on top of her head. Luchie was deep in conversation with Jose, the gardener, her arms folded across her chest. When Flor appeared, everyone fell silent and turned to look at her.

"My dear," Papa said in a dazed voice. "Your ship isn't leaving after all."

WHEN FLOR TOOK her seat at the breakfast table alongside her family, she could scarcely think straight. She knew she should be upset by the news of the Japanese attack on Hawaii. Everyone else certainly was—the stunned faces of her family confirmed that—but Flor was secretly relieved. Now she could stay home and life could carry on. She would continue with her calculus class at the university. Though there had been talk of war with Japan, no one believed a conflict could last long. Perhaps a naval blockade, maybe aerial bombardment, but nothing that would drag on. How could such a small island nation like Japan be capable of mounting anything more than that?

Iris unpinned her nurse's cap and laid it gently on her lap, a move that would normally prompt Mama to scold her for her attending to her hair at the table, but everyone was too distraught to pay much attention to an oversight in manners.

"The other doctors and nurses at Sternberg have been saying

the likelihood of an attack before the new year would be absurd. I can't believe it happened today," Iris said. As a nurse for the USAFFE, the United States Army Forces in the Far East, this attack was bound to impact her work directly.

"With all due respect to your American colleagues, they have been overconfident and underprepared." Papa scooped some rice onto his plate. "They haven't been paying enough attention to how the Japanese have reinvented themselves over the last few decades."

Mama frowned. "But how could they be crazy enough to attack the United States? How did they manage such a thing?"

He glanced at his wife and eldest daughter over his wire-rimmed spectacles. "The Japanese do not fear size. They've certainly made quick work of the Chinese."

This gave them all pause. Everyone had read the newspapers. They knew of the brutal tactics the Japanese had meted out against the people of Nanking a few years earlier during an invasion of China. The looting, the widespread murdering and raping of civilians. Memories of those frightening newspaper articles and photos of bodies piled up like bricks along the Huangpu River still had the power to make Flor feel ill.

The phone rang and Iris sprang from her seat to answer it. After a moment, she returned, her face somber. "Gloria's reporting that the Japanese just bombed Camp John Hay in Baguio. Sternberg is expecting casualties today. I need to return back to work now."

Luchie, who had been carrying a plate of sliced mango, clicked her tongue. "Don't go until I feed you something."

Iris, who appeared ready to race out of the house, stopped on Luchie's command. Twenty-five years ago, newly married Pilar had hired young Luchie to be her lady's maid, and then to tend to her babies, but now Luchie operated the entire household.

Flor and Iris often pointed out that they had outgrown their former yaya's ministrations, but today's fussing felt comforting.

As Luchie packed food for Iris, Flor thought back to a trip her family had made the previous summer to Baguio, a mountainous retreat north of the city. "Could the Japanese bomb us?"

As soon as the words left her mouth, she realized how naive she sounded. Though the trip to Baguio had taken five hours by automobile, a Japanese bomber would be able to cover the same distance in a mere fraction of the time. Of course the Japanese would come to Manila. The city's bay was considered the best in Asia and the Dalisays' home in the Ermita District was only a few minutes' walk from the waterfront.

Mama picked up a notepad and began to make a list. "Luchie, Flor, and I will stock up on rice and canned foods. Iris, Jose can drive you to the hospital when he takes us to the market."

"Go on foot. It will be faster. Traffic will be a mess right now as everyone tries to shop and leave the city," Papa said, rising from the table. "I need to go to my practice, at least for a few hours. Pilar, plan on shopping for a month's worth of food."

"A month? This will be over in a few days," Mama protested.

Papa scratched his chin. "I don't think so."

"Come now. With the Americans involved, it won't last long," Mama said.

Flor and Iris swiveled their heads back and forth between their parents as if watching a tennis match. For as long as the sisters could remember, the relationship between their parents had been strained, their resentments simmering like a pot of rice over a flame. Both husband and wife were ambitious and though this had initially drawn them to each other as young university students, the responsibilities of daily domestic life often stirred up small but persistent resentments between the two.

Iris sighed and pinned her cap back on. "I need to leave. I'll be back this evening." She gave Flor an apologetic look, knowing she was leaving her behind to suffer through an argument.

Pilar and Romeo were like the Sun and Moon from the old folktale Luchie used to tell Iris and Flor when they were younger. Luchie would gather the girls in the kitchen and the three of them would peel garlic and ginger for adobo or pancit noodles. "The Sun and Moon were married but used to quarrel all the time," Luchie would say, adjusting Iris's small fingers on the knife so they'd be closer to the blade and give her more control. "The Sun would tell the Moon, 'You need me to shine.' But the Moon would say, 'You burn too brightly. You can be dangerous.' Once the Moon asked the Sun to watch over their children, but the Sun made a mistake and melted the children into stars. When the Moon came back, he was heartbroken and furious and argued with the Sun, but she refused to admit her mistake and threw sand in his face. That's why the Moon has dark spots."

Luchie enjoyed telling old folktales for entertainment, but Flor couldn't help seeing the parallels between her stubborn, outspoken mother and her quiet father, who had his own brand of stubbornness. And as Iris headed for the stairwell to leave, Flor could see that same quality running through her sister too.

"You shouldn't leave now," Flor protested. "What if there's an actual attack?"

"That's exactly why I must go. They'll need me at the hospital," Iris called over her shoulder. "I'll be careful."

Flor watched her sister's retreating figure and fingered the small golden cross hanging around her neck. How was Iris so fearless?

THAT EVENING, AIR-RAID sirens began to wail and Flor kept one ear angled toward the sky to listen for airplanes while cutting out squares of dark black fabric to cover the windows. Later, she gathered around the radio with her parents to listen to the American president address the world.

"With confidence in our armed forces, with the unbounding determination of our people, we will gain the inevitable triumph so help us God."

Mr. Roosevelt sounded so sure of himself, so certain in his belief in his countrymen, that as the rest of the night passed without incident, hope took root in Flor. *Maybe the Americans were right and this won't turn into anything too worrisome,* she told herself as she knelt in front of the crucifix over her bed to say her evening prayers. *Hawaii must have been a fluke.*

But Iris never came home that evening. Nor the next day.

By Wednesday, two days after the news of Pearl Harbor, there was still no sign of Iris. Papa tried telephoning the hospital, but the lines were busy.

Despite the intermittent air-raid sirens, there was also no sign of the Japanese. The radio reported sightings throughout the different islands and around Luzon. No one doubted they would arrive in the city, but when?

Flor paced the house, anxious for Iris to arrive, but by midday, she could wait no longer. At lunchtime, she announced to her mother and Luchie that she was going to Sternberg Hospital to see what was happening. She headed outside, her nerves jangling from being cooped up indoors for two days straight. She passed bored members of the Philippine Constabulary in their pie-plate helmets and khaki puttees, wandering around hastily erected piles of sandbags.

After the initial flurry of shopping, the streets had quieted as people stayed home, listening to their radios, waiting for definitive news. Flor was a few blocks from the hospital when a buzzing sound filled the air.

She tented her palm across her brow and stared at the sky, hazy with heat. Over the Pasig River, it looked like a flock of silver birds was heading toward the fortified thick stone walls of Intramuros, the sixteenth-century historic section of the city. Flor stopped and watched. *That* was the enemy? The tiny planes looked harmless enough, but then small canisters dropped from them and fell toward earth. After a few seconds, the ground lurched under Flor's feet and giant feathers of black smoke fanned across the sky.

Flor spun around and ran toward home. With every step, the ground buckled and cracked from explosions. When she tore into the front door, her mother embraced her tearfully while Luchie fluttered around them, clucking with concern.

"I didn't even make it to Sternberg," Flor said, furious with herself for not knowing more about what had happened to her sister.

Pilar kissed her forehead. "We will pray for Iris."

All day the family listened to the distant crashes of bombs. The planes appeared to be targeting Nichols Field and Cavite Naval Yard, both south of the city, although sometimes the house shook from explosions along the waterfront. The smell of cordite drifted through the air.

That evening when Papa lifted the phone to call the hospital and make inquiries about Iris, no buzzing sound emanated from the receiver. The phone was dead. No one dared to leave the house for fear of what they might encounter in the dark. Flor lay in the sala, drifting in and out of sleep as the radio reported the latest news, but all she wanted to know about was her missing sister.

4.

TESS

December 1941
Fort Stotsenburg

The Japanese intensified their attacks on Luzon and we scrambled to keep up with casualties. By destroying our planes at Clark Field, the Japanese expanded upon what they had achieved by sinking our ships at Pearl Harbor: now American naval *and* air power had been obliterated in the Pacific. The situation was dire, but we were finding we hated the idea of giving up.

For one thing, say what you will about General Douglas MacArthur—and that winter and spring *everyone* developed strong opinions about him, both good and bad—but he loved the Philippines and his loyalty was inspiring. It was clear that the idea of surrendering it to an invading force was the last thing he wanted to do. And he wasn't alone. All of us felt protective of the Philippines.

Did this place feel sacred because our youth had been shaped by the Depression's hardships and we were grateful for the island's beauty and bounty? Perhaps. Maybe it was our collective sense of being cornered—we were so far from home that we were going to fight tooth and nail to save what we had. Or maybe it was simply good ol'-fashioned American righteousness—we were simply appalled by a nation defeating us by playing by a set of rules we considered unfair. Everyone had seen the news of the Japanese atrocities against civilians in Nanking and then the surprise attack on Pearl Harbor came, and both events galvanized us to not let anything similar happen on our watch. Whatever the reason, we were scrambling to figure out a viable defense.

Several days before Christmas, the Japanese Imperial Army was rolling south through Luzon and the USAFFE was in full retreat. At Fort Stotsenburg, we received orders to prepare our patients for evacuation to Manila. I was in a hallway, filling crates with vials of medicine, when an orderly stopped me.

"Hey, Tess, Sergeant Willis wants to see you on the front steps."

"Me?"

He glanced at the strip of paper in his hand. "Yep, you're the one he asked for." And with that, he took off down the hallway to deliver more messages.

I smoothed my hands over my white uniform to brush off any dust and then dashed outside and found Sergeant Willis surrounded by several others. He fired off rapid orders to them before turning to me.

"Miss, you're in charge of the hospital train leaving in an hour. Keep the patients safe." And with that, he handed me a .45 pistol and a tatty green army sock full of bullets and then checked his watch, cracked his knuckles, and marched toward the quartermaster's office with nary a backward glance.

Agape, I remained rooted to the sidewalk. *What on earth was I supposed to do with a pistol?* Sweat trickled along my face, but I didn't dare brush it away for fear of setting the gun off somehow.

"Tess?"

I looked up, squinting at the figure approaching me in the blinding sunshine, and let out a small cry of relief. "George! What are you doing here?"

As he neared, a bright smile took over his face. "I was sent here for something. Figured I'd check in on my favorite nurse."

Despite my delight at his arrival, I remembered my orders and raised the gun gingerly. "What am I supposed to do with this?"

George's mouth fell open and he ducked, lifting his hands in surrender. "Whoa, Tess, what are you doing? Is the safety on?"

I cringed, embarrassed by my foolishness. "How can I tell? I was just given this and told I'm in charge of a hospital train leaving in an hour, but clearly I have no idea how to use a gun."

He approached and gently took the weapon from my hand, leaning in to kiss my cheek. "Are you packed and ready to go?"

"Yes, I knew we were leaving today. I just didn't know this"—I nodded at the pistol—"was part of the deal." Since our attack each day felt stranger and stranger. Every morning I'd awaken and there'd be a brief moment when I'd think the war had been a weird, horrifying nightmare. But then the moment of respite would flicker through me and a cold pit of dread in my stomach would take hold, and with it the realization that the nightmare was real. War was our life now.

George nodded and looked around. He picked up two crates from a nearby refuse pile. "Come with me." He led me to the jeep he'd parked nearby, tossed the crates in the back, and helped me in.

We drove a few minutes away from the base before he veered off the road, parked in the shade of a banyan tree, and signaled we should get out. He grabbed the crates and reached under his seat to produce an empty bottle of Coca-Cola, and then he constructed a target out of the crates and bottle. Turning to me, he began explaining the basics of using a pistol.

I was listening, of course, but at the same time my heart pumped as if I'd been running sprints. For the previous few weeks, my nervous system had been working overtime. Between the thrill of seeing George again, the gun, and the evacuation—not to mention the lack of sleep and strain brought on by the daily enemy bombing raids—I was keyed up, but somehow managed to listen and then fire off a few practice rounds at the target. I wish I could boast I'd been a crack shot on my first try, but nothing could have been further from the truth. To my surprise, George seemed satisfied with my attempts and glanced at his watch, saying we needed to go.

Once we were back in the jeep, I turned to him. "So what are you doing here? You just had a sixth sense I needed pistol instruction today?"

He took off his cap and wiped his forehead, before looking straight at me. "I haven't been able to stop thinking about you. I had to come back and make sure you're safe."

The directness of his admission stunned me. "Safe? Ha, that was last season's style. Full-on panic is the only look people are wearing now."

He smiled sadly and handed me the sock full of bullets. "I'm here to check on the readiness of Filipino fighting forces in Pampanga Province. Within the next twenty-four hours I'll be heading back to Manila."

"Will I be able to see you there?"

"Of course," he said, turning on the ignition. In silence, we drove back toward Stotsenburg. I gripped my seat with both hands as he navigated the vehicle around bomb craters dotting the road.

"I'm looking forward to being back in the city," I ventured. "Out here, it's been hard to know what's going on."

"Prepare yourself for a lot of changes."

ONCE WE RETURNED to the hospital, I hesitated before climbing out. A steady stream of doctors, nurses, and soldiers flowed past us carrying supplies and equipment. I glanced at George, trying to memorize his face. His straight nose, high cheekbones, and the permanent crease between his eyes, a result of his tendency toward thoughtfulness. There were so many things I wanted to say to him, but at the same time, I was tongue-tied. It was entirely possible we would never see each other again.

I looked at the pistol in my lap. Under my hot, perspiring fingers, the thing was cool, its metal surface shiny and smooth. "They must really think the end is near if they're expecting me to fight." I meant it as a joke, but neither of us laughed. "But really, how on earth will I know when to use this?"

"Listen to what your gut's trying to tell you," he said quietly. And then he surprised me. Despite the fact that his jeep was parked in a busy spot and half of Fort Stotsenburg was marching by, he reached for my shoulders and kissed me hard on the lips. Catcalls erupted from nearby, but George couldn't have cared less. If anything, he gripped me tighter and I leaned in for it because what the heck did we have to lose? For the last two weeks, horrors had been everywhere and as a result, we were punchy and a bit reckless. After a minute, we broke away, both of us breathless and grinning like we'd lost our minds.

"Was that your gut talking? Or maybe another part of you?" I asked, giggling.

"Could you get in trouble for that?"

I looked around. "I don't know, but what are they going to do? Send me home?"

"That's the spirit. See you in Manila?"

I hopped from the jeep and winked. "Thanks for the warning, soldier."

WITH VIRGINIA'S AND Sally's help, we managed to load the patients onto the train and the three of us settled into a row of seats as the trip got underway. Between the rhythm of motion and the heat in our car, the men grew quiet and drowsy. Periodically we checked on them, but everything was going along swimmingly. It wasn't until we reached the outskirts of the city that the shrill sound of an air-raid siren interrupted the quiet. From outside the window, a cluster of incoming enemy planes approached us, low and in formation. Dread filled me and instantly my legs began to quake. Our train jolted to a stop.

Along with the sirens, the buzz of Mitsubishi engines overhead created chaos. Patients stirred from their lethargy to cover their ears, writhe, yell, and scream.

Several men tried to rise from their bloody litters.

"Hey, fellas, calm down," Virginia called out, but delirium swept through the compartment like a tidal wave.

"Get me the hell out of here!" one patient cried.

Another man's eyes bulged as his face split into a manic leer and he started laughing uncontrollably. "I don't want to die!" he yelled before dissolving into loud sobs.

Sally looked at me, aghast.

I glanced out the nearest window to see the approaching planes and my fear heated into fury. What kind of enemy targets a hospital train? A sense of protectiveness overcame me. Perhaps if I'd had more time to think, I would have been surprised by this because the men were supposed to protect us, but suddenly that's not how it felt. There was no way I was going to let this poor group of damaged souls suffer any additional injuries. Not that day. "Go block the exit doors," I murmured to Virginia and Sally.

As they darted to the back of the compartment, though my legs were shaking, I clambered onto my seat and stood over the men, glowering with the most ferocious expression I could muster. "Stay in your seats!" I yelled. "Quiet down and don't move! *Don't even think about moving!*"

To my amazement, they fell silent and stared at me, wide-eyed and openmouthed. Virginia and Sally took their places at either end of the compartment and braced themselves against the frames of the doors. The planes bore down on us. Though I remained standing, inside I was praying like I'd never prayed before. *Please let us survive this. Please let us survive this*, I chanted to myself. Instinctively we ducked, covering our heads with trembling arms, but the planes roared past, fixed on a target beyond our train.

As quickly as the enemy had arrived, it vanished from view.

I could have wept with relief, but this was no time to let my guard down. Instead, I steadied myself by holding on to the wall and kept on glaring at the men. "Everyone remain calm. Stay quiet. We'll come by to check on you momentarily."

From the far ends of the compartment, Virginia and Sal gave me triumphant grins, and though my knees were practically knocking together with the residual fear still careening through my system, I bit back a smile and continued trying to look as fearsome as possible as I hopped off my seat.

When I bent over to check on a patient's sutures, one of the other men whispered raggedly to his neighbor, "Damn, now why doesn't MacArthur put *her* on the front lines?"

"War would be over in a jiffy," murmured another.

I looked up to see who was talking, but all I could see was Virginia, a few rows away, smothering a laugh.

Later that evening, once we'd settled our patients and retired to a break room at Sternberg Hospital, Virginia and Sal gave the other nurses and doctors a rousing reenactment of my command on the train. As we all dissolved in laughter at the improbability of Virginia, Sally, and me serving on the front lines, little did we know that was exactly where we would soon find ourselves.

5.

FLOR

December 1941
Manila

Three days after we received news that the Japanese had bombed Pearl Harbor, as Flor and her parents were eating breakfast, Iris appeared in the doorway of the dining room. Her once-white uniform was now black. She moved as though sleepwalking and staggered into her sister's arms.

"Ate, you're home," Flor murmured, squeezing her tightly as their parents folded in around them.

"They sent me north to Fort Stotsenburg. The airfield was bombed. It was a mess" was all Iris said. Flor helped her sister to her room, where Iris undressed and collapsed into bed.

When Flor returned to the kitchen to recover the remains of her breakfast, flashes of something white outside the window caught her eye. She crept into the back garden and found sheets of paper fluttering between the jasmine blossoms creeping up the back of the house. She plucked one from the vine and read:

"People of the Philippines: America seized your country forty years ago and since then, you have been abused, exploited, neglected, and treated as an inferior race."

Flor read the message several times before slowly crumpling it.

Since the United States had arrived in the Philippines for the Spanish-American War and then stayed, her family had directly benefited from the close relationship between the two countries. Members of the Dalisay family had visited the United States numerous times for educational purposes and to visit relatives who had emigrated to places in California. Flor's father had studied in California as part of the Pensionado Program, a US government–sponsored initiative to cultivate democracy in the Philippines by educating promising Filipinos at its own universities. Similarly, her mother had received an American Red Cross scholarship to study nursing at Columbia University, and later, Iris took advantage of the same opportunity. Along with these personal connections, Manila bustled with new modern infrastructure, railways, and facilities, all engineered by the United States. The proliferation of schools across the country? Those wide boulevards crossing Manila? The neoclassical buildings around Luneta Park? Annexation to the United States had led to these improvements and others.

Along with attracting Americans, Manila had a long history of welcoming people from all over the world. A walk along the city's busy shopping thoroughfares would reveal a wide range of languages and skin colors, a result of being one of Asia's busiest ports, a former Spanish colony, and a territory of the United States.

But the crumpled leaflet in her hand contained an important truth: a division ran between the white people in the Philippines and everyone else.

If Flor went to the Manila Hotel and tried to have a meal at one of its restaurants, though she might not be told directly to leave, her brown skin guaranteed that she would be stared at and whispered about by the white people surrounding her.

In fact, a number of places in Manila would not welcome the Dalisays simply because of the color of their skin.

Though she avoided thinking about it, there was no way to deny that many of the Americans and other Europeans who resided in Manila considered their Filipino neighbors to be inferior. This division led to a complicated relationship between many Filipinos and Americans and helped to explain why the Dalisays wholeheartedly supported full Filipino independence and self-rule, a milestone many of their countrymen also eagerly awaited.

Flor gathered the other leaflets and balled up each one, but when she went into the kitchen and tossed them into the garbage pail, a cold prickle of doubt ran up her arms.

Inferior race. Inferior race. Inferior race . . .

No matter how hard she would try to dismiss the leaflets as ugly propaganda and forget about them, she couldn't stop those bold blockish black-printed words from circling her mind.

OVER THE NEXT couple of weeks, the Japanese bombardment continued and American military installments throughout Luzon were obliterated, one by one. Despite this, the people of Manila seemed to assume the trouble would end quickly once American reinforcements arrived, but then came news that the Japanese Imperial Army's General Homma had landed with a large number of troops at Lingayen Gulf. This force was on the offensive, marching south through Luzon.

The citizens of Manila reeled. People scrambled to stock up on final provisions and many fled the city for the provinces, jamming the roads. At dusk, the streets emptied and looters trashed Japanese-owned businesses while Japanese saboteurs began setting buildings aflame to sow disorder. Between the air raids and fires, sirens blared through the long dark hours of each night.

Flor and Luchie stripped the house of valuables. Important documents, several thousand pesos and American dollars, the kitchen's knives, an old hunting rifle, a bolo knife, jewelry, and their liquor collection—all this they buried in the backyard beneath the chicken coop. Iris continued nursing at Sternberg, Papa attended to his patients, Mama worked at the Red Cross, but Flor's university canceled classes.

The day before Christmas, Iris marched into the dining room as Flor finished eating lunch with her parents. "General MacArthur is hoping to spare us any more damage and is going to pronounce Manila an open city on December twenty-sixth, so all military personnel and equipment must leave immediately. We're being sent to the Bataan Peninsula," she said. "I leave this evening."

"Tonight?" Luchie covered her mouth, horrified.

"The jungle? Even without the Japanese making trouble there, it's a dreadful place to go," Mama said.

"Don't leave," Papa said. "Stay and work here. I can obtain you a job at St. Luke's. At least consider the Red Cross, and you can still work in the field, but you'd be with a neutral party."

"The Japanese are coming and I've been ordered to retreat with my USAFFE colleagues." As if to make her announcement more dramatic, the thunderous sound of a bomb erupted somewhere nearby, perhaps a warehouse at the port. Iris cleared her throat and then said, "Our boat leaves this evening and I must be on it."

Everyone fell silent. Iris and Flor never disobeyed their parents.

Luchie lowered her head and skittered into the kitchen.

Flor braced for Papa's response. But he sighed and looked away.

While it had been staggering to see the Americans losing to the Japanese, to see Papa defeated was even worse.

Amazed, Flor turned to study her sister. Iris stood unwavering in her slim-cut khaki skirt, well-tailored blouse, and clean saddle shoes. At her side, she carried the beautiful leather suitcase she'd bought with one of her first paychecks. Iris was extremely proud of that suitcase and saw it as a symbol of her freedom. The sisters had spent an entire afternoon meandering the artfully curated displays at H.E. Heacock's, the city's most stylish department store, savoring the air-conditioning and debating which suitcase Iris should buy. In the end, she selected one made of dark brown leather, the color of mahogany, and brass trim that gleamed.

Flor watched as Iris accepted stiff goodbye embraces from her parents and Luchie. She wanted to tell Iris not to go, but knew any attempt to change her sister's mind would be futile. Iris had never backed away from a fight. Whenever any of their schoolmates had taunted Flor for being quiet and shy, Iris always came to her defense, telling the girls in no uncertain terms to mind their own business and be kind. Her sister had always appeared invincible, but now this war was coming for her.

Flor's heart twisted as she looked at Iris's brave smile. Her sister would soon arrive in a wilderness known for its pythons, malarial swamps, and packs of wild boar—how would she defend herself? Her beautiful leather suitcase would be no match for the jungle.

6.

TESS

December 1941
The Bataan Peninsula

That year the war began, it was easy to forget about the holidays. On Christmas Eve, Head Nurse Josie Nesbit found us eating turkey sandwiches in Sternberg Hospital's small break room. "Ladies, pack away your nurse's uniform because it might be a while before we're working under normal circumstances again." As she spoke, she pointed at a couple of crates next to her feet. "Once we leave, you'll be wearing these coveralls and combat boots."

I frowned. We had only been in Manila for a couple of days. "Where are we going now?"

"Bataan," Josie said, maintaining a level look, but we could see how her jaw tightened as she spoke. "General MacArthur's going to declare Manila an open city in hopes of sparing civilians from more enemy bombing. That means all military material and personnel must evacuate. The army's strategic planners have designated Bataan as being the best spot for us to maintain a defense while waiting for reinforcements."

We fell silent. The Bataan Peninsula was a mostly uninhabited mountainous stretch of jungle that formed one side of Manila Bay. To get there from Manila, you could take a boat across the water to reach it or undergo a long overland trip north out of the city and then start heading west across Luzon. I'd never met anyone who had been to Bataan. I'd also never met anyone who'd expressed any interest in *going* there. It was said to be a land full of dense malarial jungle, steep hills and ravines, and untamed terrain teeming with the type of wildlife I could do without: snakes, monkeys, and wild pigs. There was no sugar-coating this moment: the mighty US Army was in full retreat to an untamed location and it was mind-boggling. A prickle of horror ran up my neck.

It was Virginia who broke the tension by reaching into one of the crates and removing a stiff square of folded khaki-colored canvas. "Y'all know I'm a real stickler about wearing white after Labor Day so I, for one, applaud this announcement, Josie, thank you." She unfolded the new uniform letting the stiff coveralls fall against her. "Hmm, size 40, huh? So you're leaving us some room to grow? That feels optimistic, given recent menu items."

We chuckled nervously, looking at our turkey sandwiches.

"I know. Ladies, I asked if these were supposed to be tents or uniforms, but this is what they've given us, so we'll make the best of things as we always do." Josie smiled apologetically. "Tess is good with a needle. Maybe if you're nice to her, she'll help you out with some alterations. Now go pack up. I want you back here in an hour. You're leaving by boat and it departs this evening."

I picked up one of the boots. "But these are huge too!"

Josie shrugged. "Layer up your socks, I guess."

As we exchanged doubtful looks, Dr. Curtis, one of our favorites among the older staff, reached for Sally's arm. "Be safe. I'm scheduled to leave in a convoy heading out on East Road in the morning. We'll see you ladies there."

"I'll be sure to set up the record player first thing," Sally said, patting his shoulder fondly. Though Dr. Curtis claimed to be too old to attend parties at the OC, at one of our recent impromptu evening dance sessions in the hospital's break room, he'd revealed himself to possess the smoothest fox-trot in Manila. To his delight, we now quibbled over the honor of being his partner.

We said our goodbyes and headed to our nearby rooms. Curlers, lipstick, a couple of dresses, cold cream, sanitary supplies—silently, I fumbled to pack my things into duffel bags with shaking hands and then we gathered in front of the hospital to load into the trucks that would take us to meet our boat. I fretted aloud about not seeing George.

"Keep your hair on; he works in intelligence. If there's anyone who knows how to find people, it's him," Virginia said as we climbed into a truck.

Sally tied a scarf around her head to ward off dust. "I'm sure he'll track you down as soon as he can."

OUR CONVOY TO the waterfront hadn't even made it four blocks when the familiar roar of Zeroes made my stomach drop. Again? No matter how many times this had happened already, the terror that filled me always felt fresh. As the silver bellies of the planes appeared overhead and machine-gun fire strafed the crowd, we slid from the backs of the trucks and slithered along the dusty ground to the nearest open doorway. Around us, everyone screamed and cried as they fled their vehicles, carts, and bicycles to hide under bushes or follow us into buildings. This happened every twenty minutes or so, and each time my insides turned to liquid. Frazzled, filthy, and exhausted, we finally arrived at the waterfront and loaded onto the boat that would spare us the slow overland trip. From our spot in the stern, we awaited nightfall, anxiously studying the sky.

Iris and Gloria, two of the Filipino nurses, stared across the water at the burning city. "What will happen when the Japanese arrive here? I'm so worried about my parents and sister," Iris murmured.

Sally cast a guilty look at me. We missed our families too, but the upside to being so far from home was that our loved ones were safe back in the States.

"Where do they live?" Sally asked.

"Ermita."

"What a beautiful neighborhood. I enjoy walking those streets and admiring the lovely old houses," Sally said. "Are your parents worried about you?"

Iris exchanged a look with Gloria. "They're not thrilled. Funny, they've sent me halfway around the world to New York City before, but it's the jungle a few hours away that scares them most."

Well, that got our attention, and everyone turned to look at Iris in surprise.

"You've been to New York City?" Mabel asked.

"Yes, we both have." Iris gestured at Gloria. "We studied nursing at Columbia University."

I didn't know much about Columbia University, but I sure knew about New York City. I'd always wanted to go, but could never have dreamed of affording such a trip.

Until that conversation, I hadn't paid much attention to the Filipino nurses. They tended to stick to themselves and rarely socialized with us. When we had arrived in Manila, our supervisors made it clear that bringing a Filipino guest to a place like the OC was forbidden, so those restrictions had naturally led to a division between our two groups. If someone had asked me for an explanation for this division, I'd have been hard-pressed to describe it as anything other than the natural effect of the different spheres we moved within, but really, what was natural about it? It was a strange arrangement.

At home in Washington state, I'd never encountered much in the way of class and racial distinctions in my everyday life. The school I'd attended was composed of the children of Scandinavian and Irish immigrants, mostly farmers and fishermen. We were all poor. It wasn't until I'd arrived in Manila that suddenly I found myself amid a city brimming with people of different races and dramatic variations in social class. At our quarters on base, a staff of Filipino cooks and housekeepers looked after us, a luxury I'd never imagined before. Based only on the whiteness of my skin and the American passport in my pocket, my status had been elevated, and while I enjoyed these benefits of our new home, I was still uncomfortable with how to navigate this strange world and its many unspoken rules.

Sally leaned her elbows against the railing of the ship. In the tropics, darkness fell with the swiftness of lowering a curtain so we strained to see what lay ahead. "I hope your family remains safe and we'll be back here soon. This can't last too long."

"When do we set sail?" Mabel asked impatiently. "This rig better make it across the bay. You know the water's filled with sharks and mines and who knows what else? Could be subs out there."

"What are you trying to do? Scare us to death?" Sally asked in a small voice.

We shrank from the railing, but remained mesmerized by the reflection of flames on the surface of the black water. The fires burned so brightly around the port that Virginia had been using the light to sit on one of the benches and read. How on earth could she focus on a book? I squinted to see the title: *The Good Girl Gone Bad*. Despite the scariness of our current position, I smiled. While many of the women tucked the Bible into their bags, Virginia was never without one of her beloved romance novels.

"For crying out loud, enough of this nonsense about sharks," Virginia said, putting her book down. "Let's not forget, we have a secret weapon with us—the Pacific Cup swimming champ of California—and she's got a bunch of medals in her duffel to prove her expertise! Trust me, I've seen them." She turned to Nell. "You'll save us, won't you?"

"I'll make sure I save everyone, but you." Nell rolled her eyes. "Don't think I haven't forgotten what a mess you made of our cabin aboard the *Saratoga*."

"Is that why you didn't come to Stotsenburg with me?"

Nell nodded. With the impassive expression on her face, it was hard to tell if she was joking. "From now on, I'm going to bunk as far away from you as possible."

"I know you don't really mean that," said Virginia, wrapping the Californian in a hug. "Now, who wants to join me in singing some Christmas carols?" And without waiting for an answer, she launched into "Jingle Bells."

Nell leaned her head against Virginia's and joined her. Soon we were all singing and for a little bit, our spirits felt buoyed by holiday cheer.

UNDER NORMAL CONDITIONS, the trip across the bay should have taken several hours, but given the zigzagging nature of our course around the minefields, it was early morning when the coast of Bataan came into sharper focus. The first rays of morning's mango-colored glow licked across the dark sky. The water's surface was calm, its glassiness almost oily, and as the sun rose, a golden hue washed over everything. It was impossible to tell where the hazy sky ended and the ocean began. Small sprays of fish disturbed the mirror-smooth water and gulls wheeled overhead. Even in war, sometimes beauty surrounded us. The gentle roll of the boat and the motionless air lulled everyone into quiet, and I leaned against Mabel's shoulder while Sally closed her eyes and rested her head atop her knees.

Our boat nudged into the dock around seven in the morning. Spirals of concertina wire across the white sandy beach caught the light and sparkled.

Despite the loveliness of our surroundings, we were utterly drained, hot, and low on holiday cheer.

As we gathered ourselves on the beach, carrying crates of medical supplies off our boat, the ground beneath our feet trembled. A nearby copse of fire trees quivered as if anxious. Seconds later, the familiar sound of Mitsubishi motors roared overhead.

Our early morning fuzzy-headedness evaporated as we dropped everything, raced across the sand, and threw ourselves into ditches lining the waterfront. While we squirmed along the ground, searching for cover, the crimson setting suns painted on the sides of the planes glared at us like angry eyes.

"Bastards!" Sally screamed, lying facedown on the ground while puffs of red claylike dirt filled the air, kicked up by the strafing from overhead. How many of these attacks could a girl survive? I feared the luck that had gotten me this far was due to run out at any minute. Placing my hands on either side of my head to stabilize myself, I curled into a ball and begged the heavens to save us.

After a few seconds, a tickling sensation came over my hands. When I looked at them, a cluster of small red freckles appeared to dart across my skin like a school of fish. Horrified, I looked closer. They were tiny red-colored ants and they swarmed the dirt around us.

"Hell's teeth!" I cried out, crawling away from the ants, while trying to remain unobtrusive to the planes. Mabel followed me, and we wriggled into a different ditch, but clumps of sawtooth-edged cogon grass sliced at our hands, leaving raised red lacerations across our skin.

When the planes finally departed, we sprang to our feet to dust ourselves off. Remarkably there were no injuries from the enemy, but Bataan herself seemed bent on giving us a run for our money.

"Could this Christmas get any worse?" Mabel grumbled.

"It's like Louisa May Alcott said: Christmas won't be Christmas without any Japanese presence," I said, flinching at the sting of ant bites across my hands.

"Ohhh, I love reading *Little Women* at Christmas," mused Virginia. "Well, shoot, now I'm getting real homesick."

It was then that the shouting of the boat's crew caught our attention. We squinted down the beach at them and watched in disbelief as our ferry listed to its side and sank.

Virginia put her hands on her hips. "So now what? How are we supposed to build a hospital without supplies?"

A new whining sound surrounded us. Clouds of mosquitoes encircled our group, drawn to the exposed flesh of our faces and necks. They were large and brown and we batted them away, but they were more relentless than the Zeroes.

"Ugh! Mabel, why did you have to ask if things could get worse?" I cried.

Just then, two trucks rumbled to the wharf and stopped. A sunburned man leaned out from the driver's window of the first one, grinning widely. "Well, what do we have here? A Christmas miracle? Looks like a bunch of angels have landed."

"If we're so miraculous, things out here must be worse than we thought," I called, slapping at mosquitoes. "Any chance you can give us a lift to Hospital No. 2?"

"Even if those weren't our orders, think we'd say no to you, beautiful?" he asked.

As the men hopped from their trucks, the taller driver clapped the shorter one on the shoulder. "And to think, Greasy, you said Santa would never find us here."

"Pleased to meet you." I nodded to the shorter one. "Your name's Greasy?"

He ran his oil-stained hands across his pink nose, leaving a smudge, and his white undershirt strained at his soft middle as he stretched. "Sure am." Then he pointed at his buddy. "And this here's Six."

"Enchantée," Virginia said, extending her hand to Six.

"Six, huh?" I asked, appraising the lanky, bony-shouldered fella. While I could see where baby-faced Greasy's name came from, Six's was less obvious.

"See how tall and skinny he is? Just like six o'clock, get it? Six o'clock Special, but the fellas just go with Six."

"What's the special part?" Mabel asked.

"Trust me, I've got some special talents." Six smirked, swinging the loose end of his twine belt in a small circle. If his suggestive expression hadn't looked so goofy, we might have been put off, but with all that had gone wrong, we could only laugh.

Six gave us a good-natured grin that revealed a missing incisor. "Now where's all your luggage and equipment?"

"Y'all are in luck." Virginia waved at the few crates and duffels we had managed to grab as we fled the boat. "This'll be quick. Most of our equipment's at the bottom of Manila Bay."

The men turned to see only the ship's antenna poking out

from the water and its crew looking dejected as they sifted through the few items they'd managed to salvage before abandoning the craft.

Greasy shook his head. "Guess that captain was on Santa's naughty list."

WHEN OUR TRUCK turned onto East Road and we saw the columns of retreating bedraggled American and Filipino soldiers filling the highway, our hearts sank. Intermingled with the USAFFE troops were frightened refugees and sluggish carabao pulling carts filled with chickens in bamboo cages, grubby bedding, and household supplies. The sun was already blazing. Heat and fatigue muffled the sense of emergency, but I had no doubt an early morning overhead bombing raid could turn everything into chaos in an instant.

As I sat in the back of the truck, I closed my eyes. Ant and mosquito bites stung at my hands and neck, my stomach was tight and hollow with hunger, and my nerves felt shot to hell. At that moment, I would have given anything to be back in rainy and cold Tacoma with Sue. The sense of having a target on my back at all times felt like more than I could handle. My eyes opened a crack and I studied my friends. Did they feel this way too? Virginia had accepted a smoke from Six when we loaded onto the trucks and she sat beside me quietly, now taking long slow drags on the cigarette. At one point when she held it out in front of her, I could see a faint tremor in her hand, and suddenly tears blurred my vision. I snaked my arm around her shoulder and pulled her toward me and she curled into my side as Sal pressed into me on the other side. Yes, I was stuck in some forsaken place awaiting an attack, but I was filled with gratitude for these women who surrounded me. I'd known them for less than a year, but crisis had cemented our friendship into something solid and reliable. In an upside-down world, these women were my ballast.

We inched along the congested highway, our ears cocked toward the sky, and then without warning, our truck veered into the dense jungle on a pitted one-way road, plunging us into towering monkeypod and mango trees. Talahib and cogon grass closed in around us, making our path invisible. After several minutes we reached a clearing.

"Here we are," Six announced.

We stared. Below the thick canopy of acacia and mahogany trees, rows and rows of bamboo bunk beds, chairs, tables, and shelves had been built.

"This is it?" asked Mabel.

I looked around in disbelief. "Are there any buildings?"

"Nope, what you see is what you get. At this fine establishment, everyone gets a garden-view room," Greasy said, waving away the smoke of the cigarette dangling from one side of his mouth. "I'll tell you what, this place looks a whole lot better than it did a week ago when it was a dark, sweltering patch of jungle. First the bulldozers cleared some spaces for the wards, and then almost every piece of furniture you see was made by hand."

"Impressive," Sally said.

"Sure is. Gals, it's been a real honor, but we've got a few other transports to make. Get settled in and good luck. No offense, but I'm hoping if I'm ever lucky enough to engage in a little pillow talk with one of you, it's not because I'm a patient. Know what I mean?"

He winked at Virginia, who gave him a playful shove as we called out, "Merry Christmas!"

IN THE JUNGLE, there was nothing to do but work. Over the first few weeks of January, more and more patients arrived and soon all seventeen wards were packed with over two thousand men. Japanese bombing raids continued on nearby airfields and the booming of tank fire made the ground tremble constantly. After a couple of buildings were constructed with galvanized steel roofs, some soldiers climbed on top of them to paint red crosses indicating we were supposed to be off-limits from any attacks, but few of us had any faith the enemy cared about such distinctions. Because the hospital sat on the front lines, shrapnel and shells from American antiaircraft guns fell over us every hour of the day. We couldn't wait for reinforcements from home to arrive.

One morning as we gathered for breakfast, the familiar voice of President Roosevelt came over the radio and Sally shushed us.

"I give to the people of the Philippines my solemn pledge that their freedom will be redeemed and their independence established and protected. The entire resources, in men and material, of the United States stand behind that pledge."

"Good." Sally nodded. "We won't be doing this too much longer. More of our boys will be here any day now."

We all cheered, buoyed by President Roosevelt's pledge. If our trusted commander in chief was promising relief, why would we doubt him?

7.

FLOR

January to February 1942
Manila

It was a new year unlike any other. A huge banner bedecked City Hall that read: *Open City - Keep Cool - No Shooting*. By the first Saturday of January, Japanese officials had installed themselves in the Manila Hotel, former home to General MacArthur before he retreated to Corregidor, the fortified island at the mouth of Manila Bay. Flor and her parents emerged from their house and joined people waiting on the Escolta, shifting from foot to foot, wondering what to expect from the parade of troops that would appear at any moment. A tense silence hung over the crowd. And then the Japanese soldiers appeared. Row by row, they poured through the city's streets, the rhythmic *clomp, clomp* of their hobnail boots providing a steady beat to the procession.

Though some soldiers marched down the wide boulevards, many others arrived on tiny bicycles, pedaling in silence, rucksacks strapped to their backs. Their olive-colored uniforms were soiled and wrinkled, their hair unkempt. They wore odd-looking little hats with flaps hanging down over their ears. Despite their messages urging solidarity, the soldiers looked unfriendly, hardened, and lean. Flor watched their angry expressions and shivered.

When the wind blew toward the city, she could smell the smoke and hear the sound of big guns. Across the bay, American and Filipino forces continued fighting the Japanese in the jungles of the Bataan Peninsula and from the fortified island of Corregidor. At night, the western sky was lit with fires and flashes of artillery. Could the USAFFE hold steady and turn the tide against the Japanese? Flor desperately hoped so. All she could think about was Iris, but with each soldier that passed, her optimism sank.

To her left and right, tears coursed down people's faces as they watched the soldiers invade their city. In preparation for entering Manila, Japanese bombers had blanketed the city with leaflets printed with the same message:

We are not at war with you! We are at war only with the American devils! Do not shed your blood for America!

The Japanese promised solidarity, but all the propaganda in the world couldn't allay the sense of shock and fear hanging over the civilians of Manila. Luzon was a big island, protected by the largest democracy in the world, yet it had taken only twenty-five days for the Japanese Imperial Army to engulf it. How was that even possible?

ONLY TWO DAYS after their arrival in Manila, Japanese soldiers began erecting checkpoints on almost every block. An evening curfew was imposed on the city, and the time was moved an hour ahead to be synchronized with Tokyo. Japanese military trucks inched down the blocks of Ermita, the neighborhood where the Dalisays lived, the trucks' loudspeakers blaring,

"Enemy nationals must report to the University of Santo Tomas by Tuesday night. Pack only what you need for three days."

Three days? No one believed that.

"Who are enemy nationals?" Flor asked of Papa as they stood at the sala's window, their heads cocked, listening to the instructions coming from farther up the street.

"Anyone who's a nationality considered hostile to the Japanese. The Americans, English, French . . ." He paused, staring at the sky lost in thought. "Canadians, Australians, Greeks, Danes, Dutch, and I'm sure there are more, but I can't keep track of everyone."

"Santo Tomas will be crowded," Flor said.

"I'm afraid so. I must go to work now, but please stay home this afternoon. I don't like the idea of you and Luchie encountering any of these soldiers roaming the area."

Flor agreed, but later, after Papa went to his office, she slipped down their narrow street to observe the checkpoint on Dewey Boulevard. From a distance, she could see the distinct rotund figure of Mr. Huerta, one of her neighbors who ran a popular photography supply store located on the Escolta. As he approached a guard, the Filipino puffed on a long, thick cigar. The guard took his papers, flipped through the pages, and then placed them down on a small table beside him, nodding he was done. When Mr. Huerta reached for them, the guard's hand moved as quickly as a cobra strike. He nabbed the cigar from Mr. Huerta's mouth and plunged it onto the backside of the Filipino's hand, grinding it into the man's flesh as if it was a pestle in a mortar. A horrible sizzling sound provided the low notes behind Mr. Huerta's screams. The guard cackled, pushing the man to the other side of the checkpoint before tossing his papers after him. Openmouthed, Flor watched the exchange and then turned to flee for home, feeling sick to her stomach.

That night, when her parents returned home from work, she embraced them tightly and relayed what had happened.

Papa gave a weary nod. "Yes, I wish I could say that type of behavior is a surprise. Between the bombs and fires, I've been busy, but now there are also injuries from the guards and soldiers. And many of the Japanese who have been working as laborers here suddenly find themselves in positions of power and they're enacting their own petty revenges too."

Mama nodded. "Before you go anywhere, Flor, you must go sit outside in the garden to darken your skin. The Japanese pay too much attention to people with fair complexions."

But after seeing what had happened to her neighbor, Flor didn't want to go anywhere. And where was there to go? Her school had been closed permanently after the Japanese took one look at the building's handsome facade and decided to requisition it to use as offices for their occupying forces. She would like to have visited a few friends but didn't dare risk a confrontation with any of the Japanese soldiers roaming the streets. She resented the fear that now overcame her when she considered leaving her own home. It made her think back to the leaflets in their garden. Weren't the Japanese treating Filipinos as inferiors?

TWO MORNINGS LATER, at the breakfast table, Papa rose to leave for his office. "Flor, can you go through your ate's room and remove anything that associates her with the USAFFE? In case we're searched, we should hide her belongings to avoid any retribution for her association with America. In fact, please remove all her personal items so we won't have to explain her whereabouts. I've left an empty crate in her room so you can pack everything into it and hide it below the kitchen." He didn't look at her as he spoke. Iris's service with the USAFFE had always been a point of pride for the Dalisays and Flor knew her father was being pragmatic, but it was galling to hide Iris's association with the Americans, much less the very fact that she existed.

After Flor finished her cup of sweet and creamy tsokolate, she went to her ate's room and stood in the doorway. Since Iris had left for Bataan, Flor found herself often sneaking into her sister's room at night and climbing into her bed to sleep there. It comforted her to breathe in the scent of jasmine on her ate's pillow and see the photos of Iris sprinkled around the room. Sometimes she would open the wardrobe and run her fingers along the silky blouses still hanging neatly in a row. She missed Iris so much that it hurt.

She sat at the edge of the bed and gazed around the room. On the top of her ate's chest of drawers was a framed photo of Iris with her closest friend, Gloria. They were atop the Empire State Building in New York City waving at the camera. Flor loved hearing Iris's stories about her trip to the United States, but this was exactly the type of item that could get them in trouble with the Japanese. She lifted the photo and placed it in a crate and then reached for the ribbons Iris had won in a YMCA tennis tournament. She stacked them in the crate too. When she had removed everything of Iris's, she took the crate, went into the kitchen, and opened the trapdoor to the crawl space below the floor. After she lowered the crate into the space, she straightened, staring down at it in the darkness of the silong. It looked like a coffin. Luchie stood at the edge of the small trapdoor and wrapped an arm around Flor.

"Your ate is fine. This will help keep us safe."

Flor nodded and Luchie folded the trapdoor back into place, covered it with a rattan mat, and crossed herself.

IN EARLY FEBRUARY, Mama cornered Flor in the sala one morning. In her hands, she held a stack of folded clothes Flor had never seen before. "Darling, I need you to get changed. You and Luchie are going to Santo Tomas to deliver food to Mrs. Stone." Mama thrust the pile into Flor's arms. "Put these things on. Don't make yourself look too pretty and the Japanese will pay no attention to you."

Flor remained in place, staring at the clothes in her arms.

"Don't look so horrified," Mama added. "Think about our friends stuck in that place. Mrs. Stone has taught you piano for years. She needs our help."

Papa stopped as he passed through the room on his way out of the house. "I'll check to see about Jose going instead," Romeo said.

"He's already busy enough. Flor doesn't have school and she's been moping around. Having a purpose will do her some good and she needs to get out of the house." Pilar sighed. "But Flor, don't forget to read the posters plastered everywhere instructing us how to bow properly. The Japanese have no patience for mistakes, but don't let them frighten you."

Flor hoped her father would continue to protest, but he merely shook his head so she took the skirt and blouse and went to her room to change. Everyone's suspicions had been correct. The three-day stay at the University of Santo Tomas had turned into something longer. Every single one of their American friends had been imprisoned, including all the women who had served as Mama's volunteers at the Red Cross.

Despite Flor's misgivings, within a few minutes she had changed into the plain clothes and was striding along Dewey Boulevard bound for Santo Tomas, clutching a canvas sack filled with canned goods and clothing.

Luchie hurried alongside her. "Remember, don't look any of the soldiers in the eyes."

Flor made an impatient noise.

At each checkpoint, they did as Mama instructed. Neither woman looked the guards in the eye, they didn't speak, and they bowed deeply. After being waved through, they boarded a tranvía, sat, and avoided looking at the other passengers. The streetcar, normally noisy with the sound of gossip about the best prices at the market stalls, was quiet as no one wanted to draw attention to themselves. Using a few tricks of mental calculation, Flor tried to occupy herself by multiplying large numbers while Luchie murmured Hail Marys the entire trip.

After they crossed the Pasig River and left the modern architecture of Manila's commercial district, the streets narrowed, and colonial-styled bahay na bato buildings drew closer together, a patchwork of ground floors constructed of stone with upper levels styled from nipa, wood, and a combination of Spanish and Chinese architectural flourishes. The savory smell of fried meat floating through the open windows made Flor's stomach growl.

When the tranvía neared Santo Tomas, they disembarked and rushed along the high walls mounted with barbed wire. At the main gate, a noisy crowd of Filipinos encircled the guard's booth. Vendors carried trays of rolls and pastries or offered baskets of mangoes, small fish, and clothing. There were also many Filipinos crowding the entrance eager to help their imprisoned Allied friends by bringing them food, clean laundry, and supplies.

Reminding herself that the sooner she delivered the goods, the sooner she could go home, Flor searched out a path into the masses and she and Luchie slid to the front of the line. When they reached the guard, he asked for their papers, flipped through them with barely a glance, and then dug through the sacks the women carried. When he pulled out a tin of canned peaches, his face brightened, and he slid it into his pocket. Flor kept her face neutral.

"Day pass for you both. Do not take anything out of here. No messages, no packages, no nothing," he said, pushing them through the line and out to the other side of the building where internees pressed toward the visitors, their faces a portrait of desperation and stress.

"*Girl, what's the latest from Bataan?*"

"*What's the Voice of Freedom reporting?*"

"*Is MacArthur saying anything about what he plans to do next?*"

Flor cast a backward glance at the guardhouse, but none of the soldiers were watching her. "Our men are still fighting," she whispered, aware how feeble her update must have sounded to these people yearning for news.

"Mrs. Stone?" Flor called out. "Does anyone know Mrs. Stone?"

A firm grip tightened on her upper arm. "Flordeliza!" When Flor turned, Mrs. Stone pulled her into an embrace. "Before we left for this hellhole, your mother told me you'd help me. God bless you."

Over Mrs. Stone's shoulder, Flor surveyed the campus. Before the war, she had once visited Santo Tomas for an academic conference. The Main Building with its tall tower, mounted crucifix, and facade filled with statuary had impressed her, and the well-tended grounds of the school had been covered in green grass and flower beds, but now Flor gaped at the place's transformation. First, the stench. She almost gagged on the overwhelming rank smell of raw sewage. Across the plaza and surrounding lawn, people lay sprawled in clusters underneath hastily constructed lean-tos of nipa, corrugated metal scraps, and palm thatching. Piles of trash lay festering in the sun. Flor's heart lurched at the thought of her beloved piano teacher and others being forced to live in such squalor.

Finally Mrs. Stone let her go and tugged Flor and Luchie through the crowd to where a small knot of women had gathered below a banyan tree. "This is Pilar's girl, Flor, and her yaya."

Flor cringed. She knew how American women believed Filipinos to be overprotective of their daughters. Once, when she and Luchie had stopped at the Red Cross office to retrieve a shopping list from her mother, she overheard the snickers of the other women.

Isn't Pilar's daughter almost twenty? Why does she still have a chaperone?

It's so Victorian.

Flor's face reddened at the memory. Though she too sometimes chafed at the traditional way things were done in Manila, she resented being criticized by outsiders. The fact was that no self-respecting young woman of her social class would be out and about in Manila without being accompanied. Until she had an important job like Iris or married, this was the expectation.

Now, facing the others, Mrs. Stone held Flor in place as though she was a trophy. "Thank god we have help on the outside."

Mrs. Stone took the sack and rifled through it. "Corned beef, beans, rice, oh good. Thank you. And feminine necessaries, thank heavens."

To Flor's amazement, Mrs. Stone began to weep. One woman patted her friend's shoulder absentmindedly, but the others remained unfazed, and Flor realized that displays of emotion like this must have become commonplace within the prison's walls. The deterioration of these women's appearances was just the beginning of their degradation.

Suddenly Flor recognized several of the faces from volunteering with the Red Cross. These were the housewives she had seen leaving her mother's office for afternoon bridge games at the Bay View Hotel, wearing stylish day suits, pearl necklaces, white gloves, and immaculately coiffed finger waves and chignons. Now their faces sagged with fatigue, stains and wrinkles marred their cotton housedresses, and their hair hung in greasy hanks. When they lifted their hands to their mouths to muffle their excitement at the arrival of something as mundane as corned beef, the skin of their arms appeared tattooed with infected welts and sores.

Luchie pointed to one of the women's inflamed wrists. "What happened?"

"Bed bugs and mosquitoes," the woman lamented.

"We need mosquito nets desperately," another pleaded.

"And if your mother could also send some sodium sulphate, dysentery is rampant. And given there's only one loo on each floor, this has become quite a problem," a woman with a British accent explained.

Flor nodded, trying to hide her horror.

"Can you deliver this?" a woman asked, thrusting an envelope toward Flor. Several others murmured in agreement and pushed folded papers toward her, but Luchie shot Flor a stern look.

"I . . . I don't think I can take those," Flor stammered. "I could be searched."

The women lowered their messages, their disappointment plain, but Mrs. Stone had regained her composure and wouldn't be deterred. "You're a clever girl, Flor. Memorize a couple of them. Next time, you can memorize and deliver a few more."

Flor agreed and listened carefully as three women relayed messages to her. She repeated the addresses for delivery several times until the women were satisfied. And then she and Luchie left. Outside the gate, they leaned against the wall. Flor took a deep breath against the drowning sense of helplessness that choked her. Though she often wished she could come and go unchaperoned as Iris did, at that moment, she was relieved to have Luchie beside her.

"It's not safe for us to linger," Luchie said after a minute. "We must go."

Flor hated leaving the camp behind without doing more to help, but what was she supposed to do?

THE NEXT DAY Flor and Luchie set out to deliver the messages from the women at Santo Tomas. When Flor had arrived home the previous evening, she had written everything down though it felt impossible to forget anything. The desperation of the internees, their sorrow, it was all seared in Flor's memory. All three messages from the internees had been pleas for money, clothing, food, and requests to check on their abandoned homes.

Their first two destinations were in Malate. The first was a home belonging to a Spanish woman who eyed Flor and Luchie dubiously.

"We visited Santo Tomas yesterday," Flor explained. "The internees are in a terrible situation with little food and plumbing. Your friend Mrs. Mason needs money and any canned food you can spare."

The woman exchanged skeptical looks with the maid standing beside her and then smoothed her dress, glaring at Flor. "And who are you?"

"Señora, I don't have a handwritten note from your friend, because I couldn't take anything out, but she also asked that you check on her home. Mrs. Mason said your housekeeper will know where they left a key and she's asking that you go inside and take her Limoges china. It's all she has left from her grandma Bea and she'd like you to keep it until she's free."

The woman's eyes filled with tears in recognition. "Dios mio, I'm too late." She pointed through the gaps in the thick eugenia and bottlebrush separating her property from the Masons, and though it was hard to see, Flor could make out movement. "They're taking over the house."

Flor moved to peer through the bristly hedge.

"Don't get too close," Luchie scolded.

But Flor inched forward, peeking through the leaves. Framed by the Masons' front door, a pair of Japanese soldiers appeared, hauling a rolled-up Turkish carpet. A moment later, four men emerged from the front door guiding a grand piano set on wheels. Next, an ornate platera with a marble counter and drawer unit made of tindalo wood was carried out with a soldier at each end. Item by item, the house was being emptied of its former owner's belongings.

"Come back!" Luchie ordered in a loud whisper and Flor returned to her side.

With her hands clasped at her breast, the Spanish woman was lamenting, "How the Japanese will win the war armed with Limoges china, I have no idea, but they're stripping the homes of enemy aliens and moving themselves right in. And honestly, who knows when they'll start taking our things too? What will you tell Señora Mason?"

Flor had no idea.

"Well, come inside," the Spanish woman said, guiding Flor and Luchie into her foyer. "We will fetch some things for our dear friend."

A few minutes later, the woman and her maid reappeared

with a bag clanking with canned foods. "Inside, there's an envelope of cash. Por favor, tell Mira I couldn't save her grandmother's china and I'll never forgive myself. When you deliver this, please come back and tell me what else she needs. I will talk to our neighbors and friends and get even more." Then the woman pulled Flor so close, she could see the gold fillings in the woman's molars as she spoke. "But this is the most important part of the message: tell her though my country is neutral, my heart is with her and I will do everything in my power to keep her family alive. You will remember this, *sí*?"

"Yes, of course."

As Flor plodded away, she felt a heaviness far greater than the canvas sack knocking against her hip. She could barely conceive the enormity of what the people in Santo Tomas were losing. It was too much.

She turned. "Manang Luchie, do you think someone's helping Ate Iris?"

The older woman nodded and crossed herself, yet she didn't give Flor a comforting smile, but instead grimaced, wiping the sweat from her brow. "Let's keep going."

THEIR NEXT STOP was the same. All over Manila, the houses of so-called enemy aliens were being requisitioned by the Japanese Imperial Army and anything of value inside the homes was delivered to the waterfront to be shipped to Japan.

Their third stop was within the historic section of town, Intramuros. They visited a Filipino family on Victoria Street, delivered the message, and added to their haul of food and money. As Flor and Luchie headed home, they encountered a crowd gathered around a speaker standing in front of San Agustin Church. Flor stopped and stood on her toes to see better.

"We don't have time for this," Luchie murmured, but Flor wouldn't budge so she sighed. "Fine, we'll listen for a minute. Only a minute."

On the old stone steps, a Japanese man clenched a bullhorn. "Friends, our mutual enemies are the people of the white race who have tried to exploit you and our brothers living in nearby lands." His voice echoed off the square's stone walls. "You have been subjugated for centuries. This church, this very one"—he gestured behind him—"was built by the Spaniards in the late 1500s as a means to bend you to a superstitious European way of thinking."

At this, Luchie made a disgusted snort, but Flor kept her eyes on the speaker as he rolled up his sleeves.

"Look at the color of my skin," he bellowed. "It is exactly like yours. You and I are closely akin to each other. I stand here before you to assure that we Japanese are your friends. We belong to the same corner of the world. If we work together, we can build a better, more prosperous Asia!"

He raised his arms as if to summon applause, but no one in the audience stirred. He tried again, yelling, "Asia for the Asiatics!"

One by one, people peeled away silently, their gazes downcast.

"Enough of this nonsense," Luchie groused and she nudged Flor to keep moving. Flor hefted her heavy sacks—by now she carried two of them—and made her way toward Puerta de Santa Lucia, her arm muscles burning from their weight, but more than anything physical, it was the weight of Flor's thoughts that slowed her pace. Her mind churned as they left the speaker behind.

"Manang, you carry heavy loads. Want a ride?" an old cochero called to Luchie.

Flor turned to see the cart pull alongside their path. Though they had planned to walk the short distance home, the women nodded, sliding their sacks onto the cart, and climbed up. They passed through the large stone gateway and turned onto Bonifacio.

"You hear that man speak?" the cochero asked, giving the reins a slight shake.

"We did," Luchie replied. "Heathen."

The cochero nodded and grunted.

Ahead, a Japanese soldier stood on the side of the street, but suddenly he stepped into traffic to hail a Chrysler limousine. When the automobile stopped, the soldier flung the door open and yanked the driver out.

"Bow!" the soldier screamed.

The driver, a Filipino, bowed deeply, but when he straightened, the soldier slapped him across the face and then slid into the car, revved the engine, and roared off down the boulevard ahead of the cluster of stopped traffic.

Flor watched the Filipino man stare down the busy street and felt her face heat with anger on his behalf. In their pamphlets, radio addresses, and speeches, the Japanese spoke of unity, but their actions seemed to continuously contradict their promises. How could they expect to be believed?

The cochero waved at the man and yelled, "Get in!"

The man approached the carromata with a dazed expression and hoisted himself onto the bench, giving Luchie and Flor respectful nods.

The cochero lifted his straw hat to the newcomer. "I'll take you wherever you need after I drop these ladies off."

The man rubbed his face gingerly where he had been slapped.

"I'm sorry to say the sting of that will not go away anytime soon," the cochero said, keeping his gaze on the street ahead.

"I've been driving this cart for forty years, but never has a Spaniard or American slapped me. The Japanese can insist we are friends and equals all he wants, but none of it's true."

FOR THE NEXT several weeks, Flor and Luchie returned to Santo Tomas with food and medicine. Every evening when Luchie retired to her apartment on the first floor of the Dalisays' house and the place fell quiet, Flor took to listening to the Voice of Freedom broadcasting from Corregidor so she would have news for the internees. The Japanese were jamming the incoming signals from San Francisco and London, but the news from Corregidor still arrived clearly, describing how American and Filipino forces continued to resist surrendering. The Germans were now bombing the Mediterranean island fortress of Malta with bomb tonnage that was estimated to be double of what had been dropped on London. The Japanese were marching through Borneo and had taken Kuala Lumpur, the capital of Malaya. They invaded the Dutch East Indies and the Solomon Islands and were on the verge of seizing Rangoon. The speed of the Japanese Imperial Army's progress through Asia was alarming.

ONE NIGHT IN late February, Flor and Papa were playing chess in the sala after dinner. Mama sat beside them reading the latest Agatha Christie novel, *Evil Under the Sun*, when a pounding at the door interrupted their tranquility. Flor's first thought was that it might be someone with news about Iris and she jumped from her seat, but Papa raised a hand to stop her.

"Open up!" a man's voice yelled.

Mama dropped her book and reached for Flor's hand. They both stood, watching as Papa crossed the room and disappeared down the terrazzo stairs to open the main door. Footsteps pounded toward them and four soldiers appeared in the sala, glowering at the Dalisays.

An officer stepped forward, speaking in clear English. "Who lives here?"

"My wife, daughter, and I," Dr. Dalisay said, bowing deeply. "We have a housekeeper and gardener with their own apartments downstairs." When the Dalisays straightened, each produced their identification papers for the soldiers. Meanwhile, the officer who appeared to be in charge paced the room, studying the ornamental wooden carvings gracing the walls and the regal portrait of Papa's grandfather, a stern-looking man, wearing a stiff traditional barong tagalog.

"You have taken down your antenna outside. This is good."

Papa nodded.

"Where are your kitchen knives?"

"We turned them in at a checkpoint," Papa lied as he led them into the kitchen and the officer immediately began opening cupboards and searching through them. Each time the man passed over the mat covering the trapdoor to the crawl space, Flor's pulse raced faster. When he was satisfied to find no contraband, he turned back to Papa. "Open your wallet."

Dr. Dalisay removed his wallet from his pocket and handed it over. The officer unfolded it and pulled out the recently issued military pesos. "You have the new money. Good." He pocketed several of the bills before tossing it back. Flor's heart seemed to be beating in her throat as she watched Papa catch the wallet and calmly return it to his pocket.

The officer led them back into the sala, where he spotted Mama's copy of *Evil Under the Sun* lying on the chair. He prodded it with his baton.

"Who is reading this?" he demanded.

"I am," Mama said smiling graciously.

"*Evil Under the Sun?* It's anti-Japanese," he said, a sneer on his face.

"It has nothing to do with the emperor or Japan," Mama said. "The book is a murder mystery set in England."

The energy of the room shifted. The soldiers suddenly perked up attentively as if they were hounds catching the scent of a meal. The officer took a step closer to Mama, glowering. "You are correcting me?"

"I just wouldn't expect you to read a silly murder mystery. That's all." Mama smiled as she spoke, but Flor could see the blood draining from her mother's face as she realized her mistake.

Papa stepped forward, his hands raised in surrender, but the soldiers moved to cut off his path toward his wife.

The officer raised his baton, and waving it with a flourish, a small iron spiked ball appeared, attached to the baton by a leather strap. Before Flor could react, he swung the blackjack toward her mother. The instrument whistled through the air and landed with a sickening *Splat!* on the bare skin of Mama's shin below her hemline, the sound like an overly ripe melon falling to the ground and splitting open.

Mama shrieked and doubled over, but the officer continued to thwack at her legs. She rose halfway to hide her face from the blows, but he kept striking.

Flor let out a small cry, but the officer paid no attention to her. He didn't even look at Mama as he hit her. No, his gaze was locked upon Papa. A smug expression stretched across the officer's face. With each blow he rained down upon Mama, his grin widened as he tested Papa's reaction.

Papa strained against the soldiers' arms and they loosened their grip, eager to see what would happen next.

"No, Romeo!" Mama screamed.

He froze, staring at her, realizing that if he retaliated, he would be setting off a much more horrific series of events.

Without breathing, Flor watched the silent back-and-forth between her parents. For a flash, Papa's eyes appeared to plead, but Mama's steely glare locked him in place. With each hit, Papa's face purpled in fury while Mama's twisted in silent agony.

Sensing he was not going to get the reaction he'd hoped, the officer's interest waned and as he spun the blackjack in a final sweep, a ribbon of blood unfurled itself through the air, splattering across everyone's faces. The soldiers guffawed in appreciation.

Mama collapsed to the ground but didn't make a sound, and the officer slapped Papa on the shoulder as if it was all a joke. The Japanese exited. Until the downstairs door slammed, the Dalisays remained frozen in a macabre tableau before hurling themselves toward Mama.

"Oh, Pilar," Papa moaned, holding a lamp over her legs to inspect the damage.

"I was a fool to contradict that monster," Mama cried.

Flor sucked in a breath. In the soft yellow orb of light haloing her mother's shins, the extent of her injuries became visible. The blackjack had flayed the flesh, leaving a pulpy mess of blood, ligament, and glimpses of bone. Mama covered her eyes with trembling hands as she tried not to scream in pain, but it was the look of shock and anguish on Papa's face that stunned Flor most. In the course of several minutes, he had aged by twenty years. His hair suddenly looked grayer, the skin on his cheeks and neck sagged, and his eyes blinked repeatedly in horror and shock.

He appeared to feel Flor's gaze, because he collected himself. "Bring me a basin of hot water, towels, and my doctor's bag," he ordered. As Flor ran to the kitchen, a hot, hard fury ignited in her chest. She didn't need a rifle or knife to fight the enemy. She would devise her own strategy.

8.

TESS

January to March 1942
The Bataan Peninsula

At Hospital No. 2, the news grew worse and our morale shriveled. Malaya. Burma. Thailand. Hong Kong. The Dutch Indies and Borneo. The Japanese mowed through Asia with alarming speed. Singapore had prepared for a sea invasion, but instead the Japanese attacked from behind, emerging from the Malayan jungle on bicycles. England, the mightiest military force for centuries, offered little defense for this unexpected attack and surrendered. The shock of these defeats left us speechless.

So what kept us going? The promise of reinforcements. Every day we prayed for their arrival.

I'd wake in the early hours of morning to the commotion of monkeys filling the bamboo thicket composing our quarters. As soon as the sun rose, the air would be hot, the humidity heavy. Before opening my eyes, I'd try to picture a fleet of American ships appearing on the horizon, steaming straight for us. There was a part of me that truly believed if I imagined the ships hard enough, they'd appear.

"Sal, what do you say?" I'd whisper, pushing my mosquito netting off my damp, sweaty skin, and pulling my coveralls off a vine. "Let's see if our boys have arrived."

"Yes, yes," Sally would mumble, fumbling to dress. We'd stumble from our bunks and climb a nearby hill for a view of Manila Bay. From this spot, we could see several islands, and beyond them, the horizon. I'd always study Corregidor, only three miles off the tip of Bataan, and wonder if George was there, conferring with MacArthur. We'd survey the bay in silence with only the constant thud of howitzers booming along the coastline.

None of us in the Army Corps of Nurses had attended Basic Training, so we didn't know anything about weaponry before arriving in the Philippines, but proficiency is born from necessity, and when you're under fire, you quickly recognize the difference in sound between Browning automatic rifles, M-1 carbines, and Nambu 8 mm pistols, and you learn to gauge the enemy's location. While we went about our daily activities, we developed the instinct for staying alert to the sounds of our surroundings, and from our perch on the hill, first thing in the morning, we actually felt safe—at least for a few minutes.

WITH EACH PASSING week, our impatience for reinforcements increased. One morning in the middle of February, Sally and I scanned the horizon, searching for a glimpse of American ships. "Darren says our guys must be getting closer," she said. "They'll get here soon, right?"

I nodded. "According to MacArthur's latest announcement, help is on the way. I sure hope they bring food. I'm getting tired of mystery stew. I almost miss K rations."

With a sigh, we descended the steep hill to return to Hospital No. 2. "Look how big my coveralls are getting." Sal's voice was hoarse and she didn't give her usual laugh.

A week earlier, Darren had proposed to Sally and everyone

in the hospital was starved for joy and fixated on the happy couple, wanting a piece of the excitement. We felt starved for joy. Shortly after the news of the engagement began to circulate, Dr. Curtis pulled me aside. "Listen, Tess, if Sal's looking for someone to walk her down the aisle, please tell her I'd be honored to do it."

"Aww, I'll bet she'd love that. You should tell her yourself."

"Well, I don't want to put any pressure on her. Maybe she's got someone else in mind."

"If she can't be home with her own family, I'm sure she can't think of a better person for the honor."

He flushed and I'd felt a hitch in my throat at the older man's concern. I squeezed his arm before hurrying away.

Surprisingly, the only person *not* excited about the proposal was Sally.

At first, her reticence puzzled me. Since meeting Darren she'd planned to marry him. But then I began to notice something. During the few times we'd have a quiet moment, she always pulled out letters from home or hunched over a piece of paper and wrote to her family with an intensity bordering on mania. I couldn't even remember our last mail service. With the Japanese blocking the Pacific shipping lanes, nothing was getting in or out—but that didn't seem to matter. Sally missed home. I suspected the idea of marrying Darren without her family to witness the event made the isolation and desperation of our situation increasingly stressful for her.

Before the war, one of Sally's favorite pastimes had been imagining her future wedding. One afternoon, not long after we'd arrived at Fort Stotsenburg, we sat beside the swimming pool at the Officers' Club and she'd described what she envisioned.

"I want to have it at the beautiful Catholic church we attend in Muskegon. My sisters will wear pale pink full-skirted gowns and hats—I saw the hats in a spread from *Good Housekeeping* and saved the picture. My brothers and Darren will wear dark suits and my father will walk me down the aisle, of course. My bouquet will be made of lily of the valley—I got that idea from my cousin. Hers was the sweetest thing. And my dress will look like Wallis Simpson's with a high neckline and cinched waist. Don't you think that would look flattering on me?"

I nodded, struggling to recall the newspaper photos of the Duchess of Windsor's dress.

"What will yours look like?" she asked.

"I'm not sure. I've never really thought much about it."

Sally's mouth fell open. "You've *never* imagined your wedding?"

Flustered, I tried to come up with something. I could barely remember my sister's wedding but was almost certain she'd worn a simple dove-gray serge suit, nothing fancy.

Virginia adjusted her swim cap. "Not everyone obsesses over their fantasy wedding. Me? I plan to elope and spare my future husband the craziness of my family."

Again, Sally looked incredulous, but she must have decided we were hopeless because that was the end of the topic.

Now, Darren's proposal was making the desperation of our predicament obvious.

"Clearly Darren thinks you're just as beautiful as the day he met you, so don't worry about those darn coveralls," I said.

"He wants us to get married now, but I was hoping to wait for reinforcements. I figure if I'm going to be stuck getting married during this war, at least if we wait for a ship, some of the navy fellas will be wearing white. Maybe they can loan me something. Do you think I'm crazy?"

I stumbled through some rattan vines and righted myself,

breathing heavily in the swollen humidity. Given the carnage surrounding us every day, it was hard to rationalize waiting. Who knew what was going to happen next? Getting married was against regulation, but no one appeared to be enforcing it. Supposedly Hospital No. 1 had thrown two weddings the previous week. "A wedding could be a great way to lift everyone's spirits, including your own."

"True." Sally swatted at mosquitoes haloing her head. "Damn these things. Have you seen how low we're getting on quinine?"

"Josie told me we need to stop taking it as a preventative measure and save it for the sick guys."

"But then we're all going to have malaria soon."

We quieted, picking our way through the thick creeper ferns and batting at the clouds of mosquitoes encircling us. Smears of blood streaked any patches of our bare skin, not necessarily because of our nursing duties, but because we were constantly smashing the attacking pests. Because our skin was always sweaty and sticky, the remnants of a crushed mosquito wing or legs stuck to us like flecks of confetti after a party. I wore the grisly carnage proudly, hoping that other mosquitoes would get the message and buzz off. Unfortunately the damned things were relentless and oblivious to my warnings.

As I pushed aside a clump of waist-high cogon grass, my stomach clenched painfully. Along with mosquitoes and the malarial fevers they spread, filthy bluebottle flies bred quickly in the open-air latrines and then climbed all over everything, so everyone had dysentery—nurses, doctors, kitchen and support staff, and patients. The more time we spent trapped in the jungle, the more precarious our health became.

"Maybe Darren and I should just go ahead and have the ceremony."

The anxiety in Sal's voice made me stop and turn. "Hey, we're going to make it through this. Our boys are giving it their all."

"I know, but Tess, come on. It doesn't look good. Have you gotten any word from George?"

I attempted a smile as we reached the edge of the mess hall's clearing. "No, but I've been telling myself no news is good news."

"Good point, but boy, it would be nice to see him. Maybe he'd have some scoop from the top brass."

"Some scoop would be good," I said, pouring a mug full of the boggy junk being passed off as coffee. The real stuff was long gone. Every day, more and more supplies dwindled. Toilet paper? All but a distant memory. Sugar and butter? Dream on. A cigarette? If you were fine with smoking foul-smelling leaves scavenged from the jungle floor, Greasy and Six always had some to spare when they visited.

"Maybe when George shows up, he'll bring real coffee from HQ," Sal said.

I hid my face behind my mug. Keeping busy seemed like the best way not to think about George, but even when I was racing from bed to bed tending to wounded and sick men, it only took a bright pair of blue eyes or a self-deprecating smile and I found myself worrying about him.

Virginia waved at us from the bamboo table where she sat with Mabel and Nell.

"Today's coffee's only half strength, but incoming fire is already full-bore," Mabel announced. We groaned.

At another nearby table, Iris was deep in conversation with a Filipino soldier named Vincent. Iris and Gloria had been moved to Hospital No. 3, which was operated by the Philippine Army Medical Service, but occasionally they'd stop by our wards to help with patient transfers. In the last few weeks, I'd seen Iris and her soldier together and it made me smile to see romance blooming in the midst of so much heartbreak and hardship.

I turned away from them to find Virginia holding a piece of toast out toward me. "The only thing I want to see coming at me full-bore is a nice big navy carrier," she said. "What did y'all see on this morning's hike? Anything good?"

We both shook our heads and forced smiles. Reinforcements would arrive any day. They had to. Our reserves were empty.

BY EARLY MARCH, we were working around the clock, no matter how ill and hungry we felt. Our wards were filled beyond capacity. How was it possible we still had enough men to fill the lines and keep fighting? With our quinine stores exhausted, malaria afflicted almost everyone. Somehow Sally, Virginia, and I had managed to escape contracting it, but most of the other nurses hadn't been so lucky. Josie commanded us to keep a close eye on the surgeons because if one turned feverish while operating on someone, it only took a moment of delirium for him to make a mistake and turn an injured man into a dead one.

As our caseload increased, a few nurses were transferred permanently from neighboring hospitals. Iris and Gloria were among the new arrivals. In the space that had been designated as our nurses' quarters, we shoved a few extra cots into the clearing and helped our friends move in.

"Iris, how about you accompany me on rounds today? I'll show you the ropes," I offered.

"Sounds good," she said, shoving her battered suitcase under her new cot.

Unfortunately, during our first shift together, we were assigned to the gangrene ward. Between the sickly sweet smell of infection, the wounds festering with bubbles, and the bloated limbs, this ward was by far the least desirable. Gas gangrene was caused by bacteria living in the soil, and once it infected a wound, the afflicted limb quickly deteriorated and often the only solution would be amputation. As we walked down the long path to the ward, kept distant because of its horrendous smell, I apologized that she was stuck with such a depressing first set of rounds.

"Aren't you using the new treatment here?" she asked. When I shook my head, confused, she hiked her coveralls up on her thin frame and nodded. "The doctors at Hospital No. 3 have discovered that if you free the wound of its binding, clean out the infected muscle and bone, and let the sun and fresh air get into the infection, it kills the bacteria. In just the last week that we started doing this, the results seemed almost miraculous."

Within minutes of arriving at the ward, Iris was showing the other nurses and doctors the new strategy. "I promise, it works. Try it," she urged everyone. So we did. And sure enough, a swift improvement within our patients happened almost overnight.

"Y'all are real angels, you know that?" a captain said as Iris and I checked his infected leg a few days later and found the swelling down, the ugly festering gone. "When I first got here, I thought I was a goner."

"Have some faith," Iris said cheerfully as we took our leave of him.

"If my sister could see me now, stuck in the jungle, treating these awful injuries, I don't think she'd believe it," I said to her as we finished our rounds and stood at the edge of the clearing, updating charts.

Iris's bright smile faded. "I know, my family warned me against coming out here, but honestly, I'm more worried about them. I wonder how bad life in the city has gotten under the occupation."

"It's hard to believe we're only a short boat ride away and yet we have no news of what's happening there. I assume they're not getting any word about us either."

It frightened me to think that while our conditions in the jungle felt harrowing, it was entirely possible that life was equally challenging, or maybe even worse, in other places too. We'd been telling ourselves that once outside help arrived, our situation would improve, but what if the war was so bad in other places, there was no help to send?

ONE MORNING WHILE I was making rounds, Greasy and Six appeared. Through their sunburns, I could see dark purple shadows circling their eyes and while Six was as bony as ever, Greasy's uniform appeared looser too. From across the ward, Six waved his arm and strode toward me carrying a large canvas sack. "I'm no fashion expert, but I think I found something for Sal."

"Huh?" I asked, my brain slow moving from fatigue and hunger.

"Remember what we talked about last week?" he pressed.

Greasy and Six often visited Hospital No. 2 with deliveries, and a week earlier when they stopped by, I'd told them to keep an eye out for something white for Sally to wear so she might gin up a little enthusiasm for a jungle wedding.

Greasy had nodded. "I've always enjoyed a good wedding, as long as it's some other poor son of a bitch who's taking himself off the market."

Six chuckled before turning his attention to me. "Couldn't you use a sheet or two to make her a dress?"

"Lord no," I said. "Take a look around. All our bedding and

bandaging is so grubby and stained that even our best efforts to launder it are practically useless. She'd look like some sort of ghost bride if we scare up anything from here."

The men nodded, their expressions sober.

Our wards resembled something from a nightmare. We no longer deemed the Japanese our most dangerous enemy. Aside from the thousands of small insectile vectors of death circling our heads, malnutrition and hunger preyed on us with greater efficiency than anything the Japanese could muster. The number of people packed into Bataan far exceeded what army planners had envisioned. Half rations had been ordered in early January so by late February, the situation was desperate. Our injured and sick men, their systems already strained by malnutrition and hunger, were not recovering.

The meat in the mess hall's thin stews became more and more unrecognizable so the men hunted and foraged for carabao, camote, calesa pony, python, wild pig, iguana, deer, dog, and monkey—and this last option was by far the most disgusting. Stringy and tough, monkey meat did a number on everyone's weakened teeth. And the worst part? Its human shape made you feel like you were eating someone's baby brother.

So we settled for one meal a day: a weevil-infested spoonful of rice and a piece of corned beef the size of a domino tile. Sometimes we got a little stew. No matter what we were handed in the chow line, our stomachs still grumbled. The human body requires one thousand and five hundred calories to survive and army rations had us down to about one thousand; you didn't need to be particularly good at math to see how this was going to work out.

I reached into the dusty canvas sack that Six thrust at me and pulled out a pile of cream-colored silk. "Oh my goodness," I said in amazement. "How on earth did you get this?"

Six jammed his hands into his pockets bashfully and looked at the ground. "Don't get too excited yet. I got a parachute off one of the grounded pilots, but I figured it's the right color for a wedding dress and it could look kinda fancy and special. Don't you girls like that? Fancy and special stuff, I mean."

I swallowed past a lump in my throat. That Six had come up with this idea on his own was the sweetest thing I'd ever encountered. "We do, actually." I shook out the parachute and yard after yard of silk billowed around me. "The only problem is that we're buried under work right now. I don't know if I have time to make her something out of this."

Greasy held up a shiny black Singer sewing machine. "Would this help?"

As if the parachute hadn't stunned me enough, seeing a motorized sewing machine here in our godforsaken stretch of jungle was almost too much. "Where did that come from?"

"Best if you don't ask a lot of questions," Greasy said. "I kinda borrowed it from the quartermaster, but if we play our cards right and I return it by tomorrow night, no one will be any the wiser."

"Tomorrow night?" I quickly calculated the number of hours I'd need to whip something up that was presentable. "I don't know if that's enough time."

"Ah, come on, miss, you gotta figure something out," one of my patients, a wounded lieutenant, called to me.

As I surveyed the rows of hopeful faces turned toward me, Josie Nesbit entered the clearing. "What's happening here?" she asked.

I held out the parachute. "Greasy and Six have brought this so I can make a wedding dress for Sally, but we're so busy . . ." My voice trailed off as the sounds of disappointed muttering filled the ward.

Josie nodded at the Singer in Greasy's hands. "And you managed to procure a sewing machine?"

"If I return it by tomorrow night, no one will be any the wiser that it's on the lam," Greasy said.

Josie gave a brisk nod. "Well, then, Tess, I don't know what you're waiting around for. You better get to sewing."

"But what about my shifts?"

"I'm sure the girls can cover you while you work on a gown. Healing can come in many forms. I think it's pretty clear a wedding is exactly what Hospital No. 2 needs right now, don't you?"

At that, my patients lying in the bunks perked up and whistled.

"All right!" I pointed at Six and Greasy. "Come on, let's take it to her."

"Don't worry about us," Six said. "Greasy and me got stuff to do. You girls just keep us posted on when to come by for the wedding."

"No sir, you're not off the hook yet. Follow me. I want you both to see Sally's expression when we show this to her. Come on, Greasy!" I insisted, leading the men toward the ward where I knew Sal was working. "I'll be right back, boys," I called to my patients and they continued cheering.

We found Sally bent over a stack of charts. "Sal, look what Greasy and Six have brought you."

Her brow furrowed as she took in the bundle of silk clutched to my chest, but when she spotted the sewing machine in Greasy's arms, amazement widened her eyes. "Holy mackerel," she breathed, looking back and forth from the silk to Greasy and Six. "You fellas found this stuff for me?"

"We heard you were thinking about getting hitched and figured you might want something new to wear," mumbled Six. "I reckoned Tess could sew you a dress out of this parachute."

The nearby patients leaned from their bunks for better views and began cheering and catcalling. Just like that, the entire mood of the ward shifted from wretched to riotously happy.

"Who knew Six was some kind of fashion designer?" a patient shouted, laughing.

"Zip it, Gene," Sal scolded, but she looked anything but stern. Suddenly she glowed as if lit from within. "Thank you!" Before Greasy or Six could say anything, she leaned forward and kissed Greasy's cheek and then rose to the tips of her toes to do the same thing to Six. For once, both men were speechless.

"I only have twenty-four hours to make you look like the Duchess of Windsor, so we'd better get moving," I said.

She took the parachute from me, lifted it overhead, and twirled, beaming at everyone. Some of the other nurses, including Virginia and Mabel, appeared, drawn by the commotion.

"What's going on?" Virginia asked.

"Folks, who's ready for wedding tomorrow night?" Sally shouted.

And with that, everyone erupted in applause. A wedding was just the tonic we needed in Hospital No. 2 to lift our spirits.

THE NEXT AFTERNOON I headed to my shift in the open-air surgery theater underneath a huge balete tree, whistling as I thought about Sally and Darren tying the knot later that evening. I'd just put the final stitches into Sally's impromptu gown and it was ready for her. I couldn't believe we'd pulled it off, but all the nurses were more than happy to pick up my rounds while I sewed, and I'd even managed to finish the dress a couple of hours early.

As I picked my way over the balete's roots spreading across

the leafy ground like thick and muscular tentacles, a shiver ran over me. The Filipino nurses believed that this open-air surgical theater below the balete tree was haunted. Or cursed. Or maybe both. Whatever the exact issue, they avoided it. Local superstition held that baletes served as enchanted gateways for dwarves, demons, and fairies, but the Americans on staff shrugged and we carried on using that ward. We were too busy and tired to concern ourselves with such notions.

I arrived at the edge of the theater and squinted into the shadows to see Darren and Mabel checking over the surgical instruments lined up for us on a bamboo table.

"Well, look who's decided to grace us with her presence," Darren called out, chuckling.

"Sorry I'm running behind. I was just chatting with your bride," I said, pulling a face at him. "So what's first on our schedule for this afternoon?"

Mabel had just reached for a chart to answer my question when suddenly, overhead, the unmistakable whistle of a bomb pierced the air.

I froze, my gaze locked on Mabel.

Before any sound reached me, the air seemed to expand and a wave of wind crashed over me, creating an overwhelming pressure in my ears and skull. I felt briefly suspended and then a second later, everything exploded. A roaring sound tore at me. I was ripped off the ground with the air being sucked from every bit of my body while tiny burns scorched along the bare sections of my arms and face. Bamboo shards, big shiny pieces of gabi plant, shreds of khaki uniform, and streaks of blood filled the air.

CRASH! My body hit the jungle floor, and lying on my back, I strained to breathe, clutching at my throat until I was gasping.

I opened my eyes to swimming vision. Overhead, the lacy

canopy came into focus. Flames licked at the leaves and vines. A mattress had been impaled on the bough of a tree.

I couldn't hear anything.

I sat, taking big ragged breaths and boxing at my ears.

Only silence.

Next to me a severed arm dangled from some bamboo. I turned to my side and retched as pain throbbed in my head. With a final heave—*pop!*—my hearing cleared.

A chorus of screams filled the jungle.

Out of instinct, I ran my hands over my legs, then my arms, and then my scalp and face. It only took a couple of seconds. Aside from being dizzy with a raging headache, nothing seemed amiss. I climbed onto my hands and knees, not trusting my balance enough to stand. Only a few feet away, Mabel lay on her side, bloody, her coveralls completely blown off her bottom half. I gasped and crawled to her while my gaze searched our surroundings for something to cover her. A beige-colored tarp had been flung to the ground nearby and I grabbed it and dragged it to her, placing it carefully over her legs while crying, "Mabel? Mabel? Can you hear me?"

Underneath the smattering of freckles that dusted her forehead and cheeks, she appeared pale and lifeless. Her slack features and limp posture were a far cry from the girl with a pouty smile and the moxie that had fueled her prewar career as a barnstorming stuntwoman. I clutched her shoulders and leaned in close enough so my breath stirred the fringe of ginger-colored lashes brushing her cheeks. "Mabel, blink twice if you can hear me," I shouted, panic filling my voice.

Her lashes fluttered, and I held my breath.

When her eyes opened, I exhaled and tears of relief spilled down my cheeks.

"What happened?" she gasped.

"A bomb hit us and it blew off the lower part of your coveralls. I think some shrapnel got you."

Mabel stared at her bare legs peeking out from under the tarp and said, "At least if I'm going to get caught looking indecent, I should have gotten a little fun out of it, don't you think?"

"Oh honey, thank god your sense of humor isn't AWOL." I kissed her forehead, my lips trembling. "Now sit tight while I find someone who can help."

She nodded, her pupils huge.

My legs shook as I rose slowly. The air felt syrupy with heat, humidity, and thick smoke. I coughed. The smell of hot metal and charred flesh swirled through the burning clearing with a sickening pungency.

"Darren?" I called, searching the debris. "Darren?"

And then I saw him.

His head of short blond hair rested in a thicket of molave, facing away from me. One of his arms twisted from his torso at an unnatural angle.

"Oh god, no," I murmured, stumbling across the clearing toward him.

When I reached him, I grabbed his shoulders and tried tugging, but blood had dampened the foliage underfoot and I slipped to my knees, realizing with horror that his right leg was missing from the knee down. Part of his jaw had also disappeared, and I let out a cry.

"Hold on." Harold, an orderly, appeared beside me and began to extract Darren from the underbrush, while I watched helplessly. I reached for Darren's neck to check his pulse.

"Tess, it's too late. He's gone." Harold laid Darren's body on the ground and covered him with a white sheet. When he straightened, he handed me his canteen. "Here, have some water and take a few deep breaths."

I experienced a flash of Darren's proud expression from when I revived that boy back in Manila before the war came to us in the Philippines. Many doctors would have taken credit for saving that kid, but not only had Darren recognized my quick thinking, he admitted to his own mistake. I squeezed my eyes shut, willing that when I opened them, Darren would sit, push the sheet off, and give me his lopsided smile that always seemed to say, *Can you believe that just happened?*

Instead I heard a gasp and whimper and turned to see Sally standing at the edge of the ward, her hands over her mouth, staring at the sheet covering Darren.

"Oh, Sal, I'm so sorry," I said as the best friend I'd ever known collapsed against me.

AFTER THE DIRECT hit to the surgical theater, I offered to work more shifts. I needed to stay as busy as possible. The first night after Darren's death, nightmares began to plague my sleep. Flames, the whistling of bombs, bloodied comrades—these images filled my mind's eye in a constant loop, and judging by the cries from the other nurses' cots, I wasn't alone. The state of constant vigilance required to survive being under siege left me feeling as though an increasingly brittle piece of twine was holding me together. With every passing hour, it frayed closer and closer to snapping.

Rousing Sally for our morning hike to the top of the hill to check for American ships became increasingly difficult. One morning she flat out refused to join me.

"No," she mumbled, her eyes hollow and complexion unnaturally pale.

"But don't you want to be able to spread the happy news

about being saved?" Virginia coaxed, sliding next to Sally and stroking her cheek.

Sally faced away. "They're never coming. It's too late."

Virginia and I exchanged troubled looks. Darren's death had sucked the vitality from our young friend, and the bubbly and energetic version of Sally who could entertain us with dramatic readings of her family's letters had vanished.

Voices from the dark recesses of our minds were getting louder and louder, enticing us to lie down and give up, let our bodies be consumed by the jungle. I understood the temptation to surrender to these voices, but we *had* to hold on a little longer. Since late December, President Roosevelt and General MacArthur had been promising that American reinforcements were on their way to the Pacific theater, and it was now the beginning of March. They had to arrive soon. The alternative was unthinkable.

ONE AFTERNOON SHORTLY after Darren's death, I entered a ward during rounds and found George standing in front of me, chatting and handing cigarettes—real ones—Marlboros!—to a couple of injured troops lying in their bunks.

I let out a small cry and ran toward him, taking both his hands. I hadn't seen him since Fort Stotsenburg and could hardly believe it was really him. "Hiya, stranger."

"Are these fellas giving you a rough time?" He bobbed his chin toward my patients and they sniggered.

One of them, Frank, winked at me. We'd amputated his left arm the previous week, but losing a limb had done little to slow down his wisecracking. "Now, Tess, what do you want with him?" Frank asked, jabbing his right thumb at George. "I can do more with one arm than he could dream of managing with two."

I rolled my eyes. "Hey, have any of you seen my surgical thread?"

"Huh? Why?" Frank asked.

"Because I'm ready to sew your mouth shut, that's why," I said with a laugh.

"Sweetheart, nothing can stop me. Even sewn shut, I'll still be able to pucker up!" he said before blowing me a kiss.

Shaking my head, I turned to George. "It's quite the party here. Dances every night. The latest frocks from Paris. Texas steaks for breakfast, lunch, and dinner." The mere mention of steak made my mouth water and immediately I regretted it.

Virginia came through the foliage, wiping sweat from her face, and she smiled, spotting George. "Well, well, look who the cat dragged in."

George pulled a brown bag from his breast pocket and handed it to her. "I come bearing gifts."

She peered inside and shrieked, pulling out a small cobalt blue jar. "Noxzema? Oh, Georgie, you're a real gem! You sure know the way to a girl's heart."

"Just trying to keep our finest gals in silk and caviar," George said.

Virginia peered in the bag. "So where's the silk and caviar?"

"Must have left 'em in the jeep," George said.

"Now don't go getting our hopes up with lousy jokes, soldier. Save those bombs for the enemies."

We all laughed.

"Virginia, will you cover me for a few minutes?" I asked.

She grinned. "You two, scram."

I reached for George's hand and we hightailed it out of there.

"Where's Sal? I've got something for her too," he said, following me toward a bamboo bench by the river.

We sat and I hesitated before filling him in on what happened to Darren. George pinched the bridge of his nose, taking in the news. "I'm sorry."

It had been over two months since I'd last seen him and I'd pictured this moment of our reunion differently. Without looking in a mirror, I was keenly aware that I was no longer the bright and shiny creature who had first captivated him. That felt like a lifetime ago. Now a turban covered my greasy hair and it had been months since I'd worn any makeup. My filthy coveralls hung on my thinner-than-usual frame, and I could smell myself—not good. Not only that, but at any minute it was possible my stomach would cramp from dysentery and I'd need to make a run for the latrine. If romance needed a whiff of fresh mystery to stay alive, our affair was about to be pronounced dead on arrival.

"How are you?" he asked.

I searched for an answer, something chipper and witty, something that showed I still had my sparkle, something that would keep him sitting beside me. With George in my life, I could pin my hopes and dreams for the future on him, but if he abandoned me, it would shatter the flimsy bit of reserves I'd managed to cling to. Let's not forget, I'd once been the girl who could raise the dead; now I could scarcely raise my chin. To my mortification, tears filled my eyes and immediately my nose began to itch and run. His expression softened and he wrapped his arm around me.

And we sat there, saying nothing, listening to the ack-ack of the artillery guns.

I breathed in the salty seawater clinging to George's uniform, the gritty sand, and the smell of exertion, feeling grateful for this small moment of peace. I might have even started to doze off because I had the sensation of falling and jerked to attention with a gasp.

"You all right?" he asked.

"Some date I am. I can barely keep my eyes open."

"Don't worry, I'm not taking it personally. Trust me, I understand."

"Those army planners have really stepped on every rake in the yard, huh?"

He scraped his hand across the stubble on his cheeks. "That's an understatement. In fact, I may have to use that exact phrasing in my next report to General MacArthur."

"So really, how bad is it?"

Instead of answering, George reached into one of his pockets with his free hand and tugged out a flask.

Without asking what it was, I raised it to my lips. Bourbon? Whiskey? Who cared? Whatever it was, it burned down my throat, tasting wonderful and awful at the same time. I wiped my lips with the back of my hand and coughed. "That stuff's almost lethal. I'm not sure I have a tongue anymore."

He took a swill, nodding. A mortar landed within a quarter of a mile away and we both flinched. "This place is too close to the action," he said.

"You never answered my question."

He ran his index finger down my cheek and I could practically hear the scritching sound it made trailing through the grit on my skin. "You're too smart for your own good, did you know that? A loyal soldier knows not to ask too many questions."

Undeterred, I rolled my eyes, but snuggled a little closer. "But where are our reinforcements? We're desperate. Honestly, I'm not sure how much longer everyone can hold out. The other day one of the girls cracked a tooth on a small pebble in the gruel we call rice, and we're making tough choices about who's getting anesthesia when we do surgeries. And to top it off, the damn Japanese have lousy aim. They're firing on us morning, noon, and night, despite the fact that we're supposed to be exempt from the action."

George tucked the flask away, not meeting my gaze. "Our guys aren't coming."

I stared at him, my breath caught somewhere south of my throat, but north of my solar plexus. "What?"

"We're on our own. Washington's decided to focus on the war in Europe. Once it's settled, they'll turn their efforts toward us."

"But . . . but that will be too late."

He nodded as antiaircraft fire cracked in the distance.

"So what's going to happen?" I whispered. "There's nowhere to go. Soon there will be nothing to eat, no medicine."

"MacArthur's relocating to Australia tomorrow."

That news hit me like a sharp kick to the shins. It was bad enough to learn our country was turning its back on us, but now to learn our leaders were fleeing? Wasn't the captain supposed to go down with the ship? This was too much. "He's leaving? We're being abandoned?"

"The announcement will be made in the evening. The brass in Washington's afraid he'll fall into enemy hands which would be a real propaganda disaster. But I'll be staying here to help Wainwright."

George's voice was so calm, so rational. Wasn't he angry about this betrayal? I sure was! I was about to let forth, but something in his eyes stopped me. Those dreamy blue eyes the color of the bay appeared glassy with sadness and his expression looked wistful. He was just as heartbroken as I and didn't bother to put up a brave front. My heart warmed with the realization that he respected me enough to give me the news straight. From the moment we'd met, I'd been captivated with his unguarded honesty. It was actually almost funny: How on earth was this man sneaky enough to work in military intelligence?

I took a deep breath, recalibrating my attitude. After all, what other choices did I have? At least I was stuck with a group of men and women I had grown to respect and love. So what if lousy old MacArthur was leaving? We still had plenty of good leaders left. I thought of Josie Nesbit and Dr. Curtis. Yes, I was in good hands. I could endure this. "All right, so what's the plan now?"

"Onward," he said, nodding as if convincing himself.

I almost laughed at the absurdity of his statement. Instead, I took George's chin between my thumb and forefinger and kissed him sadly on the lips.

9.

TESS

April 1942
The Bataan Peninsula

They came for us a month after George's visit. I was hovering behind Dr. Curtis's right shoulder, ready to irrigate a shrapnel wound, trying to see the operating table in the dusky shadows. Iris stood across from us, transfixed by the careful movement of Dr. Curtis's fingers as he navigated the injury. Under the best of conditions, visibility in the jungle was a challenge, but given the sudden influx of injured men, we were conducting surgeries well into the evenings. Murky light lent the scene an underwater quality, exacerbated by our pruny, waterlogged skin and sodden hair, clothes, and bedding—the extreme humidity and our own sweat dampened everything.

An increase in action had marked the last few days, and smoke now drifted through the air, obscuring our vision even more. We had to raise our voices over the rat-a-tat of small-arms fire sounding increasingly closer, solid evidence that rumors of the arrival of Japanese reinforcements were true.

Harold, the orderly, appeared. "Tess and Iris, you two need to come with me."

I kept my eyes on Dr. Curtis's hand, concentrating hard on these final steps of our procedure. "Ten more minutes, please."

"No, I'm afraid you both must come now." Harold's serious

tone brokered no further discussion. Everyone in the operating theater turned to look at him.

Dr. Curtis's head bowed for a second. Though a mask covered most of his face, his brow furrowed in worry, prompting fear to race down my lungs and settle in my gut like a brick. He nodded at Iris and me. "Go on, girls. We're going to miss you."

"Please let us stay a little longer," I begged.

"We've been so busy that the charts are a mess," Iris added. "I really need to give the staff some updates on our patients."

Dr. Curtis cut us off and spoke quietly. "Orders are orders. We've known this moment was coming. Trust me, we'll do everything we can for the boys." He paused and when he started speaking again, emotion thickened his voice. "It's been an honor to serve with you both."

When I looked at Iris, I saw her face fall. My vision swam with tears as Harold helped untie our masks and slide off our aprons. It took all my willpower not to embrace Dr. Curtis and the orderlies who stepped in to take our places. Though only a few months had passed since our arrival in Bataan, we'd become a family. These men—our colleagues, our patients—I hated leaving them. With the enemy rapidly approaching, didn't we need to stick together?

Our jungle wards, always noisy with birds and monkeys chittering, the creaking of bamboo, and sounds of the men calling out to one another, laughing and groaning—all of it seemed to fall silent as we walked away. My service alongside these men represented the most important time of my life. My ability to help my colleagues and patients had reshaped how I viewed myself. A year earlier, I'd arrived in the Philippines as a young, foolish girl, but now I understood the importance of sacrifice, loyalty, and honor. How was I expected to leave it all behind?

We pushed past the branches of glossy gabi leaves and ropes of dangling rattan and I allowed myself to guess where we would be going next. There was really only one place left: *Corregidor.* Despite the heavy bombardment being unleashed upon it, the fortified island had an underground bunker currently housing American forces. We would be retreating to live like rats in the Malinta Tunnel. How long could we be expected to hole up there? When would supplies run out?

As we trudged through the wards, passing cot after cot of silent men, I felt the weight of their dejected expressions. They didn't say a word but merely watched. Abandoning them to the enemy felt like a bad burn—of course it hurt, but not just on the surface. More than anything, the pain accompanied a shame that lodged itself deep in my stomach, overcoming me with a horrible feeling of nausea. Those men were willing to sacrifice everything with their fighting, yet we were being forced to leave them when they needed us most. We nurses lived by a code—the Nightingale Pledge. Didn't our promise to serve, heal, and stand by our troops mean anything?

By the time Iris and I reached the other women clustered around a convoy of sedans, anger heated my face. Virginia waited for us on the edge of the group, the same fury burning in her eyes, but before we could say anything, she turned. I followed her gaze to the middle of the group where Josie stood facing Colonel Gillespie.

"General Wainwright has ordered your corps to evacuate to Corregidor," Colonel Gillespie said.

I felt the other nurses beside me tense. We had all known evacuation was coming, but there was no denying that retreating to the Malinta Tunnel was an act of desperation. Once we landed on Corregidor, it would be our final stand.

But Josie, ever the planner, was taking problems one at a time. She surveyed the four sedans in front of us and shook her head. "There's not enough room for my nurses in those."

"Only the *American* nurses are going," Colonel Gillespie said.

Josie was a greyhound of a woman, lean and angular, but in the flash of an eye, with her shoulders thrust back and her chin set, she became a bulldog. "Sir, in good conscience I'm not leaving my Filipino nurses behind. If they can't go, I'm not going either."

Not a single one of us dared to breathe. Josie's audacity in resisting a direct order was shocking. But she was right. We'd been serving as a unit since the beginning, and the idea of a portion of us being left behind for the enemy was a terrifying prospect. I glanced at Iris and saw fear stamped across her face. We all knew what had happened in Nanking a few years earlier. No one wanted to imagine what lay in store for a group of women left behind.

A vein pulsed on Colonel Gillespie's sunburned neck as he stared Josie down, but she didn't blink, didn't give an inch.

After a long pause, he gave a small nod. "I'll notify HQ to expect a bigger group." He turned to a subordinate, signaling to add another vehicle to the convoy.

"Thank you, sir." Josie bowed her head and then turned to point at Iris and me, her face pale and strained, but relieved. "Get only what you can carry. *Now.*"

In the face of Josie's insubordination on the group's behalf, my misgivings about being forced to evacuate faded. I took a deep breath and ran, setting off the *pop, pop, pop* of brown ipilipil pods underfoot. In our nurse's quarters, ragged books and scratched records lay scattered across the cots. A few old dresses hung limp from the rattan vines. I grabbed my duffel and jammed my toiletries, mosquito net, and small stash of undergarments into it, but what else was there to take? By that point, we had so little. Maybe a stub of lipstick. A beloved family ring. A favorite pair of socks or scarf. The jungle's humidity and the bugs and rats had made quick work of our old letters from home.

I took a final look at our ring of cots and breathed in air thick with the nearby river's skunky odor. We hated the jungle, but we'd survived. We'd learned to shake out our bedding for snakes before climbing into it. We'd learned that a circle of dark, smooth rocks lying below the largest balete tree near the river provided the most comfortable spot to kneel and bathe, to wash our clothes. We'd carved paths for ourselves through the mahogany trees and the thick tangle of molave. Though this place had challenged us at every turn, we'd made it our home.

Ready to go, I turned to Iris and found her eyes filled with tears.

"What's wrong?" I asked.

"I'm not going to be able to say goodbye to Vincent. I don't even know where he is right now."

I thought of each time I left George and how we never knew if we would see each other again. The ways this war was transforming our interactions—the casual goodbyes, the gallows humor, the clinical detachment we took in estimating risk, the intensity of our friendships and romances—it was almost inconceivable and yet now it was all we knew. It was how we faced each day. It was the way we coped with the overwhelming uncertainty that would have paralyzed us if we gave ourselves time to contemplate it.

There was nothing I could say to make Iris feel better, so I simply took her hand. Sometimes all we could do was focus on the next step in front of us. Bound together, we sprinted back to the line of waiting sedans. Six stood sentry next to the final automobile in the group and waved for us to hop in.

"We've got to hustle," he said, lowering his voice. "The road to Mariveles is taking a lot of incoming fire and rumor has it the peninsula's being surrendered tomorrow morning. If we don't catch one of those boats out of Mariveles, things are going to get real ugly so let's get you girls out of here."

My gut twisted as a huge explosion made the nearby bamboo and mango trees shiver. The enemy was getting closer and closer. Six shifted the sedan into gear and stomped on the gas, sending us careening down the hill toward the bay. *If* we reached Corregidor, there would be nowhere else to go. There would be no more retreating.

10.

FLOR

April 1942
Manila

After her flogging, Mama remained in bed for the rest of February and all of March. Like storm clouds, the shape and colors of the bruises on her legs slowly shifted from angry crimsons and violets to ominous greens. Gradually, she left her bed to creep around the house with a cane, but she could not return to work at the Red Cross. She moved painfully and Flor knew she feared hobbling down the streets and opening herself to the possibility of more abuse by the Japanese soldiers roaming the city, looking to stir up trouble by preying on the vulnerable.

Determined to defy Japanese orders, Flor insisted on continuing her trips to Santo Tomas every week, and Luchie accompanied her. Word of their trips spread to their neighborhood friends, and more and more canned foods started arriving on the Dalisays' kitchen doorstep. Sometimes envelopes stuffed with pesos appeared too, nestled in between the stacks of cans. Since the arrival of the Japanese on Luzon, the price of food had skyrocketed, so every peso helped, but Flor also decided to give cash directly to the internees so they could buy what they needed at the in-camp canteen and from the black market. She sewed a skirt with a pocket tucked under the hem and stored the peso bills there to evade the guards' notice. When Luchie realized what Flor had done, she fussed about it being too risky, but Flor refused to back down.

"I don't want the guards to get a single centavo. We can't afford to lose any of it," Flor said. She understood the enemy now. Their words of unity meant nothing. Not anymore. She was determined to strike any blow she could against the enemy.

"Well, then I should sew one into my skirt too and help," Luchie said.

"No, don't. Your parents rely on your income. Let me take on this risk. I'll pass along the messages and anything that could cause trouble."

"If you get in trouble, we both will. They'll know we're together."

"Then we need to stop arriving as a pair. We should pretend we don't know each other and try to keep as separate as possible. I'm serious. I don't want any trouble for you."

"You've grown so bossy," Luchie huffed, but as she turned for the kitchen, Flor could see a tender expression on the woman's face.

WHEN FLOR FIRST handed Mrs. Stone an envelope with cash neatly arranged inside by denomination, it was the rare occasion when the American was rendered silent for several seconds.

"Our friends sent this?"

"Yes, and strangers. And I've decided to start taking written messages out. We can put them here," Flor said, lifting the hem of her skirt to reveal the secret pockets she had sewn.

"Thank you," the American murmured.

On some days when Flor left the house, she could hear the thunderous rumble of artillery fire on Bataan. At the market stalls, the sound of laughter and the babble of gossip had quieted. Everyone in the city knew Americans and Filipino fighters were suffering. Though the Voice of Freedom reported many USAFFE victories on Bataan, reinforcements had yet to arrive from the United States. No one could fool themselves into believing the war was going well.

One afternoon in April, Flor was sitting in the kitchen organizing her next delivery to Santo Tomas when Papa appeared in the doorway. He carried his medical bag and slid a business card from his suit pocket. "Remember Pablo and Rosario Bautista? They own a restaurant and they're looking for a new bookkeeper. I wondered if this could be a good job for you."

Flor took the card and studied the name of the restaurant: Café Rosario. She had seen it before and admired the cheerful red-and-white-striped awning over its front door. She also remembered the menu's delicious-sounding Pancit Palabok, sautéed rice noodles in shrimp sauce with ground chicharron on top. Her mouth watered. "I've taken an accounting class before," she said, thinking aloud.

"That's what I figured. They have a son fighting for the USAFFE on Bataan. You'll remember them. When you were much younger, sometimes you would accompany me to visit Mr. Bautista and the two of you would play chess. Afterward, Mrs. Bautista would feed you her delicious saba con hielo."

"I remember that. Those sweetened plantains were the best."

"Keep your voice down, so Luchie doesn't hear that." Papa smiled. "I said you would pay them a visit and discuss working together."

Flor nodded. She missed her school assignments. She missed the neat logic of how numbers could be managed in predictable ways. Surrounded by so much uncertainty, the idea of a job that relied on precision and an understandable order of operations appealed to her. There was also the very practical concern about money. Every week the prices of food and basic supplies continued to rise and rise. "Thank you, Papa. You know I can do this type of work in my sleep, right? I can do more advanced math than this will require."

He ruffled her hair. "I know, but it's a job and there aren't many of those around these days."

Flor nodded. "I'll meet with them on Friday."

THE NEXT MORNING, before Flor and Luchie planned to go to Santo Tomas, they left for the market in hopes of obtaining coffee beans, an item that was becoming increasingly hard to find. The American internees loved their coffee, though, and Flor was eager to see Mrs. Stone's delight when she handed her a sack of the beloved beans. When they reached Dewey Boulevard— now renamed Daitoa by the Japanese as part of their campaign to rid the city of all vestiges of the Americans—Flor froze at the sight of headlines plastering a newspaper stand.

Bataan Collapses!
36,000 U.S. Men Feared Lost

Though the sky was almost white with heat, goose pimples rose on Flor's arms and legs.

"What is this?" Luchie cried, pointing at the papers.

Flor pushed five centavos toward the newsboy and skimmed the *Tribune*'s front page. It made no mention of the women who had been there. What did this surrender mean for Iris? Where was she? Flor pictured her captured in a place like Santo Tomas—or worse, Bilibid Prison.

The paper only praised the surrender as a wise decision by

the Americans to spare further bloodshed. There was a photo of Filipino civilians being fed by Japanese soldiers in a show of goodwill, but the article reported nothing about the fate of surrendered USAFFE fighters and support medical staff.

"What does it say?" Luchie demanded.

"Nothing specific. Nothing useful." Flor crumpled the paper and hurled it into a trash can.

Now only the USAFFE forces still fighting on Corregidor separated her country from complete control by the Japanese.

When Flor and Luchie visited Santo Tomas that afternoon, the women crowded around them asking about the surrender. Mrs. Stone didn't make any of her usual jokes that day, and before Flor left, the American held out a piece of paper, wrinkled and worn. "See if you can find out anything about these men."

Flor nodded, knowing these were the husbands of many of the camp's women. The names were written in pencil by different hands, some appeared smudged, the script wobbly and uncertain. To add the name of a beloved to this list meant acknowledging the realities of the situation and these realities were too awful to contemplate.

ON FRIDAY, FLOR and Luchie visited Café Rosario. Papa had told her that the Bautistas would be in their apartment above the restaurant, so the two women rounded the corner into the backyard, passed a large chicken coop filled with clucking birds. When Flor knocked on the apartment's door, the fuchsia-colored flowers on a large bougainvillea vine next to the door trembled. She looked up. A window slid open a few inches before closing quickly. Concerned, Flor and Luchie looked at each other. Moments later, Mrs. Bautista opened the door and tugged the women inside.

"We were hoping you would come," she whispered.

Though she was a large woman, Mrs. Bautista flew upstairs toward the entresuelo with surprising speed. Once they arrived in the mezzanine, she pulled Flor and Luchie into a small room, where her husband stood by the door. There, in the far corner of the room, lay an unconscious white man wearing a torn and bloody US Army uniform.

Luchie stiffened. "Oh no."

Flor inhaled sharply. "Who's that?"

Mrs. Bautista pulled the door shut behind them. "We don't know. I found him hiding in my chicken coop this morning. He was delirious. It looks like he's been shot."

"You both managed to carry him up those stairs?" Flor asked.

"He's only skin and bones. We knew things were bad on Bataan, but judging by the looks of him, it's been really bad. His wound might be infected. We have no idea what to do with him."

Flor didn't either. The penalty for hiding an American soldier would be death for the Bautistas. And if Flor and Luchie helped and got caught, they'd be executed too.

She took several hesitant steps toward the man. A bloom of blood had darkened the entire right side of his body from his chest down. The skin on his nose, forehead, and sunken cheeks looked cracked and painful from sunburn, but he was as white as the belly of a milkfish. How on earth had he gotten here from Bataan? And had Mrs. Bautista found him too late? Flor did a quick calculation. If she went to the risk of involving Papa, would this man still die? And if he did, how would they dispose of a body?

At that moment, the man groaned and his emaciated hand, which had been clutching at his chest, moved to reveal his name tag stitched over his pocket: Pvt. Morris.

Now he was no longer a lost soldier. Flor knew his name. She leaned in and gently lifted his dog tag from around his neck.

> **Luroy Morris**
>
> **Mrs. Eugene Morris**
>
> **12 Wren Ridge**
>
> **Watson, OR**

Somewhere across the Pacific Ocean, a woman waited for news of her son. Someone would miss Luroy.

Since her mother's beating Flor *had* decided to take on more risk—well, this was her chance. She took a deep breath and made a decision. "I need to get my father. Manang Luchie, you don't have to be a part of this. You can go home."

But Luchie let out an impatient snort and waved a calloused hand to silence her. "No. I've been with you since your first breath, and the Japanese can't scare me away now. We'll do this together."

BY THE TIME Flor, Luchie, and Papa hurried to the Bautistas' building, it was afternoon. The city's curfew fell in place at midnight, giving them several hours to help Private Morris. When Luchie and Flor had arrived at her papa's practice, they gave him the briefest description of what had happened and he hadn't hesitated. He'd asked them for information on the gunshot wound, and Flor had shrugged. "I don't really know what hit him or where it hit, but he's lost a lot of blood."

Papa nodded, filled his musette bag, and they left, moving through checkpoints without incident. Outside the front door of Café Rosario, he turned to Luchie. "Flor can stay with me, but please go home to help Señora Pilar."

Luchie cast a wary look at Flor, but nodded. "As you wish, Dr. Dalisay."

"If it gets late, we'll telephone and stay here," he said.

With a grumpy sigh, Luchie left them.

By the time Papa and Flor climbed the stairs at the Bautistas', the soldier's condition had deteriorated even more. His chest rose and fell at an irregular pace, but Papa washed his hands and got to work, giving the man a shot of morphine and then cutting off his uniform and assessing the injuries. When Papa pulled out a scalpel, light-headedness caused Flor to avert her eyes. While Mrs. Bautista leaned in to assist, Flor busied herself with filling and refilling basins of boiling water and keeping a steady supply of clean towels on hand.

Dusk approached and Papa continued to work on Private Morris.

He managed to clean out the wound and stitched the man up before curfew. As Private Morris slept, Papa handed Mr. Bautista several vials. "He can't be moved. Keep him drinking water and try to get some rice in him. Replace his dressings every four hours. I think it's best if I don't return unless it's absolutely necessary, but Flor can come and go unnoticed. If his condition changes, call our house."

"When do you think he'll be ready to leave?" Mrs. Bautista asked.

"Let's give it a week and see how he's doing." Papa placed a comforting hand on her shoulder, but the woman gave a worried shake of her head and her husband wrapped his arm around her shoulders.

"I just keep thinking of our children out in the jungle," she lamented. "Someone will help them like we're helping him, right?"

Flor took Mrs. Bautista's hand in her own. "You keep him safe and I'll figure out what happens next."

The Dalisays left and headed home in the darkness. "How will we get him out of there?" Papa asked.

"I don't know." A desperate feeling clawed at Flor's chest. She had no idea what to do. There was no easy formula to solve this problem. "I just keep thinking about Iris."

Papa nodded. He raked a hand through his hair and Flor could see how it trembled. "I thought of her the whole time I was working on him. I've been praying that if she needs help, someone will be there for her, but I can't do a job like this again. Your mother relies on me now completely and I'm the only one with a job in our family. The Japanese secret police, Kempeitai, are everywhere these days. If those agents come for me, I'll disappear into Fort Santiago's prisons and then who would support you and your mother, Luchie and Jose? I must be very careful now." He swallowed. "I've already failed your mother once. I'll never forgive myself for what happened that night."

"You must forgive yourself. None of us did anything wrong," Flor spoke, suspecting her father wanted to hear her say that she would not participate in resistance activities either, but she could make no such promises. She did not want to worry him, but she would not lie.

Papa's pace lagged as a silence stretched between them. He finally said, "One of the doctors who worked with your mother at the Red Cross just returned from a trip to Bataan to provide aid to the surrendered soldiers. I ran into him the other day."

Flor's pulse quickened. "Did he know anything about Ate Iris?"

"No, but he described what happened in the jungle as a scene from hell. The Japanese didn't plan for so many prisoners and forced many of the men to march from Mariveles to the train in Capas, where they sent them to a prisoner camp. But that march . . ." Papa faltered. "Many of the soldiers were starving and thirsty. The Japanese showed no mercy and killed those who struggled to keep pace. Thousands have died."

An image of Iris holding her suitcase and standing in their house's doorway flashed through Flor's mind. What would the soldiers do to her beautiful sister? She reached for Papa's medical bag and took it from him. "Could Iris have been forced to march?"

"I don't know." The mix of hope and sorrow etched onto Papa's face almost broke Flor's heart. "When Private Morris is lucid, you need to talk to him and find out as much as you can. Maybe he'll have an idea of what's happened to Iris. But Flor, you must be careful. I don't like the thought of your involvement in such dangerous work."

"For as long as I can remember, you've always been quoting President Quezon by saying 'we prefer a government run like hell by Filipinos than one run like heaven by Americans.'"

An amused glint came into Papa's bloodshot eyes. "So you've been listening to me."

"I have and I've been studying the difference between what the Japanese have promised and how they've treated us. I've concluded that we must be free of all of them. I can play a role in achieving our freedom. I'm being careful, but I can't stand by and do nothing. You raised me to be a thinker. To be someone who cares. You raised me to want more. And that's what I'm doing. I'm trying to help."

"I know, I know," he groaned, taking her arm in his. "Why do you and Iris have to be so stubbornly idealistic?"

"Because we're your daughters."

He looked away, but before he did, Flor thought she saw tears misting his eyes. Were they from pride or sorrow? Since the war began it felt like the two had become inextricably linked.

FIVE DAYS AFTER Dr. Dalisay visited, Flor and Luchie returned to the Bautistas' house. Private Morris was sitting up in bed, a game smile stretched across his thin face.

"I don't know how I got lucky enough to land above a restaurant, but someone was looking out for me," he said, forking caldereta into his mouth. The aroma of beef, garlic, and tomato sauce made Flor hungry, but she tried to ignore the food. "Private Morris, I'm relieved to find you looking so much better." With the Bautistas and Luchie watching, she sat on the chair next to his bed. "How did you find your way here from Bataan?"

He placed his fork beside his plate and then rubbed his hand along the stubble of his face. "The surrender wasn't pretty. We were ordered to hand over our weapons and empty our pockets. The enemy took it all. Let me tell you, they have a real hankering for watches. By the time they'd finished swiping all our stuff, some of those fellas were wearing six of them on one arm. When it became clear there weren't enough trucks to get everyone off the peninsula, they made us start marching." His brow furrowed and he gazed down at his plate for a moment. "It was a real rough treatment, what happened to a lot of the boys. At one point, a few of us were able to peel off. We hid in farmhouses and made our way to Orion in the dark of night. A few locals helped us and one arranged for a fisherman to get us here."

"When were you shot?"

"That happened down on the waterfront here in Manila. The three of us who'd escaped decided our best move was to split up. We'd just left the boat and I'd set off on my own when a guard appeared and popped me one. I managed to drag myself a few blocks until I saw that chicken coop out back. Curling up inside there is the last thing I remember."

"It was a good hiding place."

"I'll say."

"My sister is a nurse working with the USAFFE. She was sent to Bataan, but now we have no idea where she is."

"Jeez, I'm sorry. I'd hate to think of a girl being stuck out there. Like I said, it was pretty rough."

Flor tried to keep her voice steady. "Is there any way she would have been forced to march?"

"Nah, I doubt it. A girl? No." He shook his head emphatically. "She was probably part of the big skedaddle of folks trying to make the crossing to Corregidor before the enemy took over. Yep, now that I think about it, I'm willing to bet—not that I've got any money—that she's safe and sound on the Rock. I'm sure your sister's doing just fine."

Flor nodded, but glanced at Luchie and the Bautistas. Judging by the sound of heavy artillery coming across the bay each day, Corregidor was far from being safe and sound. Mrs. Bautista, head down, hurried from the room. Flor and Luchie thanked the American and excused themselves.

They found Mrs. Bautista washing dishes in the kitchen.

"Your father worked a miracle on Private Morris. The poor man took a walk around the apartment this morning and looked pretty steady," Mrs. Bautista said, keeping her eyes trained on the suds in the sink. Luchie picked up a dish towel and helped her dry. Their host seemed to keep her head at an angle as if listening for a sound outside the house, and her hand revealed a tremor when she raised a plate to scrub at it.

"How are you?" Flor asked gently.

"It feels like I haven't slept a wink since that man arrived. I've been praying for him and for your ate and my Felipe." She put the plate down and clutched the counter with both hands. "I keep expecting the Kempeitai to arrive in the middle of the night and drag us down to Fort Santiago, but I can't just send that poor boy on his way. He won't make it two blocks before a guard spots him."

"Manang Luchie and I will take a walk around here to see what the checkpoints look like. Maybe we can figure out a route."

"But to where? He'll never be able to cross the entire city to get to the mountains. And I don't know anyone at the waterfront who can ferry him somewhere. If I open that door, we'll just be throwing him to the sharks."

"Let us think. We'll come back tomorrow," Flor said.

"Before you leave, I'll feed you both."

But neither woman had any appetite and they left without enjoying any of Mrs. Bautista's cooking. As they walked the blocks surrounding the Bautistas', trying not to draw attention to themselves, they saw checkpoint after checkpoint, guard after guard. Each time Flor spotted one, she felt as though she glowed with guilt. When they reached Rizal Park, they stopped.

"Manang, I don't know what to tell the Bautistas. I don't know how we can possibly get that soldier out of there safely."

Luchie stared at the walls of Intramuros, seemingly lost in thought. "It's Wednesday, so let's go to church for the novena to Our Mother of Perpetual Help. Maybe God will have an answer for us."

The women walked to Malate Church and sank into a pew.

After several minutes, a priest named Father Callahan glided along the nave but stopped when he spotted them.

"Good afternoon, ladies. Kamusta?"

Flor shook her head. Tears welled in her eyes and she began to weep.

Father Callahan sat in the pew a row ahead of them and turned to face the women, his eyes wide with concern. "Miss Dalisay, we've been praying for your ate."

His pale skin, ginger hair, and freckles made Flor pause. "Father, how is it that you haven't been sent to Santo Tomas?"

"Ireland's considered neutral. Call it the luck of the Irish, I suppose. Now, how may I help? Your burden appears heavy today."

Luchie leaned forward. "Father, if we confess something to you, must you report it to the authorities?"

"I'm bound by the sacred seal of confession to keep words to myself. I may counsel ye to go to the authorities yourself, but I'll not reveal a word."

Luchie nodded at Flor, so she took a deep breath and told him about the Bautistas and Private Morris. She expected to see the priest look surprised, but his expression remained still. Confessing the secret made her feel lighter. Her stomach settled. Suddenly she found herself describing her smuggling at Santo Tomas too. Through it all, the priest merely watched her. When she finished, he bowed his head a moment.

"This church supports the needy and destitute of Manila by distributing food. The produce comes from our gardens, the eggs from our chickens. We run carts filled with these goods and other sundry items all over the city and sometimes beyond."

Flor stared at the priest as he ticked off the ways the parish supported the community, but it was the phrasing of *all over the city and sometimes beyond* that caught her attention. She glanced at Luchie, whose eyes had also brightened. He smiled as the realization of what he was offering dawned on their faces.

"Aye, we may be able to help your soldier," he whispered.

11.

TESS

When our transport craft docked at Corregidor at sunrise the morning after our swift evacuation from Hospital No. 2, no one rushed to disembark. Instead we found ourselves drawn to looking back at Mt. Samat rising from the mist. Our trip to the island had been frantic, the roads to Mariveles filled with soldiers desperate to catch a boat for Corregidor before the peninsula was surrendered, and in the chaos, our car had become separated from the convoy. We had arrived in Mariveles hours late, and after a chaotic scene on the beach at midnight, Six managed to arrange our passage on the last boat departing Bataan. While our small craft chugged away, streaks of tracer fire revealed panicking men wading into the water and trying to escape the enemy by swimming to Corregidor. We watched them vanish into the darkness, our hearts in our throats at the anguish of the situation.

In the gilded light of early morning, we looked back at the coast of Bataan only three miles away, wondering what would become of our dear friends like Greasy, Dr. Curtis, Harold, and countless others.

The toll of living in the jungle revealed itself when we lined up with the other nurses who had arrived on Corregidor directly from Manila, four months earlier. Those of us who had spent time in the jungle appeared feral. Our hair had grown wild, well beyond regulation off-the-collar length, our coveralls were in tatters, our cuts in rations had left us underweight and gaunt, and our sallow skin glowed with a dull sheen of malarial fever sweat.

At the sight of us, Captain Davison recoiled. She was a serious, sharp-eyed woman and I got the impression little could surprise her, so her reaction to our beleaguered state said something. "For those of you who were on Bataan, please march straight to the quartermaster and retrieve some new army-issue khaki skirts and button-up short-sleeve blouses. And when you've got your new uniforms, burn those things," she said, pointing to our ragged attire.

As we departed, Virginia pinched the filthy fabric of her coveralls and whispered, "These things are so lived in they could probably walk around on their own."

"Maybe they could cover our rounds in the hospital while we go take naps?" I suggested wearily.

In those first few days, it was easy to get lost in the Malinta Tunnel. We were told that from a bird's-eye view, Corregidor resembled a tadpole, but we could only take people's word on that since we were whisked underground immediately. The island's mountainous main body, where the ruins of Fort Mills could be found, connected at Malinta Hill to a thin tail of the rest of the low-lying island. There, the main tunnel, a straight-away about 800 feet long, was carved right through the hill's base. Branching off the main tunnel, the Army Corps of Engineers had built a series of smaller tunnels called laterals.

It was in these laterals that we could find the hospital, offices, mess hall, barracks, and the quartermaster. In short, everything that composed a normal military base existed within the Malinta Tunnel complex. The place was an extraordinary feat of planning and constructed so no dead ends existed, but we often found ourselves disoriented, wandering from lateral to lateral in search of our destinations, especially at first, and our disorientation was exacerbated by the fact that bright electrical lights illuminated the ceiling and walls of the tunnels at all hours. Time of day could only be established by a look at a clock. No view of the sky existed unless we exited one of the main entrances and peered outside.

At first underground living offered some advantages. Dug deep down under Malinta Hill, we felt safe. The hospital resembled what we'd left behind in Manila in the sense that the wards contained iron cots with white enamel bedside tables, refrigerators, a dental clinic, laboratories, a dispensary, kitchen, dining hall, and our sleeping quarters—not a single item constructed from bamboo could be found in the tunnels. After the messiness of jungle living, we all agreed that the best part of our new home consisted of the flushable toilets, sinks, and showers with running water. But how long could this facility be maintained? Did enough supplies exist here to keep us stocked with medicine, food, fresh water, electricity, and weaponry through a prolonged siege?

Since the fall of Bataan, with over a hundred of us nurses now residing in the Malinta Tunnel, our section grew very popular. Any time the men found themselves with free time, they visited and suddenly our social lives hummed with gatherings and events. When we weren't working, our hours were filled with card games, sewing and knitting circles, and impromptu dances and sing-alongs. Though these provided precious time for letting our hair down, we missed many of our friends from Bataan, and I often wondered what had become of Dr. Curtis, Greasy, and Harold. Were they still alive?

Six, now stationed on Corregidor, often dropped by to visit us in the hospital lateral and somehow he always managed to bring gifts, like canned peaches, playing cards, and chocolate bars. He especially kept an eye on how Sal was faring. Everyone worried about her. She never danced or sang anymore. She didn't sit around and gossip. Instead she tended to lie on her bed and write letters home that would never be mailed. When Six stopped by, he always brought her fresh pens and paper, along with goodies like chewing gum and any sweets he could find.

Though George came and went from Corregidor on missions, he was another regular in our hospital lateral, and I saw him frequently. At night, we'd sit outside the main entrance, talk, and look at the stars.

That April we celebrated Virginia's twenty-second birthday. I'd managed to trade a ball of yarn for a lightly used romance novel, and Nell surprised everyone by wielding an unopened bottle of Johnnie Walker. She had developed quite the knack for coming into possession of highly desirable rare items, a result of her card-playing skills. Since our days aboard the USS *Saratoga*, she'd demonstrated no mercy when it came to poker and though the men knew adding her to a game would result in lightening their wallets, they kept inviting her, hopeful for some flirtation, but she kept her own counsel, her poker face legendary.

One evening, George and I sat outside, enjoying the cool breeze. Somewhere in the dark beyond us, a harmonica hummed out a sad melody.

"Remember when we met in Manila?" I asked, thinking back to nights filled with music, gin and tonics, champagne, powdered faces, spotless white dinner jackets, and the swish of satin dresses.

"How could I forget? That feels like a dream now, doesn't it?"

"Yes, exactly. It does. If that was a dream, is this our real life now?" Even to my own ears I sounded crazy. "Actually don't even bother to answer that. *Real life?* What am I talking about?"

But when I glanced at George out of the corner of my eye, he nodded, considering my question. "This feels like a nightmare."

"Maybe real life was what happened before we came to the Philippines."

"No, that wasn't it either."

I smiled into the darkness, grateful he was trying to understand what I was talking about. "So what is real life? It feels like this war, this nightmare, will last forever and become our new normal."

"It won't."

"Are you sure? Because I can't imagine the end anymore. What are we doing all this for? What will life be like?"

George was quiet for a long time. "This is a test. Eventually we'll win and go home and that's when real life begins—the two of us together without a war. Someday we'll sit side by side, staring out into the evening like this, but we'll be on our own porch back in our own country."

As he spoke, my mouth fell open and I was thankful he couldn't make out my expression in the darkness. *We were going to live together after this?* The tight wires holding me together loosened, but at the same time, I couldn't breathe. This was romance during wartime. Emotions arrived quickly, promises even quicker.

He chuckled at my silence and knocked his shoulder into mine playfully. "It may not be gin-soaked parties every night, but a life with you sounds like the best thing that I can imagine. What do you think?"

His voice was so low that I leaned toward him to hear better and his warm breath on my neck made me feel like I was paper next to a flame, my skin curling toward the heat. I wrapped my arms around his shoulders and pulled him toward me and we kissed long and hard. I wasn't entirely sure what we had agreed upon, but at that moment, despite the wreckage surrounding us, everything felt promising.

After a few minutes of this, a pair of soldiers walked behind us, their boots kicking bits of sand onto us. They must have caught sight of our shadow and they whistled and laughed. George pulled away and I shook my head a little to regain my balance. He cleared his throat. "Listen, I've got something I need to share with you, but don't tell anyone. I mean *no one.* Understand?"

I frowned at the abrupt shift in his tone, but nodded.

"If all goes well, two navy seaplanes are arriving tomorrow for a quick stop," he said. "When they leave, they're taking some people out and going to Australia. MacArthur has ordered me to leave on one of these planes and I've snagged you a seat too."

The cogs of my brain struggled to process his words. Planes. Leaving. Australia. "What?"

"Some of MacArthur's staff is leaving, several older officers and dependent family members, and a few nurses. I've arranged for one of them to be you."

"Which other nurses?"

"I don't know. The department heads are making the decision."

"You're going to Australia?"

"Yes. With you."

"And we would stay there?"

"We'd stay for the duration of the war, but chances are that I'd be heading back here on some undercover missions. And of course, to chase the enemy off eventually."

I frowned, taking this in. The feeling of walking away from my colleagues and patients in the jungle still hurt like a fresh wound. That we'd heard our men had suffered horrific atrocities at the hands of the enemy after the fall of Bataan didn't help my pain. Six arrived with us on Corregidor and we saw him often, but I felt sick when I thought about Greasy and the rest of our colleagues we left behind. And what about our patients? How could I be expected to walk away again? And how could I leave the other nurses, my good friends?

He continued, "You can work in Australia and when we regain territory in the Pacific, you can travel and remain near the front lines if you want."

But I didn't care about the front lines. I cared about my corps of nurses. As I looked at the dark edges of George's silhouette, I was torn between my sense of duty and friendship and how I felt about this man. I swallowed hard. "I don't want to lose you."

"Then come with me. You know our days here are limited."

This was true. Too many of us were packed into the Malinta Tunnel. With the increase in new mouths to feed, how much longer would we be receiving two meals a day? In the nurses' quarters, we were sleeping in what Josie called "hot beds," letting one nurse sleep while the other worked, and then reversing. And in an ominous sign of things to come, over the last week the generators had begun glitching and now the lights flickered every time the Japanese bombed us.

George spoke quickly. "I know you hate the idea of leaving the others. I do too, but Hirohito's birthday is late next week and our intel says they're softening us up. An invasion is coming. It's just a matter of time. The Japanese Imperial Army has promised to deliver the Philippines fully surrendered to the emperor as a gift."

"You're asking me to make an impossible choice."

"Tess, I'm afraid of what's coming. The Japanese haven't signed the provision in the Geneva Convention about the treatment of prisoners. We all know what happened in Nanking and what they've done to our boys on Bataan—" George's voice broke and his warm hands encircled my own. "Please come with me."

"But maybe they'll repatriate us. Could they use us as a prisoner exchange and send us home? After all, what are they going to do with a bunch of women prisoners?"

He shook his head. "I don't want to imagine it."

My gaze drifted overhead to the stars and I couldn't help myself from thinking about home. What was Sue doing at that moment?

The temptation to leave Corregidor was strong. It was a completely reasonable offer to accept. Nurses would be leaving, so why shouldn't I be one of them? I stretched my legs out in front of me and that's when I realized something. Compared to many in my corps, I was in pretty good shape. Sure, I was tired and probably anemic and suffered from bouts of dysentery, but others were suffering from malaria and dengue. And then I pictured Sal, lying listlessly in her bunk.

"I'm sorry." I paused for a second, dreading the words I was about to say. "But I can't leave the other nurses. You need to take Sal in my place. She's struggling."

"Maybe I can get you both out."

"No. There are other girls who are sick. They should go."

"Please don't be so stubborn."

But my mind was made up and I plunged on with my plan. "You have to make sure Sally's on one of those planes. Do you promise?"

"Yes, I'll get Sally out, but—"

"No." I raised my hand to stop him. "Please don't ask me again. I need to stay."

"You don't need to be a hero."

I stiffened. A year ago, when I'd arrived on the decks of the *Saratoga* to set sail for Manila, I'd lived a small life. I was lonely and knew little about friendship. But since I'd been here in the Philippines, I'd become a part of something bigger than myself. This sprawling group of nurses and doctors and soldiers had become my family, and while serving alongside them, I'd learned I could withstand fear and deprivation and help others. That shy orphaned farm girl was half a world away and in her place was someone I barely recognized—but I liked her a lot. Now I was strong, independent, and resourceful. Though saying no to George hurt like hell, I knew it was the right answer.

"I'm not trying to be a hero," I said. "I'm simply sticking with the job I came here to do. Please don't make this harder than it already is. My orders are as important as yours."

"I didn't realize how committed you'd be to staying." His voice sounded sad and I hated that I was making him feel that way.

A few yards away, Virginia's husky laugh rose over the others sitting huddled in groups around the entrance to the tunnel. Several voices threaded together in song:

There's a yellow rose of Texas
That I am going to see
No other fellow knows her
No other, only me.

George then took my hand and laid something cool and smooth across my palm. "This was my grandfather's watch. Wear it to count down the minutes until we're together again. We'll win this, though it's going to be tough, so don't give up hope. You have to survive whatever comes next because I'm coming back for you."

I closed my trembling fingers over the glass of the watch's face. A low cloud obscured the stars and the wind picked up and tugged at my hair. I shivered. "I'll be here."

THE SEAPLANES ARRIVED the following evening in a small cove on the southern side of Corregidor. An hour before they were scheduled to land, Captain Davison told twenty nurses they were being reassigned from Corregidor to Australia. She gave them only a few minutes to assemble a small bag and said not to tell anyone about the planes, but a secret like that was impossible to contain. Soon the hospital laterals buzzed with news of their departure.

Several of us gathered around Sally, who wrung her hands. "I shouldn't leave you gals."

"Nonsense," Virginia said. "And if you don't shake a tail feather and get moving, I'll take your spot."

"When you get to Australia, will you mail these for us?" Mabel asked, pushing letters into her hands.

"Of course. Do you really think we'll make it?"

"Yes," I said. "Soon you'll be back in Michigan."

"I'll miss all of you," Sally said.

"We'll see you when this is over."

Sally nodded and when I wrapped my arms around her shoulders in an embrace, she felt so frail, so light. With my chin pressed against her temple, I said a quick, silent prayer that she'd make it back home.

We led her out to the main tunnel to find the larger group. Across the crowd, I spotted George.

I'd met with him again earlier that morning. He'd found me while I was on my rounds.

"Can I talk to you?" he asked.

I placed my clipboard down and nodded. Around us, nurses and officers brushed past and I racked my mind for a place where we could speak privately. Every inch of the laterals bustled with busy people. After leading him to a few places that wouldn't work, we ended up in an area where several supply cabinets were pushed against the walls.

"Stand there." I pointed to a spot on the wall between two of the cabinets.

"This feels an awful lot like what my grammar school teacher ordered us to do when we were naughty. Do I need to face the wall too?"

"Hmm, I'm not going to comment on your extensive experience with being naughty," I said, suppressing a giggle as I opened the supply closet doors and tucked us behind them against the wall. Beyond the gap between the doors, glimpses of my colleagues flashed past, but I turned to George, only a couple of inches away, and tried to forget about the outside world. This was it. Our final few minutes together.

"You want to know if I've changed my mind, don't you?"

He nodded, his blue eyes wide and pleading.

I bit my lip. When I'd collapsed into my cot the previous night, my head hummed with questions. Why not leave this place? How could I possibly let George slip through my fingers? Shouldn't I save myself? But for all the buzzing in my mind, my heart was steady. I could come up with a million reasons to rationalize leaving for Australia, but I knew I'd never feel good about making that decision. *Never.* I couldn't leave. I couldn't abandon my friends and colleagues or my orders. I had to do the right thing, no matter how much it hurt.

"I'm staying. I must."

For a second, George closed his eyes, defeated, but then he opened them and forced a smile, clutching my wrist where his grandfather's watch lay against my skin. "All right. I'll be back as soon as I can. Don't forget about me." And then he kissed me and I sank into him, wishing we could have stayed like that forever.

Now, from across the lateral, with my eyes locked on his, I raised my wrist and tapped on my new beloved watch. *Come back for me*, I murmured to myself, blinking back tears.

Less than a minute later, the small group left for the seaplanes.

As I turned to drag myself back to the hospital laterals, Virginia stopped me. "You were supposed to leave, weren't you?" she whispered. "Did you give up your spot for Sal?"

"No," I mumbled, not wanting to get into it.

She gave me a long look and then kissed my cheek. I knew she didn't believe me.

"You're a good friend" was all she said.

ON ONE OF the last evenings of April, Iris and I were wrapping bandages in a supply area when an enormous boom rocked Malinta Hill. Immediately the overhead lights snapped off. We'd grown accustomed to flickering bulbs, but a full blackout was new. Complete darkness took over. Without the fans blowing, the tunnels grew sweltering within seconds. Sweat dripped down my spine while panic snaked through my insides. Voices called out to one another, but my sense of direction had vanished. Dizziness overcame me.

"Iris? Are you still here?"

"I haven't moved," she said in a wobbly voice. "Where are you?"

Right then, a flashlight flicked on. "Ladies? Everyone still here?" Billy, one of the orderlies, held the light overhead, sweeping our area.

I exhaled with relief at the small beam of light. Beyond us, shouting echoed in the main lateral. Billy swung the flashlight in that direction. "Better go see about the commotion," he said moving away. Iris and I trailed him, close as a tail on a kite.

"That was the biggest explosion we've heard yet," Iris said as we ran along the lateral. "What was it?"

"The enemy's supposed to have installed a few new big guns on Bataan," Billy said. "Could've been a 240."

The thought of such big shells blasting at our boys elicited a keen needling of fear. We'd become accustomed to cleaning up 125s and those were grisly, but survivable. Could soldiers walk away from the business end of a 240? I dreaded finding out.

As soon as we reached the main tunnel, a press of bodies sprinting toward the big entrance swarmed us. We joined the maelstrom, tripping over each other, stumbling, and struggling to stay upright in the chaos.

When we reached the tunnel's slatted iron gate, it was shut. Several corpsmen were leaning against it, their arms spread wide, hands clenched against the slats as they strained to open it. Outside the gate, the sound of desperate screams pierced the night.

"Watch out!" a voice, hoarse but recognizable, yelled.

Next to one of the corpsman trying to open the gate, Virginia bent over and removed something from where it hung stuck between the slats.

In the spotlight of someone's flashlight, she raised a dismembered forearm and let out a faint cry. I pulled her away from the gate as more flashlights strobed the area behind her, revealing a gruesome scene of limbs, hair, and bits of uniform jammed within the gate's slats. We fell silent for a second, but then leapt into action.

Some huddled over extracting the human remains from the gate, while others banded together to open it. An orderly pushing a wheelbarrow stopped next to Virginia and she bowed to it, placing the arm down as if sliding a sleeping baby into a cradle.

When she stood and faced us, she looked as terrified as I'd ever seen her. There were no snappy jokes, no winks, but she started talking in a monotone. "I was making my way out to the entrance for some fresh air and then the loudest explosion I've ever heard threw me onto my back. Its force was enough to knock the gate shut. All those boys who were standing around, smoking and talking, they—" She broke off. We didn't ask for more. We didn't need to.

THAT NIGHT WAS one of the longest of my life. The blood. The mangled, burned flesh. It was like nothing I'd seen before, and by that point I considered myself battle hardened. Under the narrow beams of flashlights, we worked for hours trying to patch up the boys who could be saved. Overhead, the concussive pounding of bombs indicated another morning had arrived. My ears ached from the change in pressure. The entire tunnel system seemed to quake.

We learned later that fourteen had been killed upon impact, but the list of injured stretched well beyond seventy.

As I made my rounds feeling faint with hunger, I found Six lying in one of the bunks, mumbling to himself with delirium. The whites of his eyes flashed as his writhing revealed a nasty stomach gash. His left leg had disappeared. Seeing him made me forget my hunger, and I pulled a stool next to his bedside and searched for a way to bring him some relief.

Since our arrival Six had made himself indispensable by delivering coveted prizes to us—cans of sliced pineapples, a sack of sugar, a bottle of gin, playing cards, cigarettes, and once even a whole ripe mango. We had no idea how much these things cost him or how he found them, but grateful, we dropped everything to flirt with him whenever he appeared. His sweet and generous demeanor secured him favored status above the many other men who came sniffing around.

"Six, tell me you weren't one of those tunnel rats out there when that monster hit."

"Bad luck, huh?" he said, his voice faint. "You know my mama lives in Dayton, right? With my three sisters?"

"I do."

"You'll write to them for me?"

I held a glass of water to his lips and gritted my teeth in frustration at the wanton randomness of catastrophe during wartime. How bending over to fix an untied boot could allow you to dodge a bullet. How picking the wrong seat in a jeep could have deadly consequences. How moving a few feet to the right to check out a friend's photo from home could save you when a mortar hit. All the *should haves* and *could haves* meant nothing when you were caught in the wrong place at the wrong time. It slayed me to wonder which variable had gone wrong for Six. He blinked slowly and when his eyes reopened, their light dulled like a cloud passing over the sun.

"I'll write and tell them what a good friend you've been. I'll remember you forever, Six. We all will," I said softly, taking his hand, hot and dry with fever. I felt for his pulse, counting it against the second hand on George's watch. With every passing second, the flutter in his wrist grew weaker.

His eyes were closed, but a faint smile twitched on his lips.

A squeeze on my shoulder made me look up to see Nell

standing over us. The other nurses and doctors hurried by, each consumed with the steady stream of patients arriving as a new day of bombing began, but Nell and I stayed with Six. After a few minutes, his pulse disappeared.

"Don't tell anyone he's gone yet," Nell whispered. "I'll be right back."

I remained with Six, thinking that somewhere on the other side of the globe, his mother and sisters were carrying on with their day having no idea of what they had just lost. Amid the swirl of action surrounding me, I tried to give weight to the moment, to honor his significance. I was glad I hadn't left for Australia. By that point, I'd witnessed the passing of many men's lives and each one had left an ache, but losing Six felt profoundly humbling. He'd lost his future but given us ours. If his sacrifice was to mean something, we had to keep fighting to survive.

Nell reappeared and bent over Six to pin one of her athletic medals from California on his chest. She turned to look at me, sheepish. "Is that foolish? It's all I've got."

I shook my head. "It's perfect."

DESPITE OUR RESOLVE to fight on, Corregidor was weakening. On the second day of May, the Japanese launched a blistering bombing offensive that lasted for a solid twelve hours. The tunnel's main entrances each had a bulb that glowed either red or green, depending on how safe it was to go outside, and as conditions on the island deteriorated due to constant bombardment, the bulbs always seemed to be stuck on red. No one knew exactly how many millions of pounds of explosives were dropped upon us, but according to the orderlies, outside of the tunnel, the island was pulverized and engulfed in flames. The air inside the hospital laterals thickened and heated with dust and smoke.

Every time I swallowed, it felt like a handful of splinters had caught in my throat. Our underground lair grew stifling and claustrophobic.

Iris found me scarfing down a quick meal of slop du jour and slapped down her own bowl before sitting beside me. "Lieutenant Garron just told me that we have less than a month's worth of electricity and water stored."

I wasn't surprised. "Have you heard anything about Vincent's whereabouts?"

She shook her head. "Haven't you said no news is good news?" When I gave her a sympathetic smile, she sighed. "Hopefully he made it off Bataan."

"We spend a lot of time hoping for things these days, don't we?" I pushed my empty bowl away and tried to yawn to bring a measure of relief to the pressure building on my eardrums. I was thinking of George and wondering where he was and when I would see him again. Did I dare hope it would be soon?

Iris lifted her spoon and considered her gruel. "Hope's the only thing we've got."

12.

TESS

On May 5, we knew something was different. Blasts from overhead shook us as soon as the morning shift began and the laterals rumbled as if a Northern Pacific train was roaring through them. The air in the tunnels felt hot and the walls seemed to press in on us. Our gallows humor, which had grown very dark since arriving on Corregidor, reached an entirely new level of morbid. It was the only way to release the relentless tension we all felt.

"Incoming patients!" an orderly called out. "Hustle up while we've got the widest range of models and styles. This sale won't last long!"

"Oh yeah?" Virginia sighed as she bent over a newly arrived unconscious patient. "Seems like today's the biggest sale day of the year."

"And I'm all out of cash," I said, tending to a dislocated shoulder.

"You're in luck because we take credit," the orderly said, placing another fellow beside me to be treated.

And it went on like that all morning and afternoon.

At one point, the blowers turned off and the heat and smell of cordite grew so unbearable that we ran from cot to cot placing wet gauze over the faces of our patients to bring relief.

"Why don't I hear the ambulance horns anymore?" I asked Mabel.

"The roads outside have been destroyed and they can no longer reach us," she whispered.

That afternoon, Captain Davison and Josie called for a brief nurses' meeting. Their expressions, always serious, now looked frayed and grim. Everyone was exhausted. "We fear an invasion is coming tonight. You must remain in the hospital laterals at all times, no matter if you're on duty or not. We must stay together. Keep your Red Cross armband on and your gas masks within reach."

After we received these instructions, Mabel tucked her gas mask under her left arm and even from a few steps away, I could see how her hands shook.

"Hey, your face is so long, you're going to trip over it. Chin up," I urged.

"But what if the Japanese run a tank right into here?" she asked. "What if they use flamethrowers? It'll be like shooting fish in a barrel. We don't stand a chance." Her whisper turned into a squeak with those last few words.

Nell rounded on her, her eyes flashing with fury. "Stop talking, just stop!"

It was so unlike Nell to speak, much less snap, that the three of us stared at one another.

"You heard the captain," I said after a beat. "We need to stick together, keep cool heads. Let's focus on our patients. That's all we can do right now. Make them as comfortable as possible."

OVER THE NEXT few hours, the number of visitors to our section increased as men stopped in to say goodbye. At one point I turned and found an officer I'd once treated for malaria waiting for me.

"You gals are always at it, aren't you?" he said, marveling at the rows and rows of wounded filling the lateral. "At this rate you'll have worked so much overtime, you should be able to take all next year off."

"Ha, I wish that's how it worked."

"Well, it should! Someone ought to x-ray Wainwright's chest and see if his heart's still in there."

"Now you're talking."

His face grew solemn. "So, listen, before I head out, Tess, I was hoping I could give you a couple of things for safekeeping. You've always been real good to me." He pushed an envelope into my hands. "I know you won't be able to mail it anytime soon, but my ma's address is on there. It's a little heavy because it's got my watch inside and a few other small things. Can you manage it?"

"Of course," I said, tucking it into my pocket. A visit to the hospital lateral was the last place a soldier wanted to go before heading out to fight. Seeing the wounded was the surest way to drain yourself of courage. The fact that these men were acknowledging the unlikelihood of their return was too heart-rending to dwell on, so I nodded briskly and gave my brightest smile. "But I won't get too attached to it because I'll bet you'll be back in a jiffy, safe and sound."

His face beamed with relief. "I sure hope so. Thank you. And thank you for your service. You gals have been real troopers."

Along with our hearts, our pockets grew heavier and heavier throughout the night as more and more of the men stopped by to thank us and entrust their belongings to our safekeeping before heading out into the field.

Virginia brushed past me, heading in the direction of the

main tunnel. "A runner just arrived and said the enemy's landed at Monkey Point. I was just ordered off my rounds and told to head to the admin lateral to help destroy paperwork. Maps, memos, cash—we're shredding it all."

The ground underneath me seemed to tilt as I pushed my matted, sweaty hair out of my face and retied it at the nape of my neck. My body buzzed with nerves and adrenaline. *The Japanese were less than a few hundred yards away.* I squeezed my eyes shut and prayed with all my might that our boys could hold.

As the hours crawled toward morning, the nature of injuries began to change. For the last few weeks, we'd received many injuries to the feet, back, and buttocks as men had thrown themselves into foxholes during mortar attacks, but now we were seeing the damage incurred by face-to-face fighting. Torn gashes from bayonets. Shredded intestines, detached livers. Small gunfire was destroying internal organs in ways that were impossible for us to treat. The dead were being piled like cordwood in any available space.

Two orderlies lingered after unloading an officer with a gunshot wound to the head. From the man's bruising and the clear fluid leaking from his right nostril, I guessed that he had sustained a basal skull fracture.

"We've got it." I waved the orderlies away.

"The bulb by the entrance is red. We're not supposed to go outside yet," one muttered.

Dr. Lewis, a normally calm and reticent type, spun toward them as he pushed his wire-rimmed glasses up his nose. "Get back out there and do your goddamn jobs!" he barked before turning to me and the unconscious patient. "I don't think this poor dogface even has a shot. And where are we going to put him?"

I watched the men scurry away and almost pitied them, but

the truth was that if Dr. Lewis hadn't told them off, I might have. Instead, I gave the doc's shoulder a pat, a tight smile on my face. "Don't worry about it. Leave it to me."

I hurried away to locate space in the adjacent lateral for our latest arrival. From one of the nearby operating tables, the whir of a blade and a scream ricocheted off the concrete walls and I cringed, knowing someone was losing a limb without anesthesia.

IT WAS HALF past ten the following morning and I was off duty, but unable to sleep, so I sat with a group of patients reading *Great Expectations*. Mabel sat beside me knitting.

"What are you making now?" I asked.

"A mitten."

"Just one? What the heck do you need a mitten for? It's hotter than Hades here," one of the men said.

Mabel shrugged. "I only have this one ball of yarn and I keep knitting it and then unraveling it. Doesn't matter what I make, but I like to keep my hands busy."

No one questioned her. We understood.

I stopped at the end of the chapter and the *click, clack* of Mabel's needles filled the space around us.

Another man lying in bed tipped his head to one side. "Hear that?"

In the distance, the mournful sound of "Taps"—a song usually only played in the evening when the flag was being taken down for the night—drifted toward us. Without speaking, we understood what was happening. Out in the main tunnel, our beloved Stars and Stripes was lowering. Those of us who could stand did so on trembling legs. I rose with my hand over my heart and felt it *thump, thump, thump* against my palm.

Surrender.

It was inevitable, yet unthinkable.

In our hearts, we had known this moment was coming for days, weeks, maybe even months, but our minds had refused to believe it. Big, hot tears rolled down my face. How had it come to this? We had fought so hard. In the naval yards of Cavite, on the golden grassy plains north of Manila, along the white sandy beaches of Bataan and in its dense mountainous jungles—our men had fought on despite starvation, malarial fevers, intestinal distress, eyesight weakened by vitamin deficiency—everything. And we nurses had fought to save every life brought to us, no matter how ruinous its state. And that was just around our section of Luzon! We knew American forces were still fighting throughout the other islands, but Corregidor had been the hub. Everything hinged on the control center here.

When the final mournful notes cleared, we looked at each other's tearstained faces.

"Think they'll march us out and shoot us?" one patient asked in a low tone.

"Nah, they won't waste the bullet on ya."

"If we're lucky they'll bring in the flamethrowers and we can go out in a blaze of glory."

"You smell so bad, you'll be going out in a blaze of something, but I don't think it'll be glory."

And then it grew silent until one man whispered, *"When's the US ever surrendered to another country like this before?"*

I stared at the men's dejected faces, the glistening tracks of tears streaking through the dirt and smoke on their faces. Everything inside me quivered. What was next?

BY LATE AFTERNOON, the surrender was complete. The shelling ceased and an uneasy silence blanketed the island. Any patient who could walk was escorted outside where the men were gathered to be processed and imprisoned somewhere nearby on the island. We worried, knowing they needed food, medicine, and rest—three things they were unlikely to receive from our captors.

Captain Davison gathered us women in the main tunnel and we fell into three lines, awaiting instruction. A group of Japanese officers appeared in clean, starched uniforms, shiny black jackboots, and gleaming swords hanging from their belts. The highest-ranking man walked down the line inspecting us in silence. This was the first time I'd seen our enemy up close, but instead of gaping, I stared straight ahead, trying to stay calm. Out of the corner of my eye, I could see that as the man passed Mabel, he stopped, bent over, and picked at the hem of her skirt between his index finger and thumb, staring at it intently. I was holding my breath and tried to exhale, but what was he doing? *What was about to happen to us?*

The officer straightened, looking confused. He kept walking and then stopped in front of Nell, surveying her up and down. The other officers joined him and they spoke in Japanese, gesticulating at Nell's extraordinary height with curiosity. One of the men scratched his head and stared at us. It dawned on me that they had no idea why we were here, who we were, or what to do with us. After a minute or so of debate, they walked to a spot in front of us and the man who had pawed at Mabel's skirt cleared his throat.

"You are now prisoners of the Japanese Imperial Army on behalf of the Great Emperor Hirohito."

Our jaws dropped, gobsmacked at his perfect English.

"Yes, I speak your language. I attended university in California. My name is Captain Sato." He went on to explain his rules about curfew and meals, but blood thundered in my ears. I could hear nothing. This man had come to our country and lived with us, yet now warred against us? A keen sense of betrayal flared within me. Until now, this had been an enemy with whom I thought I had little in common, but now I knew he had walked my country's streets, sat in one of our classrooms underneath our flag, eaten in restaurants side by side with us, and after these experiences, he was still bent on destroying us? But then I realized something else: they must have been wondering how a bunch of American women had ended up on an island in the Pacific, far from home, on the front lines of a war. Really, how had any of us arrived here? There was suddenly a very real sense that we were all tiny figures playing roles in a much larger drama that none of us fully understood.

But then he clapped his hands together. "We will take a picture now." Before we knew what was happening, Japanese soldiers were using their bayoneted rifles to herd us toward the main entrance.

Dazed, we turned stiffly and walked toward daylight. With each step, the smell of smoke and death grew closer. Until now, leaving the tunnel had been a respite, but judging by how our pace slowed, everyone seemed to realize the outdoors would not bring the same relief it had before our capture.

We crossed the threshold into the sunshine and staggered in its sudden brightness.

I blinked, shading my eyes while trying to adjust to the blaze of white heat. White *everything*. My saddle shoes vanished into a thick dust underfoot. Grit blew in small cyclones, dancing along the rubble. Where had the trees gone? As far as I could see, a wasteland surrounded us, and the smell was beyond anything I'd ever encountered. I gagged, pulling my handkerchief from my skirt's pocket to hold over my nose. Huge charred logs lay in a pile down the hill from us, but as my vision cleared, I realized I wasn't staring at logs.

They were corpses.

In the heat, abandoned bodies had bloated several times beyond their normal size and blackened as they prepared to burst open. I turned away and vomited. Virginia gasped and followed suit, and several more followed. We were then herded into a couple of swaying lines and a photographer snapped a few pictures, but as soon as he finished, we streamed back into the tunnel like a cauldron of bats, desperate to escape the grotesque remains and devastation surrounding us.

And so began our lives as prisoners.

13.

FLOR

In early May a cart rolled into the circular driveway behind Café Rosario, ostensibly to collect food donations from the restaurant to be delivered to the poor, but before crates of plantains, sugar, eggs, and bread were loaded, Private Morris slid into a fake compartment the priests had created within the bottom of the cart. About twenty minutes after the priest stopped the cart behind the café, he drove it away, rolling through checkpoints with nary a second glance from the sentries.

Flor hadn't asked where the priests planned to take Private Morris. The less she knew, the better.

Several days later, Flor and Luchie visited the church in the early afternoon, a quiet time. The women lit candles, took seats, and waited for Father Callahan to spot them, but instead, a seminarian stopped and whispered, "Father Callahan is awaiting you both in the administrative area at the back of the church."

The women found the priest in his office sitting behind his desk. After waving away their thanks for helping Private Morris, Father Callahan got down to business. "The men from Bataan have been taken to Camp O'Donnell. According to locals, conditions for the prisoners are terrible so we've found locals around the camp who are willing to help us smuggle in food and money to keep the men alive. There are a number of military wives at Santo Tomas who have husbands there. Do ye think it's possible they'd be willing to offer more funding for food and medicine for the men?"

"Maybe. Can we find out who's there? The women will want to know," Flor said.

"There are about seven thousand inmates. I'll try to obtain a roster, but I fear men are dying every day so just because a lad's listed doesn't mean he's still alive."

"I understand."

Father Callahan nodded and removed a camera from his desk. "We're going to issue new identification papers for your trips to Santo Tomas. At the main gate, do the guards record your names?"

"No."

"At some point that will probably change. In the meantime, it would be wise to use a different set of papers so we don't leave a trail connecting ye to this church. The next time ye come here, I'll have them ready." He pointed to a spot by the window. "Stand there so I can take your photos in the light."

"Father, Luchie isn't transporting any contraband and we pretend we don't know each other during our visits."

"I see, so there's no need for her to carry false papers?"

"No," Flor said, standing and moving to the spot by the window.

As Father Callahan finished with the photo, another priest poked his head inside the office. "The radio's reporting that Corregidor's surrendered. The Philippines are now in full possession of the Japanese."

The news hit Flor like a blow to the chest. How had the United States, one of the largest countries in the world, been defeated by such a small island? Her lip began to tremble. When she glimpsed Luchie's stricken expression, she felt even worse. What did this mean for Iris?

Father Callahan tried to lead Flor to a chair, saying, "I'm sure General Wainwright will be able to arrange special care for the nurses."

But Flor couldn't move.

"Father, we must go home," Luchie said.

Luchie's words lit something within Flor. Yes, she needed to leave. She needed some sign of her sister. Without saying a word, she bolted from the church's offices. Outside, the sun's brightness almost hurt. Blindly, she ran for the waterfront. When she reached the bay, she doubled over, resting her palms above her knees as she strained for breath, fighting back tears. Ahead, a thin marine layer still hovered over the water like a ribbon of organza, so Flor couldn't see beyond a few miles, but Iris was somewhere out there—Bataan or Corregidor or maybe even a horrible place like Cabanatuan.

"I'm too old for running like this, Flordeliza," Luchie said, catching up. "Now don't assume the worst."

"I can't bear to think of my ate out there, suffering."

Luchie clasped Flor's shoulders and looked into her dark eyes. "She's strong. Don't you think you'd feel something if she had perished? Have some faith."

As Luchie murmured a prayer, Flor closed her eyes, turning inward. Did she feel anything different? A shifting in the atmosphere? A cool tingle in her bones? A hollowness in her chest? She placed her palm over her heart, felt its ferocious beating. She didn't feel defeated. She was furious at the prospect of someone hurting her sister. Her hands curled into fists at her sides. Her body burned with life and that was the sign she needed.

Flor opened her eyes and stared toward Corregidor. Her

sister *had* to still be on that island—*alive*—tending to the men who needed her. She refused to imagine any other possibility.

ON MAY 24, Flor and her father attended Sunday morning mass at Malate Church. As the priests at the front chanted and the acolytes swung censers filled with incense, the cloying scent of oil and tallow filled the nave. Flor knelt and as she prayed to keep Iris safe, sweat dripped down her spine and the backs of her legs, trickling along the creases behind her knees. Finally the service ended. When she and Papa reached the doorway to leave the church, Flor caught a knowing look from Father Callahan before he bowed his head in farewell. As she passed, he slid the new identity papers from his black cassock and she tucked them into her waistband. It was so crowded that she hoped no one had noticed. Flor and Papa left the stuffiness of the church, spilling outside with the rest of the congregants to stroll home.

At Taft Avenue, they slowed, puzzled by the crowd gathered at the edges of the wide boulevard. Flor searched everyone's faces, trying to ascertain what was happening but people looked right through her, searching a spot farther down the street. Flor craned her neck and gasped.

Rows and rows of men flowed down the middle of Taft Avenue like a river, their faces grim and skeletal, their uniforms in tatters. They staggered and limped and leaned on one another. When the pace of the marchers slowed too much, Japanese soldiers carrying truncheons swung at the men, yelling.

In horrified silence, the crowd, composed of many who had just left church services throughout the city, watched as the Americans dragged themselves block by block toward Bilibid Prison. One soldier staggered past and tripped, lying splayed on the street. The cords of his neck strained as he struggled to keep his head out of the horse manure that now covered the pavement since gasoline shortages had rendered most automobiles useless. A Japanese soldier approached and began hitting him with a baton. Slowly, painfully, the American rose to hands and knees. With his face screwed into an expression of anguish, he teetered to his feet and continued to drag himself along, step by step. Flor found herself weeping and when she looked at the people surrounding her, everyone's faces shined with a glaze of tears.

If the Japanese had staged this miserable display to show the people of Manila how far the mighty Americans had fallen, they miscalculated. The spectacle caused something to shift in the crowd. Spines straightened. Frowns deepened. Resentment toward the occupiers solidified. Flor felt the change in her countrymen at the base of her neck as if a breeze was ruffling her collar. People along the route held out bananas, while others threw cigarettes and candies toward the men, hoping to show their solidarity.

As the parade of tragedy passed, Flor and Romeo held hands tightly. *Where was Iris?*

14.

TESS

June 1942
Corregidor

After what felt like a long six weeks of close living in the tunnels with our captors, the Japanese moved us aboveground to the ruins of Fort Mills Station Hospital. At first, the shock of seeing the island denuded of its greenery rendered us silent, but signs of life persisted amid the wreckage. As we trudged uphill to Topside, we searched our surroundings for some sign of where the men had been imprisoned. Corregidor wasn't big and we knew they had to be nearby, but we had no idea where. Did they have shelter? Clean water? Food? We feared the worst.

Underfoot, in the dusty cracks of the craters and fissures of concrete, shoots of bamboo fought their way toward the brilliant sunshine. In the distance, turquoise waters edged with lacy white foam still pushed and pulled upon the black volcanic sand beach at the base of Malinta Hill. That was the thing about life in the tropics. Nature was a force that couldn't be stopped.

A few days of living in the fresh air and sunshine revived us. The Japanese left us alone to tend to our wounded and a sense of relief came over us. Our skin brightened. Almost overnight, the persistent coughing that had punctuated life in the laterals vanished. My chronic earache caused by the fluctuations in pressure from living underground finally eased. Gardenia trees bloomed around the fractured walls of the old base, filling our wards with their sweet fragrance. Snowy egrets marched through the ruins of nearby Mile-Long Barracks in search of food. For a few days, we had a reprieve, but of course, it didn't last.

At the end of June, the Japanese announced we would be leaving Corregidor, but they gave no details about our destination. Would we be reunited with our colleagues and patients somewhere on Luzon? Could we be repatriated through a prisoner exchange and sent home? In the bay, a large freighter awaited us and we had no idea where it was going, but we hoped to see the men who'd been separated from us during the surrender. Not a day passed without us worrying about them.

That final night on the island, as I lay on a cot amid the old hospital's blasted walls, I sensed someone moving nearby. When I cracked my eyes open, a shadow appeared. I froze as it crept closer. Soon a man stood beside me. I stopped breathing. The scrape of calloused fingers crept along my arm to my wrist, and I tried to hold still, to not flinch though my heartbeat sped into a gallop.

I opened my mouth to scream, but no sound emerged from my lips, only a gasp.

Fingers circled around my watch—*George's* wristwatch—and it slid off my arm. A Japanese soldier leaned closer and my entire body quivered in terror. After a moment, he turned away. My mind raced. Should I react? Slide from bed and give chase? Fight back?

No.

As much as I hated losing my one tangible reminder of George, it was not worth risking something far worse.

During my shifts, I'd taken to wearing the watch hidden on

a long loop of string around my neck, but when I was in bed, I wore it on my wrist. I'd lie in the darkness listening to it—*tick, tick, tick*—taking comfort in the knowledge that his skin had once warmed the leather band that now touched me. Not only was it my single physical reminder of George, but that watch had counted the fading pulse of many of the men who'd died under my care. Its significance was immeasurable to me.

And now it was gone.

As the fright of the encounter wore off, my jaw clenched. I'd been cursing the enemy ever since they'd bombed sleepy Fort Stotsenburg back in December. Each time I'd discovered a new mosquito bite on my skin, I'd cursed them. Each time I'd dipped my spoon into a bowl of soup and raised it only to find a thin broth, I'd cursed them. Each time I hoped my patient would pass out so I wouldn't have to excavate his wound while he held back screams, I'd cursed them. I thought I'd run out of curses, but losing that watch took my anger one step beyond what I would have thought possible.

I understood it was unlikely I'd see the watch again, but lying in my bed rigid with fury, I vowed I'd live to see the hour when we won the war. No matter where they sent us, no matter how long it took, no matter what I had to do, I'd survive.

15.

FLOR

May to September 1942
Manila

After the sad display of American prisoners being marched through the streets of Manila, Flor and Papa rushed home, hoping to find Iris. But there was no sign of her. Where were the rest of the prisoners from Corregidor? With every passing day of May, Flor hoped for Iris to return home, but she never appeared. June came and went and still, the Dalisays received no word about Iris.

At the beginning of July, Flor and Papa attended afternoon mass. On their way home, when they turned the corner onto their narrow street, a familiar figure was visible ahead, opening their gate. She carried nothing and looked slight, her shoulders stooped.

"Iris!" Flor shouted and they ran to her. Up close, they could see the raggedness of her hair and dull exhaustion of her eyes. As she collapsed into Papa's arms, Flor stared. Iris was nothing like the bright-faced woman who had left them seven months earlier.

They brought Iris inside and when Luchie brought her some scrambled eggs and a small loaf of pandesal, Iris's shoulders rose as if she was shielding her food from the others, a movement that struck Flor as both feral and desperate. Papa's brows knit together as he watched how she gobbled her meal.

Afterward, as Flor helped Iris bathe and dress in pajamas, an image of those struggling American soldiers weaving weakly down Taft Avenue flashed through her mind. "So the Japanese let the women go?"

Iris rubbed at her eyes. "On Corregidor, they packed us into a ship. There were some men aboard it too, but when we reached Manila, we were separated from them. Once they had us women alone, they ordered those of us who were Filipino to leave, but they kept the American nurses." She shuddered. "When we were on Corregidor, there were rumors of girls being captured in Manila and brought to the island to serve and"— Iris winced— "*comfort* the Japanese."

Flor pondered this, but then she understood. Her stomach tensed. "What happened to those Filipinas? Were they taken from the island with you too?"

"No, if they survived their imprisonment, I'm sure they were killed."

The leaden way Iris delivered this information stunned Flor.

"I fear for what will happen to our American friends," Iris said faintly. "Both the nurses and the men. It won't be good."

"Try to sleep," Flor said, easing her sister into a prone position. "I will find out what happened to the other nurses."

But Iris didn't answer. She was already deeply asleep.

As Flor shut the door to her sister's bedroom, she pulled her new false identification papers from her waistband.

Lily Benipayo.

She studied her new name and smiled.

IN THE MORNING, Flor and Luchie visited Malate Church to ask if Father Callahan had gotten word of the American nurses' fate.

"They've been taken to Santo Tomas, but they're isolated from the civilians and being kept in a convent right next to the camp's walls."

"Why are they being kept apart?" Luchie asked.

"They probably don't want the nurses telling the other internees about the harsh imprisonment of the men. The Japanese want to avoid an angry group of wives stirring up trouble."

"Will they remain in isolation?" Flor asked.

"Who knows?" Father Callahan said, sliding a folder of notes from Cabanatuan to hand across the table to Flor. She removed the small papers and placed them into the secret pockets sewn into her skirt's hem. Once she had the messages for Santo Tomas hidden, she and Luchie left.

OVER THE NEXT week, Iris woke several times to eat and drink water, but mostly she slept. While she convalesced, Flor and Luchie delivered food and messages to the Package Shed at Santo Tomas and then they walked around the corner, following the prison's high walls until they reached the small convent.

"You should stay back," Luchie said to Flor. "Remember, we don't want to be seen together."

"Can you carry this one too?" Flor asked, sliding her sack off her shoulder.

Luchie grunted as she lifted Flor's sack alongside her own and marched toward the convent's gate.

Flor watched Luchie hand the bags over to the guards. The men nodded, shrugging, and took the supplies past the gate, heading toward the front door. When Luchie returned to Flor, her expression appeared irritated. "Lazy men. I hope that food makes it to Iris's friends and the guards don't end up eating it themselves."

THE FOLLOWING WEEK, as Flor sat at the dining room table, packing supplies for her next trip to Santo Tomas, Iris drank her coffee and watched.

"I want to come with you," she said.

Flor hesitated, balancing three cans of Ovaltine between her palms. "The trip across the city is a long one. We encounter many checkpoints and guards. Are you sure you can manage it?"

Iris stirred her coffee, her jaw tense with annoyance. "Yes, I can do it. I want to help."

Flor knew there was no dissuading her sister. "Fine, we leave in an hour."

WHEN THEY REACHED the block where Santa Catalina was located, the women slowed. "It will just be the two of us," Luchie said to Iris. Flor remained behind and watched the women proceed to the convent's gate. When the guards approached, she could see Iris step forward to speak to them and gesticulate toward the convent. Iris appeared to be arguing with the guard and Flor stiffened. Why couldn't her sister just come and go without making a scene? As far as Flor was concerned, the critical part of their forays to the camp relied upon not drawing the guards' attention. She wanted to be easily forgotten.

From where Flor stood in the shade of a building, she watched as the guards took the bags from Luchie and Iris, and then the women waited at the gate, staring at the convent, looking expectant.

With every passing minute, Flor's worries grew. Why were Luchie and Iris still waiting around?

But then, just when Flor could stand it no more, her sister's posture changed. Suddenly Iris raised her hands and waved at the building's windows happily. She blew kisses. Iris must have convinced the guards to notify the women that she was outside. Flor smiled, shaking her head at her sister's nerve.

When Iris and Luchie finally returned to her, Iris was beaming. "We did it! We made the guards take the bags directly to my friends and then the women came to the windows and saw us. Now they know we're trying to help them." Iris looked back and forth at Flor and Luchie. "You don't understand. When we were stuck on Bataan and Corregidor with no word from the outside, it was the loneliest feeling. I want my friends to know they're not alone. We're here to help."

"I was just worried," Flor said.

"One thing I learned on Corregidor is not to show those guards any fear. I don't think they expected us to argue with them and I used that to my advantage."

"Lord have mercy," Luchie muttered, glancing skyward.

"Don't worry, Manang Luchie; from now on, Gloria and the other nurses from our group will accompany me to Santa Catalina and we'll help our imprisoned colleagues on our own." Iris bit her lip. "I can't believe they're stuck in that dreadful place. We need to do whatever we can to help them survive."

Luchie and Flor exchanged pleased looks. Though Iris was upset, Flor knew a little anger could be a good thing to revive her sister's courage and fighting spirit.

OVER THE NEXT few months, Iris's expeditions to Santa Catalina seemed to help her recovery. Through July, August, and September, twice a week, Flor, Luchie, Iris, Gloria, and a group of the Filipino nurses traveled to Santo Tomas to deliver bread and sugar, fresh fruit and nuts, sewing kits, yarn, sanitary supplies, and clothes to the inmates. Iris gained back most of the weight she had lost, but she remained quieter. Her trademark vivaciousness had faded. Every night, as Flor drifted into sleep, she'd feel Iris slide into bed next to her. Sometimes Flor would awaken in the dark to feel Iris's heart pounding through the thin cotton of their pajamas. Iris would mumble and cry in her sleep, her muscles twitching. When morning came, they never acknowledged Iris's nightmares. After a lifetime of being the sister who needed bolstering, Flor felt surprised to be the stronger one. She didn't quite understand what had led to Iris's diminishment and she longed to ask questions about what had happened in the jungle, but she knew her sister didn't want to think about the past.

Iris had never been one for keeping secrets, so Flor waited, hoping her sister would reveal more when she was ready.

16.

TESS

When we left Corregidor in early July, six months had passed since we'd last laid eyes on Manila. Oh, how the beautiful city had suffered! An eerie quiet muffled the waterfront, once the busiest and most colorful in all of Asia. The stately buildings that lined the harbor now appeared boarded up and abandoned. Unkempt, broken, and filthy, Manila was a mere shell of her formerly glamorous self. When we peered out toward the bay, murky clouds of oil marred the once-turquoise water. Burned-out hulls of ships jutted from the bay at odd angles like blackened icebergs and the tips of submerged mastheads suggested that more ruins lay below the surface.

Our captors drove us to a civilian internment camp in the north of the city and dumped us in Santa Catalina, a convent located just outside the walls of the former university. A hazy period began. One week? Two? A month? The only mark of time's passage was the pattern of sunlight slanting through the convent's large windows and its gradual fade to darkness, but none of us counted the days. We spoke little and slept around the clock, recovering from the stress and illnesses that had plagued us for months—malaria, dengue fever, dysentery, sores, coughs, tinnitus, malnutrition, and more. Meals were delivered, but I had no recollection of what we ate. Eventually we woke and fell back on the routines of our army training: scrubbing our rooms to a high shine, organizing our meager possessions, and mending our uniforms. The only interruption in the monotony of our captivity was when Iris, Gloria, and the other Filipino nurses came with deliveries of food, needlework supplies, medicine, and clothing. Spotting their bright faces outside of Santa Catalina filled us with hope and gratitude. We hadn't been forgotten! Whenever word of their arrival filtered through our rooms, we beelined for the front windows, jostling for spots to glimpse our friends, wave, and smile. Those brief moments of contact with the outside world became as critical to our well-being as food and water.

In late August, Captain Davison called a meeting. We piled into the cramped hallway and I was struck by how tired our leader looked. Her gray hair had grown from its utilitarian short cut into something longer and unruly. The war had been hard on all of us, but I could see that it had taken a particularly painful toll on the older women, especially those who felt the weight of leadership and responsibility for our welfare. When the captain cleared her throat, it sounded phlegmy and thick, but she shook off Josie's offer to speak on her behalf.

Captain Davison rose from a chair, surveying us. "Ladies, I've just received notice we're being transferred into the larger camp immediately. They want us out of here within the hour."

A chorus of groans met this announcement.

"So we're being folded in with the civilians?" a nurse asked.

"For the time being, yes. The Japanese have no experience with women in the military. It's obvious they haven't the slightest idea what to do with us." Captain Davison clapped her hands to stir us from our sullen stupor. Though physically diminished, she had lost none of her impatience. "Go pack up, please."

The air in the hallway bristled with frustration. We had worked hard to be taken seriously in the military, so I could understand the annoyance my colleagues felt at the prospect of living among the old men, women, and children of the camp, but after being trapped within the confines of Santa Catalina, the prospect of widening our range of movement appealed to me.

By evening, we were jammed into our new accommodations: three classrooms on the second floor of the campus's Main Building. It was tight. We'd be sleeping head to toe in bamboo cots, separated only by a space of six inches. Though privacy was a thing long gone, this level of crowding was something entirely new. You couldn't even sigh in the new rooms without ruffling someone's hair.

When Virginia, Nell, Mabel, and I headed to the dining shed for dinner, a cluster of people blocked our way. A young woman with two children glanced back at where we stood. "You gals are the new arrivals?" she asked.

"Guilty as charged," Virginia said.

"Well, get used to this." She glared down the long line of people. "This is your main occupation now—waiting. For meals, the lavatory, all of it."

"And I assume dinner is worth the wait, huh?" I asked.

The woman sighed and turned away.

I AWOKE THE next morning to the loudspeakers blaring the Andrews Sisters boogie-woogieing their way through the upbeat lyrics of "Don't Sit Under the Apple Tree." With the warning about waiting still fresh in my mind, I pushed aside my mosquito net and hurried to the lavatory, but apparently I was already too late. Seventeen—yes, I counted—*seventeen* bleary-eyed, yawning women stood in line ahead of me.

"Isn't this an odd choice of music for first thing in the morning?" I asked no one in particular.

An older woman chuckled. "It's hard to sleep through, that's for sure. But sometimes the song choices provide hints about news from the outside."

With renewed interest, I cocked my head to listen more closely. "So what's happening with apples?"

The woman shrugged. "The fellow who runs the announcements probably just has a thing for the Andrews Sisters, but a fresh apple sure sounds good right about now. Say, has anyone told you gals about the Package Shed yet?"

"Huh? No."

"Gather up your money and head down to the main gate in an hour. Vendors are allowed to come in and sell fruit, maybe some bread, and other odds and ends."

As I waited for my turn at the toilet, I contemplated this information. The prospect of anything edible that was fresh sounded dreamy, but I had run out of money long ago. When I'd finished my business, I hurried back to our room to fill the others in on these new developments.

"Is it a black market?" Mabel asked after I finished relaying the Package Shed information.

"I don't think so. It all sounds aboveboard, but we need money to buy things," I answered.

Everyone's expressions fell. Not only did we not have any money, but we had few things left in our possession that even warranted bartering.

"Let's go down to this Package Shed place and get a lay of the land," Virginia said.

An hour later, we followed a crowd of internees to the main gate and found it already baking in full sun. Sure enough, a lively exchange was happening. Vendors circled around the area holding trays and baskets filled with food, sewing and knitting materials, and clothes. One man carried two baskets filled with sugary puffed rice. *"Ampau!"* he called, strolling through the crowd, the baskets swaying as they dangled from a bamboo bar running across his shoulders. A Filipina passed me exhibiting a tray filled with flaky pastries topped with coconut and it took all my willpower not to snatch the entire batch and run. Ripe mangoes, nuts and candy, Ovaltine, canned milk—for the right price, it could be ours. With envious eyes and watering mouths, we watched a brisk business ensue until we could stand it no more.

We plodded back to the Main Building, our heads bowed in dejection. "I was ready to rip a sweet cake out of a little old man's hands," Mabel lamented.

Virginia pulled her shirt's sweaty collar from her neck impatiently. "Nell, put an ear to the ground and find out if there are any standing poker games or something. Maybe you could win some cash."

Nell swatted away a fly. "It wouldn't be enough to supplement our meals for long."

In the plaza of the Main Building, we paused and looked around the campus, all of us quiet, lost in our thoughts. The reality of our situation was becoming clear. Sprinkling the expanses of lawn around the buildings were rows and rows of internee-constructed shanties with handmade street signs like Hollywood Avenue, Broadway, and other well-known landmarks from home. This place was like a small city teeming with amenities from tailors to cobblers to an internee-run coffee shop, but little good did it do us since we couldn't afford something as simple as a thimble.

Mabel scratched at a mosquito bite. "I know it's a bit foolish when we consider all the things we need right now, but I'd love to get my hair cut by someone who knows how to add a bit of style. Do you think there's a salon here?"

"I'm sure there is," I said. "But we need to figure out a way to pay for it."

Everyone nodded. At that point, life in Santo Tomas didn't appear too bad. Sure, overcrowding was a problem and prison life was monotonous, but the internees possessed a measure of autonomy, and after our dire months spent on the front lines, we knew boredom to be a luxury. We could adjust to our new surroundings, but with so many temptations available at every turn, it was only a matter of time before one of us did something desperate to procure additional food or shoes or some desirable item. On the front line, the enemy had been clear. We needed to defeat the Japanese Imperial Army. Here in prison, without the urgency of battle and a clear sense of purpose, I sensed the threat was shifting. The enemy might no longer be an outsider, but the warring forces within each of us. If we were going to survive in this place, we needed a plan and purpose. And some money.

A WEEK PASSED—SEVEN full days of being tantalized by things we couldn't have. In the dining shed, the blue-tinged watery lugao, crunchy with weevils, did little to lift our spirits. Petty arguments broke out and factions developed between us on everything from how best to manage the raging bedbug infestation to who should be cleaning the stinky pigeon waste from our windowsills.

Captain Davison called for another meeting under the shade of a large banyan tree. "Our former lodgings at Santa Catalina have been converted into a new camp hospital and we will be its nurses. Each of you will be expected to serve four hours a day, seven days a week. We will dress in our uniforms and re-turn to our previous code of conduct."

"So we're going to spend our days lancing boils and putting lotion on mosquito bites for civilians?" a nurse called out.

"What better things do you have to do?" one of the others shot back.

"Ladies, these last few weeks have proved that inactivity will be the death of us. Our survival depends upon our bonds of sisterhood and service. Whatever lies ahead, we need to meet it with a sense of purpose and professionalism, the very things we were trained for. We're going to spend our days doing what-ever is required to tend to the medical needs of the people of this camp. I expect there to be a range of necessary services from the mundane to more complicated surgeries, but what-ever the task at hand, it is my expectation—nay, it is the *army's* expectation—that you will do your duty to the utmost of your capabilities, no matter the patient or procedure. Do I make my-self clear?" At this last question, the captain placed her hands on her hips and regarded us with a piercing glare. Suddenly everyone seemed to sit a little straighter, and out of the corner of my eye, I could see hands surreptitiously rising to smooth down hair and blouses. If I'd been concerned the captain was no longer up to the task of managing us, those concerns were now gone.

At dinner that evening, the prospect of work seemed to have invigorated everyone's low morale, so I brought up an idea I'd been mulling over. "Returning to work has reminded me that we're still getting paid by the US government, which means that somewhere in a bank at home, our accounts are being filled with our paychecks."

"So are you saying we'll return home when this is all over and discover we've become millionaires?" Mabel asked, smirking.

I wagged my finger at her. "You wish, but, no, because we're going to start spending it as soon as possible."

"How?" Nell asked.

"Well, obviously there are people in here with real cash on hand. What if we could secure ourselves a loan?"

"From who?" Virginia asked.

"Well, that's what I don't know," I confessed. "Anyone have any bright ideas?"

From behind us, a small, clear voice piped up, "You should try the Wack Wack Club."

I turned to see a young girl sitting at a table by herself. Her short dark bobbed hair lay flat and silky smooth despite the humidity, but the most arresting thing was her striking pale blue eyes. She watched the four of us with a startling intensity.

"What did you say?" Mabel asked, addressing the young girl.

The child stood, abandoning her empty plate, and pushed her chair up to our table. "I'm Frances Burns," she announced solemnly, holding her hand out to shake mine.

Impressed by the girl's temerity, I bit back my smile. "It's a pleasure to meet you. I'm Tess," I said, before introducing the others.

"Aren't you a serious little thing," Virginia said, giving her most winning smile.

Frances studied Virginia, and then, unimpressed, turned back to me.

"If you're looking for someone with money, you should go talk to the Wack Wack men," she said. "They play golf every day on the playing field by the tennis court. Everyone knows they're rich. Do you golf?"

"No," I answered.

"But I do," Nell said. "In fact, I have a pretty good stroke."

"Of course, you do," Virginia grumbled. "Is there any sport you don't play well?"

Nell shrugged. "Not that I can think of."

Frances nodded her approval at Nell. "The men will like you. What exactly do you want from them?"

"We're going to ask them for a loan," I said. "We just need someone to invest in us, knowing they'll be paid back when we go home."

"They'll probably say yes. I think the only reason they golf is so they can get away from everyone and talk about women. I see them at meals and sometimes I go and watch them play and they don't pay any attention to me because I'm so young, but they'll pay attention to you."

"How do you know so much about these men?" I asked.

"My father was a member of the Wack Wack Country Club before the war. He likes to golf, but hasn't been playing much lately . . ." Her voice trailed off awkwardly. I glanced at the other table she had just abandoned. She looked too young to be on her own, but I didn't see anyone who resembled a mother or sibling anywhere nearby. When she saw me studying her, she said, "If you want, I can take you and Nell to meet them tomorrow. They're always losing golf balls over the wall, so if you want to get in good with them, you should try making some of your own like this." She pulled a knit ball from her pocket and gave it a small toss before catching it and holding it out for me to inspect.

"May I borrow this for the evening so I can figure out how to make more like it?" I asked.

I could see reluctance as she gazed at the ball, a slight flush of embarrassment creeping over her cheeks. For the first time since joining us, she actually seemed like a child—at least for a moment. "Yes," she said slowly. "But please be careful. I'd like it back tomorrow."

"Of course. I won't let anything happen to it." I slid the ball into my skirt's pocket. "Thank you, Frances. Isn't it our lucky day that we've run into you?"

Right then, a harried-looking woman with a toddler on each hip bustled through the area to our table. "Frannie? Good Lord, I've been looking all over for you. How many times have I told you to not go out of my sight?"

"Sorry, Mrs. Blake," Frances intoned in a way that made it obvious she did a lot of apologizing to this woman.

"I hope she wasn't bothering you, ladies," Mrs. Blake said.

"She wasn't bothering us at all. In fact, she was giving us some helpful information." I watched as Frances reluctantly rose and took one of the toddlers from Mrs. Blake's arms.

"I can only imagine what fanciful bits she was telling you. Only eleven, but my goodness, the moxie on this one. She has far too many opinions for her own good." She pursed her lips, looking down at the child. "You should smile more, Frannie. You'd look prettier."

Frances simply stared back at Mrs. Blake without changing her expression a whit. "It's Frances."

The woman frowned. "I have my hands full, that's for sure, and this one"—she nudged Frances—"isn't nearly as helpful as she ought to be."

The toddler in Frances's arms poked her in the ear, yet the girl did nothing to stop the baby. If anything, her eyes assumed a glazed-over vacant quality as if she was off in a world far away.

"Actually we could use some occasional help from a young girl like her," I said. "Sorting bandages, things like that. I'm happy to keep an eye on her any time."

At that, Frances blinked and I could tell she was back from her dream world. Her eyes brightened.

Mrs. Blake hiked the baby back up on her hip. "Well, she certainly has no interest in helping me with these little ones. She's almost more trouble than she's worth. I suppose it wouldn't hurt her to start learning a trade like nursing."

"How about she finds me midday tomorrow? Honestly, she would be a big help."

"Fine. Noon."

"I'll be waiting under the large banyan by the plaza."

"She'll be there." Mrs. Blake nodded and she tilted her head toward Frances. "Enough dillydallying, Frannie. Let's go back to the others. Who knows what the older ones have gotten into."

As Frances shuffled away with the toddler squirming in her arms, she turned back to me and I winked at her. The edges of her mouth quirked upward slightly and if I didn't know better, I'd have said she almost smiled. Almost.

"What a strange child. So serious," Mabel said as we rose to leave the mess area.

"Let's keep our fingers crossed that these Wack Wack fellas will help us," I said as we headed back into the Main Building. For the first time in weeks, a small loosening of relief unspooled inside me. Hopefully with Frances's help, the golfers would loan us some money and we could buy the things we needed.

"That Mrs. Blake was a real piece of work. Can you imagine being cooped up with her all day long? No wonder her children cry so much. I'm sure we can find some things to keep Frances busy and out of that dreadful woman's hair," Mabel said.

"I'll bet you were a child like Frances. Watchful and independent," Virginia said quietly as we reached our rooms.

I thought of Frances's unsmiling face. Virginia was right. I had been that serious child, and while my older sister had never made me feel like a burden, I could relate to that faraway expression that had come over Frances's face while Mrs. Blake had spoken about her as if she wasn't there. I knew what it was like to feel alone in the world, to dream of escaping to a new one.

THE NEXT MORNING, Virginia, Nell, and I headed back to Santa Catalina to resume our nursing responsibilities. For the first time in a month, I felt wide awake. It was strange to return to the convent and see its transformation into a bustling medical facility. I walked my ward, checking on patients, until I came upon a cot with a man lying unconscious. I checked his chart and froze upon seeing his name.

I pulled aside one of the nurses who had arrived from the original camp hospital. "Do you know anything about this man?"

"Well, you can see he has complications from severe beriberi." Indeed, both his legs had swelled to ghastly proportions.

"Does he have any family who come to check on him?"

"It's a sad case actually," she said, lowering her voice in a conspiratorial tone. "Apparently his wife left Manila for California last fall to visit a dying relative and she took their oldest two children with her, but then war broke out and now the family can't reunite. The wife and two children are in the US while the rest of the family is stuck here."

"So who's still here with him?"

"He has a young daughter. Poor thing. She's been shuffled onto some other families to look after her since her father's taken sick. It's quite worrisome, of course. I fear he's terribly ill and may not be able to hold on much longer. If he gets much worse, we might try transferring him to Philippine General Hospital. We're allowed to send serious cases there."

"And what will happen to the girl?"

"Who knows? These are far from normal times. One of the families will have to take her in, I suppose. At least for the duration of the war. She's at a vulnerable age."

I looked at the dying man with a heavy heart and thought of his daughter, Frances, and her serious expression. No wonder she acted older than her age. Absent a mother, she had faced this war and captivity on her own and bore the anxiety of tending to a sick parent. Her narrow shoulders carried a large burden. For the rest of the morning, I felt distracted. Seeing Frances's father and contemplating what lay ahead for the girl dredged up all kinds of memories of my own, and I felt wrung out by the time our shift ended.

When we reconvened in the convent's lobby to walk to campus together, Nell took one look at me and stopped. "What happened?"

"Did you forget how much work nursing is?" Virginia asked, pushing open the door.

"Frances's father was one of my patients," I said. As we made our way back to the Main Building on campus, I explained what I'd learned and Virginia's teasing expression shifted to concern.

"Poor girl," she said with a sigh. "We'll have to keep an eye on her."

"As if you're a good influence," Nell muttered.

Virginia made a face at her. "I'm just as upstanding a citizen as you are. In fact, I'm wonderful with children. Maybe I should join the three of you and meet the golfers today."

"The last thing we want to do is make a big fuss over her and scare her off," I said.

"And you can't even golf," Nell said to Virginia.

"Oh honey, I can swing a lot more than a golf club."

I snorted and knocked my hip into Virginia's playfully. "That's what we're afraid of. The last thing this place needs is a bunch of old-timers dead from heart attacks. We just need the loans."

We entered our classroom and Virginia pulled off her uniform and flopped onto her cot in only her slip.

"Stay here and read for a bit or do something to keep yourself occupied until we get back," I said.

"Fine, I've got a new project anyway." Virginia pulled a battered notebook out from under her pillow, and then rolling onto her stomach, she began writing. "I'm working on a romance of my own."

"Tell me more. Do you need a reader?" Mabel asked dropping onto the foot of Virginia's bed and looking at her expectantly.

"I'll be ready soon."

"I want to read it too," a nurse named Rosemary called from two cots over. "We could use a little romance in here."

"Amen," I heard Mabel say as Nell and I set off to find Frances in the plaza.

FRANCES WAS RIGHT. The men of the Wack Wack Club couldn't believe their good luck when we appeared. Not only were they delighted with the new batch of balls that we had sewn the night before, but they were even more thrilled to stand behind Nell and watch her take some practice swings. When we explained our need for money, the men nodded, pleased with the prospect of government-backed loans.

"Do I get to keep you as collateral?" one of them asked, looking Nell up and down wolfishly.

"Nope," she said, not bothering to soften her refusal with any other niceties, but the man didn't even notice.

"Probably a good thing because my wife would throw me out

on my backside," he said, chuckling and elbowing the other fellas as they guffawed. Nell, Frances, and I departed, flush with the knowledge that we'd soon have money to spend.

"It was a mistake not to bring Virginia," Nell murmured as we walked away. "If those old farts keeled over from heart attacks, maybe we could have inherited all their money."

I laughed, but Nell remained serious. Sometimes I couldn't tell what was happening in her head.

THE RAINY SEASON—JULY, August, and September—came and went in a wet and gloomy blur. Our nursing shifts kept us busy, but in the hours that we weren't at Santa Catalina, time stretched before us in a long, boring spells of tedium.

Mr. Burns's condition stabilized, but he remained in the hospital so I tried to keep close tabs on Frances. She should have been growing taller, but like many children in the camp, she only seemed to lose weight, no matter how many things I slipped from my plate onto hers. I worried about her. At a time when her world should have been expanding, it had shrunk cruelly.

Few material luxuries existed during my childhood, but the freedom to roam and explore had always been a salve to my loneliness. I'd wandered our land, looking for birds' nests and rabbit tracks. I'd admired the irises that grew during spring and searched for raspberries, strawberries, and blackberries, depending on the month. I'd immersed myself in new discoveries about the creatures that lived around me and how plants grew and blossomed. But here in Santo Tomas, the children were trapped in a barren, dusty playground surrounded by guards who scolded them for laughing and running. I feared discovery could only come in learning about new levels of deprivation and cruelty.

None of us were thriving at Santo Tomas, but what would the long-term consequences of such a wretched confinement be on the camp's children?

17.

FLOR

September 1942
Manila

One afternoon in September, when Flor, Iris, and Luchie returned from Santo Tomas, they found a man wearing a suit and tie standing at their front door. Flor estimated him to be a couple of years older than her. He was handsome with high cheekbones, thick and wavy dark hair, and wide-set eyes.

When Iris spotted him, she let out a small cry and then froze. At the sight of this stranger standing outside of their front door, Luchie moved in front of Iris and Flor. "How may I help you?"

He smiled sadly. "I'm Dr. Ernesto Marcial and am hoping to speak with Iris Dalisay."

Iris blanched. She grabbed Flor's hand and didn't let go. Luchie raised a brow, but Flor shrugged to show she didn't know what was happening either.

Luchie cleared her throat. "Please, come upstairs, Dr. Marcial. I will fetch you a cold drink while you speak with her."

They climbed the stairs in silence and upon reaching the top, Luchie led the group to the sala before departing for the kitchen. Iris tightened her grasp on Flor's hand as she sat. Pilar entered the room and introduced herself to Dr. Marcial. "How may we help you?" she asked.

The man gave a small bow. "Mrs. Dalisay, I'm afraid I'm here with sad news. My family recently learned that my older brother, Vincent, is dead and it's our understanding he had become good friends with Miss Iris while they served together on Bataan."

Iris squeezed her eyes closed and made a small animal-like sound from deep in her throat, a sound Flor had never heard before. Pilar stroked the space between Iris's shoulder blades before turning her attention back to the young man. "I'm so sorry for the loss of your brother. We're grateful for his service, but I know this is of little comfort to your grieving family."

The man nodded, his expression sorrowful. "My parents received a note from his corps informing us that he died of typhoid at Camp O'Donnell."

Luchie had returned to the room with a glass of cold lime juice, but she hesitated upon seeing how Iris's shoulders shook as she listened to Dr. Marcial. Luchie met Flor's gaze. Who was this Vincent? But Iris's quiet sobs gave them no time to ask questions.

Dr. Marcial reached into his suit jacket's pocket and pulled out a letter. "He also wrote this for you, Iris, and my parents asked that I deliver it."

He held it out, but Iris kept her hands over her face so he offered the letter to Flor and she accepted it.

An awkward silence. "I can let myself out," he said.

Flor followed him to the top of the stairs and before he descended, he turned to her. "I'm going to return in a few days to check on your sister. My brother would have wanted me to." It wasn't a question; he suggested it gently, and Flor got the impression she could have discouraged him. Instead she nodded. "That would be fine, Dr. Marcial."

"Please, call me Ernesto," he said.

When the door closed behind him, Flor realized she was still holding Iris's letter. The thin paper wrinkled easily between her fingers and there was no seal on it. Briefly, she considered reading it, but even as the idea flicked through her mind, she knew she couldn't do that. She returned to the sala and watched Pilar stroking Iris's back. So much had been left unsaid about Iris's time away—why? Why hadn't Iris told Flor about Vincent?

THE FOLLOWING WEEK, Flor was coming home from meeting one of her bookkeeping clients when she found Iris and Ernesto sitting on a bench in the Dalisays' small garden.

She greeted them, feeling awkward to interrupt, but Ernesto stood and smiled kindly. "Your sister says you're an accountant."

Flor blinked. "I was studying mathematics at the university and thinking of becoming a professor, but the war has upended that plan so I suppose I am an accountant. At least for now."

"This war won't last forever. Hopefully you'll be able to return to your studies when it's over." His expression turned sheepish. "After we received news about Vincent, I got in touch with a few of his friends who are working for the guerrillas, hoping I could be a doctor for them." Flor and Iris looked shocked, so he hurried to add, "I wanted to do my part in trying to help win this war, but they turned me down and told me to stay at the hospital. Apparently it's helpful to have a doctor in the city who's friendly to the underground."

"I should get back to nursing," Iris mused. "It would be good to have a purpose again."

"I can get you a job at Philippine General, where I work," he said. "Our staff is terribly overworked, and we could use the help of someone as experienced as you."

THREE DAYS LATER, Iris had a nursing job at Philippine General. That night she sat on the edge of Flor's bed, brushing her hair like she used to, and Flor could almost pretend that nothing had changed, that there was no war. "After Ernesto introduced me to the head nurse, I thought the woman was going to ask me to start working right then and there." Iris lowered her hairbrush. "I've enjoyed getting to know Ernesto. Until he visited, it had almost felt like Vincent was a vision from one of my fever dreams, but now I know he was real."

This was as much as Iris had said about Vincent, and Flor wanted to ask more. How had they met? Who was he? What had it felt like to fall in love? But she sensed her sister's reticence on the subject, so she didn't push. Iris was finally shedding the jittery, hunted quality that had marked her since returning home from Corregidor and Flor didn't want to reverse any of her ate's progress.

Throughout September, when Iris worked daytime shifts, Ernesto often walked her home in the early evenings and she would call to their upstairs windows, urging Flor to come down and chat with them in the garden. Iris's buoyancy and confidence was back, and she and Ernesto regaled Flor with funny stories about their patients.

One evening, Iris rubbed her hand across her forehead and sighed. "I'm tired and am heading inside, but you two should stay, don't mind me." It all happened quickly and after Iris vanished, as Flor turned to raise her hands apologetically at Ernesto, Luchie appeared and took a seat on the garden bench, looking at them expectantly.

"I'm sorry. I don't know what came over her, Ernesto. Maybe she doesn't feel well?" Flor toed at a paver stone, feeling uneasy, both at her sister's swift departure and Luchie's arrival.

"We had a patient from Santo Tomas today and I think the woman's pitiful condition rattled her."

"I didn't realize the camp sent cases to the hospital."

"Only when the patient's needs exceed the medicine that the camp can provide. The Japanese don't approve many of these cases, but occasionally it happens. It helps that Santo Tomas is being run by a civilian department. The camps housing American soldiers like Cabanatuan are regulated by the military and medical procedures must happen within the camp's walls, but civilian-run camps seem to have a little more freedom to make their own procedural decisions." Ernesto's serious expression turned more jovial. "But enough work talk. On my walk home with Iris, I asked if she thought *you* might want to take an evening stroll with me before dinner."

"Me? A walk?"

"It looks like your two legs work, so yes, I was thinking you could join me for a brief loop around the neighborhood. Manang Luchie, would you join us too?"

"It must be quick because dinner needs to be on the table shortly," she said gruffly, but the older woman stood and took a spot next to Ernesto, appraising him closely. Apparently she approved of what she saw, because she gave Flor a small nod.

A mixture of delight and embarrassment seized Flor. She had assumed Ernesto was interested in her sister. It made sense. Most men were. But when she glanced over her shoulder to the sala's windows, Flor was almost certain she spotted Iris smiling before sliding into the shadows of the house. Flor exhaled and placed her accounting ledger on the bench, feeling her face color. "Yes, I can join you."

"Wonderful, thank you," Ernesto said and three of them walked out the front gate with Luchie in between the two young people.

They passed a bush of rosal and Ernesto plucked a bloom and handed it to Luchie. "Manang, this is a lovely color on you."

She brushed off his compliment, but beamed, tucking it into

the breast pocket of her blouse. "What a sweet man you are." She gave a sideways smile at Flor. "We've been walking all over town lately and my foot's aching so I may slow down a bit, but you two can carry on. Just don't get too far ahead."

As she dropped back a few paces, Flor flushed and Ernesto smiled.

"Before I arrived at your front door, had your ate Iris mentioned Vincent?" he asked, leaning forward slightly to peer at Flor's face.

Flor hesitated, embarrassed to admit how little Iris had confided in her. "No. My sister and I have never kept secrets from each other, so I haven't been sure how much to ask her."

"Maybe she wasn't keeping a secret from you, but keeping her pain to herself so as not to burden anyone else with it."

"But it wouldn't have been a burden to me."

He nodded. "I know, but I suspect the front lines were worse than anything we can imagine. She wants to protect you."

Flor darted a look at his face. She imagined him delivering painful news to his patients in his kind, gentle way and suspected he was a good doctor.

"At work, I see that all the time," he said.

"My sister's never been one to keep a romance secret, so I know it must have been a painful loss. It's so sad."

"It is, but I'm glad my brother found love before he died."

Flor smiled. She liked the way Ernesto looked at things.

18.

FLOR

One afternoon in October, when Flor and Luchie took seats in a pew at Malate Church, Father Callahan sat in front of them immediately. Since summer, when the men at Camp O'Donnell had been relocated to Cabanatuan, Flor, Luchie, and the priests had been smuggling messages and provisions to them.

"There's an outbreak of diphtheria at Cabanatuan and the death toll is rising," he whispered. "We have a contact at a factory on Mindanao that's secretly producing enough serum to inoculate the men, but we need money to buy it. Do you think your network can provide enough?"

"How much is needed? The cost of food keeps rising. Each week we're able to afford less and less," Flor said.

"We're working our contacts too." He slid a sheet filled with calculations toward them.

"Five thousand men need to be inoculated? That's a lot!" Luchie said.

Flor quickly calculated the number of households they visited and how much each family could be expected to offer. "If we try to raise that much, I fear we'll tap everyone out."

"I understand, but see what you can do." Father Callahan ran a hand along his furrowed brow. "This outbreak has the potential to devastate the prisoners."

"How soon do you need the money?" Luchie asked Father Callahan.

"A week."

Luchie gave Flor a dubious look, but shrugged. "We can try."

Since Pilar's beating over six months ago, Flor had been getting headaches, and now the dull throb of one started behind her eyes as she sat in the church. The heavy aroma of incense felt as if it was smothering her. "Let's see what we can do," Flor said, jumping to her feet, eager to leave.

On the front steps of the church, she shrank into a shadow and leaned her forehead against the cool facade of the stone building.

"Are you sick?" Luchie asked, reaching to place a hand on Flor's forehead.

Flor turned away. "No, I'm fine. Just worried. How are we going to find this money?"

Luchie chewed her lip thoughtfully. "Stay calm. We will think and pray."

But Flor didn't want to pray. The numbers simply didn't add up. There was no way their network could produce that kind of money. With her headache in full force, Flor hailed a tranvía, although as she counted out the coins they needed for the ride, she cringed. These days, every centavo felt precious. When the streetcar stopped, she and Luchie climbed aboard and watched as three Japanese soldiers followed, paying nothing. The men pushed through the passengers and gestured at three older Filipinas to abandon their seats. The women rose, bowed low, and sidled away from the soldiers while everyone else stared straight ahead. Flor could feel the tension from the other passengers as they ignored the snickering soldiers.

Over the summer, the occupying Japanese had become increasingly bold. In restaurants and stores, they expected meals and goods to be discounted or even free. Ernesto had invited Luchie and Flor out for ice cream one evening, and they had been in their café seats for only a few minutes before the maître d' approached and asked them to leave their table. A pair of Japanese officers waited behind the café owner, their gloating expressions obvious to all. But Ernesto didn't budge. His expression darkened and he remained seated.

"We must leave," Luchie pressed as Flor eyed the waiting officers anxiously.

Ernesto, normally calm and cheerful, had moved slowly to rise, folded his linen napkin, pushed in his seat, and sighed before exiting the café. Many shared his resentment. As Filipinos watched their occupiers demand more and more concessions, anger seethed within the city.

THE NEXT DAY, Flor and Luchie decided to delay their next visit to Santo Tomas until they knew more about the diphtheria outbreak at Cabanatuan. The last thing the wives at Santo Tomas needed was one more worry.

That evening, Flor turned the radio on for the Voice of Juan de la Cruz. Since Corregidor had fallen, the Voice of Freedom had gone off the air, but this new mysterious Filipino radio personality had taken its place with reports from London and San Francisco, and the Japanese hadn't discovered the source of the rogue radio station. At first, a blast of static filled the sala, but then a man's warm baritone spoke:

My Filipino friends, keep the fires of hope in your hearts alive. These are dark times, but freedom will win.

He went on to report that Stalingrad was now completely

encircled by the Germans and the situation appeared dire. The Japanese and Americans were locked in fierce battle on Guadalcanal, part of the Solomon Islands. The RMS *Laconia*, carrying civilians, Allied soldiers, and Italians POWs, had been struck by a U-boat and sunk, killing an estimated 1,632 people.

Flor turned off the radio. The war was not going well for the Allies. If she was going to be able to help the camp prisoners for months, and maybe even years ahead, she needed to pace her requests for assistance. Asking neighbors for large sums of money for the serum was out of the question. She stood and slid back the capiz-shell window, breathing in the sweet smell of night-blooming jasmine to try to calm the swirl of questions in her mind.

"Flor?"

She turned to see Iris tromp into the room and hurl herself onto the settee. "Good heavens, what a day."

Flor slid the window closed so they couldn't be overheard and took a seat next to Iris.

Iris stretched out her legs onto Flor's lap and sighed. "I just took care of a patient who's entertaining the Japanese every night even though they killed her husband. He was one of the soldiers out on Bataan who died during the march off the peninsula."

"Is she Filipino?"

Iris nodded slowly. "Mixed, I'd say. She's fair-skinned, although definitely some Filipino blood in her."

"How's she entertaining the Japanese?"

"She owns a nightclub that's become popular with them. She came to the hospital for stitches because apparently an officer got carried away and sliced open her hand with a smashed glass. She'll be fine, but she was furious. I told her I'd served for the

USAFFE on Bataan and Corregidor and she wanted to know everything." Iris chewed a fingernail.

"Did you catch her name? Or the name of the club?"

"In fact, I did." Iris smiled, removing her feet from her sister's lap. "She offered me free drinks for my service. Her name's Yasmin Matthews and she owns Club Sampaguita. It's near the waterfront."

Flor was intrigued. This mysterious woman had Philippine papers, a thriving business, a dead American husband, and was bitter toward the Japanese. Perhaps she was exactly who Flor and Luchie needed to add to their network.

"MANANG LUCHIE, I have a new prospective client. Can you please join me for a visit?" Flor asked, tucking a blank book-keeping ledger under her arm.

Luchie grumbled about having a full list of tasks for the day, but she dried her hands and untied her apron. "Will this take long?"

"Hopefully not," Flor answered.

The two women walked toward the waterfront. When they reached a white gate and the sign for Club Sampaguita, Flor stopped. Luchie looked horrified. "Here?"

"Yes, this nightclub is owned by a woman who could solve our money problems," Flor said. When Luchie folded her arms across her chest and didn't move, Flor added, "Ate Iris met her at the hospital yesterday and recommended we pay her a visit."

Iris's endorsement seemed to work because Luchie relented, although she shook her head and stomped up the path to the club's door, her footfall heavy.

They entered and found a few workers wandering around the main room, preparing tables for the evening's guests.

"May I help you?" an attractive Filipina asked, giving a small bow to Luchie. The young woman wore a spangled costume that consisted mainly of a peach-colored satin brassiere and high-waisted bathing suit bottom. Her neckline was trimmed with bugle-beaded fringe. As the woman moved, the fringe undulated in a way that reminded Flor of the colorful anemone she'd once seen during a visit to the city's aquarium. She had never seen an outfit like this and could only imagine its effect when the woman danced.

Luchie stared, openmouthed until Flor nudged her, lifting an accounting notebook. "Yes, I'm looking for Señora Yasmin."

"She's getting ready for tonight, but please have a seat at the bar." The dancer signaled at a figure in the back before turning to the women. "Want anything to drink while you wait?"

"No, thank you," Flor answered.

"Not even a Coca-Cola?"

Luchie surprised Flor by sliding onto a stool in front of the bar. "We would welcome Coca-Colas. Thank you."

Flor followed Luchie's lead and also took a seat, admiring the rows and rows of colorful bottles gleaming in front of her. Judging by the dao wood interior, the clean linens on the table, and the extensive collection of liquor at the bar, this club was doing well. Flor wondered how much it took in each night. While the girl poured them both Coca-Colas Flor watched as a young man gracefully moved around the room neatly arranging votives and small vases of white jasmine flowers at each table. When he glanced at her, Flor could see kohl outlining his eyes and he appeared to have streaks of rouge running along his cheekbones. She had never seen a man wearing makeup before, but then again, she had never been inside a nightclub either.

"Do you like what you see?" A woman slid onto a stool beside Luchie and pointed a lacquered fingernail toward the young man. "Isn't Carlos gorgeous?"

Luchie leaned slightly away and kept her eyes on her drink, but the woman looked unperturbed by the snub. If anything, the club owner seemed to view it as a challenge and she leaned forward, allowing the top of her black silk kimono to gape open and reveal an impressive décolletage. "So, manang, are you here to be a singer or dancer?" the woman asked while covering up a dramatic yawn. "Most of my showgirls are young, but I always like to keep up with the times and have something on hand for everyone, don't I, Naomi?"

The dancer behind the bar filled a glass with water and pushed it in front of Yasmin. "Yes, you've got the most beautiful staff in the city."

"Says one of my top dancers." Yasmin winked at Luchie and Flor.

Naomi, the dancer, lowered her lashes and pouted flirtatiously over her shoulder before strutting away.

Yasmin turned back to Flor and Luchie. "I'm not hiring right now, but I shall keep you in mind for the future."

As the woman spoke, the color of Luchie's face blazed, but she maintained silence.

The club owner then leaned forward to get a better view of Flor. "So, do you have some Spanish in you? You're fairer and taller than most. With a light complexion like yours, I'll pay more. I'd need to see you in costume first, of course, but eventually I might have something. You have a shy demeanor that many of the men here respond to, that's for sure. How old are you?"

Flor could feel waves of frustration rolling off Luchie and decided it was time to end the teasing, so she shook her head and pushed her blank ledger forward. "Neither of us are here to be showgirls. I'm an accountant."

Yasmin barked with laughter. "An accountant, huh? I don't think too many of the fellas come here looking for that." She reached up to her hair, adjusting one of the curling rollers that had slid slightly out of place. Her smooth skin glowed the tawny hue of wet sand, and her thick, long hair was so black it radiated a blue sheen. Flor guessed Yasmin to be somewhere around thirty and didn't doubt that she was part Filipino, but wondered what other blood was mixed in.

Flor nodded at Yasmin's bandaged hand and spoke in a low voice. "I know you were at the hospital yesterday. You told a nurse about a recent trip to Bataan."

Yasmin's flirtatious expression morphed into something more guarded. She glanced around the bar. Only a few of her employees wandered around. "Tell you what, Miss . . ."

Flor had not yet said her new name aloud. She held up her chin. "Call me Lily."

"Miss Lily, why don't you and your friend bring your drinks back to my private apartment? Your timing is good. It's been very busy here lately and I've been wondering if I should hire a bookkeeper. I've got some receipts we could review, but they're in my sala."

Flor nodded and the three rose and retreated through a door next to the stage and into a hallway. They entered the second door on the left and stepped into an ordinary sala with no sign of it being adjacent to a nightclub. There was also no sign of an American husband. No photographs, nothing. Yasmin gestured at an upholstered chair and Flor sat, keeping her face impassive. This was the dicey part when she had to gauge how much to reveal to this stranger. She kept the ledger on her lap and reminded herself to not hold it too tightly, to relax.

Yasmin fingered her hand's bandage. "Who are you? Why do you want to know about Bataan?"

"According to my nurse friend, you and I may have some interests in common. You told her you're unhappy with your clientele. Tell me, how is it that the Japanese are willing to visit a club owned by an American?"

Yasmin reached for a silver cigarette case, held it out as an offering, and then when neither guest wanted one, she went on to light a cigarette for herself with a shaking hand. "I've owned this club for years. I don't know exactly why the Japanese like it so much. I think they can't really figure me out. My mother was Filipino, my father American, and one of my grandparents was Chinese. All this makes me a little ambiguous and I think people see what they want to see. This place is small, maybe a little mysterious, and I really do have a beautiful and talented staff, probably the best in the city." She snorted. "The Jai Alai and the Stork Club have nothing on us."

"But why aren't the Japanese more interested in your American husband?"

"They know nothing about him. There's no paperwork for my most recent marriage. It wasn't legal. I'm still married to another man, a Spaniard, but he disappeared seven years ago. When I met Peter Matthews, I fell head over heels, so even though it wasn't official, we got married last fall, right before the war started. I wanted to think of myself as his wife."

"And how did you get to Bataan?"

"I don't know how much the nurse told you, but here goes: Peter worked for the US Army and he went missing when Bataan fell. I managed to get myself over there with a Red Cross convoy. At a hospital outside of Mariveles, I learned that Peter had been killed after the surrender. Several of his corpsmen witnessed it." A slight tremble entered her voice on the last few words, but she cleared her throat and started again. "He stopped at a well for a drink of water but was murdered by a Japanese soldier. Some would probably say it wasn't murder, it was war, but I call using a machete on an unarmed sick surrendered soldier murder."

Flor liked Yasmin's nerve. They regarded each other cautiously.

Yasmin blew out a long plume of smoke and stood, heading toward her kitchen, where she dropped to her hands and knees, opened a cupboard, reached into the back of it, and removed a false wooden panel, revealing a secret compartment. She removed a stack of papers and photographs and returned to Flor, spreading them on a table. Flor lifted a photo of Yasmin posed with a handsome man in an American army uniform. Several other photos of them together lay on the table. "I've had to hide any sign of Peter. I never bring anyone from the club back here, but of course, you just never know who's going to drop in these days, do you?"

Flor nodded.

"Every night the Japanese are in my club tossing back drinks and leering at me and my girls, and yet I plaster on a smile and try to carry on as usual, but inside I'm just so angry. I miss Peter with all my heart and feel so helpless. I can't even publicly mourn the loss of him. I suppose at least I'm bilking the enemy of their money, right? I'll just keep leading these men on, taking their cash, and spending it on beautiful clothes."

This was Flor's opening and she leaned forward. "What if I had a suggestion for how you could use that money to fight back in your own way?"

Yasmin narrowed her eyes. "You want to take my money? You still haven't told me who you are."

Flor took a deep breath. Though she didn't want to reveal her real line of work, Yasmin had told her enough that Flor decided she could be trusted. In vague terms, she told Yasmin about the men at Cabanatuan and explained the smuggling network and how they were transporting food, money, and material to the prisoners. She pulled the long list of the men's names that Father Callahan had given her and showed it to Yasmin and then followed it with the last receipt of the food and money she and Luchie had sent to the camp.

Yasmin studied the documents. "If Peter survived, he would be there. He would have needed you."

Though Flor had been building this network for almost eight months, hearing Yasmin say that Peter would have needed them struck a chord. A year ago she had been a university student worrying about exams and studying overseas, but now she was helping to run a smuggling network right under the noses of an enemy who had beaten the United States. She had learned more in the last year than she ever had in school. Flor sat straighter. "Yes, he would have needed our help. And now there's an outbreak of diphtheria raging through the prisoners. Our people have access to a serum, but we need money for it. Your club appears to be very successful. Any contribution will make a big difference. You could save the lives of many men."

Yasmin ground out the remainder of her cigarette. "I'll give you as much as I can. Anything. When I think of what the Japanese did to my Peter, I want to—"

Flor held up her hand. "I know, I can only imagine how you feel, but you can't let your anger and desire for revenge guide you with this work. It will make you reckless and lead to mistakes." She tapped her fingers on her accountant's notebook. "Before the war, I was a math student. I particularly like statistics, and the study of chance contains an important lesson for us. If we're careful and rational, we can help a lot of people, but at a certain point, a mistake will be made. We will be discovered and it's very possible we'll be killed. So we need to do everything in our power to hold off that inevitability for as long as possible. Do you understand?"

Yasmin nodded slowly. "So if it's not anger that makes you do this, what is it?"

Flor didn't want fear to govern her life anymore. It was as simple as that. If she and her neighbors ever wanted to live freely, they needed to rid their country of occupying forces. All of them. Japanese and American. Of course, she was angry about her family's suffering, but that no longer prompted her to risk her life on a daily basis. "Since the beginning of this occupation, I've watched how the Japanese have treated us. They've claimed solidarity and promised independence, but their actions do nothing to support their claims. To defeat this enemy, we need to unite around a cause that's bigger than our personal injustices. We must fight for freedom. If the Kempeitai come for me and I'm going to face whatever pain they incur, I need to know my sacrifice will benefit others. My small actions must ignite something larger."

Yasmin looked skeptical. "And we're working with priests? I never would have imagined this place getting some religion."

Flor laughed. "For your own safety, we won't tell you exactly who they are. And we won't tell them who you are either."

"When you speak to your priests, what will you call me?"

Luchie leaned forward and spoke for the first time. "The Abbess. And we'll call this place the Convent. It won't be strange to be talking to the priests about another church."

Flor and Yasmin laughed and crossed themselves.

"I'm right, you know," Luchie said, a twinkle lighting her eyes.

"Somewhere up there, my mother is a happy woman to know

I've become an abbess. Now how much money is needed for the serum?" Yasmin asked.

Flor opened the notebook and tried to not look apologetic as she pointed to the figure.

"Give me two nights and let's see what I can do." Yasmin stood and twirled the belt of her kimono.

Flor thought she had misheard Yasmin. "Only two nights?"

Yasmin bent over and her kimono gaped to reveal one of her breasts. She ran two soft fingers along Flor's jawline. "Like I said earlier, I'm the best," she whispered. "Now if you'll excuse me, I need to make myself beautiful enough to drain the pockets of every man who walks in that door tonight."

WHEN FLOR AND Luchie entered the club two days later, Carlos offered them seats at the bar and set tall fizzing glasses of Coca-Cola in front of them. When Yasmin appeared, she slid two envelopes toward Flor. "One is receipts. The other has everything we talked about and there's extra to help with other expenses."

Flor peeked inside the envelope to see a stack of bills. Amazed, she tucked the money inside her bag, but kept the envelope with receipts on top of her notebook. When she looked around the club, she realized everyone had disappeared.

"My staff and I had a chat," Yasmin said. "We can do more than just make money. The officers who come in here fancy themselves very important. They love to boast about what they're doing and where they've come from. With a few drinks in them, their tongues really loosen up, so we've realized if we listen and urge them on a bit, we can obtain all kinds of information. Troop and ship movement, cargo, news from outside, who's in town—we can pass all this along to you if you think your people might be interested."

Flor glanced at Luchie, who looked intrigued. The club's location so close to the busy waterfront could definitely be useful. "Our people would be very interested. If we come by three times a week, will that be enough?"

"Yes, but if I have something urgent, can you provide me with a phone number? If you get a call with only one ring, that's a signal to come here immediately."

Flor nodded. "That can be arranged, but do you think the information will be reliable? If it's noisy in here, everyone's drinking—"

"None of us are drinking anymore," Yasmin said. "From now on, my staff will only be drinking fake cocktails."

Flor raised an eyebrow, but Yasmin chuckled. "Everyone wants to do their part. By the time this war is over, my crew will have the best acting skills outside of Hollywood."

Flor smiled as she spread the receipts in front of her and they reviewed the club's take over the last few days. Yasmin's confidence in her club was not misplaced, and a wave of relief filled Flor. Business was strong. With a steady stream of cash coming in, they would be able to make a sizable improvement in the quality of life for the men at Cabanatuan, but the risk was also increasing as she and Luchie added more people to the network. How long could they keep their work a secret?

THE PRIESTS DELIVERED the serum to Cabanatuan and the outbreak was contained, but not before it took the lives of many men. Several weeks later, when Father Callahan handed Flor a list of the recently deceased, she scanned it and winced. Mrs. Stone's husband was listed.

"How do we tell her?" Flor asked the priest.

He gave a small shake of his head. "Gently."

But Mrs. Stone didn't take the news well. As the weeks passed, the American woman appeared to fade into distraction and listlessness more and more. One week, a different woman awaited Flor's arrival at the Package Shed. She slipped Flor a message. When Flor left the camp, she pulled it from her waistband and read it before handing it to Luchie.

Mrs. Stone is in the hospital suffering from a severe case of nerves. Please find a new contact at the camp.

Mrs. Stone had been a vital connection, but Flor could understand how the monotony of prison life, compounded with the additional blow of losing someone you loved, could break a person's spirit. Flor needed a new Santo Tomas contact and she needed one fast.

"What do we do now?" she asked Luchie.

"When they're not working at the hospital, your ate and Gloria have been visiting their American nurse friends and taking them supplies. Maybe they'll have a suggestion."

Flor nodded. "Let's pay a visit to Philippine General."

19.

TESS

October 1942
Manila

One morning in October I awoke with a headache. My legs wobbled as I dragged myself to the hospital for my shift. I wasn't even over the threshold of the main ward when Mabel took one look at my chattering teeth and waved me over to an open bed. I tried to protest, but my mouth wouldn't work. Words refused to form. And when had my mouth ever been so dry?

The white walls softened, undulated, and merged into the whiteness of the sheets to form a strange, foggy cloud. Nothing made sense anymore. Nothing looked familiar. At one point, it felt like small crabs were crawling all over my body, poking and pinching me. Above me, black crows circled me and I batted them away. I screamed and cried. And then I was underwater, swimming, diving and spinning, and then surfacing for a minute only to sink again. When I awoke, I didn't recognize my surroundings, but the crows had disappeared. A good sign, I supposed. I drifted back to sleep.

When I woke again, a woman stood beside me, her face obscured by the chart she was writing on. She lowered it and asked, "Tess, how are you feeling today?"

I blinked at the familiar smile. Could it be? Or was I having one of my strange fever dreams? I tested my voice. "Iris?"

"Tess, good to see you awake. We've been worried about you. You've suffered a terribly high fever brought on by malaria."

"Where am I?" I croaked. My arms and legs weighed thousands of pounds and my exhaustion felt so complete, every inch of me ached.

"Philippine General Hospital," she said. "The staff at Santo Tomas decided to send you here for special care so now you're my patient. Was this your first bout of malaria?"

I nodded and had so many questions, but my mouth was parched. Iris saw my distress, poured a glass of water, and held it to my cracked lips.

As the cool liquid poured down my throat, I decided to risk moving the muscles of my jaw. "At one point, I thought I was being attacked by crows," I rasped.

"That must have been when the Dominican priests from Santo Tomas prepared you to leave. It's remarkable you didn't catch malaria until now."

I blinked and my eyesight cleared. Iris looked healthy. She'd gained some weight and her skin had brightened. "Thank you for those wonderful packages of food and clothes that we've been receiving at camp. I can't tell you what a difference they make."

She nodded. "How's everyone at Santo Tomas?"

Before I could answer, a doctor entered the room and took the chart from Iris. "Ah, the patient's awake."

"Yes, although she's weak and dehydrated."

The doctor wrote something on the chart and handed it back to Iris. "Patient should remain under our observation for at least four more days, given the severity of her recent fevers. And if they return, we will reconsider lengthening the stay."

The doctor's visit drained me and I closed my eyes as he retreated.

WHEN I AWOKE next, the room was filling with nightfall's marine-colored shadows. A small figure sat in a chair beside me. I squinted to see better.

"Frances?" I whispered.

The little dark head shot upward. "Yes?"

"What are you doing?"

"My father was sent here, but . . . now he's gone."

"Gone?" I asked dully, my brain struggling.

"He died." A small sob escaped the child and she buried her face in her palms. Suddenly I understood. Before I could say anything, the girl climbed onto my bed to curl up beside me, her head nestled against my shoulder. She trembled.

"I'm so sorry," I murmured, running my palm down the silkiness of her hair. "I don't think I've told you this, but my parents died when I was ten."

She pulled away to look at me. Even in the murky light, her pale blue eyes gleamed with tears. "What did you do?"

"My sister, Sue, and her husband came to live with me. She raised me. She's still back at home and I miss her very much."

"I miss my mother and older sisters."

"You'll see them again." With the girl's small warm body leaning against mine and my shoulder damp from her tears, I felt a surprising tug inside me.

On a fall afternoon many years earlier, after Sue and I had buried our parents, we walked away from their gravestones. At the top of a hill in our orchard, she stopped suddenly and sunk to her knees next to me, pushing away the tendrils of my hair that clung to my cheeks, damp from the day's drizzle. She looked me in the eyes. "Esther, I'll always be here for you, no matter what. Though we'll miss them terribly"—she bobbed her chin toward the matching mounds of freshly turned rectangles of dark soil—"I'll take care of you." And she had. I'd never doubted her.

Now I would take care of Frances—it was more instinct than conscious decision. This impulse to love, protect, and sacrifice for another, it didn't take us sharing blood to forge it, but lay somewhere deep in the heart. The bond was an instinct, a force as ungovernable as gravity.

I tilted Frances's small pointy chin toward me and looked deep into her eyes, the same way Sue had pulled me from my grief. "Frances, I'll take care of you. Someday when this war is over, we'll find your mother, but in the meantime, I'm here."

She clung to my side like a barnacle. Her trembling ceased, and after a few minutes, her body slackened. With her knobby spine below my hand, the rise and fall of her breathing reminded me of the rhythm of the ocean, of waves lapping the shore, and I too slept.

FOR THE REST of my hospital stay, Frances remained with me. During my final morning, a nurse took Frances to the canteen for breakfast, while Iris checked my temperature, vital signs, and signed off on my departure.

"Where's Stalingrad?" Frances asked, returning to my room.

"Russia," I said. "Why? You planning a trip?"

She wriggled back into her seat and looked at Iris and me. "There are a couple of Japanese guards outside talking. Apparently the Germans are running into problems outside of Stalingrad. Sounds like they're suffering big losses."

"They told you this?" I asked.

"No, I overheard them," Frances said with an apologetic wince. "I know I'm not supposed to eavesdrop, but I couldn't help it."

Iris and I stared at her, dumbfounded. For a flash of a moment, I wondered if I was back in a fever dream so I spoke slowly. "Frances, do you speak Japanese?"

"Yes, we lived in Tokyo a few years ago when my father was establishing a business there. I can't read or write it, but I can understand it. Pretty much."

"Does anyone know this about you?" Iris asked.

Frances thought for a moment and then slowly shook her head. "I guess not."

My mind raced. How had I not known this? Then I realized that if this news about Stalingrad was true, it was the first indication of Germany struggling. The Japanese would never broadcast this news on the local radio station. If Frances could understand what our guards were saying, we could learn all kinds of interesting and useful information.

"Don't tell anyone," I told Frances. "This will be our secret."

Iris clutched my arm, not removing her gaze from Frances. "Wait here. I have someone who will want to talk with you."

Iris left for a moment and returned with another young Filipina. They closed the door behind them. "You understand Japanese?" the woman asked Frances.

She nodded.

"I'm with a group working against them. We move money, medicine, and messages between Santo Tomas and the Allied prisoners at other camps. With your ability to understand Japanese"—she nodded at Frances—"you could be a big help for us if you could listen for information from the guards at Santo Tomas."

"What kind of information do you want?" I asked.

"News about what's happening in the war and information about troop movements, the arrival of important Japanese people, and anything that could help plans for smuggling and sabotage." She looked at Frances. "Do you think you can do this?"

Frances nodded. "The children's dormitory and playground is right by one of the guardhouses, so I can hear them easily."

"But can you keep a secret? You mustn't tell any of your friends at camp," the woman said.

Nonplussed, Frances shrugged and pointed at me. "Tess is my only friend."

I squeezed her to my side. "Isn't this dangerous for her?"

"Living in that camp is dangerous, no matter what you're doing. No one will suspect a child of working for the resistance. As long as you two say nothing about her ability to understand Japanese, hopefully she will go unnoticed."

"Does this make me a spy?" Frances asked.

"Yes, and you can only tell Tess what you know. You two can work together." She turned from Frances to me. "You will meet me outside the Package Shed. Although they don't search me on my way out, please write down your messages on small strips of paper that I can easily hide in my clothes. Our handoffs will be fast, no time for conversation. You'll call me Lily and our story is that we met when I was a laundress at Sternberg Hospital and became acquaintances and now I bring you food. That's all. If you're ever questioned, you don't have to know anything else about me. I also have another prisoner contact, Don Davenport. You'll meet him in a few minutes on the transport back to camp. You two can coordinate how to work together."

Iris checked her wristwatch. "They need to leave."

Lily nodded. "Good luck. Tess, I'll be at camp on Tuesdays and Fridays."

20.

TESS

October 1942 to September 1943
Manila

When Frances and I went outside to the courtyard to board our transport back to Santo Tomas, several people boosted us aboard the truck, but one man made no effort to help. He remained seated, one long leg crossed over the other, observing Frances and me with a distant, cool expression and just like that, I knew immediately that he was Don Davenport, our contact.

At Santo Tomas, we disembarked and he led me toward one of the camp gardens, where we could talk without being overheard. Frances followed us.

"Excuse me," he said to her. "I need to talk with your . . . ?" He looked at us in confusion, unable to figure out our relationship.

"It's fine. She can stay," I said. "So you must be Don Davenport."

"Yes, and I take it you're Tess?"

She nodded.

He cast a final annoyed glance at Frances and then focused on me. "Anyway, some of the men and I have built a radio that we keep underneath the floor of my shack. It can receive news reports from as far away as San Francisco and London."

"Ah, so is this the source for the news that sweeps through the camp?"

"Most of it, yes. And now apparently, the resistance wants these headlines to pass on to the prisoners at Cabanatuan. They send in what they call Cheer Sheets, notes with the latest news stories to help give the fellas a morale boost. I'll write up these news stories, but then we need to add them to whatever you're producing. Sorry, but why did they add you to this operation?"

"I'm working with someone who understands Japanese and is listening in on the guards for useful information."

Davenport gave a skeptical shake of his head. His hair was dark, streaked with gray, and like many of the men in camp, he wore it longer than would customarily be the style, yet his face was clean-shaven and inscrutable. "Bill Millhouse? We've got him listening to the Japanese? How the hell's he pulling that off?"

I looked at him, confused. "Who's Bill Millhouse?"

Don's eyes narrowed. "I've been in Manila a long time and know almost everyone here. Millhouse, a Brit, is the only man who I know that speaks Japanese in this place and I can't possibly see how we could risk him getting close enough to hear anything useful."

"He's not the only person who understands Japanese. I do too." Frances put out her hand. "My name's Frances Burns."

"Frances, we're not supposed to tell anyone," I said.

"But he's working with us."

Don stared at her for a moment. "Are you related to John Burns?"

"I'm his daughter."

He looked over her head at me. "How old is she?"

Irked, I said nothing and looked at her. "I'm eleven," she answered.

"This can't be serious. She's a child!" he scoffed.

"Normally I'd never suggest her taking such a risk; however, these aren't normal times. Frances understands Japanese and no one knows that except for the two of us. Think of the advantages she can offer."

Don paced the scrubby grass, lost in thought, while I reined in my mounting impatience. I fanned at the hot afternoon air with my hand until I could contain myself no longer. "Listen, she has an uncanny way of moving around this camp unnoticed. She hears everything and is very observant. She runs errands for me and the other nurses and is constantly slipping between the Main Building, the children's quarters, and Santa Catalina without anyone looking at her twice."

"Good Lord, this is what we've been reduced to? Using little girls as spies?"

I stiffened. Why *not* a girl? "The fact that you're dismissing her so quickly is exactly what makes her effective. No one pays attention to young girls. Invisibility is her advantage. And on top of that, she's sharp as a tack. Trust me, she'll exceed your expectations."

Don shook his head impatiently. "That won't be hard since I have *no* expectations for this foolishness."

After he stomped away, Frances turned to me. "What's so hard about listening to a radio and writing down the news? Why does he think he's so important?"

"Good question. I suspect he's touchy because he knows your work will be more valuable. Let's just ignore him and do our jobs."

AND SO OUR operations commenced and 1943 brought us some good news. From Don's radio, we learned the Soviet Red Army defeated the Germans outside of Stalingrad that winter, a major blow to the Axis powers. And then several days before Don caught it on the radio, Frances overheard our captors drinking and bemoaning the Japanese loss of Guadalcanal, the first significant American victory in the Pacific. These bits of good news buoyed our spirits for days, but more important than the news reports about battles was when Frances learned that a high-ranking Japanese official would be arriving at Nichols Field air base and traveling by motorcade to Manila. I imagined the plans guerrilla groups could make with this. She also learned that a celebrated Filipino war hero refused to collaborate with the Japanese and they were furious. If word about his reluctance got out, it would a propaganda nightmare for the occupiers. When I shared these findings with Don, he rubbed his chin.

"Your girl is getting good intel," he conceded. "But remind her to be careful."

It took all my willpower to refrain from rolling my eyes. As Frances wandered along the edges of the children's playground, looking bored and alone, no one would have guessed she was listening to the gossip coming from the windows of the nearby guard's shed and memorizing all of it so we could relay the news to Lily.

One morning in March, a commotion broke out outside the Package Shed. One of the old Filipinos who sold candy dropped his basket and a pile of letters spilled out across the exit. I'd just made an exchange with Lily and moved to the outskirts of the area, but the shouting of the guards caused me to stop and spin around to see what had happened. The guards pounced on the old man, furious at the sight of contraband leaving the camp. They punched him several times before dragging him away. Lily and I locked gazes before she vanished down Calle España. I tucked my shaking hands into my skirt's pockets and fled to the Main Building.

That evening, Frances found me in the dining shed. "The guards tortured that vendor and then walked him through the Annex so he would identify the two men who were giving him mail. They're going to make an example of them tomorrow morning at roll call."

I barely slept that night. If my messages had been found, Lily would have been beaten, questioned, and possibly executed. During her beating, would she have been able to withhold information about me? And if I was beaten and tortured, what would I reveal?

The next morning we assembled in the plaza. Two men, a Brit and a Dane, were tied to posts facing us. Though I didn't know them well, I had treated each of them for minor ailments at the hospital. There were almost four thousand people in the camp, but as nurses, we knew many of our fellow prisoners because at some point, almost everyone needed treatment for a medical issue.

The camp commandant paced the space between the two men and the rest of us. The sun blazed overhead and flies darted from one spectator to the next, reveling in the perspiration dripping from our bodies. "Sending messages out of this camp will not be tolerated," the commandant yelled. "Let this be a lesson!"

Two guards began whipping the men's backs. Each lash whistled through the air and struck their flesh with a sickening smack. The sound of impact was horrifying enough, but it was the dull, restrained groans of the men and the way their bodies melted inch by inch to the blood-soaked dust surrounding them that broke my heart. The way they struggled to maintain a measure of dignity and downplay their agony as if to protect the rest of us—it made me rethink everything.

Were we taking unnecessary risks? Surely there were other radios in Manila. But then I thought about the unique value of Frances's reports. Despite the importance Don attached to his own news, we both knew Frances's information had become critical to the underground.

I searched the crowd and found Don watching me. When our gazes met, he arched his eyebrows as if to say *what now?* Despondent, I shook my head.

The whipping ended. We were forced to file past the unconscious men.

"Look closely!" the commandant ordered.

I looked at the shredded flesh on their backs and bile rose in my throat. I had seen plenty of gruesome injuries, but this wasn't a battlefield wound. This had been inflicted in cold blood. One man had power, the others didn't. I stumbled toward the Main Building. When I stepped inside the lobby, suddenly the walls seemed to constrict on me. I was back in the ruins of the aboveground hospital on Corregidor with a man hovering alongside me. I could barely breathe. The sensation of George's watch being slipped off my wrist crawled over my skin with clarity, as if it had happened yesterday. Though I hadn't worn that watch for long, I missed it. Between the sense of violation and the anger and uncertainty that had swept through me moments earlier at the sight of the men being beaten—something hot, jagged, and angry took root inside me. I needed to do everything in my power to hurt the enemy and help win the war and that meant I needed to figure out a way to keep getting messages out. I returned to our classroom, searching my brain for a way to fool the enemy.

Later that day, as I headed to my afternoon shift at the hospital,

I passed a cluster of women washing clothes and bedding in the community tubs. They gossiped and sang as they scrubbed and hung the laundry on the public drying lines. Those with money sent their laundry out of the camp, but many internees did their own, a laborious job. I slowed, watching the white sheets ripple in the faint breeze. They reminded me of pieces of paper waiting to be written upon.

THAT EVENING, I traded my yarn for another nurse's white thread and began stitching onto a white sheet.

Frances sat beside me, watching. "I can barely see what you're sewing."

"That's exactly the point."

"That no one can read it?"

"No, silly. Our messages will be hidden. We can send Lily out with a basket of laundry and even if the guards start inspecting what's leaving the camp, it's unlikely they'll detect my stitches."

That night I sewed Frances's latest report onto a sheet and loaded it into a basket, along with several pillowcases and rags. No one seemed to notice my project because Virginia was reading her latest chapters from the romance novel she was writing, and the nurses had gathered around her enthralled.

The following morning, I went to the Package Shed and waited. Lily handed me a sack of canned food and I gave her the laundry basket. She looked at me quizzically. "Check the sheet closely," I said quietly, before turning to leave. Lily nodded.

OUR NEW SYSTEM worked well because it took place in plain sight. Needlework was the perfect disguise for our deception. When I wasn't at the hospital, I was stitching messages onto the laundry that Lily brought me and no one paid any attention. When I needed more white thread, I asked the internees on kitchen duty for the empty canvas bags that the rice arrived in and as I unraveled those bags, Frances rolled the unfurled canvas thread around sticks we used as spools. Guards walked right by me as I sewed and they never paused to look at what I was creating. It seemed that sewing, long considered the banal work of women, could be used for subversive purposes.

Each time Lily visited me, we exchanged laundry baskets. She would take my linens stitched with messages and return them on her next visit, cleaned, pressed, and with the stitches torn out. As the months passed, searches on people departing the camp grew commonplace. The guards pawed through Lily's laundry basket half-heartedly, feeling for contraband items, but it never occurred to them to inspect the laundry itself. More months passed and messages that would have devastating consequences for our captors slipped right through their careless fingers.

One evening, almost a year after Frances and I had first started working with the resistance, she found me in our nurses' quarters. It was September and the rainy season was underway. The room reeked of mildew. Frances left her muddy leather shoes at the doorway and came to sit on my bed across from me. I had an exchange planned with Lily the following morning and was stitching Don's news that Italy had surrendered to the Allies.

"A typhoon is coming," she whispered. "The Japanese aren't announcing it because they don't want the guerrillas to take advantage of the chaos this storm will bring."

Much of Manila lay at sea level, and between the bay and the

Pasig River, a storm surge could have catastrophic results for a city unprepared for such an event. I hurried with my stitching about Italy so I could add this message about the storm. Heavy rainfall pelted at the window near my cot. Hopefully our information wouldn't be too late to be helpful.

21.

FLOR

September to October 1943
Manila

Getting by in occupied Manila became a delicate balancing act between pretending everyday life was carrying on as normal while coping with the fact that *nothing* about life was normal. Store shelves were empty. Schoolchildren learned how to speak Japanese. The occupiers carved neighborhoods into zones and designated civilian leaders to report any suspicious activity. Occasionally Filipinos disappeared, hauled away by the secret police, the Kempeitai, and no one dared ask questions.

Guerrilla groups smelled opportunity in the air and infiltrated the city with increasing confidence, blending in more and more with civilians to recruit and sow disorder. Mayors, policemen, businessmen—anyone seen as being pro-Japanese was a target for attack. Earlier in the summer, a city official had been shot three times while playing golf, yet remarkably he survived. Every day the Kempeitai loaded more and more Manilans into the dungeons of Fort Santiago to answer for these crimes.

With Luchie's help, Iris and Gloria continued to supply the interned American nurses with food and the other supplies they needed, while Flor continued smuggling messages, money, medicine, and materials back and forth between Santo Tomas and Cabanatuan. They were also supplying eyeglasses, books, and painting supplies—items that showed the prisoners were getting stronger, not only from the food and medicine, but also from the hope they found in the messages and news from the outside.

Despite this progress, during the rainy season, traversing the city to visit Santo Tomas grew unpleasant and increasingly risky. For one thing, each month residents of the city received a ration of one small bar of rough soap, and by the end of September, judging by the smell of the passengers on the streetcars, those bars were gone. Furthermore, the weather always caused delays for the streetcar schedule and irritable guards at the checkpoints began hassling people for no substantive reason other than the gloomy weather and persistent dampness shortened tempers. One morning, when Luchie fumbled to locate her paperwork at a checkpoint, without warning, a guard slapped her, splitting open the tender skin over her eye. While Iris and Gloria continued on to the camp, Flor and Luchie abandoned their trip and instead had Dr. Dalisay stitch up the wound in his office.

Four days after Luchie's injury, the women attempted a trip to Santo Tomas again. The rain fell like blades, cold and sharp, quickly soaking their hair and clothes. When they reached the gate into Santo Tomas, the guards waved them through distractedly. Tess, the American nurse, approached Flor. "Sorry, this load's a real mess," she said as they exchanged baskets. Dread prickled Flor's damp skin for she understood the warning. She nodded and fled the camp.

Flor and Luchie braved the large puddles consuming the city's streets and took the sodden laundry basket straight to Malate Church. By the time they entered the back door into the church's warren of administrative offices, both women were bedraggled and impatient.

"Father, I think there's urgent news in today's load," Flor said, dumping the wet laundry onto the floor by the priest's desk. Because of the gloomy weather, the light was bad, so they spread the sheets across a table next to the window, squinting to read the words the white thread spelled out on the white sheets.

When they found the section about the typhoon, Father Callahan blew on his cold hands. "We'll start spreading the word, but I fear our warning will come too late for many. You should hurry home."

Flor saw Luchie tense. Her parents lived in a low section of the city, near the Pasig River. "Manang Luchie, you should go warn your family. There could be a dangerous storm surge. If you need, stay there until the storm has passed or, if there's time, bring your family to our house."

Luchie accepted her offer and fled from the church so quickly that Flor's fear of the storm grew sharper. Under normal circumstances, Luchie would never consider leaving Flor unchaperoned outside of the house. At the prospect of being on her own for once, a giddy excitement warred with her concerns about the storm.

She left the church and sloshed her way through the wet streets to Philippine General Hospital, where she found Ernesto making rounds. Her wet hair clung to her forehead, and rivulets of rain streamed down her legs, pooling around her feet.

"Where's Manang Luchie?" he asked, looking around in surprise.

"A typhoon is on the way, but the Japanese aren't issuing any warnings," she said once she caught her breath. "Manang Luchie has gone to alert her family."

Ernesto cocked his head. "How do you know about this storm?"

Flor hesitated. "I heard the rumor at the market."

His brows knit together and he tugged her into a room. She smiled, thrilled at the prospect of being alone with him, but when the door closed behind them, a terrible stench made her gag.

"What is—?"

"Shhh," Ernesto said and pointed. There, on a bed, lay a woman. Her face was swollen beyond recognition, and filthy clothes hung off her in shreds. Even without any medical training, Flor could see the woman had a broken arm and ankle. Flor backed out of the room as quickly as she could.

"Why did you take me in there?" she demanded once they were back in the hallway.

Ernesto glanced around before whispering, "I know you're doing something other than just bookkeeping, and I'm sure it's connected to your visits to Santo Tomas, but you must be careful. That woman was found outside of Fort Santiago. The Kempeitai show no mercy toward anyone. If you're caught, your father's connections to the government, the fact that you're a woman—none of it will matter. You'll be brutalized. You *have* to be careful."

"I *am* careful."

Ernesto winced. "It's just that I care about you, Flor. I don't want to see you hurt."

Flor softened. "I care about you too. That's why I don't say anything about what I'm doing. I want to keep *you* safe. Now I need to find Ate Iris and go home to help my family prepare," she said and slipped out of the hospital as quickly as she had arrived, but her excitement at being on her own had vanished.

THE RAIN INTENSIFIED. Jose moved upstairs from his ground-level apartment and slept in the kitchen. Luchie did not return and the Dalisays fretted, worrying about how the river would rise and threaten large swathes of the city. Darkness overtook the sky and the wind screamed outside. Water puddled in front of the windows. Two days into the storm, the power, telephones, and electricity failed. On the third morning, Flor and Iris placed pails throughout the house to catch rain from leaks in the roof. By the fourth day, Flor began to worry about their fresh water supply and she filled every bowl, pitcher, glass, and tub with water from the taps. On the fifth day, the rain stopped.

When Flor slid open the kitchen window to peer into the back garden, it looked as though a pond had formed. Only the tops of their hedge and the gateposts marking their property poked through the water.

"There's flooding up to the fourth step," Iris called from the stairwell leading from the front door.

Flor feared for the rest of her city. Too many people were teetering on the brink of destitution to withstand a crisis like this.

WITHIN FOUR DAYS, the water receded. Jose, Flor, and Iris cleaned the silt from the two servant apartments, but a smell of mildew lingered. A tired-looking Luchie reappeared with her mother and father at her side. They moved into her apartment and Luchie took Jose's place sleeping on a small pallet in a corner of the kitchen.

"Your parents can stay for as long as they need," Mama said.

"My brothers are rebuilding the house, but it was almost entirely ruined. They will only stay for a few weeks," Luchie said. She didn't explain how they survived so the Dalisays didn't press for details.

A week later, Luchie discovered an entire load of laundry had disappeared from their drying lines.

"Could the wind have blown it away?" Flor asked, peering into the garden from the kitchen window.

Beside her, Mama looked horrified. "No one would take our sheets and underclothes, would they?"

Papa and Jose entered the kitchen, their faces grim. "The entire garden next door has been picked over. Every edible thing was stolen," Papa said.

"The laundry may have been stolen, but we still have food in the garden. Come nightfall, I will watch over the yard," Jose announced.

"No, we don't know if these thieves are armed," Papa said. "It's not worth risking any danger to you."

"Then I will harvest what I can now," Jose said, heading down the stairs.

Luchie opened a cabinet and ran her fingers along the baskets and cans of food, inventorying how many meals she could produce from what they had. Knowing how the market's shelves were almost bare, Flor knew they had to make the most of everything they could find.

THE STORM DROVE desperate people to take alarming risks. Prices rose on everything from coconuts to cotton. Nothing was safe from theft anymore. And it wasn't simply individuals driven to crime. Cartels were forming, emboldened by the possibility of charging outrageous prices on the black market, but the Japanese provided little help to the struggling civilian population. Instead, they mounted a distraction.

For months, the Japanese had been dangling independence and self-governance in front of the Filipinos, but few believed the promises. In the middle of October, on a hot day that made the rainy season feel like a distant memory, Flor accompanied Iris and Papa to the Legislative Building to witness the Japanese-sponsored independence ceremony. The entire event was a sham, everyone knew it, but Papa's presence was required due to his association with the Ministry of Health.

Ernesto met them at the Legislative Building and stood at Papa's side. Throughout the ceremony, Flor tried to catch Ernesto's eye, but he never glanced her way. Flor stewed. If Ernesto wanted her to quit her resistance work, she would have to refuse. Their courtship of the last year had been the bright spot in her life, but she couldn't stop working with the priests. Too many people relied on her and she was careful. The work was worth the risk. Flor folded her arms across her chest and exhaled impatiently. How much longer would this ceremony last?

Several long speeches ensued, and then the band struck up the first few chords of the Philippine national anthem. In the distance, the clang of church bells rang out. Inch by inch, the Filipino flag rose up the pole in the center of the crowd.

When it reached the top, Flor was surprised by the poignancy of the moment.

She forgot about the scorching sun overhead, her tension with Ernesto, the smug expressions on Japanese officials, and the empty promises of the day's speeches. For her entire life the Filipino flag had always flown below another country's. First, the American flag, and then the Japanese. And before she had been born, it had been under Spain's flag.

Today the flag of the Philippines fluttered by itself.

The sight gave her hope. She was surprised by how much it affected her, given that they knew the Japanese had no real intention of ceding any control.

But still, the image of the flag on its own wouldn't be easily forgotten, not by Flor and not by her countrymen. It was why she was risking her life for the resistance. Out of the corner of her eye, she glimpsed Ernesto blink away a tear. He looked at her and winked and her heart soared. Someday Filipino independence would be real. But she knew that a hard and dangerous stretch lay ahead. The Allies were on the offensive, and this would mean life in a city governed by an angry, defensive enemy would become more volatile and threatening than ever. At the same time, Filipinos were desperate and people with nothing to lose can be a powerful force.

22.

TESS

Ｎew guards are coming," Frances whispered to me one day when we left the dining shed after breakfast. "The military is taking over the camp."

My heart stopped. The Japanese Department of External Affairs, a civilian agency, had run Santo Tomas since our arrival and allowed us leeway in many ways. Everyone knew that if Santo Tomas were to be turned over to the military, like Cabanatuan, we were in for trouble. The horrific conditions of military war prisons had become legendary—and feared.

Sure enough, two days later a caravan of trucks stormed through the main gate, and the men emerging from the vehicles weren't the usual guards. These were soldiers. Truck after truck roared through the gate, delivering more and more of them.

Our lives changed overnight. The new commandant instituted a curfew, and everyone had to evacuate the shanties by four in the afternoon. The number of vendors allowed to enter the Package Shed area was reduced, although somehow Lily still managed to get inside. Toilet paper disappeared. Electrical appliances were confiscated. Lunch was eliminated so we were down to two meals a day, and calling them meals felt generous. Guards patrolled the camp carrying rifles affixed with bayonets. The Japanese expelled the handful of Filipino doctors and nurses who had been working alongside us in the wards.

On top of these challenges, the demeanor of our captors changed. Under civilian rule, the guards had largely ignored and neglected us. Now under military rule, they harassed us. Searches became commonplace. Brutality increased. One guard, Lieutenant Sagawa, was particularly cruel and quick to slap a baton against anyone who wasn't moving quickly or bowing deeply enough. We took to calling him Saggy because everything—his pants, his belly, but most of all, the features on his face—sagged. His expression was perpetually pulled downward in a sneer.

One evening when Nell, Mabel, and I were returning from our shifts at Santa Catalina, he stopped us outside the Education Building.

"Late! Late!" he shrieked.

"We're nurses," I said, thrusting my armband with its medical cross in his direction.

But he didn't care. "You line up!"

The three of us fell into line facing him. In the distance, faces crowded the windows of the Education Building, where many of the men were housed. Their anxious expressions made me step closer to Mabel. *What did Saggy want?*

"Slap each other," Saggy commanded, pointing at Nell and Mabel. "You two start."

Nell blanched as she faced Mabel. "Just do it," Mabel muttered under her breath.

Nell brought her hand back and half-heartedly hit Mabel across the cheek.

"Harder!" Saggy stamped his feet. "We stay here until you do it right!"

"Do what he wants," Mabel whispered, her eyes smarting above her reddened left cheek.

Nell bit her lip and then hit her a second time, though again, it was obvious she hadn't tried very hard. Saggy stepped so close to them, his spittle rained upon both women as he yelled at them. This time Nell wound up, and though she was openly weeping, she hit Mabel hard and the sound cracked through the hot evening air like a shot.

"Now you!" Saggy pointed a stubby index finger at Mabel, then me. By this point, he was laughing and holding his sides. Three other guards stood behind him, hopping up and down, energized by the cruelty in the air.

Mabel turned to me, tears streaming down her cheeks. A trickle of blood ran down the left side of her face where the tender skin above her eye had been cut.

"I'll be fine," I said without moving my lips, but my heart thundered in my chest. I'd developed a case of ariboflavinosis, an ailment caused by malnutrition that produces painful sores on the lips and inside the mouth, so any impact to my face was going to hurt more than usual. "Let's just do this once."

When she hit me, stars speckled across my vision. The coppery taste of blood filled my mouth.

I could barely even hear Saggy yelling over the pounding of blood in my ears, but even though I knew I couldn't really hurt Mabel by slapping her, the humiliation of this exercise made fury burn like a fever. Shame and anger smoldered in Mabel's eyes too. Blood dripped from my lips as I reeled back to hit her and then she turned to dole out the final blow to Nell.

And then it was over. Saggy and his goons sauntered away, jeering and laughing uproariously while the three of us drooped in stunned exhaustion.

"Tess, your mouth," Mabel cried, wiping at the bloody mucus dripping from my chin. "I'm so sorry."

"It's fine, let's just get back to our cots." I felt furious with my tears, the guards—everything. "I have a little salt and can try a rinse."

"Look what I did," Nell said, sniffling and hiccuping as she touched the injured spot above Mabel's eye. "You might need stitches."

Mabel shrugged. "Good thing we can fix each other up."

As we turned to go, we caught sight of the men still crowding the windows of their building. Many were weeping and it occurred to me how helpless they must have felt watching us abused. The men had no way to come to our defense and the guards had known that. The location of our punishment hadn't been accidental and the blatant cruelty of this hurt far more than the stinging of my sores and the burn of our faces.

MORALE IN SANTO Tomas plummeted. Throughout the winter, we saw the effects of wounded psyches manifest as physical ailments in the hospital.

"I think we need to show these monsters that they can't defeat us," Virginia suggested one evening as we sat in the dining shed, eating slimy lugao.

"How?" Nell asked.

Virginia thought for a minute. "What about some sort of performance? It's been a while since the little open-air theater's been used. Don't you think a talent show would be fun? We could keep the commandant happy by having a few Japanese songs in it, but for the most part, people can show off their talents."

"What kinds of acts are you envisioning?" a nurse named Rosemary asked, pushing her spectacles up her shiny face. "I could enlist my chorus to sing a song or two."

"That would be perfect," Virginia said, warming to her idea.

"So many people here have been taking classes, this could be the opportunity to show off what they've learned. We could have an art exhibit as part of it too."

"I could juggle," Mabel said. "Maybe I could teach some others so it could be an ensemble act. How about I teach a juggling class?"

"I'd like to learn to juggle," Frances said. The idea of our serious little Frances doing something like juggling made us all grin at one another.

"Virginia," I said, "this is a great idea."

THE FOLLOWING DAY, Don and I met by the classrooms for an exchange. We strolled along one of the paths, but before he started telling me the latest news from his radio, he cleared his throat. "When you first began stitching those messages, I was skeptical, but I must tell you how impressed I am. It's been over a year, and no one's figured out your system."

I stopped walking. "Don Davenport, are you giving me a compliment?"

He jammed his hands into the pockets of his patched trousers. "I suppose I am. Don't get used to it."

I laughed, but before I had time to say anything more, Virginia appeared.

"Tess, here you are," she said. "I've been looking all over for you. I was going to ask if you could put your sewing skills to good use and help with talent show costumes, but"—she beamed at Don and then looked at me expectantly—"first, please introduce me to your friend."

"This is Don Davenport. He was the editor in chief of the *Manila Star* before being stuck in here."

Virginia clapped her hands together with delight. "Why, I

need someone who's well-connected and knows how to get the word out about an event. Something's telling me you could be the *perfect* man for this."

I darted a glance at Don, expecting him to appear horrified at being enlisted into something as pedestrian (I imagined that would be *exactly* the word he'd use to describe such an activity) as a talent show, but instead a flicker of amusement passed over his face. "I'm flattered you'd consider me perfect for anything."

I blinked. Was he flirting with Virginia? In the year I'd been working with him, he'd scarcely smiled, yet now he was suddenly charming. What was happening?

"If I may be so bold, could I snag you to chat for a few minutes about what I need?" she asked him.

He crooked out his elbow at her with a debonair flourish. "Your wish is my command. Shall we walk?"

"I'd be delighted," she said, clasping both hands around his arm. They took a few steps away, before Don snapped his fingers on his free hand, remembering something. He paused to glance over his shoulder at me. "Sorry, Tess, were we done?"

I forced a smile. "Yes, I'm done with you."

"See you in a bit, Tess," Virginia trilled and off they went.

Stunned, I remained planted. Why was I so irritated?

TALENT SHOW REHEARSALS filled the next month. Everyone was talking about the upcoming performance. Between her work at the hospital, her romance writing, and her efforts to produce the show, Virginia was the busiest woman at camp. I barely saw her, but when I did, all she talked about was Don.

"Did I tell you that he'll be performing too?" she asked one morning as we picked at our meager serving of gruel and banana.

I almost fell off my chair. "He is? What's he going to be doing?"

"He's going to recite poetry." Virginia's face took on a dreamy expression. "You should see him when he says his lines. He is *so* handsome." Virginia rested her cheek on one palm. "He's just wonderful. He's traveled and has so many amazing stories of adventure. Do you know he once hunted tigers in India?"

I held back from rolling my eyes, but I felt quite certain Don had never even held a rifle, much less hunted tigers.

Frances interrupted. "He didn't actually kill one, did he?"

"Fortunately, no. They're such magnificent creatures, aren't they?" she asked, petting Frances's hand. "In fact, he has a very self-deprecating sense of humor and goes on and on about what a lousy shot he is."

Self-deprecating? Was she really talking about the same Don Davenport I'd known for the last year? "Isn't he a little old for you?" I asked.

"Oh, honey, what does it matter? I've been thinking a lot about Sally and Darren recently. They're a good reminder that you must seize romance when you get the chance. Why wait around? Falling in love is a blessing and I for one don't plan to squander the opportunity. I'm tired of romance only happening on the pages of my manuscript."

"Hear, hear," Mabel chanted, raising her tin cup of lukewarm water. "To love!"

Frances wrinkled her nose, but also raised her cup.

I raised my mine too, but my heart felt heavy. I didn't want to begrudge Virginia any happiness, but it was hard for me to feel enthusiastic about Don. On top of the fact that he was not one of my favorite people, he was working with the resistance— did Virginia know that? Was it my place to tell her? With my friends, I had withheld the nature of my own resistance work because I didn't want to put any of them in danger. Was her association with Don putting her at any more risk than she was at by being my friend?

That night when I tucked myself under my mosquito net, I tried to remember how it had felt to kiss George on the waterfront that first night I'd met him. It had been two years since our whirlwind of a romance. Had I been a fool to let him get away? While I was stuck withering down to nothing in this prison, it was completely possible he had met someone else and moved on with his life. What were the chances he was still waiting for me?

In the cot beside me, Nell snored lightly. Sheets rustled throughout the room. Someone muttered in their sleep. Outside the window, a dog howled and another one answered it. I tried to imagine George's face in my mind's eye, the way his smile had conveyed safety and trust, but maybe it was because I was tired or trying too hard, or maybe there were just too many distractions, but I couldn't picture him. I wished I still had his watch ticking on my wrist, but I had nothing. It almost felt like he'd never existed.

IN MARCH, THE morning of the show, I awoke early to finish stitching my newest batch of messages before my nursing shift started later that morning. Frances entered the nurse's quarters carefully carrying a stub of a bruised banana for me.

"Thank you, I'm not sure I'll have time to get to the dining shed this morning," I said.

"You're not missing much." Frances sat cross-legged in front of me. "You have a meeting tomorrow?"

"I do. Almost done with this. I'll be ready."

Most of the women in our crowded room had gone to breakfast and no one was paying attention to us, but Frances leaned forward and whispered, "Men are being taken from Cabanatuan and put on ships for ports in Japan and Manchuria to be used as slave labor in mines and factories. I just heard the guards saying that seven hundred men are leaving Cabanatuan today and being sent to the waterfront here in Manila to board a ship."

My mouth went dry. Seven hundred? That was no small number. How many of those men would have wives and families here? After our own brief overcrowded, steamy trip from Corregidor to Manila, I had little doubt of the misery of a longer one. Those men had survived a death march to arrive at Cabanatuan only to now face the horrors of ocean transport and slave labor that awaited them?

I looked at the pillowcase where I was stitching the latest war news. Everyone believed the Allies were on the verge of launching a major offensive in Europe, but no one knew where or when. We all desperately awaited this attack because the sooner the war ended in the west, our corner of the world would receive more attention from the Allies. I looked for space on the pillowcase to add the news about Cabanatuan. This information would be important to the network.

Virginia entered the room and brightened at the sight of Frances and me. "Just the gals I was looking for! Can y'all please join me down by the northwestern garden plot?"

"I need a few minutes, but I'll try to get down there soon," I said.

Virginia put her hands on her hips. "What on earth is so important about that pillowcase? Please, I need you now. Urgently!"

From Virginia's stern expression, I knew we had to go with her.

As we walked out of the Main Building, a group of women sat under one of the acacias working on costumes for the evening's show. I counted three who had husbands at Cabanatuan and my vision swam. Without concrete information about who was being sent away, I couldn't say anything and start a panic, but I hated the secret I carried.

When we arrived at the garden plot, Mabel and Nell awaited us, looking confused.

"What's going on?" I asked.

From a spot beneath a shrub, Virginia bent over to remove a small bouquet of weeds tied with a pale pink bow and she handed it to Frances. She raised her chin proudly. "Don and I are getting married right now and you're our witnesses. Frances is my flower girl."

Mabel laughed. "My, aren't you two fast operators! But why on earth did you pick today? You've got a show to put on in a few hours!"

They'd only known each other for about a month but who were we to argue? In the camp, a month felt like a year. Virginia gazed at Don adoringly as he approached with one of the Dominican priests who was housed on campus. Don smiled. "My wedding present for my new bride will be my performance tonight at the show."

I smiled. Whatever my personal feelings about Don, a wedding was exciting. It had been so long since anything like this had happened. The priest nodded and the most unexpected wedding ceremony of the war got underway. When it was done, and the new Mr. and Mrs. Davenport embraced and kissed, I felt a pang of sorrow as I found myself thinking about Darren and Sal. If only they had gotten their chance. And then I pictured George and missed him with such intensity that my chest hurt. *Why hadn't I married him back on Corregidor?*

In this pathetic garden full of the dried husks of our old crops, I saw signs of how hopeful we had once been. Yes, the Americans were coming back, we all knew as much, but as our conditions worsened every day, I feared they may not arrive quickly enough to save us.

THAT EVENING, INTERNEES streamed from every corner of the camp onto the expanse of plaza in front of what Virginia had taken to calling the "Little Theater Under the Stars." I sat next to Frances and watched how her face lit up during a dance number. The beautiful, clear voices of Rosemary's choir prompted plenty of toe-tapping and humming along to the music, and there was a comedy act that had the entire audience rocking with laughter, but it was Don's recitation of Elizabeth Barrett Browning's poem "How Do I Love Thee?" at the end of the night that left everyone speechless, tears streaming down their faces.

> *I love thee with a love I seemed to lose*
> *With my lost saints. I love thee with the breath,*
> *Smiles, tears, of all my life; and, if God choose,*
> *I shall but love thee better after death.*

The way he gazed at Virginia as he spoke tightened my throat. "Who knew Mr. Davenport was such a romantic? He's always been so snooty." Frances took my hand in hers and squeezed it, her palm hot and sticky. "People in love can be full of surprises, can't they?"

I nodded, holding in sobs I knew would choke me if I let them out. I'd never imagined Don to be the kind of man to stand in front of an audience and recite a love sonnet, but he had. Wonders never ceased.

That evening, as we sat under the flickering white lights hanging from the frame of the stage, basking in the goodwill brought forth by the show, fear and misery felt far away, at least for a few minutes. We were a group of people who had been thrown together under the worst of circumstances, yet we had forged a community, a large messy one that cared for one another no matter social strata, occupation, or nationality. We were bonded by loss, but also by a sense of purpose and common goal. All the trappings of regular society had vanished. Gone were the pricey watches, jewelry, white gloves, kid-leather shoes, finely tailored gowns, and sharkskin suits. Instead we sat shoulder to shoulder sweating through our faded, thread-bare, mismatched clothes, willing to be silly for an evening. We were a little drunk on hope and happiness and had no idea how short-lived this shot of joy would be. Life was about to become more challenging than we could possibly imagine.

23.

FLOR

June to August 1944
Manila

Even after two years of smuggling, the tremor of anxiety Flor felt when carrying contraband never went away. As she hastened to Malate Church, it was like the basket of laundry in her hands was a beehive, buzzing with an energy of its own. At Santo Tomas, when Tess handed her the basket, a rare smile flashed across her drawn face. "It's the news we've been waiting for," she murmured. Behind her, Flor heard "Over There" blaring on the loudspeaker. A rinse of relief swept through her. Had the Allies finally landed somewhere in Europe?

When the women arrived at Malate Church, they practically flew through the back corridor to Father Callahan's office, where they found the priest kneeling over a wastebasket of burning documents.

Flor looked at the small conflagration quizzically and lowered the laundry to the ground. "We have big news from Europe."

But Father Callahan shook his head. "Read whatever's in there quickly and then start pulling out the stitches. There can be no evidence of any messages. Our contacts at Cabanatuan have been compromised. The Japanese have discovered our network."

Flor exhaled slowly, but Luchie put a hand on her hip. "How?"

"We're not sure yet, but we need to cease all operations until we know more."

"But what about the prisoners?"

"Hopefully they've been storing up food and medicine." In the shadows, Father Callahan shook his head. "You should both stay away from here for a couple of weeks."

"Even to attend regular services?" Luchie asked.

"I think we should avoid contact for a bit."

Flor chewed the inside of her mouth. If the Kempeitai was torturing the people they had caught, there was no telling how much information they'd uncover. Would they connect the network to Malate Church? To Flor? To Club Sampaguita? She tried to exhale and loosen the tightness from her chest.

From the first few days of involving herself with the resistance, she knew the odds were not in their favor, but she had hoped this day would never come. Now that it had, she was afraid of Fort Santiago. If tortured, how much would she be able to endure? She cast a guilty sideways look at Luchie. And what if others were caught with her?

LATER THAT WEEK, Luchie and Flor made a trip to Santo Tomas and told Tess to stop sending laundry since they were under suspicion. When the American woman's face crumpled at the news, Flor hurried away.

They also visited Yasmin. After Flor explained how the church had ceased operations, she spread out her accounting notebook and said, "But we can keep raising money and if we can't send it to Cabanatuan, we'll funnel it to the guerrillas somehow. Don't worry, though it may feel like you're not helping, you are. Just stay patient."

But even as Flor counseled patience, she too felt the chafe of helplessness.

One morning in early July, as she brought her breakfast dishes in to Luchie, Flor leaned against the doorway. "What would you say to taking a walk by Malate Church? We could just take a peek and see if everything seems normal."

Luchie didn't need prodding. She tugged her straw hat onto her head and Flor felt guilty for how much the older woman had obviously missed going to services. As they neared the church, the streets felt quieter and less busy than normal.

Luchie placed a hand on Flor's arm. "Let me go ahead and see what's happening. I used to attend daytime services sometimes so my presence won't be unusual. Wait here."

Flor stopped and idled in front of a few shop windows, trying to look inconspicuous. Minutes later, Luchie returned, her eyes glistening with tears. "Let's go. The church's doors are shut."

Flor swallowed. In all the years they had lived in the neighborhood, she couldn't think of another time the church had closed. The women turned toward home.

"What if the Kempeitai are waiting for us?" Flor whispered.

Luchie said nothing, but crossed herself.

When the women arrived at their street, they peered down the way, searching for signs of anything amiss, yet the neighborhood appeared normal. Flor sidled along the street toward home and gestured at Luchie to stay close. At the gate, she peered over and saw nothing unusual. If the Kempeitai were inside the house, Mama was doing a remarkable job of welcoming them and carrying on as if everything was normal.

Flor thought about the contents of their house. Was there anything that would connect them to the resistance?

She pushed through the gate and jogged up the stairway into

the house and was relieved to find Mama, sitting on the settee, sewing. While Luchie returned to the kitchen, Flor chatted with her mother for a few minutes and then went back to her bedroom. She slid open the window and gazed across the skyline of tile roofs, of church steeples. The Japanese would lose the war, that much was now clear, but how hard did they plan to fight to hold on to the Philippines? A sense of an impending collision hung over the city as everyone waited for what was coming next.

IN AUGUST, AFTER Luchie served dinner and then retired to her apartment downstairs, Flor sat at the table bent over one of her accounting ledgers when the sound of fists pummeling the front door crashed through the quiet of the house. The Dalisays stared at each other and Flor stiffened. So the time had come. In a strange way, she felt calm. She had known this day would arrive. For one last time, her mind darted through each room of the house, mentally checking for any signs of incriminating evidence. Her accounting books held no secrets. She felt confident she had covered her tracks. Whatever was coming, she needed to face it head-on. Hopefully Luchie would be spared any association with Flor's smuggling.

"I'll get the door," she said, noting the tremor in her legs as she stood.

"No, I will," Papa said and there was a new fierceness in his voice. He didn't signal for anyone to hide. Though the pounding on the door was growing more insistent, he paused and clasped Flor's hand for a second.

She swallowed and remained standing, waiting.

24.

TESS

By August, hunger consumed us. The Santo Tomas Ladies Baseball League canceled its season since no one had the energy to play. In the meal lines, sometimes people fainted as they waited for food. Cases of beriberi, pellagra, and scurvy filled the camp hospital, along with people suffering headaches, joint pain, anemia, incontinence, and vision problems—all a result of malnutrition and early signs of starvation. The commandant of the camp had closed the Package Shed to all deliveries of supplemental food and materials. Despair hung as heavy as the humidity that blanketed the camp.

In a weird response to our slow starvation, a recipe exchange craze struck us. We spent our free time discussing elaborate imagined meals and carried around dingy notebooks filled with recipes that we traded and spent hours copying down in painstaking detail.

On a muggy, rainy afternoon, I sat on my cot copying a recipe for chocolate cake. Virginia sat next to me, absorbed in writing her novel. It was hot, so miserably hot. We were too hot to talk, too hot to complain, but I missed stitching messages. They had been my lifeline to the outside world. A few weeks earlier as I walked home from a shift at the hospital, Don fell in beside me.

"Has Frances heard anything recently?"

"I told her not to spy on the guards since we can't do anything with the information. Why subject her to any additional risk?"

"There's a group that's sneaking out over the wall every few weeks to pass information and retrieve food."

"Does Virginia know you're doing that?"

"I'm only listening to the radio and recording the messages. I'm not young enough to risk climbing over the fence anymore."

"And you're a married man," I reminded him.

"That too. Still, don't mention anything to Virginia about it."

I'd never divulged our resistance work to her. I hated keeping secrets, but it was safer for her not to know.

A few cots away from where I sat with Virginia, Frances lay on her side, playing checkers with Mabel. The young girl's thin face had an unusual flush. A large stack of Mabel's checker pieces lay beside her elbow, but Frances seemed unusually listless considering the size of her lead. Normally competitive, Frances had a tendency toward talking nonstop when winning. I frowned. I was about to ask what was wrong when a commotion outside our room interrupted the quiet of the afternoon.

"Room inspection!" Saggy's voice hollered. "On your feet! Into the hallway!"

We tripped over ourselves, tangled in mosquito nets and bedding, and fled from the room. From my vantage point, I could see the guards tearing through our belongings and tossing contraband items toward the door. One guard picked up a banana from Nell's cot, peeled it, and jammed it into his mouth as he continued the search. I heard a small sound of dismay from her direction but didn't dare console her. Instead I looked around for Frances. The girl had disappeared.

Inside our room, Saggy reached Virginia's cot, picked up one of the notebooks she had been using to write her romance, and flipped through a few pages. With a sneer, he grabbed a dagger from a band around his calf and proceeded to cut through large chunks of the notebook's pages. I darted a glance at Virginia and could see her jaw clench and sweat bead on her upper lip. She stared straight ahead, her hands bunched into fists, pressed against her sides.

At that point, none of us had spotted what was happening below our windows in the plaza.

When the guards swept out, we busied ourselves with reassembling the chaos of our room, picking up the tossed bedding and spilled personal effects.

But then the sound of yelling reached us.

We beelined for the door and hurried down the stairs, moving faster than we had in months, and we were swept down into the rain-splattered plaza, along with streams of other internees. Frances appeared like an apparition in front of Virginia and me, her eyes wide with fear, her sopping hair plastered around the sides of her thin face. "They have Don," she said.

Virginia gasped and pushed past her, leaving us to trail her through the crowd. When we reached the front, three men were positioned between guards, their clothes bloodied and torn. Soaked from rain, the thin cotton of their shirts revealed the ridges of their ribs. Don stood in the middle. He locked eyes with Virginia and then me. A shudder of horror turned my stomach. The Japanese must have discovered his radio.

I wrapped my arm around Virginia's waist to prevent her from doing anything to draw attention to us. If the guards knew we were connected to Don in any way, it could bring about more trouble and reprisals.

"These three men have violated numerous rules and they are subjected to die by firing squad," the commandant announced.

Over the drumming of the rain, his voice shook in fury. Beside him, the guards raised bayoneted rifles.

A collective groan of horror emerged from the internees surrounding us.

Don stared at the firing squad, his expression as inscrutable as ever. I tried to swallow past the scream rising inside me and it felt like a handful of nails was caught beneath my breastbone. Helpless, I simply watched.

I'd always known we might get caught, but now that the moment had arrived, my body suddenly numbed with disbelief. The only thing that roused me from my state of shock was Frances's nails digging into my arm. When I looked down at her, she stared straight ahead as if in a trance. I rubbed the rain from my brow.

"Fire!"

A battery of shots rang out.

The men slumped to the ground, landing in puddles that quickly reddened with blood. The sound of the shots echoed off the distant stone walls and buildings of the camp. My gut twisted. Beside me, Virginia's knees buckled. Nell and I steadied her.

With the rain soaking our hair and clothes, an angry ripple crossed the crowd like a wind stirring the surface of a lake. Sensing a change in the air, the guards tensed and raised their rifles at us.

"Curfew starts now. Go back to your rooms immediately! No dinner!" the commandant bellowed.

But no one moved. Virginia had jammed her fist in her mouth and though I could feel her trembling, no sound emerged.

"Now!" he repeated. In silence, the crowd dispersed.

Virginia turned to me, her eyes wild. "You knew he was up to something, didn't you? Why didn't you stop him?"

"I . . ." I started to whisper miserably, but stopped. What could I say?

But then I heard a small cry.

Beside me, Frances sank to the ground.

"Frances! What's wrong?" I bent to lift her. She felt boneless and light. Heat radiated from her skin. Her glassy eyes looked right through me. Stunned, I cradled her in my arms and turned to Nell and Virginia. "She's burning up."

A gap widened around us as people realized the girl was sick. No one's immune system had defenses anymore and illnesses ripped through the camp without mercy. With a painful jolt of realization, I knew our thin, frail Frances was in serious trouble.

Over Frances's limp body, Virginia and I stared at each other. She fixed a final murderous glare at me, but then shook her head and took a deep breath. "Well, don't just stand there, come on. Let's get her to the hospital."

"But what about the curfew?"

"Damn the Japanese and their curfew. This is an emergency!"

I squeezed Frances to my chest and followed Virginia.

As we reached the edge of the plaza, a guard stopped us. "Go back to the Main Building. Curfew!"

Virginia stepped forward and the soldier raised his bayonet, aiming it at her chest. "Listen to me, this child is seriously ill. It's an emergency, don't you see?" She gestured at Frances clutched in my arms and then she leaned toward the man, raising her index finger to scold him as though he was nothing more than a schoolboy, her voice low, insistent, and angry. "You will let us take her to the hospital right now. We are nurses and we will not be stopped until this patient is safe."

I held my breath, waiting for the soldier to do something terrible, but Virginia didn't waver and continued to stare at him, her expression thunderous. The soldier looked surprised and glanced uneasily at Frances's prone form in my arms. We all stood there, facing off, unmoving, until he lowered his rifle and stepped aside. "You go to the hospital, but stay there until curfew's lifted."

We nodded, but Virginia took a final look at where Don lay on the plaza before turning away and tightening her jaw. Her shoulders were set and she hunched forward against the rain, a portrait of determination if I ever saw one, but I couldn't bear to think about how much leaving Don's lifeless body must have cost her. Love, a force she put above everything, had failed her.

25.

FLOR

August to October 1944
Manila

Four days?" Papa repeated the Japanese officer's words.

"We give most people a couple of hours to leave, but you're receiving a more generous offer due to your connection with the Ministry of Health." The officer ran a finger along the dark narra carving in the foyer. "We'll be back and you should be gone. Four days. You understand?"

Papa nodded.

With every passing day that summer, more and more members of the Japanese Imperial Army flooded into Manila. Housing had become precious and the occupying force thought little of pushing Filipinos from their homes. Though the war had turned against them, their overwhelming presence in Manila made it clear they had no plans to surrender the Philippines. Not without a fight.

When the Japanese officers left, the Dalisays gaped at one another. Flor couldn't believe it hadn't been the Kempeitai at the door. She had received a reprieve—for now. She exhaled with relief and turned to survey their home. She had lived in this house her entire life. A crack ran through one of the Machuca tiles in the kitchen from when Luchie had first taught her to cook and Flor dropped a pot. In her bedroom, one of the capiz shells in her window could be slid out of its frame. When she and Iris had been young girls, they would remove the shell and peer out the window at the next-door neighbor's handsome son when he had played in the garden with his friends. Small irregularities like this filled the house. They were signs of home. How could she be expected to leave all this in the hands of strangers? And what should she take? What could be left behind?

And most importantly, where would the Dalisays go? Most of their friends were losing their homes too. Those who remained had no room to spare.

When Flor slid into bed that night, she stared into the darkness. In four nights, a soldier would lie in her place. Or maybe several would be packed into this room. A strange language would be spoken within these walls. Stiff, ugly uniforms would hang in her wardrobe. All signs of Flor would be erased. The years the Dalisays had spent building a home would be undone in a matter of days. The sting of this injustice affected Flor more than she expected.

At the same time, she was being offered an opportunity to disappear. The priests from the Malate Church had vanished and she feared the Kempeitai would soon be looking for her. If she moved now, how would they know where to find her? She needed to figure out a way to stay in the city, to keep working for the resistance, and be close to Ernesto. Perhaps she could move in with Yasmin.

The next morning, the Dalisays sat at their dining room table for breakfast. Flor studied the china plate in front of her, the same one she had eaten off for more than twenty years. Luchie was telling her parents that each household on their small street had been ordered to leave, but most only received a few hours to pack their belongings and flee.

"We should go to my sister's in Pampanga Province," Papa announced. "Her farm is safer than staying here in the city."

Mama nodded in agreement.

"I must stay here because of my job," Iris said. "I'll move to Gloria's apartment in Malate, near the hospital. Her parents are leaving for the country too. Papa, if I look after Flor, could she live with me?" Iris reached for Flor's hand under the table and squeezed it.

Papa looked stern. "Flor should accompany us. This city is unsafe right now. When the war ends and her university reopens, we will come back, but until then, no."

"Yes, Papa, I understand your concerns, but I fear I will miss all of you so much. What if Manang Luchie and Flor remain with me? Gloria's apartment isn't very big, but Flor and I can share a room. Their presence would bring me great comfort."

When Luchie entered the room carrying two mugs of tsokolate, Papa studied her. "Luchie, what would you say about staying in Manila with Flor and Iris? I know you'd like to remain near your family so perhaps this arrangement could work. What do you think?"

Luchie looked to Mama, who nodded back at her. "Oh, Luchie, I hate the idea of leaving the girls behind, but if you were to stay with them, I'd feel so much better."

"But who will accompany the two of you to the country?" Luchie asked.

"Jose," Mama said.

Luchie nodded, relieved. "All right, it would be best for me to stay near my family."

The rest of the meal was quiet.

Japanese ships packed the harbor. Soldiers filled the city's sidewalks and they were angry. At the same time, more and more guerrillas were slipping into the city and moving among them, disguised as civilians, waiting for opportunities to strike back at the occupiers. The situation felt combustible, yet Flor couldn't imagine leaving.

THE DALISAYS PACKED only what they could carry. When Ernesto came to the house, Romeo asked him to take several volumes from his beautiful medical library and what books Ernesto didn't take, they decided to bury. Flor and Iris dug up the trunk in the backyard. They removed the liquor and sent Jose off to trade it for food. Then they reclaimed the cash, identification documents, and jewelry, before reburying the trunk now filled with an old rifle, kitchen knives, valuable books, china, and photographs. Piece by piece, Flor watched as their home crumbled away.

BY SEPTEMBER, MANILANS began to watch the sky. The Americans had to appear soon. They had vanquished the Japanese at Guam and established a radio station that reached Luzon. Finally the residents of Manila could listen to news reports that weren't Japanese propaganda. Tucked into their new rooms at Gloria's apartment, when Flor, Luchie, and Iris first heard the twang of an American accent coming over the airwaves, the sisters cried with joy and twirled around the small sitting room, laughing, giddy, and out of breath. Even Luchie jumped from her seat and broke into a funny dance. According to the radio, an American attack was imminent and planes had already been spotted over Luzon.

In an effort to keep people from witnessing an American air attack on ships in the bay, the Japanese erected barricades blocking anyone from visiting the waterfront. They also drove trucks through the city, ordering residents to black out their windows. City dwellers were threatened with losing their electricity permanently if they failed to comply, yet most households rebelled by turning on as many lights as they could.

Flor and Luchie were outside Club Sampaguita's front gate one afternoon when the first sound of a cannon boomed. Flor peered overhead. A formation of eighteen planes swooped toward the city. Her breath hitched in her chest. Yasmin, Naomi, and Carlos bolted from the club's front door and they gathered in the street. Neighbors joined them and everyone stared at the pale blue sky. Though the hot sun seared down on them, no one moved to the shade. As the planes neared the bay, huge explosions shook the ground.

The antiaircraft cannons hit several of the American planes and they fell from the sky, leaving smudges of smoke behind them as they plunged into the water, but most of the planes managed to drop their payloads exactly where they were intended: on the warships, freighters, and tankers moored in the harbor. Within thirty minutes, the sky over the water darkened with smoke as dozens of fires burned and oily fumes spiraled upward. Despite the foul air blowing over them, elation filled Flor. The end was near. She imagined the internees at Santo Tomas and the joy that must have seized the camp. In the space of a few seconds, Flor dared to picture her family reunited, a wedding with Ernesto, perhaps she could return to her studies. The possibilities of a life without war multiplied. She had waited three years for this moment.

"*Mabuhay!*" Flor cheered, raising her hands overhead. Never before had the greeting been more poignant and meaningful! *To life! Welcome!* Soon, everyone was screaming and embracing.

Each crash and boom from the bay sent up a hurrah from the crowd and people overwhelmed the blockades and raced to the waterfront to view the spectacle.

When the raid ended, Flor returned to the club with Yasmin and the others. When Carlos flicked the switch to turn on the lights, the power had been cut.

"Never mind about that," Yasmin said. "Let me open a bottle of champagne!"

She handed Luchie the first glass. Everyone cheered as Luchie said, "I don't even remember the last time I had a drink."

"It's gotten too pricey to waste on ourselves, but today's a day to remember," Yasmin announced, raising her glass. "So when will the Americans land? Later this week? Two weeks from today? It won't be long now!"

FOR TWO DAYS American planes zipped across the Manila skyline, bombing boats in the bay and warehouses along the waterfront and riverfront, but then they disappeared. From Malacañang Palace, the puppet Filipino government declared martial law, but it did little to alleviate the threat of danger at night. As food became increasingly scarce, bands of thieves roved the streets, looking to steal anything that could be traded for food and liquor.

While Iris continued to work every day, Flor and Luchie's waking hours became consumed with locating food. They filled their pockets with a mixture of Filipino and Japanese military pesos to see what they could negotiate, but bare shelves greeted them at the market and at stores.

One day in early October the women obtained two bags of rice from a market vendor who had always been partial to Luchie. The women hid the rice bags in their baskets and dropped the first one off at their new apartment and took the second to Yasmin, but when they arrived at Club Sampaguita, a padlock hung on the front gate. The women scampered around the block to the alley running behind the buildings and padded along the narrow path to the club's back door. When Flor knocked, she also called out Yasmin's name quietly.

Yasmin pushed the door open, squinting into the bright sunlight. Her eyes widened when she saw the bag of rice and she ushered Flor and Luchie inside.

"You've closed the club?" Flor asked.

Yasmin, normally clad in glamorous gowns and suits, now stood before Flor wearing a dowdy cotton flower-printed housedress. Her hair was pulled back into a bun and her face looked younger when bared of any lipstick, rouge, or kohl. She gestured to her friends to sit at the kitchen table. "I'm taking it week to week. This week we'll be open only on Saturday night. I can't locate enough alcohol to stay open seven nights a week, and even if I could, the streets are too dangerous for my staff to travel home after closing. On Saturday, they'll sleep here, but no one wants to do that more than once a week. We're playing with fire, because even if we can stay in here under the protection of the Japanese officers, all of them are in such bad moods, I worry the men will hurt us. We need to make enough money to survive, but I don't like relying on the Japanese to keep us safe." Yasmin lit a cigarette and inhaled deeply. "I've been approached about helping the resistance more." She explained the new mission and when she finished, she raised her brows at the women. "So can you help too?"

Flor thought for a moment. "I need to speak with my ate and Gloria, but I feel confident they'll support this, but"—she turned to Luchie—"your family relies on your income. You don't need to do this."

"No, we need this war to end. If this will help us win, I'll do it," Luchie said, setting her chin resolutely.

Yasmin rested her cigarette on the edge of her ash tray. "Talk to Iris and Gloria and then let me know if the plan will work. The resistance needs us in two days," she said.

FLOR CONFIRMED THE new arrangements with Iris and Gloria and then spent the next couple of days filled with anticipation and saying nothing to Ernesto about her new resistance work. What good would it do to involve him? The less he knew, the safer he would be.

Two days later, when the two faint knocks on their door came at midnight, Luchie switched off the apartment's lights. Iris and Gloria were working three overnight shifts at the hospital so they weren't home. Flor cracked the door to find a solitary figure waiting outside. In the darkness, there was no seeing his face, no checking who they were allowing into the apartment, but there was no time to waste. She pulled the man inside. They held their breath, listening for any sound from outside the building. Every muscle inside Flor seemed to twitch. The man was tall, much bigger than expected, and he seemed to fill the dark space around them. The sudden intimacy of the moment was jarring. Trapped with a stranger, Flor bit her lip, uncertain what to do next. For a moment, she felt a flicker of doubt.

"Lily?" the man whispered.

In the dark, she smiled. As her nerves evened out, Flor became aware of the man's breathing, his solidity next to her. The trace of saltwater rose from his clothes and she guessed he had come from the bay. Since the beginning of the war rumors of American submarines plying the waters around Luzon had circulated. Fishermen reported the sea parting to reveal the emergence of a sub hatch and then US Navy men would appear and regale them with cigarettes and old American newspapers and magazines.

"Welcome to Manila," she whispered.

"Thanks. Wish I had more time for sightseeing," he said.

Luchie switched on a lamp and served him a basic meal of scrambled eggs and tinned sardines. When he sat on the wooden chair, it creaked and he laughed, stretching out his long arms and legs. "What can I say? They make things big in Montana." He then smacked the side of his head. "I just said more than I should have, huh? I'm not supposed to tell you where I'm from, right?"

"If.they catch us, all that will matter is that you're American."

His face turned grave. "Thank you for doing this. I know it's risky."

"Just don't tell us how you got here or where you're going next."

"Got it. They're coming for me tomorrow though at four in the morning and then I'll be out of your hair."

Flor smiled and sat across from him, watching his dinner-plate-sized hands fork the eggs into his mouth at an astonishing pace, and when he finished, he pulled a chocolate bar from his pocket and handed it to her.

Her mouth watered at the sight of the candy and she grinned at Luchie. "We can split it."

He chuckled in a mischievous manner. "You can each have one. I've got more." He revealed a second bar and handed it to Luchie.

Luchie lifted it with a reverence normally reserved for something holy and she held it aloft, savoring its heft.

"What's wrong?" he asked.

"It feels so heavy," Luchie said.

"We haven't seen chocolate in what—three years?" Flor asked, not taking her eyes off the candy. She unpeeled the foil and admired the precise lines of the bar's squares. When she lifted it to her lips, she closed her eyes, breathing in the fragrance of sugar and the sharp tang of cocoa. Under her teeth, the bar cracked with a satisfying snap. Her tongue danced along the chocolate's smooth surface and in the heat of her mouth, it softened and melted, sending bursts of sweetness that shot right through her and made her smile. It had been so long since food had brought her such delight.

Something like pity flashed in the American's eyes, but he tried to hide it with a brisk nod. "Please promise me you'll eat the whole thing."

Flor didn't need to be told twice. She was so hungry that there was no stopping her after that first bite.

26.

TESS

October to November 1944
Santo Tomas Internment Camp

Diphtheria. It was an illness that preyed on the camp's children and now Frances suffered from it. She writhed and her throat swelled so badly any sign of her jawbone and neck musculature vanished. She burned with fever. Her teeth clattered. She shivered violently.

Captain Davison transferred me from Santa Catalina to the camp's Isolation Hospital to help care for Frances and I scarcely left the girl's side. Since the first American planes were spotted a couple of weeks earlier in mid-September, the internees had become hopeful that liberation was at hand, but helplessly I watched as Frances's chest heaved and sucked, struggling for each breath. Would she make it through the night? Sometimes I wasn't sure.

"I fear for her heart," Dr. Nathan said as we stood beside her cot. Already overtaxed from hunger and stress, we knew her system to be precarious. More than anything, we needed the Americans to arrive with food and medicine. Liberation *could* save her. But we didn't know how close the Americans were, how soon they would arrive. So really, all Frances had was her own fighting spirit, and fortunately she fought her illness like a tiger. Three weeks after she had collapsed on the plaza, she clawed her way back to consciousness. She was exhausted, but alive.

On the day we planned to move her back to the main ward at Santa Catalina, where the rest of the nurses could have doted on her, red splotches arose on her cheeks and her temperature spiked again.

"Measles," Dr. Nathan sighed as he tugged on the stethoscope looped around his neck. "I'm sorry, but she'll need to stay here longer."

More days passed, and then weeks, me at her side, applying cool compresses to her burning forehead and watching the red rash creep along her pale, transparent skin.

I received a message one evening that a guest awaited me in our small ward's lobby. I left Frances to see who it was. As I plodded along the hallway and passed an open window, the sight of the nearby playground caught my eye. A few months ago, a horde of children would have been absorbed in games, but now only a few sat in the shade of the buildings, depleted and listless.

Before I turned the corner to reach the lobby, I stopped, pressing my forehead against the cool plaster of the wall. I needed a minute, just a minute, before I faced whoever wanted to see me. For three years we had been clinging to hope, to this idea that in the end, good would prevail over evil, but what if we were wrong? What if this was it? A slow slide into oblivion, into death. Why had I not left with George when I had the chance? What arrogance I'd displayed thinking I could endure anything!

I rarely allowed myself to think this way, but exhaustion and frustration had chipped away at my defenses. "Stop it!" I whispered to myself, squeezing my eyes shut. Frances needed me.

"Pull yourself together," I murmured, straightening, knowing this was no time to fall apart. After a few beats, I stepped forward, resuming my trip to the lobby.

Virginia leaned against a windowsill, waiting for me. Her collarbones jutted from her khaki uniform shirt. The skin of her hands stretched tight and shiny across the knobs of her knuckles and wrists. I halted a few paces away. "Hi," I said.

"How's our girl?" she asked.

But instead of answering, I broke down into a sea of tears. Virginia pulled me close. "She'll make it," she whispered into my hair.

After I cried myself dry, I hiccuped and wiped at my face. I swallowed. "I'm so sorry I said nothing about Don."

"I know you are. Everyone's saying there was a radio hidden below the floorboards of his shanty. You must have known about this?"

I had been dreading this moment. I nodded. Calmly, I explained how Don, Frances, and I had been working for the resistance for almost two years. Under normal circumstances, seeing Virginia rendered speechless would have been entertaining, but now I just felt like a heel. When I finished, she stared off into space for a minute before smoothing her hair and meeting my eye.

"I knew he was up to something, but what was I going to do? Demand he stop? I understand the need to resist. Honestly, I suspected you were in on it too, and there were even a few times when I almost demanded to be included, but . . . I don't know. I was afraid." She shrugged, looking more flattened than I would have ever imagined possible, but then a guard passed by a nearby window, his bayonet gleaming in the sun, and Virginia's face rearranged itself into a defiant smirk. "But I would never have dreamed Frances was a part of it. If only the Japanese understood a young girl would be part of their undoing. No matter what happens next, I'll always take great satisfaction in knowing that."

Despite my drained state, I smiled too. Frances had surprised everyone, and her intelligence had helped the war effort in countless ways, but what if she didn't survive to see the rewards of her work?

"Look, Tess, you're a wreck. Go back to the Main Building and get some sleep. I can take over here."

"Really?"

"Yes, in fact, you'll be doing me a favor. I need something to take my mind off Don," she said, and I must have looked worried, because she shooed at me. "Really, get out of here. I don't want to talk about anything. I just want to work."

I SLEPT FOR two days straight and when I awoke, I panicked and pushed aside my mosquito net, but as I tried to stand, my knees buckled. Nell caught me.

"Slow down, we've been keeping an eye on you. You're not going anywhere until you've had a bite to eat and some water." She pushed a small tin plate of mush and a piece of meat toward me. I ate it down in one gulp, and knowing how the camp's dog and cat population had dwindled to almost nothing in the last few months, I knew better than to ask what I was eating.

Nell went on, "Virginia's there now. Once you've cleaned yourself up, you can go back."

After I washed my face, I entered the classroom and found Mabel placing my uniform on my bed. "I washed it while you were sleeping."

All I could do was kiss her.

BY LATE OCTOBER, the red rash receded and Frances's fever broke, but thick, barking sounds convulsed her emaciated chest and Dr. Nathan pronounced her latest affliction to be whooping cough. Day after day, night after night, she battled for each breath. I'd never been particularly religious, but I spent that time praying, begging God to spare the child, and each prayer made me angrier and angrier. The futility of our situation appalled me. What was the point of this war? Why hadn't I left when offered the chance? And then I hated myself for being weak.

By early November, Frances showed signs of improvement and Dr. Nathan insisted I take a break and return to my classroom to sleep. Nell, Mabel, and Virginia were permitted to relieve me.

One morning in the middle of November, when I returned to the Isolation Hospital, I found Virginia reading aloud to Frances. She stopped and tucked the book into her skirt's pocket. "Look, Frances, Sleeping Beauty has arrived!"

Propped on a pillow, Frances gave a wan smile as Virginia straightened the bedsheets proudly.

I kissed the girl's forehead, noting how cool and dry it finally felt. "Your bright eyes are the best thing I've seen in ages. Even better than the American planes buzzing the city."

Frances wriggled into an upright position. "Can you keep reading?" she whispered to Virginia.

"Oh, there's plenty of time for that later," Virginia said, busying herself with pouring a watered-down glass of milk for Frances.

"What's got you so hooked?" I asked.

"Oh, nothing much," Virginia said. "We might try *Romeo and Juliet* next week. It's been ages since this poor girl went to school."

"But what do you have there?" I pointed to her pocket.

Sheepishly, Virginia pulled out *The Trouble with Blondes*.

"Are you kidding? Come on, that's not appropriate for her!"

"But she's almost fourteen!"

I was about to continue scolding until I spotted how widely Frances was grinning. "Oh, fine, if it's keeping her entertained, who am I to judge? But if she elopes from here to marry a man thirty years older than her, I hold you responsible."

"Oh pish, she wouldn't run away. I'm sure she'd invite us to the wedding, wouldn't you, sweet girl?" Virginia said, chucking Frances under the chin.

"What about your book?" I asked. "Have you been keeping up with your writing?"

Virginia smoothed her faded skirt. "I've put it away for a bit."

"But you'll keep working on it, right? Everyone looks forward to hearing you read the latest installment," Frances said.

"Sure, I'll get back to it when things settle down," Virginia said.

That book had not only been a wonderful source of distraction for the other nurses, but I knew that it was also Virginia's escape from the banality of our existence. It broke my heart to think that she was no longer writing, but I understood that it would be hard to write a romance if you had lost your faith in happy endings.

The truth was that we were running low on faith in everything.

27.

FLOR

December 1944
Manila

Every time Flor and Luchie welcomed an American operative into the apartment during the darkest hours of the night, it was both thrilling and terrifying—and far more stressful than smuggling messages in and out of Santo Tomas. Each time, the jangle of anxiety that swept through Flor as she stood in the darkness with a stranger within arm's distance almost paralyzed her. But after the initial clamp of panic loosened, she'd greet each visitor, offer a basic meal of a little tinned fish, and they'd settle down and talk about nothing important—"shooting the breeze" the men called it.

One morning at the end of December, Luchie answered the door and found her brother waiting for her. "Our father is ill. He doesn't have much longer," he said.

Stricken, Luchie turned to Flor. "I hate to leave you, but—"

"We will be fine here on our own. Please go and spend time with your father," Flor urged. "Besides, tomorrow's Christmas and you should be with your family."

Luchie scrambled to her room to grab a few possessions and when she rejoined them at the door, she grasped Flor's shoulders. "You'll stay here. Don't go out on your own. No guests." She gave Flor a knowing look.

"We have no plans," Flor said. And it was true. With so little family around and food so scarce, the holidays would be even quieter than usual this year. For the next week, no American operatives were expected to arrive.

Luchie's eyes narrowed, but her distraction was palpable, and her brother took her arm and gently led her away. When Flor closed the door behind them, she leaned against it and smiled. Though no Americans were expected to arrive, Ernesto was not working until later in the day and he usually stopped by the apartment to visit Luchie and Flor before his shift. With Gloria and Iris scheduled for an overnight shift, Flor could be alone with Ernesto for the first time. Under normal circumstances, this would be unthinkable. No reputable young woman would be alone with a man unchaperoned. But these were not normal circumstances.

She moved into the small sitting room, turned on the radio to some Christmas music, and paced, but only a few minutes passed before there was another knock. She hurried to the door, expecting to find Ernesto, but instead a young boy pushed a note into her hand and fled.

Don't forget to say your prayers tonight. —The Abbess

Flor stared at the message. This was Yasmin's code to expect an American that evening. Flor had never received such late notice of a guest. She ran into the hallway, looking for the boy, but he had vanished. The thought of being alone with an American made her breath catch in her throat. Being alone with Ernesto was one thing, but a complete stranger? She glanced at the note again, willing the wording to change. She could telephone Yasmin and tell her that tonight would not work, but as she tore the note into tiny pieces, she reconsidered her concerns. The war was coming to a close. Even though she was on her own, why not help? She had done this many times before. The men were always courteous and mindful of safety. What could possibly go wrong?

Before she lost her nerve, she raced back to the room she shared with Ate Iris to change into clean clothes because Ernesto would be arriving any minute. She would say nothing to him about the guest. Telling him now would just make things more complicated.

Minutes later, Ernesto arrived at the door. Flor covered her mouth in amazement when she saw what was in his hand: a bag of sugar.

"Where did you find this?" she asked. "Please tell me you didn't spend a fortune on it."

He looked around. "Merry Christmas! Manang Luchie will be so excited about this, won't she?"

"She would, but she's not here."

Ernesto's brow wrinkled in confusion. "Where is she?" As Flor explained, he frowned. "I should leave," he said, but Flor noticed he didn't move from his spot at the doorway so she pulled him inside, peering into the hallway first to make sure no one had seen them. As she closed the door, she smiled, suddenly shy.

Ernesto glanced at the bag of sugar still in his hands. "I suppose this is our festive treat this year. I shouldn't go until I've made sure this sugar tastes acceptable, right?" He handed it to her, grinning.

"Right, we should make sure there's nothing wrong with it." Flor's arm holding the bag trembled as she took in his golden skin and teasing smile.

"Well, go on," he urged. "Dip a finger inside."

Flor gave her index finger a quick lick and then darted it inside the canvas sack. When she pulled it out, a few granules of sugar sparkled in the sunlight. She touched her finger to her tongue and made a sound that was half delight, half sob. "It's so good."

Again, she dipped her finger, but this time she held it out to Ernesto, her face reddening as she did so. He stilled and then, keeping his gaze locked on hers, he leaned forward to suck on her finger lightly. The moment his lips grazed her skin, Flor felt a shiver run from her hand, up through her arm to her shoulder, and then it burst apart, sending firecrackers of anticipation through her.

Ernesto placed the bag of sugar on the table and Flor guided him to her bedroom in the back of the house. If Flor had learned anything, it was how quickly life could change so she held Ernesto close. Their union was clumsy, yes, but also thrilling, confounding, and comforting, all at the same time.

Afterward, as Flor lay in Ernesto's arms on her narrow bed, he traced his fingers along her rib cage. "I wish I had more food to bring, especially since it's Christmas Eve."

"It doesn't feel like Christmas, does it?"

They were silent and dozed until the late afternoon, when Ernesto unwound himself from Flor's limbs. "My shift starts soon. I'm on for the next two days because this is always a busy time at the hospital. I hope you won't be lonely."

Flor rose with him, saying she understood, and her mind raced ahead to her expected guest that evening. She braided her fingers around Ernesto's. "I'll be fine. It should be nice and quiet here."

LATE THAT EVENING, Flor fried a single egg and waited, listening for sounds outside the apartment. Shortly before midnight, two knocks made her jump. She practically leapt across the room to the door, but before opening it, she took a deep breath. Within a minute, the American was inside, standing next to her, listening for any suspicious noise outside. Flor held her breath and, out of the corner of her eye, studied the man. Tonight's arrival was tall with sandy-colored hair. "Merry Christmas," she whispered.

"Bet I'm not what you had on your Christmas list," he said, chuckling.

As she led him to the table, he took in his surroundings carefully.

"I'm sorry I don't have much to feed you. The holidays are lean this year." She placed an egg in front of him.

"Don't worry. The invasion's starting soon. Relief's coming."

"Good. We're ready." Her stomach growled as she watched him eat. She hoped he didn't hear it.

"Lily, have you been working with the resistance for long?"

She hesitated. If the invasion was almost here, she felt she could take a chance and trust this American. "Yes. I was a courier for the network between Santo Tomas and Cabanatuan before it shut down."

"What do you know about the prisoners at Santo Tomas?" the American asked.

"I haven't been in contact with anyone there since June, but it's not good. They're starving."

"Are they civilians?"

"Yes, except for a group of army nurses who arrived after Corregidor fell." She watched as the American's face stilled. He didn't touch his food, but stared at his plate without really seeing it.

"Are you looking for someone specific?" she asked gently.

"Tess Abbot."

Flor thought back to the woman who sewed her intelligence

reports. "When I was smuggling things in and out of the camp, she was one of my contacts."

Suddenly, there was a clatter from the front door. Flor froze.

"Open up," a man shouted. Fists pounded on the door.

The American appraised the room, assessing his options.

"Go to the back bedroom. There's a balcony. You can climb onto the roof," Flor whispered. "This building's connected to several others. I'll stall them for as long as possible."

The knocking got louder, the yelling increased.

"You should come too," he whispered.

Flor considered. There was no official record of her living here, so it seemed unlikely to be the Kempeitai at the door. Perhaps it was merely the authorities complaining about a blackout violation. Or making demands for lodging. These days the Japanese had many reasons to nitpick over infractions.

Running would immediately implicate her.

She shook her head. "No, I'll take my chances."

The American weighed his options, but as thuds rained down on the door with an intensity threatening to splinter the latches from the wall, he vanished into the back of the apartment.

"Coming," Flor called, walking toward the door.

When she opened it, she faced two men holding rifles with bayonets pointed at her. Both wore the dreaded Kempeitai armband and her gut knotted at the sight of its crimson kanji lettering. "Flordeliza Dalisay?"

She faltered, suddenly icy with panic. How did they know to find her here?

"Yes." She bowed deeply and the men pushed past her. She cocked an ear, listening for any sound from the back room, but heard nothing. She tried to exhale, although everything inside her seemed to wobble.

"Are you alone?" an agent barked at her.

"Yes." Thankful she hadn't sat down to join the American, she gestured at the one plate on the table as evidence.

One of the Kempeitai appeared younger than the other, more nervous, and he spun in place, still holding his rifle at the ready. The only sound came from their heavy breathing and occasional squeak of their boots on the tile floor as they peered around the apartment, finding nothing of interest. When they appeared satisfied, they prodded her with their rifles. "Come with us."

Flor's legs felt like jelly, but she nodded and led them from the apartment. Was the American watching from the rooftop? Had he run? How far could he make it in the city without being discovered?

She expected to find a truck waiting, but instead the Kempeitai indicated she should walk between them and they set off along the road. This was it, the moment she had awaited for three years. What did the Kempeitai want with her? How much did they know? The only bit of luck was that Luchie was gone. Hopefully the agency knew nothing about her. Though the air felt hot and heavy, Flor started shivering uncontrollably. She cursed herself. *Why hadn't she fled with the American? Grabbed a sweater? Left a note for Ate Iris?* Her mind spun.

She peered around the street. Was anyone watching her departure? Would anyone know what had happened? Windows remained shuttered and dark. Doors stayed closed. No sign of movement. Flor stumbled as one of the men prodded her along. She suddenly felt tiny and alone. With no one witnessing her leave, she felt as though she was vanishing.

28.

TESS

The holidays came and went and I felt like I was holding my breath, waiting for something to happen. Three months had passed since we first spotted an American plane overhead. Anticipation had grown stale. Each morning, rising out of bed became a struggle, not only because of our physical ailments—the swelling, numbness, aching joints, bleeding gums, loose teeth, incontinence—but because of the darkness that pulled at each of us, the feeling of helplessness, and our biggest fear: the Americans weren't going to arrive in time.

Our saving grace was work. No matter how slow our shuffling steps became, we made the trip to Santa Catalina to serve others. Day by day, the work saved us.

Frances left the Isolation Hospital and transferred back to Santa Catalina. I accompanied her and resumed my normal nursing shifts. One morning Commandant Hayashi arrived in our ward, demanding a meeting with the hospital's chief, Dr. Miller. Outside the frosted glass of the office door, we could hear entire the entire exchange.

"You must stop putting starvation as the cause of death on official hospital documents!" the camp's commandant demanded.

"I cannot lie about such a thing. We are not getting enough food."

The commandant stormed from the office and left. Fifteen minutes later, soldiers appeared in our ward and they dragged Dr. Miller away.

BY MID-JANUARY, SAGGY prowled the paths of camp, twirling his rifle as if he was a marching band's majorette. Everything about us annoyed him. Our slow walking. Our feeble bowing. The long lines that clogged the dining shed and the lavatory. His nightstick was kept busy hitting us for any infraction he could think of, and when he couldn't think of one, he hit us anyway.

Our guards grew increasingly quarrelsome with us—and with each other. Like a group of cats in a bag, they argued in shrill, strident voices. They also began filling the stretch between the Main Building and the front gate with weapons and barrels and they covered it all with camouflaged tarps. It did not look like they planned to surrender or leave meekly. Would they attack us? Burn us? Blow us up? We feared the worst.

A thick black acrid smoke now crept over the camp's walls, blocking the sky so we couldn't see the American bombers overhead, but we heard their handiwork. Massive explosions shook the ground. Sirens wailed. The report of artillery fire rang in the distance, along with the sound—*pop-pop-THUD!*—of nearby arsenals being destroyed. The pounding of shelling served as constant background noise. With every passing hour, the battle drew closer. The Americans *had* to arrive soon. That knowledge should have been cause for elation, but a new fear developed: What if the Japanese planned to kill us all, rather than surrender?

29.

FLOR

Crouched in a small dark cell, Flor struggled to figure out why she had been captured. Did the Kempeitai know she was operating a safe house? No, they probably wanted her for smuggling. But who gave her up? One of the priests? Had Yasmin been taken too? When Flor had been led through the hallway to her cell, she cringed at the screams of agony, the moans and weeping, and the unhinged babble of broken minds. What did the Kempeitai *do* to their prisoners?

Flor remembered that beaten body Ernesto had once shown her and shuddered. What would they put her through? Could she withstand the agonies that lay ahead? As her knees scraped against the damp, sharp stone walls of the cell that was barely as wide as she was, these questions cycled through her mind over and over.

In the darkness of her tiny cell, Flor was unsure how long she had been imprisoned. To stay calm, she tried to focus on solving math equations, but for the first time in her life, the security of numbers failed her. She clung to the walls. She tried to breathe. She prayed for strength and courage. She wanted to survive.

The sound of a latch clanking startled Flor. She squinted as light framed the opening door. Too bright!

"Come," a guard ordered.

Her feet and legs stung as she staggered to rise, but she managed to totter forward. He led her into a room and pointed to a table and chair. Behind them, a window revealed a glimmer of the bay. On the table sat a bowl of thin lugao, but no fork or spoon. She sat.

The door swung shut and she was left alone, eyeing the food. The gruel appeared to be moving, wriggling. She blinked to steady her vision. Worms. She bit her lip and hesitated. Who knew when she'd be offered more to eat? She needed to be smart and keep herself strong. With her bare hands, she dug into the rotten gruel, downing it as quickly as possible, and then she felt a little more clearheaded.

Minutes later, two men arrived, an interrogator and a translator.

"You sit like this," the translator demanded as he stretched Flor's filthy arms straight in front of her. "Place your palms down and hold that position."

Flor followed his directive, and he peppered her with basic questions. Her name. Where she lived. Family members. In her weakened state, her arms began to tremble within minutes. She watched the shaking and felt the burn in her shoulders and knew she needed to refocus. She shifted her gaze to the translator.

"Have you visited Santo Tomas since January 1942?" he asked.

Flor paused, but she knew she needed to stay as close to the truth as possible. "Yes."

"For what purpose?"

"To deliver food to the internees."

"Did you deliver anything else?"

"Yes, I brought mosquito nets and some provisions from the Red Cross."

"Did you bring money?"

Flor's mind raced, but before she could answer—*SMACK!*— the interrogator leaned forward and slapped her.

She nodded slowly. "Yes, I did."

"Did this money come from the Red Cross?"

Flor thought quickly. No real harm could come from this admission. Though she had always hidden the money so the guards didn't take any of it, it hadn't been illegal to bring it in. Before she could answer, the interrogator reached forward and slapped her again, and this time, he put his weight and fury into it. Flor felt something crack and pop in the back of her mouth. A molar loosened. Her eyes teared as she said, "Friends of the internees gave it to me. People living freely outside the camps."

"Is it true you were scheduled to sail for the United States on Monday, December 8, 1941?"

Flor blinked at the unexpected line of questioning. "I was."

"Have you at any time served as an agent of the United States?"

Right at that moment, an air-raid siren began to wail. Flor could hear footsteps running along the outside hallway. The interrogator and translator started to argue with each other and then abruptly stood and left the room. Within a minute, a guard dragged Flor back to her cell. When he slammed the door closed behind her, all sound from the outside vanished. Flor ran her tongue over her aching molar. It was definitely loose, but if that was the only injury she had sustained, she knew to count herself lucky.

30.

TESS

By early February, the guards started acting even more strangely, more on edge. One afternoon, Saggy yelled at us to stay indoors so we piled into the Main Building. Nell stood sentry in a window, peering out into the dusk for some sign of action.

The power switched off and darkness overtook us.

"They're going to burn us alive!" a voice shrieked.

"I swear, I saw the bastards putting dynamite under the stairs!" another woman yelled.

But a loud unidentifiable rumble drowned out the women's shouting. In the dark, the whites of everyone's eyes glowed. *What was that sound?* Virginia grabbed my arm, I held Frances tight.

Machine-gun fire. A snapping sound of flares. The dense, smoky air over the plaza brightened. And then—*CRASH!* Thunder rumbled at the front gate.

"Oh my god," Mabel moaned.

Nell pressed her face against the window. "Tanks! I see tanks crashing through the gates! They're coming straight for us!"

"But *who* are they?" Mabel wailed.

We quieted, listening to the sound of the approaching tank.

It stopped. No one breathed as the metallic clang of the its door opening rang across the courtyard.

"Hello, folks!" a man's voice called out. "We're here!"

An American voice!

We scrambled toward the stairs, our movement more slow ooze than wild stampede. Our cries and laughter and praying created chaos as we swarmed out of the Main Building toward the soldier waiting for us on the plaza.

Grinning, he hopped up onto the front of the tank and removed his helmet. "Say, aren't you gals a sight for sore eyes? Hello! We're your Forty-Fourth Tank Battalion from the good ol' U.S. of A!" More men emerged from inside the tank.

And at that moment, Rosemary closed her eyes and her voice rang out over the plaza.

"God bless America,
Land that I love."

Her voice contained a clarity and joy that none of us had heard in years. Different tones and accents merged as we all joined in. The voices of the soldiers served as a strong, steady, and deep unwavering force. Tears flooded my eyes.

"Stand beside her,
And guide her,
Through the night
With a Light
From above."

When we finished the song, we surged toward the soldiers and they hugged us and handed out chocolate bars, ration tins, and cigarettes with a casual generosity that we hadn't seen in three years.

"You're so big! I've never seen such handsome soldiers," Captain Davison said in a tone so girlish and naive that all of us fell against each other, laughing. The Andrews Sisters rang from the loudspeaker. There would be no sleep for anyone that night. At one point, a soldier handed me a bar of soap and I held it to my nose and inhaled. Right then and there, I decided if I ever went to heaven, it would smell just like that. Ivory soap.

AS THE CELEBRATION really got rolling, news spread through the crowd that Commandant Hayashi had taken a couple hundred men and boys hostage in the Education Building. Women peeled off from the plaza to check on the status of their husbands and sons, but most of the internees continued wandering around in a happy daze, even as the sound of the assault on Manila continued outside the camp's high walls.

Virginia, Mabel, Frances, and I were walking through the first floor of the Main Building when screams and howling stopped us in our tracks. The commotion seemed to come from one of the administrative offices so we poked our heads in the doorway to see what was happening.

"You miserable shitface!" a woman yelped, standing over someone on the floor. I pushed my way through the melee. There lay Saggy, huddled into a ball, his uniform torn to shreds. Half his right ear had been sliced off. Another woman squatted next to him, methodically placing a burning cigarette to the bare flesh of his chest.

"Cut off his balls and stuff them in his mouth," an old woman sneered.

The crowd howled with the fury of a pack of feral dogs.

I felt little surprise at the crowd's vindictiveness. In the wild emotional swings of liberation, anger was a close cousin to exhilaration. It had been simmering within all of us for three years. I put my fists on my hips and surveyed the scene. Should we walk away? Let them finish what they started? Leave the man to die in his own blood and urine? For an instant I was taken back to standing in front of the Education Building, tears streaming down my face as I wound up my arm to slap Mabel. The humiliation of that moment still had so much power over me. I gritted my teeth and eyed the blood-speckled foam on Saggy's lips. The temptation to let that horrible man suffer was great.

But then, without speaking, Mabel, Virginia, and I fell upon our nurse's training and we encircled the downed Japanese guard.

"Y'all make room," Virginia hollered. The violent orgy was over and everyone knew it.

"Go find a few soldiers," I urged Frances, and the girl vanished amid the angry faces surrounding us.

Blood poured from a wound on the side of Saggy's torso and foam bubbled from his cracked lips. "How did he get shot?" I asked the crowd. "Who the hell has a gun?"

My question prompted the crowd to drain from the room just as a pair of American soldiers entered. They scooped the guard from the floor as though he was little more than a child. Would I have lost any sleep if Saggy had been killed by the mob? No, in fact I might have slept better knowing he could never instill his brand of sadism on anyone else, but playing a small role in restoring humanity to our surroundings allowed me to breathe past a space in my lungs that hadn't received air in a very long time. No matter the nationality of the patient underneath our hands, no matter the person's history, we were healers. Watching the soldiers cart Saggy away, I exhaled. We were free, and that knowledge felt better than eating any chocolate bar ever would.

When we stepped into the courtyard to head to Santa Catalina with the Americans carrying Saggy, I realized Frances was missing.

"Where did the girl go? She's small. Brunette." I grabbed a soldier's sleeve. "The one who came to get you—what happened to her?"

"Our commander was looking for someone who could help come to terms with the enemy. He asked who in the camp spoke Japanese, and she said she does. A British fella too, but we all got a kick out of the girl."

"So she left with your commander?"

"Yep. I hope one of the press photographers gets a shot of her negotiating with the Japanese for their surrender." I must have looked panicked because he added kindly, "Don't worry, one of your nurses went with her to chaperone. A blonde. A real tall drink of water."

Virginia nodded, satisfied. "Must have been Nell."

"Think you could introduce me to her later?" the soldier said, grinning as he chewed on some gum loudly.

"Ha, she'd eat you for breakfast," Virginia said.

"I'll take my chances."

"Then sure." Virginia smiled at me, a full smile that reached her eyes. Even after three years of being locked up and starved, we could still get a date if we wanted. I glanced at my bloodstained hands and shoved them into my pockets. Or at least Nell could.

"Tell me," I said to the soldiers, "do you know anything about other American units moving in? I'm looking for George Walsh. He's in MacArthur's circle."

The jovial expressions on the men grew solemn. "MacArthur's making his way down from Lingayen, but it's slow going. The Japanese aren't giving anything up easily."

"He works in military intel and might have been running other missions."

"Listen, it's not great out there. This whole city's been booby-trapped. These bastards"—he gave the stretcher a contemptuous shake and Saggy groaned—"are fighting to the last soldier. We'll keep our ears open for your man Walsh, but this place is chaos."

"Thank you. I'm Tess Abbott."

"Got it. Miss Abbott, I hope we can deliver your man to you, but be patient. Line up all your good luck charms and pray a lot."

A FEW DAYS later, General MacArthur visited camp. He emerged from a jeep on the plaza, his signature corncob pipe poking out from the side of his mouth, and proceeded to give the boisterous crowd on hand a rousing speech. I pressed to the front of everyone, searching for George, but there was no sign of him at the general's side.

I followed MacArthur through the sea of grateful internees, studying the faces of his entourage, and then trailed him as he greeted the troops who'd set up camp inside the main gate. The smell of fried eggs and bacon made my mouth water and one of the GIs—I'd just learned that's what the soldiers were called now—handed me a mug of coffee. I drank it gratefully and looked for any sign of George among the tents and cooking fires dotting the area.

By the time I'd made it to the front gate, MacArthur loaded back into his jeep and sped off down Calle España.

A GI approached me. "Hey, sweetheart, you shouldn't be standing here. Snipers would love to make a mess of your pretty face." A series of explosions rumbled from the north, making me wince. I spotted the patch over his breast pocket identifying him as Private Higgins.

"Higgins, why's there so much water?" I asked pointing at the stream of murk running over my tattered shoes.

"The Japanese blasted a water main. Jesus, they're bent on destroying as much as they can. I know the general just told all of you we've won Manila, but we're still fighting this damn thing."

I looked at the stone wall next to me. The smell of burning rubber and something more noxious wafted over us. Would I ever find George? I was so tired, so bone-crushingly tired. I started crying.

"Oh shoot, I'm sorry." Higgins held out a handkerchief. "Don't worry, we'll fix the water and—"

A shot rang out and dinged a hole a few yards away from us on the side of the guard's hut. Higgins grabbed my arm, pulling me behind a pile of sandbags.

"I'm looking for George Walsh. He should be here," I blubbered, my tears turning into convulsive sobs. I was so tired of waiting for him.

"Walsh, huh?"

"Yes, *George Walsh*. I'd hoped he'd come with—" My explanation was lost in an outburst of nearby machine-gun fire.

"Hold on," Higgins said, squatting down and tugging my shoulder lower so we were both fully hidden behind the wall of sandbags. The grinding crunch of a tank rolling down the street cut off our conversation, but he gestured at me to follow him.

Crouched behind the wall of sandbags, we scurried away from the perimeter of the camp and deeper into where the troops had set up their tents. "There was a guy who came with the brass, but he took a group of newly arrived nurses over to the camp's hospital. I think you gals are getting relieved and will be heading home soon."

I must have looked like I was about to keel over, because Higgins grabbed my shoulders. "Whoa there. Deep breaths, deep breaths," he said, guiding me to sit on an overturned bucket.

"I'm going home?" I murmured in a daze.

"Well, I don't know for sure, but seems like you gals have earned it."

I gawked at him. If I went home, how would I find George? But also: If I was sent home, wouldn't I be free of this nightmare?

"What's going on, Higs?" another GI asked. "Is she all right?"

"She's fine. Just hungry, I think. She's looking for a guy named Walsh. Was that the name of the fella taking the new nurses over to the hospital?"

The newly arrived GI handed me his canteen and indicated I should take a drink. "I think so."

"I need to find him. I need to go there," I said, struggling to my feet.

"Hold up, you're not walking anywhere looking pale like that. Let me give you a ride." The GI jabbed his thumb in the direction of a jeep. "Want to go for a spin?"

AFTER WHAT FELT like the longest five minutes of my life, we screeched to a halt in front of Santa Catalina. Though the whine of nearby shells could be heard when the jeep's engine stopped, Higgins hopped from the back seat and proffered his arm with the flair of a gallant knight. My legs wobbled, but I laughed and climbed down so he could guide me up the steps of the convent. *What if George isn't really here?* I feared getting my hopes up, only to have them dashed.

As we pushed through the front door, a sea of faces turned toward us. Faces brightened with shiny lipstick, rosy cheeks. Faces framed by glossy, thick, curled hair. The new nurses were gorgeous. Next to them, I suddenly felt like a shriveled-up old lady. And that's when a whole new fear struck me: What if George *was* here? Would he even still want to see me? Almost three long years had passed and I could barely walk on my own. I was practically a ghost! What if I disgusted him?

My steps faltered, and against my will, my tears returned. At the expressions of pity crossing these women's faces, I wanted to disappear.

"Hey, is there a George Walsh here?" Higgins called. "I've got his girl."

And that's when I saw him. Under an archway at the far end to the lobby, George appeared. Tall. Broad-shouldered. Straight-backed. His familiar blue eyes widened at the sight of me and then he smiled, the biggest smile I'd ever seen. Behind him, Virginia and Nell appeared with their hands clasped over their heads in victory. I started to collapse and he rushed toward me, wrapped his arms around my waist, and planted a huge kiss on my lips.

When we broke apart, Virginia and Nell were dancing some sort of crazy jig. The nurses were cheering, Higgins was hollering, my friends were singing, and the whole place erupted into a joyous riot. George lifted me into the air and spun me, until everything became a blur—a big, colorful, loud blur. When he lowered me, I squeezed my arms around his shoulders and decided that no matter what came at me—the emperor, General

Homma, and the whole Japanese Imperial Army—I was never letting go of George again. That life he had promised me when we had sat outside the Malinta Tunnel, our future together? I was ready to start it right then.

But things don't always work out the way we hope. By that night, George was gone and I was alone again.

31.

FLOR

The next time Flor was pulled from her cell, she had no idea how many days had passed. She had lost count of how many times food was pushed inside her cell. Only one thing was certain: she smelled terrible.

"Come," the guard snarled.

But when she tried to stand, her legs burned as if on fire. The guard gave an impatient growl and grabbed her arm, nearly tearing her shoulder from her socket, and then he dragged her along the hallway to an interrogation room. In the distance, Flor could hear the sound of raised voices.

When they arrived in the interrogation room this time, there was no table. Only two chairs faced a black iron ring hanging from the ceiling. A cold sweat prickled Flor's skin.

The guard pulled a length of rope off his belt and tossed it through the iron ring above them. He grunted that Flor should step closer. She did so on trembling legs. He bound her wrists together with one side of the rope. With the opposite end in his meaty hands, he moved toward a cleat on the wall that Flor hadn't noticed. He pulled on the rope and Flor's wrists rose with a jerk. She let out a cry as he pulled tighter. By this point, she was hanging by her wrists. The guard eyed her feet carefully and adjusted the rope's tension.

Flor scrabbled at the damp stone floor with the tips of her big toes, trying to find purchase, anything to ease the weight off her upper body. Her wrists and shoulders burned painfully, but only the tips of her toes grazed the floor. She dangled at a height that made finding relief impossible.

"Shut up," the guard snapped.

She hadn't even realized she'd been whimpering.

Her interrogator and translator arrived and took seats, their faces impenetrable as they watched Flor twist at her binding. They briefly conferred with the guard, who disappeared. A moment later, he returned with a small table he placed next to the interrogator.

The interrogator reached into the briefcase he'd placed on the floor and removed a stack of notebooks. He placed them on the small table. Flor squinted through her blurry vision and spotted her accounting notebooks.

"You worked as a bookkeeper?" the interpreter asked.

"Yes," Flor said. As she stared at them, her vision swam. Images of the men multiplied horizontally across her line of vision.

"Who were your clients?"

If they had her notebooks, there was no use in lying. She listed each one, including Club Sampaguita. Sweat poured off her as she tried to breathe through the pain of the ropes digging into her wrists, the torturous elongating of her arms and shoulders.

As she spoke in between gasps, the interpreter jotted down names. When she reached the end of her list, an enormous explosion shook the area. Even surrounded by the fifteen-foot-thick walls of Fort Santiago, the table shuddered and the interpreter's hand slipped as he wrote, leaving a smear of ink across the page.

Again, the men began jabbering at each other. A minute later, they stalked from the room.

While she was alone, Flor wriggled and used her toes to turn herself toward the window, but she gasped as she felt the cords of her arms tear against her weight. Black smoke drifted by the window, filling the room with a pungent chemical reek. Another blast rocked the earth and Flor moaned as her shoulders seemed to tear against the pressure. She could barely breathe through the heat of the room and the panic inside her. Even if the Americans did arrive, did it matter? Would her captors leave her behind to burn?

A guard arrived in the doorway. His gaze darted toward the window, panic evident on his face.

"Please let me go," Flor pleaded. "Save yourself, but please let me out of here."

His face screwed into an angry twist and he hauled off and slapped her across the cheeks. The taste of blood filled Flor's mouth. She spit it out. He untied her and she fell to the floor, weeping.

The guard gave her a kick to prompt her to move, but her arms could scarcely hold her weight. In agony, somehow she crawled back to her cell. The voices of other prisoners filled the corridor, screaming and begging to be released.

THE SAME INTERROGATION pattern occurred several more times. Each session revealed more sounds of chaos outside the prison—shouting, explosions, sirens. Time became a blur. Flor saw little daylight and barely received anything to eat. Her mind became a churning stew of visions, voices, loud sounds, and pain. Luchie embraced her, whispering, *Have faith. I'm waiting for you.* Ate Iris, Yasmin, and Father Callahan cried,

Don't tell them about the laundry. Say nothing about the money from Club Sampaguita. Ernesto appeared and wrapped his arms around her. Were these visits real? She could no longer tell. Her head grew hot, but her feet and hands felt freezing. Her teeth clacked together, her shoulders trembled. Was she still in Fort Santiago? Was she on a boat? She had no idea.

ONE DAY, HER door clanged open. Flor cowered against the light. Two guards lifted her by her arms and let her legs drag along behind, her bare feet scraping against the sharp edges of the paving stones. Next thing she knew, she was lying outside the prison's gate.

The courtyard felt abandoned. Dark smoke snaked over her and she spluttered and coughed. In the distance, thunder rumbled. It was dark as if a storm was on the way. Flor swallowed and her dry, hot throat stung. Now she understood why Iris spoke so little about Bataan and Corregidor. Miserable, trying times do not lend themselves to being revisited. Flor wanted to forget her imprisonment had ever happened.

"Flor, I'm here," a voice whispered. Flor felt herself being lifted. She squinted into the hazy light and a familiar face came into focus above her. Luchie! Flor could have cried with relief, but she was spent and had nothing left.

"You're safe now," Luchie said.

The slightest movement set off a series of aches and stings and Flor almost laughed. She knew she'd never be safe from the memories of what had happened to her at Fort Santiago. But she also knew she could survive anything.

32.

TESS

February 1945
Santo Tomas Internment Camp

In Santa Catalina, George pulled me from the crowd in the lobby and Virginia led us to the back of the convent where a narrow stairway existed for servants.

"Virginia, I'll take care of her, don't worry," George said.

"Far be it from me to slow you down, soldier." Virginia laughed and left. George scooped me into his arms effortlessly and climbed the stairs.

"I'm so weak now," I lamented, and then poked his neck. "But why's your skin so yellow?"

"Atabrine, it's a new malaria medicine. I'll tell you what, there's a lot to catch up on," he said entering a small ward containing five beds, all empty. The glass of the windowpanes rattled as explosions erupted outside the camp's walls. "Oh, hey, guess who I ran into?"

There were so many men I'd spent the last few years wondering about. Our patients. The doctors. The orderlies. I didn't even know where to start guessing. "Who?" I asked.

"Greasy. Turns out he was rescued from Cabanatuan. He's pretty worn out, but he'll make it. When I last saw him, he was trying to score a date with a group of nurses."

"A group?" I laughed, but tears pricked at my eyes. I could

scarcely imagine how he'd managed to make it through that horrible place. "Some things never change, I guess."

"I guess not."

I watched him laugh, suddenly at a loss for words. Did he really believe that Greasy hadn't changed at all? Did he think I was the same girl he'd left behind on Corregidor? While I knew little about his life in Australia, I sensed he had no idea how hard things had been here.

George reached into his pocket and held up a can. "Look, I come bearing gifts."

"Evaporated milk . . ." I breathed, watching him open it with a knife. He added water from his canteen and placed it in my hands before turning away to sort through his pack. While his back was to me, I practically inhaled the milk and tried to lick every last drop from my lips.

When he turned and saw the empty can and my sheepish expression, his face crumpled into sorrow. "What have they done to you?"

"Nothing, I'm fine," I said, sliding the can onto a bedside table. Suddenly I was all too aware of my threadbare clothes, my toothpick-thin legs, my matted, stringy hair. Visions of the newly arrived nurses downstairs made my skin heat with embarrassment.

"Of course you are," he said brightly, though his gaze wandered along the patches and embroidery I'd added to my skirt to keep it held together. "We'll get you squared away in no time. In fact, you and the other nurses are being flown to a hospital on Leyte. All you'll have to do is sit in the sun, swim, and eat." A particularly loud explosion outside caused us to shudder.

"When do we leave?"

"This evening."

"So soon! But what about you? You'll stay here?" I could hear the panic in my voice. I'd made the mistake of letting us separate once before and I wasn't doing that again.

George sat next to me on the cot and kissed my forehead. "You'll go, but MacArthur himself approved me for twenty-four hours of R and R. I'll meet you on Leyte."

"When?"

"In four days. And I happen to have something planned for us while we're there." He pulled a small velvet box from his pocket and held it out. "Tess Abbott, will you marry me?"

My eyes almost popped out of my head as I glimpsed a solitaire diamond resting on a thin gold band. "You've been carrying that around all this time?"

He laughed. "That's all you have to say?"

"Of course I'll marry you," I said as he slid the band onto my finger. It boggled my mind to imagine a world in which he had gone to a store and bought a diamond ring sometime recently.

I spun it on my shrunken finger. "It's too big. Maybe you should keep it instead."

"Nope, it's staying with you. I'll bet one of the girls downstairs will give us a chain so you can wear it around your neck."

Tears had been threatening to spill ever since I'd seen the ring and now they began to roll down my cheeks in earnest. The idea that one of the nurses downstairs would simply give away a chain was too much for me to imagine. A week ago, any of us in the camp practically would've killed for something of value like that to trade for food.

"Pretty, isn't it?" he asked, admiring the ring on my hand, and I realized he assumed I was crying from happiness. But instead of explaining myself, I leaned forward and kissed him.

From now on, I only wanted to look forward.

BACK AT THE Main Building, Captain Davison cemented the plan for our departure. "Pack, say your goodbyes, and be ready to meet outside in the plaza in an hour. Don't be late."

As she spoke, the building shook under the impact of shells hitting the clock tower on the roof above us. Chunks of plaster tumbled to the floor and we covered our heads with our hands.

"Can we leave sooner?" Rosemary asked, squinting nervously toward the ceiling. "I could be ready in ten minutes."

Captain Davison gave a wary glance toward the main doors. "Actually let's meet inside, right here instead. Be back as soon as you can and maybe we'll leave sooner."

Nell, Virginia, and the others headed toward the stairs, but I picked my way through the clusters of nurses to find Captain Davison. "Excuse me, ma'am. What about Frances? May I bring her with us?"

Captain Davison's eyes were pink-rimmed, but her voice rang clear. "No, she will stay here under civilian control. They'll retain custody of her for the time being and will reunite her with her remaining family."

"I admit, it's an unusual situation, but—"

"The army can't take possession of a young girl. You know that." The older woman shook her head with impatience, but I remembered how Josie had stuck up for the Filipino nurses on Bataan and I refused to be put off.

"But she—"

"No, not another word about this. There's no time for this foolishness." Captain Davison brushed me aside and moved toward a circle of officers waiting to speak with her. Josie gave me a sympathetic pat on the shoulder.

"The girl will be all right," Josie said.

The smell of smoke had made its way into the building. I gestured at the haze enveloping us. "Will she? This place is turning into a battlefield."

"Have some faith. That girl is stronger than you think. Now, go and get ready to leave." Josie turned away.

I was practically light-headed with frustration, but reluctantly, I joined the other nurses upstairs. When I entered our classroom, Mabel began to hum "Here Comes the Bride" and the other girls joined in until they saw my expression. The song trailed off.

"What's wrong?" Virginia asked.

I told them about Frances and everyone's faces fell.

"Sorry, but I can see why we can't take her," Mabel said. "It's better if she stays with other children who need help. Or maybe if she stays with a family."

"You think she's better off with that awful Mrs. Blake?" I asked.

"It won't be for long," Virginia said.

But it didn't matter to me if it was one hour, one week, or one year. I'd promised I'd watch out for her. How did no one understand this?

Virginia dropped her embroidery kit into her duffel, but I noticed she shoved her pile of notebooks under her cot.

"You're not leaving those behind are you?" I asked, pointing at them. "Don't you need to finish your manuscript?"

"No, I don't want to lug these ratty things back home." She wrinkled her nose. "I'll bet a big family of bedbugs has taken up residence in them. They probably won't even pass inspection anyway."

I was about to protest, but she shoved my duffel toward me. "Knock off your nagging and pack up your stuff so we can find Frances and say goodbye, and then let's get the hell out of here.

Doesn't it feel like we've been awaiting this day forever? Just imagine the food we'll eat. The clean bedding. New clothes." Her eyes grew misty as she stared into the distance.

"I'm ready!" Nell lifted her duffel in the air. "Let's go!"

I went through the motions of gathering my few possessions. We had been awaiting liberation for so long. I could barely even imagine what normal life could be like. Three meals a day on clean china. Real shoes without holes. Clean socks and underwear. Toothpaste.

With my duffel in my hand, I followed the others downstairs, expecting a bit of time to find Frances and say goodbye, but Captain Davison and Josie were waiting for us in the lobby. "We're leaving now. The streets around here are growing more dangerous with every passing minute. Let's go through the back of the building where some trucks are waiting."

The crowd surged away, but I slowed, grabbing Virginia's sleeve. "Wait, what about Frances? We need to say goodbye!"

"She'll understand. Everyone will tell her we had to go."

Outside, George met us by the trucks and wrapped his arms around me. "I'll see you in four days," he said, kissing me. "Get some sleep and—"

I pulled away. "There's a girl that I've been looking after. Her name's Frances Burns, she's got straight, dark shoulder-length hair. She just had her fourteenth birthday. She's on her own and has no family here. Can you pass a message to her for me?"

"I'll do what I can, but I'm clearing out of here shortly too," he said. "Trust me, she'll be fine. A lot of assistance will be rolling in here within the next day or so."

Before I could say more, I was lifted into one of the trucks. The small plaza was dark with thick smoke. Tiny flakes of ash fell through the air like snow. Breathing hurt and my eyes stung. Though we were filthy and slick with sweat, the other nurses were singing and laughing, but I craned my head to peer between the tarp cover and the edge of the truck, searching the haziness for any sign of Frances. Where the dickens was she? Overhead, the sky glowed an otherworldly shade of red. If there was a hell on earth, this was it.

"Go, go, go!" a voice shouted and the truck engines roared to life. Our caravan rolled toward the gate on Calle Dapitan, and I searched the people waving at us for a glimpse of Frances. Should I have insisted on not leaving? Maybe I could have stayed behind with the new nurses and continued to watch over Frances. We could have sailed back home together.

"Stop worrying about her," Virginia whispered. "She's busy being the hero as she negotiates with the Japanese, remember?"

I closed my eyes, trying to push my guilt away. I couldn't think about Frances anymore. I had done the best I could. Everyone told me she'd be fine, so I needed to believe them.

When the truck rounded the gate, everyone cheered. The high wall of Santo Tomas receded.

I pulled the thin gold chain from around my neck and fingered the ring George had given me only hours earlier. *My new life is finally beginning.* I couldn't believe it. He had told me that he'd return and he had. As we picked up speed, my hair whipped around my face, and I smiled, suddenly giddy. Joy filled my chest. A weight lifted from me. This was what freedom felt like. I'd been waiting three long years for this moment! The war wasn't over, but it would be soon and we were finally heading home. No more waiting in line for rotten lugao, no more mosquito and bedbug bites, no more loudspeaker announcements and music blaring at us all day long, and no more sharing a single toilet with one hundred other women.

I looked around at the thin, weary-looking faces smudged with dirt surrounding me. Everyone looked happy, but stunned.

It was hard to believe our nightmare was over. Several years earlier, we had arrived in the Philippines in search of adventure, a sense of purpose, camaraderie—even a little romance—but we had experienced so much more than we'd ever imagined. Virginia, Mabel, Nell, Josie, and the others—I'd come to love these women. For over three years, they had been my whole world. I'd worked alongside them, laughed, cried, prayed, and we had made it. Since this war had begun we hadn't lost one of our own. Not a single army nurse had died. There were many reasons to account for this, but more than anything, I knew I had these women to thank for my survival. I reached for Virginia's hand and held it tightly. We all had saved one another.

33.

FLOR

Flor's eyes flickered open to see only a dishwater-gray haze. She could smell smoke.

"Ate?" she whispered. Iris and Luchie leaned into her line of vision.

"She's awake," Luchie said, a note of triumph in her voice.

"You're in Gloria's apartment," Iris whispered.

Trembling, Flor lifted her hand to study her fingers in wonderment. "My nails are so pink and clean," she mused.

The ack-ack of distant artillery fire caused the three women to flinch.

"Before I put you to bed, I managed to wash you." Iris placed a hand on Flor's forehead and frowned. "How are you feeling? On top of general exhaustion, dehydration, and hunger, I think you caught malaria in Fort Santiago."

At Iris's touch, Flor's eyes filled at her ate's kindness. "Thank you," she rasped. Her bone-dry throat ached for a drink and Iris helped her to raise a glass of water. Flor gulped it down.

"How long have I been back?" she asked.

"Four days," Luchie said. "Today is February twelfth. You disappeared on Christmas. I prayed for you every day."

"Manang Luchie did more than pray. She went to Fort Santiago and waited every afternoon to see if you had been released," Iris said.

"Where's Ernesto?" Flor asked.

"Working at the hospital. He's been beside himself with worry about you."

"We all have been." Luchie's eyes filled with tears. "I should never have left you that night."

Flor wanted to argue, but she was so tired. "I felt your prayers," she said and then she closed her eyes. More than a month and a half spent at Fort Santiago—but she had survived. If they had washed her, they'd seen the marks on her body. She was grateful they asked no questions. She felt Iris slide into bed beside her. They wrapped their arms around each other and wept.

DURING FLOR'S IMPRISONMENT, conditions in the city had changed dramatically. From what Flor could see when she peered out the window, the port was no longer the source of the flames. The fires were creeping closer. Because of the black smoke clogging the air, day and night blended together to create what felt like an endless continuum of waiting. A fine scrim of soot seemed to cover every surface in the apartment, no matter how many times they wiped it away.

Apparently the Kempeitai had returned to the apartment several days after Flor's arrest and seized her accounting notebooks. No one had been home, but returning to the apartment and finding it ransacked proved too much for Gloria. She left Manila to stay with relatives. Many of Iris's other friends also left, but she and Luchie stayed in Malate, hopeful that Flor would reappear.

Early in the siege, the power went out. Before the water was turned off, Iris and Luchie had filled the tub and a bunch of pails with water. The women had no access to radio and therefore no idea what was happening beyond the walls of their apartment. In the days since Flor had reappeared, occasionally neighbors banged on the door to yell they were fleeing for sanctuary in one of the local churches, but Flor resisted.

"We need to stay here," she said.

"But going to one of the churches will be safe. No one will hurt people in a sanctuary," Luchie said.

Flor and Iris exchanged looks. They had little doubt the enemy wouldn't hesitate to gain any advantage it could. Nowhere was safe. Not even churches. Flor realized sadly that their roles had changed. For her entire life, Flor had been protected by Luchie and Iris, but now she understood how power and cruelty worked, and she would do anything to protect them from learning the same devastating lessons she had.

After a week of being holed up in the apartment, the women were down to their final quarter bucket of water and only two cans of food. Every few minutes, the floor and furniture rocked from nearby explosions. The air in the apartment felt thick with smoke and heat. With the constant grit of soot settling on her tongue and scraping against her teeth, Flor could taste violence and destruction. In the late hours of that evening, someone pounded on the apartment's door.

"Flor? Iris? It's me, Ernesto!"

Surprised, the women looked at each other and then set upon moving away the table and chairs they had pushed against the door. When they opened it, he fell inside. Hunched over, wheezing against the smoke, he tugged off a filthy bandanna wrapped across the lower half of his face. Flor could see the whites of his eyes, those beautiful, kind eyes that had captivated her, but they now looked red-rimmed, tired, and afraid. "Flor, thank God, you're back."

She wanted only to sink into his chest. It had been too long since she had last felt his heart beat against hers, and she closed her eyes, pressing away the memory of Fort Santiago and the dangers lurking outside. Ernesto was finally *here* with her, and for the moment, it was all that mattered. Underneath the coating of grime, she could see tracks of smooth, golden skin and she wished she could kiss him. But with Luchie and Iris watching them, she settled for resting her palm atop his hand. Deep in her belly, she felt that electrifying jolt as they touched briefly. "I'm fine."

Luchie led them into the kitchen, where she lit three of the candles they had been saving. A halo of golden light danced around the room, momentarily lending some brightness to the space. Iris pushed a chair toward him and Ernesto dropped onto it, groaning.

"I have barely anything to feed you," Luchie lamented.

"You three must come to the hospital with me until the Americans arrive. It's no longer safe here. The Japanese are moving into this neighborhood and it's only a matter of days, maybe hours, before it's destroyed. We'll leave at first light."

As much as Flor feared leaving the safety of the house, she desperately didn't want to be separated from Ernesto again.

Iris's face grew pale. "But there's nowhere to hide on the streets."

"It's only a few blocks away," Flor countered.

"And we can't go in the dark. Trust me, it's a miracle I made it here tonight. The streets are mined and we need to be able to see where we're going." Ernesto's voice grew hoarse. "Nothing good will come from the four of us being captured in the dark. *Nothing.*"

The report of rifle fire made them stiffen. It sounded close. And then screams sliced into the darkness, shouting, and then more rifle shots. Silence.

"We will go with Ernesto," Flor announced.

He said, "When we leave, dress as men. If they find you're . . ."

Iris didn't let him finish. "Gloria's father left some old clothes in the big bedroom's wardrobe. We can wear those."

"Only dark clothes, please," he added, wiping his hand across his forehead. It was then that the glistening of splattered blood on his sleeve became visible.

"What happened?" Luchie fussed. "Are you injured?"

He turned his right hand toward the candlelight and inspected its front and back. "I was too late to help someone," he said in a voice scratchy with exhaustion. He fell quiet, slumped in the chair.

Flor poured a small amount of water from a pail onto a rag and began to sponge off his hands. Out of the corner of her eye, Flor saw Luchie stiffen at the intimacy of the gesture, but she said nothing. Iris watched, making no protest of the use of their diminishing water supply.

"We should get some rest," Iris said. "Ernesto, you can sleep on the couch."

He nodded and stood. They left him and retreated to the bedrooms in the back of the apartment.

Flor crawled into bed beside Iris. After a few minutes, when she heard her sister's breath even into sleep, she tiptoed from the room they shared.

She found Ernesto lying on the couch, an arm thrown over his face. She knelt beside him and whispered gently into his ear.

"Are you asleep, my love?"

He slid his arm from his face and she could hear a smile in his voice. "I've been waiting for you."

THEY ROSE IN the dark. In the kitchen, Luchie tucked their last two cans of food into her pockets as Ernesto handed them each a rag to tie over their noses and mouths. "Wear this to prevent coughing from the smoke. We must be as quiet as possible. And if they catch us, take this." He handed them each a pill. Flor studied hers for a moment. She never planned on being imprisoned again. Without comment, she tucked hers into her hair and then wrapped a rag around her head. When she looked up, she realized Luchie and Iris had been watching her, and with unsteady hands, they imitated what she had done.

Ernesto wiped soot along the women's faces to complete their camouflage. "As soon as we get outside, you're going to need to follow me exactly where I step. If something happens to me, go to the hospital, the back entrance of the same building with the emergency room. Ready?"

Flor couldn't bear to spend another minute waiting. "Let's go."

Ernesto cracked open the door and Flor felt like they were stepping off a cliff into the unknown.

A weird twilight hung over them, despite the fact that it must have only been around six in the morning. Tiny gray bits of ash floated in the air, and it almost would have been beautiful, except for the ominous silence. Before advancing through the smoke veiling the street, Ernesto studied the surrounding roofline and windows. He then slunk along the wall of the building in the direction of the hospital before turning to the women and pointing to where they should step. Flor barely breathed as they crept down the block.

From down the street, there was shouting. She lowered into a half crouch behind Ernesto.

The sudden crack of rifle fire popped from somewhere nearby.

Hunched over, they skittered along the gates lining the street, stopping every few steps to check their surroundings. When they reached the intersection, Flor gasped. The smell! Sewage ran down the street from a burst line, and a horrible stench blew with the smoke, a stench so pungent that Flor could taste it. She gagged but continued to inch forward. Craters dotted the main street and lumps lay intermittently along the stretch of road, but it took Flor a moment to realize she was looking at bloated, dismembered corpses. In her ear, Iris whispered, "Don't look at them."

The wide street, though empty of any obvious action, offered few places to hide, but they had to cross it to continue toward the hospital. Again, through the billowing smoke, Ernesto's gaze roved over the rooftops and Flor found herself staring in empty windows looking for any sign of movement, but all she could think about were those bodies. *Did she know any of those people?*

The intersection was a mess. Gashes from artillery fire had left the facades of many buildings crumbling into the streets. Through the gaping holes, Flor glimpsed kitchens, parlors, and bedrooms. Ernesto waited. Sweat trickled down her temple, but she didn't dare move to brush it away. A minute passed. And then another. It felt like hours.

Ernesto turned his head to speak, but his eyes never left watching the surrounding buildings for trouble. "Once I step into that road, follow me, stay low, and continue forward no matter what. Quickly!"

The women nodded. Flor's heart thudded so loudly, it amazed her no one seemed to hear it. Bent over, Ernesto skittered into the intersection like a crab, and before she had time to doubt herself, Flor followed suit, with Iris and Luchie behind her. When they were halfway across—PING!—a sniper found them and bullets, one after another, sprayed the street under their feet. Ernesto let out a small moan and fell to all fours, but without speaking, the sisters grabbed his arms and they dragged him, their bodies shielding his. The rifle fire continued, but Flor could barely hear it. The only sound was her own breathing. Time seemed to stretch. She couldn't even feel the weight of Ernesto. They were flying, swerving around rubble and broken glass. Step by step, they were closing in on a wall of sandbags at the other side of the intersection.

When they reached the sandbags, the women collapsed on top of Ernesto. Flor's heart throbbed at the base of her throat. The rifle shots stopped. Ernesto's head dropped to the street with a thud, and Luchie leaned over his face. "Ernesto!" she cried, grabbing his chin to force him to look back at her.

"There's a roll of bandages in my breast pocket," he said through clenched teeth, and Iris wasted no time retrieving it and binding his left thigh above where he had been shot. He kept his eyes squeezed closed the entire time.

"It's not bad," Iris whispered once she had wrapped his injury. "But can you walk?"

"Yes, with some help, but just give me a second," Ernesto panted.

It was then that the women heard a strange sound. A small wavering bleat of desperation. They looked at each other in confusion.

"What's that?" Luchie whispered.

"Shhh," Iris said, her gaze darting over the nearby rubble. And then she pointed to a spot beyond the sandbags. Flor leaned forward to see, her eyes straining and stinging against the smoke. Wriggling alongside a pile of rocks was a naked baby girl, coated in dust.

"I've got to get her," Iris whispered and before Flor had time to respond, her sister was hurling herself toward the baby. Iris grabbed her and turned back. Two steps away from their sand-bag wall, the sniper found her—PING! One shot was enough. Iris cried out, but threw herself forward into the protection of the sandbags.

"He got me," Iris muttered, holding up her left hand to reveal a bloody stump where her pinkie finger once lay.

"Take her head covering and use it to tie off the stump of her finger as tightly as you can," Ernesto instructed Flor.

Flor gagged as she wrapped the injury into a sloppy cast, but Iris didn't even notice. She was staring at the baby tucked under her right arm. Luchie brushed the dust off the baby and stretched out one of her little arms, clucking at how thin she appeared.

"Someone will be looking for her," Flor said.

"No." Luchie pointed at a dead woman camouflaged by the dust and debris a couple of steps beyond where the baby had first been spotted.

"I'll get her identification papers," Flor said.

Iris shook her head, her eyes gleaming with pain. "No, the sniper will get you."

Flor nodded, knowing she was right. With Ernesto and Iris both injured, Flor understood what she needed to do. The hospital lay two blocks away, but suddenly the distance felt like two thousand miles. Shouting and artillery fire came from the direction of nearby Dewey Boulevard. A huge explosion shook the ground beneath them and a thick cloud of dust streamed down the block like a tidal wave. They all huddled together against the prickle of flying debris.

From where the baby lay hidden against Iris and Luchie, she cried. Iris made gentle shushing sounds, nestling her closer to her chest.

Flor swallowed, studying the block ahead. She could smell

death, but more than that, she could feel it. Death hung in the silence, the stillness, the absence of light. It soaked into her pores and clung to her, making her shiver. She noted the railroad ties lying across the street as an impediment to tanks, the pillbox halfway down the block, and the piles of bricks and fragments of concrete obscuring a straight path. *What would a mine look like?* One wrong step and it would all be over.

She didn't want Iris, Ernesto, Luchie, or the baby to pay the price for her miscalculation, so she turned to them. "Follow me, but walk a few steps behind. If anything happens, just go forward. Get to the hospital. Save yourselves. I mean it."

"Flor, wait," Ernesto hissed, but she raised a hand to silence him and lifted her right foot to step forward.

34.

FLOR

February 1945
Manila

Outside a ward entrance at Philippine General, Ernesto pounded on the locked door. "It's me, Dr. Marcial! Open up," he half whispered, half shouted. Flor leaned against the wall next to the door, limp with disbelief. They had made it. Her legs shook so violently she couldn't believe she was still standing. Beside her, Iris and Luchie checked the baby.

After a minute, the door opened a crack. When the staff saw it really was Ernesto, they pulled the group inside.

"Dr. Marcial, we figured you were dead!" one of the nurses exclaimed as she looked them over. "What's happening out there?"

"It's not good. A street battle's brewing in front of the hospital," Ernesto answered. He leaned against the door after the nurse locked it behind them. "There was a lot of noise coming from Dewey Boulevard."

"The Americans are closing in," Flor said. "It shouldn't be long now."

One of the nurses frowned. "The Japanese are getting more aggressive as they lose ground."

A doctor steered the group away from the door. "From what we can see, the Bureau of Science Building has been fully taken over by the Japanese, and they've also set up a cannon in the main entrance that they're using to fire all the way over to the river. Don't go near the windows and don't open the door to anyone."

Flor studied the faces of the exhausted and frightened-looking staff. The smell of excrement, blood, and vomit was overwhelming, but she felt relieved to be part of a group. Surely, there was strength to be found in numbers.

A nurse pointed to the wriggling bundle in Iris's arms. "What's that?"

IRIS AND ERNESTO were stitched up and bandaged, and the baby was cleaned and given a small bit of milk. The sound of shelling intensified as the day wore on and Flor hoped this was a good sign. The women split a can of herring, but it did little to calm the growling of their stomachs. As evening neared, a shell crashed into one of the rooms facing the outside courtyard and screams erupted. While Ernesto and others swarmed into the smashed room to retrieve survivors, Flor, Luchie, Iris, and two other nurses quickly cleared an area in one of the labs to treat the injured. Screams and ragged wailing made the hairs on Flor's arms stand on end.

As darkness fell, the sounds from outside changed. Explosions continued, but now the thud of boots thundered outside the ward's locked door. Several times, banging and shouting in Japanese came from the hallway, but no one inside the suite moved. Nurses clapped hands over the mouths of the injured to keep them from crying out. Iris gave the baby the last of the milk and let the baby suck on her finger. They needed to stay hidden and quiet.

Hours passed. The next day, thirst began to consume Flor,

but there was no running water. The baby fell increasingly list-less. "She's dehydrated and isn't going to last much longer," Iris fretted. But there was nothing they could do. They were trapped.

The second night, again, predators stalked the hallways outside their ward so Flor, Ernesto, Luchie, Iris, and the baby moved farther into the suite of offices and took refuge in a small storage room. Leaning against Ernesto's shoulder, Flor dozed until the sound of gunfire hitting the door to the ward roused everyone.

"Quick, up!" Ernesto whispered. "Iris, in here with the baby." He opened the door to a cabinet and pointed toward an empty large cubby at the bottom. She crawled inside, curling around the baby. "Manang, you go there." He pointed at another large cubby and the older woman climbed into it. He jammed a lab coat over both women before shutting the cabinet and pushed a laundry hamper toward Flor. He pulled out the soiled sheets and Flor hopped inside and tightened herself into a ball at the bottom. "I'm sorry, I know you'll hate this, but it's our best shot," he whispered as he piled the disgusting bedding on top of her.

"What about you?" Flor whispered. But it was all happening so quickly.

Ernesto didn't answer.

From outside their lab, there was screaming, crying, and yelling, a few pistol shots, then silence. Flor breathed only through her mouth, squeezing her eyes shut.

The door to their lab slammed open. *Thud, click, thud, click.* The sound of boots circled the small room and then a grunt.

"Out, out, out!" screamed a soldier.

"I'm unarmed. I'm a doctor!" Ernesto pleaded, but he was cut off.

Inside her laundry basket, Flor dug her teeth into the flesh of her hand to stay quiet.

There was a sharp crack of metal on bone. The dull thud of a body hitting the floor. And then a pistol shot.

Flor jammed her fist against her lips to cut off the sobs building in her chest.

And then she heard a whimper. The baby.

The thud of boots neared her and slowed. She imagined the soldier studying the cabinet. She held her breath, her mind racing.

Three years of anger turned molten hot inside her. Her mother's beating; her father's humiliation; her torture in Fort Santiago; and now Ernesto—all of it. Before she had time to think, she pushed off the bottom of the laundry basket, roaring, her hands over her head.

She caught a glimpse of surprise on the soldier's face. Covered in bloodied soiled rags, she must have looked like a monster. She lunged forward, trying to step from the basket, but her toe caught on the rim and she tumbled onto him, clawing and screaming, punching and more screaming. The two of them rolled across the floor, sliding in the bloody pool spreading from Ernesto. She hit the man, slapped, and yelled.

BANG!

Underneath Flor's hands, the man's body went limp. She scrabbled out from under the mess of bloody sheets wrapped around her and her mouth fell open.

Luchie. She stood over the dead man, still pointing a pistol at his head.

Beyond her, two Japanese soldiers appeared in the doorway, bayonets fixed.

One of the men stepped toward Luchie and drove his bayonet into her. The pistol in her hands clattered to the floor. As the soldier withdrew his bayonet, she collapsed, moaning.

The other soldier approached Flor where she sat and kicked her. The tip of his boot caught her ribs and she gasped in pain as her vision swam and flickered. She wiggled closer to Ernesto. He lay on his stomach, his face turned toward her, eyes open but unseeing.

Above Flor, the soldiers congregated. *No, no, no.* One heaved his bayoneted rifle high above her and as it came down toward her, she turned to Ernesto, preferring to look into his blank eyes than the vengeful expressions on the men surrounding her.

35.

TESS

The time that followed our evacuation from Manila was a blur. First, we were taken to a convalescent hospital on the island of Leyte, where the doctors told us our only job was to sleep, eat, and relax. While I was thrilled to eat and sit outside under the shade of a palm tree, sleep didn't come easily. Nightmares plagued me. Some nights I found myself in the jungle, other nights I was lost in the tunnels of Corregidor, but what these visions had in common was Frances. In each nightmare, she'd appear, wraithlike and lifting her hands to me beseechingly. I would awaken from the nightmares gasping and in a cold sweat, worrying and feeling guilty for leaving her behind.

And then three days after we arrived on Leyte, George stepped onto the hospital's veranda as I was eating pancakes, scrambled eggs, and sausage for breakfast. Suddenly, as he leaned over to hug me, the anxiety I'd been carrying with me since leaving Manila eased.

"Are you done? Let's go for a walk by the water," he said, pointing to the beach beyond the hospital's lawn.

"I just need to put my dishes away first," I said, rising to my feet.

"Forget your dishes," Virginia said. "We'll take care of them. Get out of here and go enjoy some time with your man."

Before I could even say thank you, Nell leaned over and stuck her fork into one of the sausages I'd left behind, claiming it for herself.

"Good idea," Mabel mumbled, swiping half a pancake from my plate.

"You know, I'll bet they'd bring you more food," George said. "You don't need to eat Tess's leftovers."

The women at the table looked at him aghast. "Why would we waste perfectly good food that's sitting right here?" Virginia asked him.

"Come on, let's go for that walk," I said, steering him away from the table and toward the water.

When we reached the sand, George took my hand and we smiled at each other.

"You look a lot happier than you did a few days ago," he ventured.

"I am. It's amazing what clean sheets, hot showers, new uniforms, and an endless supply of chocolate ice cream can do to lift a girl's spirits."

He chuckled. "I'll bet. I wish I could stay here. This mop-up duty's going to take longer than we thought. Manila's a real mess and the Japanese are determined to fight this to the last man."

I closed my eyes. The last thing I wanted to think about was Manila. "How much longer do you think you're going to be there?"

He cleared his throat nervously. "General MacArthur's asked me to assist with the war crime trials that will happen sometime in about a year from now."

"*Another* year?"

"I'm afraid so."

I knew I shouldn't complain. We were alive and about to get married and that made us lucky, but still I felt crushed by the idea of a long separation. I took a deep inhalation of the clean sea air and exhaled slowly. "Well, then, we'll make the best of it. The army's flying us to California in a week and we're expected to attend some official events. When I get back to Washington, I'll stay with my sister and her husband for a while and wait for you."

"I'm sorry I'll be here so much longer," he said. "These trials will be important. We've got to hold the enemy responsible for the things they did."

I cringed, thinking back to the rumors of what had happened to the men on Bataan, to the awful stories of Cabanatuan and Bilibid Prison. I knew George was right, but all I wanted to do was forget.

"Oh, I almost forgot something," he said, digging around in the breast pocket of his uniform. "I have a wedding present for you."

"A wedding present?"

George smiled, handing over a letter addressed to me in a careful script. I opened it and gasped.

Dear Tess,

I hope you this letter finds you well. The army has been keeping me very busy, but they feed me a lot of bacon and chocolate, which is much better than what we used to eat in the dining shed. General MacArthur came back to Santo Tomas and a reporter took a photo of me with him and he told us it might end up in Life. Wouldn't that be something? I'm looking forward to *sailing for California to find my mother and sisters as soon as things settle down. I miss you. Congratulations on your wedding. I wish I was there to be your flower girl.*

Your friend,
Frances Burns

P.S.: Please tell Virginia I've read and reread The Trouble with Blondes *several times now. I think it's a good thing that I'm a brunette.*

When I finished the letter, tears streamed down my cheeks.

"Now wait a minute, that letter was supposed to make you feel better," George said, pulling me to him.

"It does. I'm so glad she's getting her fill of bacon and chocolate, but I wish she was here."

"I know you do, but she'll head home soon and be reunited with her family. Don't worry." He held me out in front of him by the shoulders, grinning. "So what do you say? Should we go clean ourselves up and get married? I don't have much time before I have to head back to Manila, and as much as I like your friends, I'd really like to enjoy some time with you *alone.*"

Laughing, I wiped my tears and nodded.

AFTER OUR WEDDING ceremony on the beach and one night spent with me, George returned to Manila, where the battle for the city still raged. I was left with a photo taken moments after our ceremony. In it, the two of us squinted into the sun, me in my newly issued olive-colored uniform proudly sporting the bronze star given to each of us nurses for our service. I held a bouquet of orchids and stood next to George, smart and handsome in his pressed clean uniform.

After our week on Leyte, the army flew our corps of nurses to Hawaii and then to San Francisco, where we had some press conferences and attended a few ceremonies and receptions. At some point someone referred to us as the Angels of Bataan, the press ate it up, and the name stuck. That we returned home hailed as angels felt disingenuous; at that point, we were shadows more than anything. We were still weary, anxious, and many of us continued to suffer a variety of health problems from our imprisonment. Sally sent us a telegram from Michigan, and some of our colleagues resented those who had left Corregidor for Australia, but Virginia and I were happy to hear she had made it home. With every passing day, we grew more eager to step out of the spotlight and resume as regular a life as we could.

IN SAN FRANCISCO, a taxicab arrived at Letterman Hospital to take me to the station where I would catch my train to Washington, but before I walked outside into the city's foggy weather, Nell, Mabel, and Virginia accompanied me down to the building's lobby and we embraced.

"Y'all stay in touch now," Virginia said, wiping away tears. "I have no regrets about being out of the war, but I'm going to miss you girls so much."

"If you need a break from the Pacific Northwest's rain, Tess, come down and visit me in Pasadena, got it?" Nell called as I pushed open Letterman's doors.

"Got it," I said, waving. I kept a smile plastered on my face, but as soon as the taxicab reached the edge of the Presidio and Letterman disappeared from view, I dissolved into tears, already missing my friends.

WHEN I RETURNED to Washington, I moved in for a bit with Sue and Dan. One afternoon in April my sister and I were on our way to a neighbor's birthday party, but before we walked out the front door, a radio announcer's voice reached me. Dan was listening to a news report about the battle underway on the Japanese island of Okinawa. I hesitated in Sue's doorway, struck by the announcer describing it as the "bloodiest battle of the Pacific." That distinction meant something to me. A dull throb started behind my eyes.

Sue, a few paces ahead on the front walk, twisted around to say something to me, but alarm widened her eyes. "Tess, are you all right?"

I hesitated, on the verge of saying maybe I'd skip the party and go lie down, but Sue tilted her head, taking me in. "You know, I think it would be good for you to get out a little. Let's give the party a try. We don't have to stay long."

Minutes later, we were in her neighbor's crowded parlor. Several large plates of sandwiches covered a table. Glistening turkey meat and ham spilled forth from between thick slabs of white bread, the crusts neatly shorn off, but the real centerpiece was a chocolate cake, sprinkled with powdered sugar, placed in the middle of the feast on a stand. Though I'd been home for several months by that point, seeing food lying around so casually never failed to shock me. Using utensils still felt awkward, especially under pressure of a public setting, and I struggled to know how much to put on my plate, how quickly to eat it.

A woman with an elegant blond chignon turned to our host. "Delores, how long did you save up your sugar coupons for that gorgeous cake?"

I didn't hear the answer because I couldn't stop staring at it, imagining the taste of cocoa, the richness of butter, and what it would feel like to inhale that powdered sugar. Mortified, I swallowed back the saliva filling my mouth.

The blonde turned to Sue and me, making a frustrated pout. "All this ration nonsense is simply ridiculous. Is it really too much to ask for a bag of sugar or coffee? I'm absolutely sick to death of scrimping and can't wait for this war to end."

A roaring sound rushed to my ears as though I was swimming and caught in an enormous wave. I thought of Okinawa and the battle being fought there, right at this moment—*the bloodiest battle of the Pacific*. Tomorrow or maybe the day after, the newspapers would report the number of wounded and dead, but for many readers, those numbers would be incomprehensible. And yet, this war had become an inconvenience to this vapid, useless woman. My hands curled into fists. I was about to say—

"Tess, my goodness," Sue cried, thrusting a cold drink into my hand. "You looked flushed. Here, have a refreshment." Our gazes met and she shook her head almost imperceptibly.

I squeezed the glass tightly, trying to contain myself. The roaring inside my head quieted, but the slight throbbing behind my eyes expanded into a full ache. I raised the drink to my lips as if I could block everyone out beyond it, and that's when the fragrance of lemons filled my nostrils. *Lemonade.* I let out a small cry as the cold, sweating glass slipped from my fingers, and that precious sugar, the tart lemon juice, and my vision of a young group of courageous and carefree men and women piling into jeeps at Fort Stotsenburg—everything spilled over. Such a waste—all of it! Suddenly I was crying, deep, wrenching, ugly sobs that shook my shoulders and threatened to choke me.

The next thing I knew Sue was steering me through a sea of surprised and curious faces, out of the neighbor's house, and toward her Packard parked on the street. That was the last party I attended until George came home.

DURING THE YEAR that I waited for George, I tried to move forward. Everyone told me I was one of the lucky ones—I'd survived the war. And this was true. I was grateful to be alive, but I was also sad. No one survives a war's front lines without ghosts clinging to them.

When George came home, he was quieter too. I'm sure he carried his own ghosts, but we never discussed them. Both of us wanted to look forward, not to the past. We bought a car and a house with three bedrooms, a kitchen full of shiny appliances. We had a baby, our daughter Nathalie. After suffering in Santo Tomas, I'd feared I'd never conceive—several of the other nurses couldn't—but when I held my new daughter in my arms and admired her wriggling arms, kicking legs, and her ability to let forth astonishingly loud squalling, I was overcome with amazement. Somehow, despite all the pain we suffer, life marches on. My baby had no patience for the fears and uncertainties that hung over me since returning from the Philippines. She wanted my full attention, and gratefully, I gave it to her.

Despite my joy in our new life as a family, sometimes I missed my nursing days. Of course, I wanted nothing to do with the war, but my friendships with the other nurses and medical staff, the satisfaction of helping patients, that feeling of purpose and service—I missed those parts of my life. For a few years, I worked as the nurse at Nathalie's school, but bandaging scraped knees, helping nudge loose teeth out, and soothing aching tummies wasn't the same. I felt an unexpected longing to reconnect with that young independent woman who'd once raised the dead. I missed her, but told myself not to dwell on the past.

George and I enjoyed twenty happy years together, until another sad time descended in 1966. It was then that an angel arrived again in my life.

36.

TESS

Seventeen days after George died, an angel arrived on my doorstep. She wasn't your typical angel. No halo, trumpet, or harp. And she certainly didn't have flowing white gowns or wings, but there she was: Virginia.

It had been twenty years since I'd last seen her, thin and exhausted, but this current version of Virginia wore bright red lipstick in a shade that screamed five-alarm fire, and it was *real* lipstick, not the kind we jury-rigged with berries and other odds and ends when we ran out of it in the jungle. She had thick, long lashes coated in jet-black mascara that clumped at the ends, sun-kissed skin, and platinum-blond hair styled to resemble Jackie Kennedy's, at least in silhouette if not color.

"Tess, my heavens, this place has missed the news that it's supposed to be spring," she said in her heavy Texas accent. Always one for expansive gestures, she made a point of raising her arm with a flourish to inspect her diamond-set wristwatch. "It's cocktail hour, isn't it?"

"It's only eleven in the morning."

"So?"

For the first time in weeks, I smiled as if seeing spring's first daffodil after a long winter. Some things never changed: my favorite angel still possessed a devilish streak.

Against the veil of April's chilly drizzle, Virginia glowed with a colorful silk scarf encircling her neck and a hot-pink cashmere sweater under a rabbit fur coat. Standing on my front porch, she looked me up and down and shivered. "It's freezing. What do I need to do for you to invite me inside?"

God, I'd missed her voice. I embraced her, pulling myself into her soft shoulder of rabbit fur, breathing in the scent of powder and Shalimar. "I'm serious," she said into my ear. "How do you live here? This weather is like a sad person's version of England, but I don't see any handsome men in kilts."

"I think Scotland's where they wear the kilts," I said, laughing. I'd been so blue that laughter felt a bit painful, like when your foot's coming back into action after it's fallen asleep, but it was also a relief. I pulled away. "I can't believe this. You're the last person I would've imagined seeing on my doorstep today."

"Of course I'd come for you." And the way she said it was so matter-of-fact, I felt a clench in my chest and feared I might cry.

As she brushed past, I caught sight of a dusty white Cadillac sedan parked out on the street. Its Texas plate appeared to have lost a screw and hung at an angle. I turned to face her. Against the muted cream-colored toile wallpaper of my entryway, she was like a sunbird who'd fluttered into the house unexpectedly, all bright plumage and exotic charm. How out of place she looked! And that's when it hit me—*really, what on earth was Virginia doing in Seattle?* The tiny hairs at the nape of my neck rose. This had to be more than a spontaneous visit. "You drove here all the way from Kingdom, Texas?"

"I heard about your loss through the grapevine and figured you might need me."

More questions must have shown on my face because she slid out of her coat and draped it on a hook before turning to me. "How about we have a drink and catch up?" It wasn't a question—it was an order. Only a couple of minutes into our reunion and she was calling the shots.

I led her toward the kitchen at the back of my house. "What's your poison?" I asked, waving to the bar cart a few feet away in the adjoining sunken television room.

"A manhattan, please."

I raised a brow.

"You know how to make one, don't you?" she asked, walking past my kitchen table toward the bay window overlooking the Puget Sound.

"Sure. I just didn't realize we were diving straight into the fast lane."

"Honey, what other lane is there?"

Good question. I shook my head, grabbing the bottles of rye, vermouth, bitters, and cherries. For the last couple of weeks as friends stopped by, my bar cart had been getting steady usage. The rye situation looked particularly dire, and I held my breath as I poured it into a cocktail glass, hoping I could get a few more drinks out of the nearly empty bottle.

"Where are you staying?" I asked, handing her a glass.

"I saw a bunch of hotels when I turned off the freeway. I'll go to one of those."

"Nonsense, stay here. I've got plenty of room and it would be nice to have some company. It's been a long time since we've bunked together. Hopefully you'll find this more comfortable than our last place."

"Cheers to that," she said and we clinked glasses and then took long swigs before lowering them to look across the rims at each other.

"So don't get me wrong, it's wonderful to see you," I said. "But really, what are you doing here?"

Virginia glanced toward the window again, and for a moment, a look of exhaustion crossed her face before a more guarded expression slid into place—but it was enough. I knew the look well. It was the one we all wore in those final days in the Philippines— fatigue, worry, and fear, of course—but more than anything, it was one of stubborn resistance.

She cleared her throat. "My husband, Roger, has thrown me out."

"What?"

"Yes, I suppose it was a long time coming, but still, I was a little shocked to have things take such a dramatic turn at this point in my life. There's a lot of backstory to this and we could be here all night, but you don't have enough whiskey on hand for that version so I'll keep it brief," she said with a weary sigh. "When we came home from the Philippines in '45, the last thing I wanted to do was stay with my parents. I wanted security, someone to take care of me, and most importantly, I wanted to start over. Along came Roger, a friend of my family's. He was a bit older, rich, and awfully smooth and confident. He turned out to be the antidote to everything that ailed me and swept me right off my feet, but after a quick wedding, the excitement didn't last. We were very different people, but we had two beautiful boys together and lived in a small town. In other words, we were going to stick it out, so I turned a blind eye to his foolishness and in turn, he provided a gorgeous home and paid for the boys to attend good schools. Our arrangement was far from ideal, but I figured I'd make do."

Nodding, I took a long drink of my manhattan.

"And then, about two years ago, I received a letter." She bent over and reached into her purse and pulled out a stack of mail before tossing it onto a nearby end table. Bright, colorful stamps glowed against the white of the air mail envelopes.

"Are those from the Philippines?" I asked.

"Yes, you should sit down."

"What? Why?"

"Because you're not going to believe what comes next."

37.

TESS

I sat down.

Virginia gave me a long look and then blurted, "Don Davenport's still alive."

I stared. What was she talking about? I had seen Don Davenport executed on the main plaza of Santo Tomas in 1944—I had seen this happen *with my own two eyes*.

She nodded and sighed. "I know, it sounds crazy. Trust me, you've never seen someone look as shocked as I was when I opened that first letter from him, but yep, he's alive."

"But how?"

"When Don was carried off the plaza by several locals after the firing squad did its business, they saw his chest rising and falling and realized he wasn't dead. Apparently botched executions weren't uncommon. Instead of taking him to be buried, the locals delivered him to a guerrilla group. Somehow Don was smuggled into the mountains, where he recovered and spent the duration of the war with the rebels."

"But why did it take him almost twenty years to get in touch with you?"

Virginia moved to one of the room's upholstered chairs and sank into it. I went to the couch across from her. "After the

Japanese surrendered, it took Don weeks to make his way back into the city. Most of Manila had been destroyed and many people were unaccounted for and homeless. Don's home in Malate was long gone and he'd lost everything. He managed to find a few freelance assignments and the Red Cross provided him with some temporary housing. The army also lined him up to be a witness for the war crime trials, but once that was over, he struggled to make sense of what to do next. A friend of his at the AP tracked down my whereabouts in Texas. About a year after the war ended, Don learned I'd remarried."

Virginia rose and poured the last drops of whiskey into her glass. "I was the only person he really knew in the US and I had a new husband. Although the Red Cross offered to sail him to California, he decided to stay in the Philippines. He convinced himself I'd moved on and that he'd be doing me a favor by not getting back in touch and turning my life upside down with the news that he was still alive."

"Oh, Virginia, I'm so sorry."

She returned to her seat. "I know; at first I was so angry about that. What gave him the right to decide what was best for me? He had no idea what my life was like. When I got that first letter, my initial instinct was to tell myself that I would have left Roger had I known that Don was still alive, but I've had almost two years to think about this, and honestly, I'm not really sure what I would have done. I married Roger because I was already pregnant with our first baby. Roger was established, he could provide, and he hadn't gone overseas during the war. While we were fighting for our lives in the jungle, he was a glorified pencil pusher in DC, sticking thumbtacks into maps of countries with names he couldn't spell, and gallivanting around the Capitol and drinking martinis with the top brass. Roger never asked me about what I went through, not once, and though this may sound strange, that was fine with me. It was a relief, actually. I didn't want to think about it."

She tapped on her glass with a manicured fingernail, lost in thought. "So what would I have done if Don had appeared in 1946 and asked me to come back? We were both so lost, so tired. Would I really have thrown away the comforts of my new home? I wish I could say with certainty that love would have won out, but it was more complicated than that. I had a baby with Roger. I didn't want to lose my son. My primary love was for my child."

I nodded. As impossible as the situation sounded, I understood.

"Don and I sent letters back and forth and it amazed me how quickly we fell right back into the ease and excitement of our relationship. Don't forget, Roger and I were living parallel but separate lives and he had no idea about Don at that point. I was waiting for my younger son to head off to college before I did anything rash. And so just as my son decided on what college he would be attending in the fall, and I was starting to think about making a new future for myself, Roger discovered our letters. It was for the best, but as you can imagine, he wasn't thrilled. Long story short: here I am. I knew you wouldn't turn me away."

"Amazing."

Across from me, Virginia's face relaxed. "With Don back in my life, I feel better than I have in years. I think we both needed a lot of time to heal from what had happened in the '40s. I even started writing again."

"Did you go back to the novel you were working on at Santo Tomas?"

"Heavens no, though I have to admit I kind of regret leaving that behind. But anyway, I started writing a new book—a romance, of course, because suddenly I believe in happy endings again. I wrote a new one. It almost took me two years, but when it was done, I sent it off to an editor at a fancy publishing house in New York City. Why not? What do I have to lose?"

I blinked. "Good for you. Let's raise a glass to that!"

We leaned forward to clink the rims of our drinks together again.

"It will probably come to nothing, but it feels so good to think about getting a fresh start in life," Virginia said. "So really you don't mind my surprise visit? I imagine this has been a hard time for you. George was one of the best."

I glanced at my one wedding photo sitting in a silver frame on the end table next to the couch. It had been taken at the convalescent hospital in Leyte where we married. George and I smiled at the camera as dazed newlyweds, squinting slightly. In our uniforms, we looked stiff and slightly overwhelmed at our status as the *happy couple*. Attaching happiness to anything at that point felt risky. The war was still being fought and George had to return to it. "He was a good one, wasn't he?"

She nodded.

"Well, I'm so happy to see you again," I said. "I can't believe it's been twenty years. Feel free to stay here for as long as you want."

"I actually don't plan to stay long. I'm planning to fly to the Philippines."

"To reunite with Don?"

"Yes." Mischief flashed in her eyes. "What would you say about joining me on a trip to Manila?"

38.

TESS

Spring 1966
Manila

Virginia and I arrived in the Philippines after an overnight at an airport hotel in Japan, and before that, a stop in Honolulu. From the small window of our plane, I gazed down on Manila, admiring how the vivid turquoise of the bay glowed with blinding intensity. I'd forgotten the saturated colors of the tropics, how the light seemed to emanate from every direction, not just the sun. When I'd last seen Manila, it had been from the tiny window of a C-47 transporting us to Leyte after we departed Santo Tomas in 1945. Now there was no sign of smoke, fire, and devastation. I marveled at how a landscape can erase the past.

I still couldn't believe I'd agreed to accompany Virginia on this trip. Back in Seattle, she had spent hours arguing that an adventure would be good for me. In the end, she wore me down and reminded me of what was important.

"I'm so sorry you lost George," Virginia had said quietly as we sat at my kitchen table in Seattle. "We've both lost a lot. But we're still young. Hopefully we have a lot of life left in us."

I'd run my finger along the rim of my cocktail glass. She was right. I was only forty-four. Since the war I'd dedicated my life to George and our daughter, Nathalie. For a few years while Nathalie had been younger, I'd worked in her elementary school as the nurse, but for the most part, I'd been taking care of my family in my home. Now, with George gone and Nathalie a student at the University of Washington, what was I going to do? Maybe an adventure with an old friend could help me sort through plans for the future.

As much as I fretted over the suddenness of uprooting myself to travel halfway across the globe, a part of me was delighted to leave the condolence letters behind, to turn the key in my front door and walk away from Seattle's gloomy skies. When I'd called my nineteen-year-old daughter, Nathalie, and found her home at her apartment near campus, she'd been flabbergasted when I described what had happened during the war.

"Why did you never tell me any of this?" she demanded.

I sighed. "Your dad and I are a different generation, darling. We don't like to talk everything out. We never wanted to re-hash those terrible years."

"It can't be healthy to have been holding all that in, Mom."

I thought of George's fatal heart attack. He had been twelve years older than me, but still, far too young to have such a dreadful thing happen. Though his doctor never mentioned a correlation, it struck me that while our minds try to forget the past, our bodies have their ways of holding on and not forget-ting our grief. "I'm sure you're right. It's probably not healthy at all."

"You should go back with your friend and help her recover the love of her life—how romantic. I'll be fine here. I'll check in on the house a few times a week."

I smiled. "You mean you'll do your laundry here, right?"

"Laundry, I'll watch some TV, don't worry, I'll hold down the fort while you're gone."

"Thank you. I'll miss you."

"It sounds so far away."

"I know, it is. But I'll come back."

BY THE TIME our taxicab rolled to a stop outside of the Manila Hotel's regal entrance, a velvety darkness had swallowed us. Even after sunset, heat thickened the air and made our clothes and hair hang limp. The brackish smell of Manila Bay, combined with the heaviness of traffic exhaust and the cloying aroma of jasmine trailing up the side of the hotel, immediately brought back the complicated nature of the tropics, the mixture of sweet and sour, beauty and ugliness.

After settling into our rooms, we met downstairs at a table in a quiet corner of the lobby for a bite to eat so we could get some sleep before our reunion with Don scheduled for the morning. Our slow trek across time zones had left me with the usual delirious sense of jet lag, but even as fuzzy-headedness enveloped me, below the table, my foot jiggled. I couldn't stop it. I felt the odd mixture of frenetic anxiety and exhaustion that I remembered from our days in the jungle, that sense of being constantly on guard.

I sensed a shift in the air and looked up. A hush seemed to fall over the lobby. The clank of silverware, the ringing of phones, the hum of voices—everything and everyone stilled, like right before a storm when the air is heavy with pressure and the leaves on the trees stop rustling and birds stop singing in anticipation of a change in the atmosphere.

Don stood only a few feet away.

He was grayer, but retained his tall, lanky posture. I knew that later Virginia would complain about the unfairness of how men often seem to get more handsome as they age—but that would wait. Right now, we both stared at him, transfixed. His eyes locked on Virginia as if she was a mirage and he didn't dare look away for fear she might vanish.

He approached, and when he came within arm's distance of her, he stopped. "Virginia."

That's all he said, but he said it with such certainty that, in an instant, I understood that sometimes time means nothing. Twenty years had evaporated.

When I looked at Virginia, big tears the size of pearls were rolling down her face. I stopped breathing. I'd never seen her cry. Not when she found the soldier's arm after the bombing at Malinta, not after Don had been shot—*never*.

"I'm sorry to surprise you like this," he said in a low tone. "I know we're supposed to meet in the morning, but we've lost over twenty years of being together and I didn't want to lose another single second."

She rose and they embraced. I looked away, suddenly feeling awkward. Why had I agreed to be a third wheel for this reunion?

After a moment, they both settled down at the table with me, hands intertwined.

"Tess," Don said, smiling broadly. "Welcome back to Manila."

"Thank you. It's so strange to be here after all this time."

"I can imagine. You'll find the city to be very different now obviously. Among the many changes: a new president, lots of construction, a thriving economy."

Plastered all over the airport had been posters of the handsome new president, Ferdinand Marcos, and his beautiful young family. "I'm eager to explore more tomorrow," I said.

"Before you make any big plans, I have a surprise for you both after breakfast."

"Haven't you served up enough surprises? I swear my hair grayed overnight after I received your first letter," Virginia pouted.

"One more," he said, stroking her arm. "You won't want to miss this."

39.

TESS

Spring 1966
Manila

The next morning after I had eaten breakfast on the lanai of my room, the telephone rang. It was Virginia. "Can you be ready to leave in about twenty minutes? Don's got something up his sleeve."

"I assume he never left the hotel last night?"

She let out a low, throaty chuckle. "A lady never tells."

My lips curved upward. "I'll meet you downstairs soon."

When the three of us gathered in the lobby, I took in the relaxed, happy expressions on Don's and Virginia's faces. When he leaned in to whisper something to her, a smile dawned across her face with the intensity of a hundred suns, a smile that eased the fear and pain and sorrow of the last twenty years. A smile that gave me hope. A smile that brought a lump to my throat.

"Good morning," Virginia said.

"It's a little hot for me, but I sure like this sunshine," I said.

"Couldn't be more different from Seattle," Virginia said.

I fanned myself with a small notepad I'd taken from my room. "I need to adjust a little, but I'll be fine."

"Make sure you drink a lot of water," Don said, and I stiffened. He always had liked telling me what to do, but then he surprised me by reaching for my hand.

"Tess, I'm very sorry to hear of your husband's recent passing," he said in an earnest tone.

"Thank you." Although my throat constricted at the thought of George, I smiled. "I wonder what he would make of me returning to this place."

"I never met him, but in the months leading up to the war crimes trials, I heard about the work he was doing. It was a tough job. He was assigned to collecting testimony from the women who'd suffered atrocities at the hands of the enemy. Most of the victims, understandably, wanted to put the past behind them. Few wanted to participate in the trials. Many feared they'd be shamed for what they had endured."

I thought back to the vague answers George provided when people asked him about the war. "When he came back, I never asked him anything," I said. "He seemed eager to put the sad past behind us, but sometimes I think back and wonder what happened to our Filipino friends. We would never have survived Santo Tomas without them."

"Remember all the food and supplies that Iris and Gloria brought us? We left Manila so quickly that there was no time for goodbyes, but I've always remembered their generosity," Virginia said sadly.

"Don, since you've been here, have you found out anything about the woman who was our contact for getting messages out of Santo Tomas? Or any of our nurse friends? Did they survive?" I asked.

Don opened his mouth to speak, but a receptionist from the hotel's main desk appeared next to Virginia. "Ma'am, I have a telegram from the United States for you," he said, handing her a slip of paper.

She thanked him, glanced at the telegram, and then looked at me, puzzled. "It's from your daughter, Nathalie." But before I could ask anything more, Virginia was reading the message with a huge smile blooming across her face. "Remember that book I told you I had written? Before we left Seattle, I'd sent a letter to the editor who has my manuscript giving her your address if she needed to contact me. Nathalie's been checking your mail and a letter arrived for me from the publishing house."

"And what does it say?" I asked, breathlessly.

"I don't know because you've raised a polite daughter who doesn't open other people's mail," Virginia laughed.

Don checked his watch. "It should be about six o'clock in the evening in Seattle. Why don't you call her? Let's find out what the editor wrote."

For once, Virginia appeared flustered. "I don't know . . . should I? Don't we need to be somewhere soon?"

"No, call her," I said, dragging Virginia toward the main desk. I waved for a receptionist's help and the same young man who had delivered the telegram came to help us so I gave him Nathalie's phone number, he arranged the call, and then he handed the receiver to Virginia. Hesitantly, she took it. We waited, holding our breath, while a series of clicks and then a distant ringing sound buzzed through the lines.

We heard Nathalie answer and Virginia asked her to open the letter and then Don and I watched her face, holding our breath. After a moment, she gasped and broke into such an expression of delight that I couldn't help myself from hugging her while Don cheered. After she hung up a few minutes later, she shook her head in amazement. "Well, I guess I need to call New York City because—I can't believe I can say this but—*an editor wants to buy my book!*"

Again, we cheered.

"It's too late in New York City, so that call will have to wait, although I swear, how am I supposed to be patient right now?"

"A distraction is what you need and I know just the thing," Don said.

"Darling, I'm not spending the day with you upstairs in my room." Virginia smirked.

He chuckled, turning to me. "How about we take our famous author out for a day on the town, shall we?"

And then Don offered us each an arm and we marched out into the sunshine, feeling on top of the world.

MINUTES LATER, WE sat in Don's car, motoring south past Rizal Park. "This entire area was completely flattened by the end of the war," he said matter-of-factly. "Almost everything south of the river was gone."

"Because of the Japanese?" Virginia asked.

"MacArthur decided there would be no aerial bombing because he was hoping to spare civilians, but as a result, the Battle for Manila was fought in close range. Certainly the Japanese destroyed much of the city in their refusal to surrender, but American shelling also contributed to many casualties as well."

Outside my window, a row of new buildings blurred past. After a few minutes, Don parked on a quiet street in front of a pale yellow stucco two-story building.

"What's this?" Virginia asked.

"You'll see." Don hopped out of the car, came around to open our doors, and then guided us to the entrance. "Ready?"

Virginia and I looked at each other, smiling at Don's mysterious invitation. We walked inside to find a waiting room filled with Filipino women of all ages, babies, and young children. The receptionist waved to us, smiling eagerly. "Mabuhay! Follow me."

We were led to a small conference room and took seats, but before Virginia and I had time to ask Don what we were doing, the door opened, and a doctor entered. Her jet-black shoulder-length hair grazed her clinician's coat and when she unwound the stethoscope from her neck to place it on the table, I caught a glimpse of her face. There was no forgetting those pale blue eyes and the way they took everything in.

"Frances," I gasped.

She stretched her arms toward us. "Welcome to the Pasay Women's Clinic. It's such an honor to have you here."

"You and Don have been in touch?" I asked, as she embraced me and then Virginia.

Frances arched a brow, looking at Don. "Well? Do you want to explain or shall I?"

Don shifted from one foot to the other and looked at Virginia apologetically. "Six years ago, Frances showed up at my office and demanded an explanation for how I was still alive. Once she'd heard the whole story, she insisted I write to you."

I thought back to the pale, thin girl from Santo Tomas who never hesitated from holding her ground with Don, or anyone else for that matter, but now I could see affection in her eyes as she looked at him.

"I actually insisted he *telephone* you!" Frances said.

"She did," Don said. "She picked up my telephone and practically threw it at me."

"But I received your first letter two years ago," Virginia said slowly.

"Well, it took me a while to work up my nerve," he confessed. "I'm sorry."

"Good grief, man, certainly no one can accuse you of moving too fast on any of this," I said, frustrated by the thought of the time they'd lost.

"I know, I know," he said, reaching for Virginia. As she buried her face in his shoulder, he closed his eyes for a moment.

Frances and I watched them and I felt myself softening toward him. I'd always judged Don harshly, yet time and again, he'd surprised me. Who was I to judge him? What did I know of the ghosts that chased him?

"To be fair, I think it was a lot easier for us to move on with our lives when we got to the United States," Frances said quietly. "But so much of this city had been destroyed. So many were displaced and struggling. For those who stayed here, life was very challenging."

"It's time to forgive ourselves for our mistakes, Don," Virginia said pulling away from him to look at Frances. "But how did you end up back here?"

Frances pulled chairs out from the table for us and we sat. "In April of 1945, the Red Cross organized many of us to sail home to the US, where I was reunited with my mother and sisters. We lived in San Francisco and eventually I went to medical school there, but I always knew I wanted to return."

"But why?" I asked. "I'd have thought this place represented a very sad chapter of your life."

A complicated series of expressions traveled over Frances's face. "It did," she said slowly, "but that period before I left proved to be defining for me. For one thing, watching you and the other nurses work in Santo Tomas was very inspiring. I wanted to be just like you when I grew up. And then, after you left, the war continued and Manilans poured into Santo Tomas in search of safety and medical help. Because I spoke a bit of Tagalog, I was often called on to translate for patients. Of course, I was too young for this, but times were desperate. People needed help.

"Many of the women who arrived had been seriously injured in all kinds of ways and I could see they didn't want to tell the American nurses and doctors what had happened. They were so embarrassed, but often they whispered details to me.

The nurses theorized that many of the feverish women thought I was an apparition, an angel maybe, because I was so small and willing to listen. I heard things that no one should have to describe—or hear, for that matter. Rather than terrify me, their secrets bolstered me. I realized how much we can endure. Especially women. I continued to help with translating, but more than anything I was storing secrets, Tess, just like you did when you stitched messages onto those sheets.

"When I arrived in California, I knew my purpose in life. Not only would I become a doctor, but someday, I decided, I'd serve women. What I'd learned in Manila was that women civilians sustained wartime injuries far different from what the men suffered. Of course, there were the physical problems, but it was the mental trauma, the fear and shame of their injuries being discovered that struck me as where I could help most. I was trained as a gynecologist, but I was also interested in helping patients heal their emotional wounds.

"When I returned here, I discovered the traumas hadn't faded with time. Several local women helped me establish this place. With money raised from my family and friends, we began building this clinic and word of my expertise spread. Few Filipinas who suffered as comfort women for Japanese soldiers survived, but those who did came to me. Many sustained all kinds of physical and emotional injuries that needed tending."

"I can't believe you've built all this. You witnessed so much misery, yet you've turned it into something positive," I said.

There was a knock at the door and a woman leaned into the room. "Good morning. Sorry we're late. I was having trouble getting my children out the door this morning."

"Ahh, come in," Frances said and two Filipinas entered. When they turned to face me, I startled at their faces, still familiar even after twenty years. "My goodness, Iris! And Lily!"

Virginia leapt from her seat to embrace Iris, but Frances wrapped an arm around Lily, smiling. "She doesn't go by Lily anymore. This is Flor Dalisay, the woman who helped us smuggle messages out of Santo Tomas. These two have been critical to helping me build this clinic."

Flor turned to me. "Tess, it's good to see you again. We're so sorry to learn about your husband's passing."

"Thank you." I shook my head. "What a surprise this is! I can't believe we haven't been in touch."

"You can't? Ha, you and I have barely even kept in touch and we're in the same country," Virginia said to me before turning to the others. "Life's been busy and we were so eager to get on with things and move ahead. I'm so glad to see the three of you. Tell us"—she leaned forward to clasp Iris's hand—"what happened after we left? How did you survive?"

40.

TESS

With six of us in the small conference room, it felt crowded. Between jet lag and the shock of seeing everyone after all these years, my mind was swirling. I rose and opened a window. I peered outside at the quiet side street. I still couldn't believe I was half a world away from home in a place I'd tried so hard to forget, but by attempting to erase the hard times, I'd turned my back on the people who'd meant the most to me, the people who'd taught me what friendship and love was. I took a moment to inhale deeply before turning back to everyone.

When I returned to my seat, Flor began to describe how a young Filipina with a keen acuity for numbers and a desire to prove herself became a courier for the resistance, and how she built connections—between nurses, priests, and a nightclub owner—to defeat a common enemy. And then when victory was within reach, resistance became riskier than ever. Suddenly she was trafficking in American intelligence agents. There was an arrest. A city under siege. A desperate escape to a nearby hospital. And then tragedy.

"Iris saved us." Flor nodded at her sister. "Manang Luchie and I had been bayoneted and left for dead, but my ate revived us. She forced us to wake, she bandaged us both, and dragged us to the basement of the hospital, all while still managing to care for that little baby we'd found. We waited, unsure if the end was near. We had no food, no water. By this point, I was suffering from fever and couldn't tell if I was hallucinating. Outside the hospital, the sounds of battle grew louder and more frightening, but at some point, people shouted *Amerikanos! Amerikanos!* US soldiers found us hidden in the basement.

"Someone carried me out of that hellhole. When we emerged from the rubble, the soldier looked down at me and grinned. And those teeth! They were the whitest I'd ever seen. And to me, he was built like a mountain. 'So Lily,' he said. 'I see you escaped the Kempeitai.'"

I inhaled sharply. "It was George?"

Flor nodded and continued, "Later, when I woke up in the care of the 112th Medical Battalion at a hospital outside the city, George came back to find Iris, Manang Luchie, and me. We cried with joy when he told us Santo Tomas had been liberated and how he had flown to Leyte to marry you. And then my tears changed. I cried about Ernesto. I was a mess. George knew what had happened at the hospital. We feared we would be shamed for our assaults. So many women suffered horrible attacks and it was hard to shake the sense of stigma that came from being left alone with the enemy, but he continued to visit and assured us we didn't need to fear our past."

I glanced at Virginia and she was nodding. When we returned home to the United States in 1945 and attended several official propaganda events for the press, reporters asked about the enemy's treatment of us and it quickly became clear that a burning question in the public's mind was if we had been "violated." Even friends and family danced around the issue, although no one ever came straight out and asked. The innuendo and suspicion disgusted me because it always implied that there had been something sordid and wrong about our service. It felt like a stain upon our survival, and if we had felt that way, I could imagine how Flor must have struggled in the conservative culture of the Philippines. I reached for her hand and she continued speaking.

"Even as George checked on us almost every evening, he continued to fight the battle in the city. Each day he looked more and more tired, more sickened by the devastation. When he arrived with a pack of cigarettes in his pocket, he confessed he'd started smoking so he wouldn't taste death in the air. That's when I stopped asking questions. I didn't need to know anything more. By that time, I'd seen the other injuries surrounding me. I'd heard of what had happened. The rapes. The burnings. The firing squads. Whole sections of the city burned to the ground. Block by block, building by building, neighbor by neighbor, the Japanese and Americans were destroying our beloved home. By the end of February, the Battle for Manila was over, but everything and everyone had been lost.

"When I healed enough to be released, George secured jobs for Iris and me with the Red Cross. He found us a place to live. MacArthur assigned him to assemble witness reports of the atrocities, and he tried to persuade me to testify, but I wanted nothing to do with the upcoming war trials. I needed to piece my life back together.

"Just as I was working again, I discovered I was pregnant. Unmarried and expecting a baby, I was ruined, but George disagreed and promised to help. Before my baby arrived, George arranged for a priest to give me a marriage certificate declaring Ernesto had been my husband. I wore a ring. When Emmeline arrived, Ernesto was listed as the father."

Flor paused a moment and looked at her hands, before clearing her throat. "When the war trials began and reports of the assaults, the rapes, and mass murders were revealed, George thought I would feel relieved and unburdened by how many had suffered assaults, but if anything, the news solidified my decision to forget the past. When it came time for him to leave Manila, I made him promise to say nothing about us. At first, he resisted, saying how happy you'd be to know we'd survived. But I didn't want anyone to know anything about me. I didn't want any more help. I wanted to move on."

"Oh, Flor, I'm so sorry. I wish I'd known. Of course, I understand being eager to forget the past. When I got home, I barely spoke of the war to my sister. When I recently told my daughter about our time here, she was shocked. But still, I wish I'd known about you."

Virginia wiped her eyes. "I have no doubt that part of our survival in Santo Tomas was because of the two of you and the other nurses who helped from the outside. I'm so sorry for what you had to endure."

"Those were hard times," Flor said. "But we managed to rebuild. I started off teaching, but then decided to start a school of my own. I figured out how to apply for a government grant and that was the beginning of my school that's located across the street."

"A school?" Virginia asked.

Flor nodded proudly. "It's a school for girls. I can take you there later."

"That would be wonderful," Virginia said.

"How did you all reconnect when Frances returned?" I asked.

Iris smiled. "I hadn't forgotten meeting her at Philippine General when you were sick. When I started nursing for the Red Cross after the war, I ran into her again. Frances ended up being quite a star in her own right. She was the girl who negotiated the surrender with the Japanese at Santo Tomas, remember? The American soldiers adored her."

"*Everyone* adored her," Flor added. "Every bigwig who came through Manila wanted to meet her."

Frances flushed. "I don't really remember."

"She's very modest, this one," Iris said of Frances.

Frances suddenly sat up straighter and snapped her fingers. "I almost forgot something important. Give me a moment," she said, hurrying from the room.

"Iris, what happened to the baby you found?" I asked.

"I gave her up to the Red Cross, but her parentage was never established so I adopted her and named her Josefina. I eventually married and have four other children."

"And you?" Virginia looked to Flor. "Did you marry?"

She nodded. "Eventually, yes, and we had three babies. My parents moved back to the city, and I've been incredibly fortunate that Manang Luchie has stayed with me to care for my children while I work. I don't know what I'd have done without her."

Frances came back into the room carrying a stack of grimy notebooks. "After you were evacuated, I went to your rooms to see if anything had been left behind and I found Virginia's manuscript."

Virginia clapped her hand over her mouth for a moment before exclaiming, "And you kept it? You've held on to my notebooks for all these years?"

Frances smiled bashfully. "This might sound crazy, but I've read this hundreds of times over the years. Whenever I missed all of you, I turned to this. What do you say about finally giving this story a happy ending?" she asked, pushing the notebooks toward Virginia.

Virginia shook her head and flipped through some of the yellowed pages. "I can't believe this still exists. Well, I guess you're right, if it's survived all these years, I'd better finish it."

We all fell into a companionable silence, smiling at one another. I couldn't take my eyes off Iris, Flor, and Frances sitting across the table from us. Though we'd grown older, I would have recognized them anywhere. "I really admire everything you've created here," I finally said, meaning every word.

I'd tried to forget this place, but it was my time here that had defined me most and set the course for the rest of my life. I'd been all too quick to try to suppress the agonies of the jungle, of the Malinta Tunnel, and certainly, of Santo Tomas, but it was during those hard times that my friendships, love, and my calling as a nurse had saved me even when I'd feared I had lost everything. Had I been lucky? Of course. Somehow the bombs hadn't hit me, the bullets had passed me. But we had also fought like hell to survive. Through helping others, both in nursing and through my acts of resistance, I found a will to live. *I had survived.* To forget the past was to deny my own growth, my power.

"If I could do things over, I wish I'd gotten in touch with you much sooner," I said.

"It's never too late. In fact, we could use your help here. You should join us."

I was on the verge of saying that I needed to go home to Seattle, but I stopped myself. For the first time in many years, I was on my own. It was never too late for a fresh start. My daughter was busy finding her own way in life. I would return to her eventually.

I looked beyond Frances at the photos of women and babies taped to the wall. To find myself in the same place as where I'd arrived more than twenty years earlier in search of a new life had a preordained quality to it. My beloved George would have been amazed to see what these women had built out of Manila's wreckage. So much was different, but at the same time, the most important things—my friends and their courageous spirits—never changed. I'd learned so much about kindness, bravery, and love from them.

It was possible to both mourn the sorrow and pain of the past, but also view it as a time of growth and discovery. Grief and gratitude can exist side by side.

From outside the conference room, the mewling of a newborn infant reached us.

Supported by the friends sitting around me, I'd once transformed from a young lonely girl into a strong and confident woman who had found her calling in healing and helping others. Why not again?

Historical Note

In November of 1943, a typhoon engulfed southern Luzon. For the purposes of this narrative, I moved that destructive and deadly storm to earlier in the rainy season of September of 1943.

* * *

Acknowledgments

Every book always ensures an adventure, and this one was no exception. An amazing group of people helped bring this story into the world. An important moment in the process came when my friend Amy Huey took me to visit her grandmother, Lieutenant Commander Teresa "Tess" Schmierer, so we could talk about her career as a US Navy nurse during World War II. Though Tess was not one of the Angels of Bataan, she represents that same generation of courageous and adventurous women who answered the call to service. Her experience is inspiring and humbling and I'm honored to have met her.

Another critical person in the development of this story came from Desiree Benipayo, author and historian extraordinaire. Des, I couldn't have written this book without you and I'm incredibly lucky for your feedback on the manuscript, your story ideas, and the patience you demonstrated with my endless questions. Along with the unforgettable tour of Manila that you gave me, your knowledge of the rich and fascinating history of the Philippines during World War II and your enthusiasm for sharing it are wonderful—thank you. How lucky that author James M. Scott introduced us! Also thank you to Johan Canlas at the Manila Hotel, to Liz DeLucia at the Manila American Cemetery, and to the museum staff at Santo Tomas University who cheerfully pulled out an archived exhibit about the school's history as an internment camp and let me spend hours studying it.

I'm very grateful to my terrific group of early readers. Tif Marcelo, Dr. Ann Chen, Kerri Maher, Erin Shigaki, Cindy Burnett, Meg Donohue, Erin Davies, Priscilla Long, and Janet Yoder—thank you!

My agent, Barbara Braun, and her associate John Baker got this book off the ground with wise counsel and by patiently reading through several early versions to help me find the heart of this story—thank you. And of course, every day I pinch myself to be working with the amazing team at William Morrow and my editor, Lucia Macro, who championed this book from initial idea to final draft. Michelle Brower and Danya Kukafka, your insight is always spot-on. Thank you all for being the best advocates an author could ask for!

And last, but not least, thank you to my beloved family, the *real* characters who inspire everything I do.

About the author

About the book

Insights,
Interviews
& More . . .

Meet Elise Hooper

Chris Landry Photography

A native New Englander, Elise Hooper spent several years writing for television and online news outlets before getting an MA and teaching high school literature and history. She now lives in Seattle with her husband and two daughters. Her previous novels include *The Other Alcott*, *Learning to See*, and *Fast Girls*. ❧

A Conversation with Elise Hooper

Q: Where did the idea for this book come from?

A: This novel was inspired by my grandfather, First Lieutenant Donald W. Baker, and his service in the US Navy during World War II, a period of his life he rarely spoke to me about with much detail. All I really knew was that he had been aboard the USS *Missouri* when General MacArthur signed the peace treaty with the Japanese delegation, and he then entered Tokyo as one of the first Americans to view the surrendered city. Thinking perhaps my grandfather's experience could serve as a jumping-off point for a new book idea, I began researching the war in the Pacific. Many excellent novels have been written recently about World War II in Europe, and I felt that the Pacific offered the possibility to find more fascinating stories.

Whenever I start exploring an idea for a novel, I tend to start in one place but land in another, and this book was no different. In this case, I began my research in Japan but found myself expanding my reading list into the South Pacific, a place where many American women also served during the war years. As soon as I read about the Angels of Bataan and Corregidor, a group of US Army and Navy nurses stationed in the Philippines, I knew I'd found my new subject. The fact that ▶

seventy-seven American nurses entered Santo Tomas Internment Camp in 1942 and all of them survived to liberation struck me as nothing short of miraculous.

Stories of resilience have always fascinated me from my earliest days of reading books like *Little House on the Prairie* and *The Diary of Anne Frank*. What gives us hope when the future seems bleak? How do we find the reserves we need to endure the unendurable? The tenacity and friendship that kept this group of women going through the toughest of times drew me right in. Little did I know that I'd end up writing the bulk of this story at a time when nurses were, again, serving on the front lines of a war— but this time the enemy was COVID-19.

Writing a war book during a pandemic might sound depressing, but it gave me a helpful sense of perspective. I took great comfort in reading, writing, and reflecting on what these women endured and how it changed them. The feelings that I experienced in 2020— the fear of uncertainty, a sense that the world had been turned upside down, occasional bouts of hopelessness—I channeled into trying to imagine what life during the war felt like for the characters of this book.

Q: How did you approach researching this novel?

A: The last of the Angels of Bataan—Lieutenant Mildred Dalton Manning—passed away in 2013, so there were no survivors to interview firsthand, although several left behind oral histories and memoirs. As I researched this story, I spotted a friend's Facebook post about her grandmother, Lieutenant Commander Teresa Walsh Schmierer, who served as a navy nurse aboard the USS *Repose* during World War II. When I told this friend I was researching a new novel about the Angels of Bataan, she generously offered to introduce me to her grandmother, so we drove up to a retirement home north of Seattle to interview Teresa. Fortunately, we managed to catch her on a day when she wasn't busy with her water aerobics class, an activity made possible by the swimming lessons she had taken seventy-seven years earlier during her navy training. While her service in the Navy Nurse Corps was different from what the Angels of Bataan experienced, meeting her brought the characters who had been rattling around in my head to life.

Like many of the characters in my novel, Teresa, an Iowan, hailed from a large farming family of modest means. She enrolled in nursing school in 1941 to develop a new skill set and see more of the world. During the war, the USS *Repose* was stationed primarily off the coast of Okinawa and she prided herself on never suffering from seasickness like many of her colleagues, including Katharine Hepburn's brother, a doctor. At one point, while visiting an officer's club in Shanghai, she met Lieutenant Clifford Schmierer, a Scout and Raider, a precursor to the Navy SEALs, and they married on May 18, 1946. In the years that followed, Teresa raised four children, continued to work as a nurse until she was seventy years old, and in 2019, she flew across the country to be honored at a ceremony at the Arlington National Cemetery's Women in Military Service for America Memorial. As I write this now in February 2021, Teresa Schmierer is strong, cheerful, and looking forward to her 102nd birthday.

After meeting the real-life "Tess" and reading everything that I could find about the Angels of Bataan, I decided to visit the Philippines because I was eager to experience the places that had shaped the nurses' lives firsthand, especially Corregidor. I'd seen the maps and diagrams of the Malinta Tunnel, but really, what on earth was this place like? What did it feel like to live underground? The Malinta Tunnel and its laterals are a remarkable feat of engineering and didn't disappoint. They were bigger and not as rustic as I expected, but it felt humbling to imagine trying to stay calm to focus on patients while bombs would have been falling overhead.

Though Corregidor has been reforested and is now home to monkeys, birds, and other wildlife, its ruins retain a spooky sense of being inhabited by ghosts. Of course, this feeling was perpetuated by the fact that my daughter and I were the only overnight guests at the island's one inn, so when the tour groups left for the day, everything grew *very* quiet. At sunset we walked through the old bombed-out remains of Fort Mills Station Hospital, and at sunrise we rambled through small tunnels dug by the Japanese, and each of these experiences left us profoundly moved. Standing on the edge of a cliff overlooking the South China Sea, it was hard not to feel far from home. Once the war began, I could imagine that the lure of adventure that pulled many Americans to the Philippines ▶

A Conversation with Elise Hooper *(continued)*

in the 1930s and early '40s must have shifted dramatically into a sense of isolation and loneliness, but being stuck on the opposite side of the world was what forged the strong bonds that helped the women of the Navy and Army Nurse Corps to survive together.

Q: How much of this story is true and how much is fiction?

A: With the exception of Josie Nesbit, Maude Davison, and several major historical figures like General MacArthur and President Roosevelt, all the characters are fictional but inspired by the real women who served in Filipino resistance and as American army and navy nurses.

According to survivors from Santo Tomas, Bilibid Prison, and POW camps like Cabanatuan, it was the support of resistance groups outside the camps that passed along food, money, and messages that made the difference between life and death. These groups were run by a variety of people from different nationalities, but it was the widespread effort by Filipinos from all walks of life that played a critical role in helping Americans survive. As I learned more about these Filipino resistance efforts, I knew I needed to develop a cast of characters outside the walls of Santo Tomas, so with the help of a group of Filipino and Filipino-American friends and historians, Flor, Luchie, Iris, and the others were born.

Yasmin and Club Sampaguita are loosely based on Claire Phillips and her Club Tsubaki, a nightspot popular with Japanese officers. Phillips and her staff funded resistance networks through their nightly earnings and passed along valuable intelligence that they learned while entertaining the enemy. Flor and her family were shaped very loosely on Florence Finch, Marcial Lichauco, and the Filipinas who worked in the "Miss U Spy Ring."

Frances Burns and her health clinic are fictional, but the idea for becoming a doctor was inspired by the harrowing stories of the assaults and rapes experienced by many Filipinas during the Battle of Manila. In addition to those atrocities, hundreds of Filipinas were forced into sexual servitude as "comfort women," a system put into practice throughout Asia during the war by the Japanese Imperial Army. Few Filipinas survived their ordeal, but after decades of shame and silence, some of these women are demanding justice. More than seventy years later, these brave survivors are still fighting to have sexual slavery recognized as a war crime and awaiting an official apology from the Japanese government. These survivors also want the abhorrent practice of "comfort women" and "comfort stations" to be included in history textbooks and historical markers built to remind people of the tragic consequences of war.

Q: During their imprisonment in Santo Tomas, did American nurses really work for the resistance?

A: In Elizabeth Norman's fascinating *We Band of Angels*, she describes how the women supported passing messages and materials to and from the camp, but there was little specific information about the logistics for this, so I created the system of embroidering messages onto laundry after reading about the Day Joyce Sheet, an extraordinary wartime diary stitched onto a bedsheet by prisoners at Hong Kong's Stanley Internment Camp. I loved the idea of women prisoners using their sewing skills as a subversive activity right under the noses of their guards.

My grandmother was a talented seamstress and embroiderer, so from the beginning of thinking about this novel I wanted to give my main character these skills too. It turned out they came in handy, not only for embroidering the messages but also for sewing Sally's silk parachute wedding dress. The idea for this unique wartime gown came from an exhibit at the United States Army Women's Museum and the original gown was worn in 1945 by Corporal Marjorie Short in the Philippines.

Q: What happened to the Angels of Bataan after the war?

A: In 1945 when the nurses were liberated from Santo Tomas, Americans were eager for good news from the Pacific. The public's appetite for the women had already been whetted by *So Proudly We Hail!* in 1943, a glammed-up Hollywood movie about the nurses starring Claudette Colbert, Paulette Goddard, and Veronica Lake, so when the Angels of Bataan (or the Battling Belles of Bataan, as they called themselves) returned home in 1945, they received a hero's welcome and the government immediately enlisted their help in selling war bonds and drumming up interest in enlistment. ▶

But reentry into American life wasn't always easy. While they had been locked up, the country had changed and moved on. No one was interested in hearing more about hardship and deprivation. America wanted to look ahead and embrace its new role as a victorious superpower. The nurses learned quickly to plaster on bright smiles, to stow away their anxieties, and to not speak of the nightmares that plagued them. They returned to their hometowns and reconnected with family members. Some married and started families of their own. Others also enrolled in school and earned college and graduate degrees. A few reenlisted and were sent to Europe and eventually to the war in Korea, and these battle-hardened nurses astonished their colleagues with their advanced medical skills.

Though the nurses received bronze stars for their wartime service, for many years those were the only honors they received. Maude Davison's colleagues petitioned for her to receive a Distinguished Service Medal, but her case was denied by the US Army Awards and Decorations Board, most likely due to a combination of sexism and political infighting. When she passed away on June 11, 1956, at the age of seventy-one, the first of the Angels of Bataan to fall, she was buried without fanfare, and, according to Elizabeth Norman's *We Band of Angels*, no one knows where to find her headstone. Finally in 2001, Maude Davison was awarded the Distinguished Service Medal posthumously. ∽

Further Reading

MacArthur's Undercover War by William B. Breuer
The Rape of Nanking by Iris Chang
A Child in the Midst of Battle by Evelyn Berg Empie and
    Stephen H. Mette
Pure Grit by Mary Cronk Farrell
Conduct Under Fire by John A. Glusman
Comfort Women by Maria Rosa Henson
Angels of the Underground by Theresa Kaminski
Prisoners in Paradise by Theresa Kaminski
Dear Mother Putnam by Marcial P. Lichauco
All This Hell by Evelyn M. Monahan and
    Rosemary Neidel-Greenlee
And If I Perish by Evelyn M. Monahan and
    Rosemary Neidel-Greenlee
The Indomitable Florence Finch by Robert J. Mrazek
We Band of Angels by Elizabeth Norman
Manila, Goodbye by Robin Prising
I Served on Bataan by Juanita Redmond
Rampage by James M. Scott
Ghost Soldiers by Hampton Sides ∾

Reading Group Guide

1. Before reading this novel, what did you know about World War II in the Pacific? Were you surprised by anything you learned? Was there anything specific you discovered about the Philippines and its occupation during the war?

2. This novel gives us a sense of what war was like for enlisted men and women on the front lines, civilians coping with occupation, and prisoners struggling with internment. How did the challenges of survival differ depending on the setting?

3. Which characters were you rooting for the most? Were there some characters you identified with more than others?

4. As Flor and Luchie become more deeply enmeshed in resistance activities, how does their relationship shift?

5. Tess has the opportunity to leave Corregidor for Australia but doesn't take it. How does this pivotal decision change her?

6. How are the themes of racism and prejudice woven throughout this story among the Americans, Filipinos, and Japanese?

7. The Filipinos have lived through many changes from Spanish colonial rule, the Spanish-American War, annexation by the United States, Japanese occupation, and then widespread destruction due to World War II. How do you see these changes impacting the Dalisays, Luchie, Yasmin, and the other Filipino characters in this book?

8. Tess tells her daughter, a young woman attending the University of Washington in the late 1960s, that they're from two very different generations (p. 338). In the last century, how have different generations handled hardship, grief, and trauma? What do you think accounts for these differences?

9. How do you think American civilians viewed the war differently from civilians from other countries who experienced the war on their doorsteps? How do you think this difference in perspective affected the Americans who came home after serving abroad and witnessing the effects of war firsthand?

10. The role of American women in the military has changed tremendously since the American Civil War. How do you see their jobs changing in this story?

11. Though life has changed since the '40s in many ways, what can we learn from the women who enlisted in World War II? ᠃

Photographs

First Lieutenant Donald W. Baker and his daughter in 1944.
(Photo from author's collection)

Lieutenant Commander Teresa Walsh Schmierer marries Lieutenant Clifford E. Schmierer on May 18, 1946. (Photo courtesy of Amy Huey)

Photographs *(continued)*

The main entrance to the Malinta Tunnel on Corregidor Island in 2020.
(Photo from author's collection)

The Fort Mills Mile Long Barracks ruins on Corregidor Island in 2020.
(Photo from author's collection)

The Main Building at Santo Tomas University once housed American army
nurses as Allied prisoners of war, but bustles with students in February 2020.
(Photo from author's collection)

Photographs *(continued)*

American army nurses wearing new uniforms after their liberation from Santo Tomas Internment Camp in February 1945. (Photo courtesy of the National Archives, U.S. Signal Corps III-SC-200726)

Discover great authors,
exclusive offers, and more
at hc.com.